Unveiled Desires

J. Wine

This is a work of fiction.

Copyright © 2024 J. Wine

All rights reserved. No part of this publication may be reproduced, stored or transmitted in any form or by any means, electronic, mechanical, photocopying, recording, scanning, or otherwise without written permission from the author, except for use of brief quotations in a book review. It is illegal to copy this book, post it to a website, or distribute it by any other means without permission.

Cover Design by 100 Covers

Model: Andrei Armiagov

Contents

Disclaimers V

1. Runaway Bride 1

2. That Seat's Taken 9

3. Better Off With A Dog 15

4. The Ice Queen Melts 21

5. The Dinner Guest 30

6. Gunpowder and Lead 40

7. A Petty Betty 48

8. Let The Tides Wash Away Our Sins 56

9. Matt Strikes 61

10. The Family Is Dysfunctional 68

11. That Baby Isn't Yours 77

12. The Iron Shield 82

13. Friday Date Nights 90

14. Sunday Family Picnic 99

15. Sunday Family Picnic, Part Deux 108

16. That Sounds Like A You Problem 116

17. The Interrogation 125

18. I Am Keeping You 134

19. Listen Up, Buttercup   144

20. Things Are Starting To Come Together   151

21. This Is Better Than Reality TV!   160

22. Safety In Numbers   169

23. The Past Is Trying To Kill US   177

24. How Are We Getting Out of This?   185

25. My Worst Nightmare   192

26. White Walls Caving In   199

27. Always The Bridesmaid   205

28. Matt Strikes Again   210

29. Hi Daddy! We're Waving At You.   216

30. IV Poles Are Dangerous Weapons   227

31. Matt Won't Go Away   235

32. Code Pink   242

33. The End of What We Once Had   250

34. Stop Playing With Your Food   259

35. Breaking Out Of This Place   267

36. Buh Bye   273

37. Buh Bye Now   281

38. Unveiled Wounds   289

39. Grace's First Ride   295

Also by J. Wine   304

About the Author   305

Acknowledgements   306

Disclaimers

FOR THE BEST READING EXPERIENCE: This story first debuted on Amazon Vella. It has undergone extensive revisions from its original form, and this is the only version available of the complete story. Sit back and relax – you're in for a rollercoaster ride.

WARNING DISCLAIMER: This book is intended for Adults 18+ only. It contains sexual situations and adult content/language.

TRIGGER WARNINGS: If you would like further information, please reach out to the author.

Cheating By Someone Not the Main Male Character

Ectopic Pregnancy

Vigilante Justice

Chapter 1

Runaway Bride

Grace

A loud moan disturbed the stillness of the church hallway as it echoed off the walls.

I stood there, dumbfounded, as more moans and groans bounced around me. I didn't want to believe it, but there was only one logical explanation that made sense. Someone was having sex in the Sunday School classroom.

I should have turned around and walked the other way, but my feet propelled me forward on their own. I was in a trance as I crept down the hall, my brain rapidly firing questions I wasn't sure I wanted answered. Pep talking my way with each step, I told myself I was an adult. I could handle whatever was going on, but in the next breath, I was clutching the pearls around my neck.

I tried not to click my heels on the linoleum floor as I approached the open door. The moans were louder, more distinguishable, but they didn't completely block out the sounds of my heart pounding in my ears.

"Yeah, baby. Just like that."

"You're so tight."

"Doesn't she suck dick like a high-class whore?"

I rolled my eyes. Did men really think we found that kind of behavior sexy? *No.* I plastered myself against the wall and tried to lean forward enough to see through the crack in the door. When nothing was visible, I propped myself against the wall and took a deep breath.

I tried again to peek around the door, and this time, my eyes focused on the woman. The skirt of the bridesmaid's dress was draped over her back, exposing her bare hips and the globes of her rear end. The delicate green chiffon flowed down her back in sharp comparison to her bare skin. When I saw the blur of a man pushing in and out of her, I averted my eyes. Shifting back to her, I couldn't look away. It was my cousin, Clara.

I quickly leaned back against the wall to catch my breath. This was the last place I needed to be. I'd die of embarrassment if anyone caught me, and there was no quick explanation that would suffice. It was pretty self-explanatory.

"You look so good sucking his dick." The voice was familiar, but I couldn't place it in my distress.

I squatted down against the wall in my Matron of Honor dress. *Here goes nothing*, I thought to myself as I tried again to get a better look. I duck-walked a few steps forward and then pivoted on one of my heels, praying no one had heard the sound. It was a mistake. A huge mistake. I quickly stuck my fist in my mouth and prayed that no one had heard the squeak that had come from me. Reaching for the door, I steadied myself so that I wouldn't fall flat on my ass as I willed my stomach not to upchuck this morning's breakfast.

My husband, Matt, was the man fucking my cousin from behind.

"He's getting married today to a shriveled cunt. You better get him off," he told my cousin, smacking her ass. The sound rang in my ears.

"She sucks like a Hoover," the other man said. I couldn't see him from my crouch, but there was only one possibility. Brandon, my sister's fiancé. They were supposed to get married in two hours.

My husband and my soon-to-be brother-in-law were spit-roasting my cousin in the church. I quickly spun back to lean against the wall, panicking.

My thoughts were racing for my sister. *Do I tell her? Do I not tell her?*

My thoughts then turned towards my situation. *What am I going to do?*

I was jealous. My hands clenched into fists as I laid them in my lap, and my back teeth were grinding as I questioned what was wrong with me. Had I done something wrong? Was I not pretty enough? Young enough? Realistically, I knew it wasn't me, but I couldn't shake the feeling that if I had just been better at life, this wouldn't be happening. It made me question what more I could have done, but none of the answers relieved any of the self-doubt I harbored.

My husband had always made love to me, and what I was watching was an animalistic sacrifice. I had never asked for anything different, but at this moment, I was curious what it would feel like to be at the mercy of two men. *No!* This wasn't porn. This was real life, and I was watching my marriage fall apart. My jealousy gave way to anger. *How dare Matt do this to me?*

Matt power-thrusted into her pussy, shoving her whole body forward. It caused her to choke on Brandon's dick. My fighting instincts kicked in. Brandon would be lucky if I didn't cut his dick off. I watched true crime shows. I could make it happen.

I didn't know why, but something inside my brain screamed at me to get proof. I was too raw to process this right now, but I'd watched this scenario play out in our social circle before. Although I didn't know what was going to happen, I needed to be prepared for the inevitable. My sister had chosen a Matron of Honor dress with pockets, and I pulled out my phone.

As I recorded, Matt's face transfixed me. After eight years of marriage, I was pretty intimate with his O face. He would smirk in the beginning. A secretive smile like he was the master, you were the puppet, and he knew exactly which strings to pull. When he knew he had you, it would widen into an actual smile. I always thought that this was the moment where we silently professed our love again. Eventually, those lips would form the perfect O shape. If I wasn't close, I would have to get there before he came. Once he did, it'd be over.

His lips were forming the O. I had to get out of here. I turned and stood, shuffling my dress shoes as quietly as I could back to the bridal suite.

What am I going to tell my sister? Will she even believe me? We were cordial, but the day our mother passed away had broken any close bond we could have formed.

My mother had been out running errands on a routine Thursday when a drunk driver had blown through a red light, killing her on impact as she sat in the intersection, waiting to turn. As a ten-year-old kid, I had missed my mom and didn't understand why she was gone. As a thirty-year-old adult, I found solace in the knowledge she hadn't been in pain.

My sister had been only five then, and we hadn't developed that closeness that people talked about when they experienced trauma. Losing my mother had been severely traumatic. I had just wanted to be left alone, and Meredith had needed a mom. My Aunt Elizabeth had stepped in to help my dad as much as she could, but it hadn't been the same.

As I approached the bridal suite, I could see my aunt pacing outside.

"Oh honey, I am so glad you're here," she told me as she grabbed my upper arms and pulled me into a hug.

"What's going on?" I allowed myself to be comforted, even though she wasn't aware of what I'd experienced.

"I am not really sure," she answered. "I walked in with a few snacks for you girls, and all hell had broken loose."

I gasped as I pulled away from her. "Do you think hell is a curse word when you're in church?"

"We might not be much longer. Your cousin Clara is missing, you were nowhere to be found, and your sister's emotional." My aunt clasped my hands in hers and rubbed them.

I didn't have the heart to tell her what I had witnessed. I discreetly tried to shake my head to clear the images away. It was my secret for right now.

Aunt Elizabeth took a step back and held the suite door open for me. I took a deep breath, steeled my nerves, and prepared for the battle that lay ahead. My aunt wasn't wrong. Meredith was sitting at the table in her wedding dress, tears collecting in the corner of her eyes as her lips quivered.

I walked over and sat across from her, clasping my hands on the table in front of me, afraid they would shake if I didn't. This was all too much to handle for one day, but I didn't want to give Meredith any reason to believe something was off. I wasn't ready to discuss what I had seen, and she'd always been good at sniffing blood in the water. She'd hound me until the words flowed out, not realizing the damage she'd cause.

When our mother had passed, our father had done the best he could with Aunt Elizabeth's help, but a lot of the daily functions had fallen to me. I had made sure Meredith was ready for school and that she had a packed lunch. After school, I was the one who had helped her with her homework and cooked dinner so that it was ready when my father walked in the door. I resented none of it, but I knew Meredith had resented me for all of it. Instead of being her sister, I became her third parent, and it had added a layer of friction to our relationship that never disintegrated.

As I sat across from her, I waited. Her eyes never left mine, but her fingers were dancing on the table, the French manicure she'd gone for yesterday making the only sound in the room. She was nervous, but the tears were trickling down her cheeks. I'd seen this before, and the only solution was to let her talk when she was ready. If I rushed her, she wouldn't talk to me at all. I didn't keep track of how much time had passed.

"Grace, I can't do this," she wailed, placing her arms on the table and laying her head on top of them. "I can't marry him."

I wanted to laugh, but that would cause more unnecessary tension. When Meredith had plopped her head onto her arms, her veil had fluffed up in a pretty cloud of tulle. It was now caught on the tips of the tiara that held it in place, making a puff shape that sat on the top of her head.

I proceeded with caution. "What's going on?" I asked her.

She sat straight up from the table, but the puff didn't fall back into place. It was even more of a mess on the top of her head, casting a shadow across her forehead. I withheld my laughter. She wouldn't think it was funny if I told her it was a halo and that she could be the devil sometimes.

"I can't do this." She hiccuped and wiped the tears from her cheeks as two big black mascara streaks appeared. "This is not my happily ever after."

Inside, I was throwing my hands up in celebration and dancing a jig on the table. On the outside, I was the one who remained calm, talking Meredith through this to make sure that she made the best decision for herself.

"Are you nervous?" I asked her. I was going to hell. This was purely for my own selfish gain. If I told Meredith that Brandon was cheating, she'd blame me because Matt was involved. I'd be guilty by association, even though I had no responsibility for any of their actions. If she decided on her own that marrying Brandon wasn't right, then I could leave his part out and deal with my marriage on my own terms. "You know, it's common to have some jitters right before your wedding."

Her sobs stopped immediately, and I watched as her face hardened, cracking her makeup. Meredith's eyes narrowed at me, and her fists clenched on the table. "It's not like that. I am about to be sick, and you just don't understand. You have a good marriage. I can't do this."

I understood more than she knew, but now wasn't the time to tell her. My marriage was in trouble, and I was trying to withhold my analysis of where it had all gone wrong for a later time. I wasn't perfect, even though Meredith was in this strange competition with herself to one-up me.

"Are you sure?" I asked again. "I was nervous when I got married, but it all worked out." It was a lie. *How much of my marriage has been a lie?*

"Yes, I shouldn't feel like this. I should be happy. I am not happy, Grace." Her forehead puckered into a frown, her mascara drying to her cheeks.

I stared deep into my sister's eyes. It was selfish, but I needed her to be absolutely sure of her decision. If she cancelled on her own, I'd be off the hook.

Meredith was right. She should have been happy, and the fear projecting from her eyes was anything but.

"Alright, get your stuff, and let's go. I'll tell Dad what's happening." I stood from the table and prepared to deal with the consequences. This felt right. Meredith might not have known what a douche canoe Brandon was, but she wouldn't be stuck with him either. From my experience, it was much easier to get in than to get out.

"Don't worry about your dad," Aunt Elizabeth chimed in. "I'll tell him what's going on, and we'll handle it. Just go, and keep me posted."

I looked at Meredith. She looked at me, and we both launched ourselves at Aunt Elizabeth.

She wrapped one of her arms around each of us. "It'll all work out," she reiterated. "Just go."

Meredith grabbed her purse and turned towards the other two girls in the room. My sister had wanted a small wedding party. She'd asked if I would be her Matron of Honor, and I'd agreed. She'd then chosen her two best friends from high school, and our cousin Clara.

I'd forgotten they were in the room, but when I turned towards them, I found them standing at the door with their purses over their shoulders in solidarity.

"We have the day to ourselves. Where should we go?" Meredith asked them.

"Let's just drive," Charlie said as she flipped a strand of her brunette hair off her shoulder. I'd always liked her because she was the voice of reason in the group.

"It's an adventure," Stella responded. I didn't know her as well as Charlie, but she'd never let my sister down. That was good enough for me.

Meredith looked at me. "Come with us," she said, not really asking me.

Matt was going to give me hell for disappearing, but I didn't care. Later on, I'd wonder if he even knew I was gone. No one had mentioned telling him I was leaving, and this question would plague me.

I grabbed my keys. "Let's go."

Chapter 2
That Seat's Taken

Grace

I felt like the mother hen as I asked the girls where they wanted to go. Like Stella had said, we were having an adventure, dressed in our bridal clothing. It was freeing in a way and yet suffocating, because I was responsible for them. I was the oldest, and I should have helped Meredith with the problem instead of running away. It would still be there when we got back.

My first thought was to take them to the beach. My mother had loved to sit on the sand and watch the waves break. It didn't matter what the occasion was. Meredith and I would run into the water to jump into the waves as she laughed nearby. Those times were some of my best memories of her.

I made the left out of the parking lot on autopilot as the girls chattered around me about nothing, but as I approached the turn for the beach, I felt like we hadn't run far enough. I had visions of Brandon and Matt showing up and ruining any happy memories we would salvage from today. Taking a quick peek in my peripheral at my sister, I knew I couldn't let that happen.

Taking the exit for the coastal highway, we made our way north with no plans, the windows down and whatever money we had in our pockets. As the girls sang along with whatever pop tune was next, I turned up the radio and smiled. It was loud and off-key, but they were happy.

Meredith's phone didn't blowup until I'd driven about an hour up the coast. My aunt had kept her word and had given us a head start.

"Do I answer it?" Meredith asked us, showing that it was Brandon calling.

"I vote no. You called off the wedding. Good riddance," Charlie said from the backseat. "I always thought something was off with him, but you were happy, so we were happy," she continued.

"I vote no too, but if you don't speak to him, he'll just keep calling," Stella piped up.

Meredith sent the call to voicemail and cranked the radio up, but it rang again. This time, she silenced the phone and left it in the cup holder. It was hard not to watch it light up fifteen more times. Brandon would call, and when no one answered, he would hang up and immediately call back.

"I have to get this over with, or he's never going to leave me alone." Meredith did a little shake in her chair to prepare. Hitting the green button on her phone, she hadn't even said hello before we heard Brandon screaming. The phone wasn't on speaker, but we heard him clearly.

"How dare you do to this to me? I will not be a laughingstock for some cheap whore."

Meredith quickly flipped it to speakerphone before responding. "Excuse me?"

"You heard me, Meredith. If I wanted a cheap whore, I could have bought one off the street and gotten my money's worth."

"You can still do that. Go pick one up, take her to the reception, and parade her to your family. You don't have the right to speak to me like that."

"So now you're going to pretend to be all high and mighty when you're just trailer trash in pearls?"

I could see her rolling her eyes as I continued to drive. He was trying to inflict as much emotional damage as he could, but she was holding her own, and I didn't think the name calling would hurt. However, I was having a hard time keeping my mouth closed. I wanted to yell out what I knew, but there was no place for it in their conversation. It would only make matters worse.

"Do you really think this is going to win me back? It actually just solidifies that I made the right decision. I want the fairytale, Brandon, and it's obvious you can't give that to me. Goodbye." She ended the call and blew out a breath.

I looked at her out of my peripheral vision again. She'd collected herself and was staring out the window as we continued to drive. I was proud that she had stood up to him. She didn't deserve to be treated that way. No one did, but in the back of my mind, there was this nagging worry that I'd let myself fall into the same pattern.

She caught me looking at her and turned in her seat to face me head on. "I feel like someone lifted a weight off of me I never knew was there. I am a little scared to admit that, but this was the right decision. He just proved he's not the right man." Her phone rang again. "Are they ever going to quit?" she asked as she looked at the screen. "It's his mom."

"You should turn off your phone. Otherwise, they'll just keep calling," Stella told her. "He probably told her you were being unreasonable, even though he's a douche. You know how they are."

"Good idea," Meredith responded, shaking her head.

I didn't have the heart to tell the girls that we were postponing the inevitable. Meredith would have to talk to Brandon one last time.

***

The sun was setting over the ocean when signs appeared for a beach bar.

"I wonder if they have food. I am hungry," Charlie moaned. "Hey, Mer! Next time you're planning to be a runaway bride, warn someone. We need snacks."

We laughed like a pack of hyenas, and I couldn't stop the snort that came out of my nose, causing the girls to laugh even harder.

"It has a four-star review," Stella piped in once the laughter had died down.

"You seriously checked Google, Stella?" my sister asked as she shook her head, turning around in her chair to look at her friends.

"Of course, I did. We're four hours from home. All we have are our wedding clothes and some money. I am not getting stuck in a slasher film." She shook her head so hard that her curls bounced, hitting Charlie.

"I am too hungry to die," Charlie growled, causing another round of laughter.

"We can try it, but we stick together. If anything is out of place, we'll get back in the car and leave," I firmly stated. I was too young to die when I had been sitting on my dreams for far too long. Being the perfect wife hadn't gotten me anywhere.

The girls and I made our way to the front door. They were oblivious, but I had checked the parking lot to make sure that there were no potential problems. We didn't want to be the bridal party caught in the wrong place at the wrong time.

This was something straight out of a TV show. There was a long bar top that sat at one side of the room, with the liquor bottles highlighted in neon behind them. In the middle was a sunken dance floor, with tables and chairs surrounding it on the main level, so you could watch the dancers from any vantage point. On the far side was a set of double doors, which I guessed led into the kitchen. We stood in the entryway, not sure what to do.

"Grab a seat, girlies, and I'll be right there," a woman called to us from behind the bar. She had to be in her late thirties to early forties, but you would have never known by the way she dressed. She had on a lime green tube top, a short jean skirt, and fishnets. To complete the look, she'd teased out her hair at least a couple of inches. The nineties had called. They wanted their hairspray back.

We ignored the chatter that hummed around the room as we walked towards an empty table. There was more than one audible whisper about a runaway bride surrounding us, but we didn't pay any attention.

We ordered, we ate, and then the girls decided they were going to line dance. They invited me to dance with them, but I declined. The place was quickly filling with Saturday night partiers, and I didn't want to lose the table.

They were having a good time, and the bar had some excellent people-watching to keep me occupied. I should have cleared my mind and just enjoyed the night, but a group of men, all wearing the same leather vests, walked in from the door on the side.

This was what I had been afraid of. I didn't have to see the patch on their backs to know they were a motorcycle club. It was time to go, but the girls were still on the dance floor with their backs turned towards me.

As I contemplated how to get their attention, a shadow crossed over the table. Looking to my left, I saw a large man pulling out the chair next to me and sitting down like he owned the whole place.

"That seat's taken," I said. I was still contemplating how to get the girls' attention without being obvious. The men that had walked in were now surrounding the girls. It looked like they were chatting them up, and my sister was all smiles. Meredith eventually faced me, and when I waved, all she did was wave back.

"Leave them be, mama. My men won't hurt them."

I channeled my inner resting bitch face and gave him a once-over. Short cropped blonde hair, blue eyes, and a ruggedly handsome face. He looked like a girl's wet dream, and he knew it.

"You should teach your men some manners," I retorted, keeping my focus on Meredith and her friends. "Right now, they're about as charming as a swarm of mosquitos at a picnic."

He barked a laugh, his blue eyes lighting up at his amusement, but I pretended like I hadn't noticed. My eyes shifted from the girls to him and quickly back to the girls.

He pointed towards the men on the dance floor. "It's not in their nature to be charming. They don't have to when they can catch as much honey as they want with a bit of sweetness. I prefer a bit of sting."

My eyes found his as he leaned further back in the chair and spread his legs wide. He was all man, and he knew how to sit to gain the most attention, and like an idiot, I couldn't look away. I gave myself one more second to admire him openly, and then I shifted my eyes back to the dance floor.

He didn't say a word, but the smirk on his lips told me everything I needed to know. He could read my innermost desires, and they were like a filthy movie, with him as the principal actor. It felt dangerous, and I didn't like it.

"So, what happened? She ditched the groom?" he asked me, pointing towards Meredith.

"Something like that," I responded. "It just wasn't in the cards."

"It never is." He smirked again, shifting in his chair. This time, I was trying not to pay attention to the way his worn jeans molded against the muscles in his thighs.

"Have you ever been married?" I asked, as a distraction.

"Nope, it's not for me."

"How do you know if you've never tried it?" It had been a long time since I had bantered with a man. It was easy, and that was when I knew I should have stopped, but I didn't.

"I don't need to put a ring on it for free pussy."

All men were the same, and that statement had just confirmed it. I'd get a dog and live by myself.

Chapter 3
Better Off With A Dog

Grace

I lost myself in the picture that I had created in my mind. I'd buy a bungalow and seclude myself in the peace. Listening to the waves crash along the beach, I'd let my dog play fetch in the water. It sounded so good that I wanted to reach out and grab it with both hands. The dream faded, and I noticed my hand was opening and closing, trying to grab that imaginary image.

"Easy, mama. I like to see you flustered like that. It's better than the ice queen. Makes you human."

I blushed at my stupidity, the heat rising from my cheeks as I tried to figure out what to say that would smooth this over. I'd been sitting in the middle of a biker bar, dreaming of a life I would never have. I should have been making my plans a reality instead of letting life pass me by.

I was mad at myself, but my first thought was to let him have it. He didn't know me well enough to make those assumptions, even though they were true. I didn't let people into my inner circle, as it was easier to ice them out so they'd leave me alone.

Before I could snap something nasty at him, the waitress came back to the table. She ignored me and looked directly at him, asking, "The regular, Sabre?"

"Sure, Dee, and whatever she's having," he said, nodding at me.

The waitress acknowledged me. "What can I bring you, girlie? Something fruity?" she asked.

"No, thank you. I am good with water," I told her, checking the dance floor again.

"Is our liquor not good enough for you? We have the premium spirits, girlie." Dee stood with her hand on her hip, and I swore she'd pop bubblegum if she'd been chewing any.

I was about done with people judging me today. "Perhaps you fried your brain cells in a mist of Aquanet, *girlie*. I am pregnant, so the water will be fine. No lemon."

A low whistle sounded from the man next to me. She had called him Sabre, and it fit him. He appeared to be laid back as he slouched in the chair, but I didn't think it would take much for him to spring into action. Appearances were deceiving, and I knew that better than most people.

"Just bring a pitcher, Dee. Thanks, sweetheart." He winked at her, smoothing over whatever damage I had caused. He waited until she was far from the table with a smile on her lips before he leaned forward and crossed his arms. "That wasn't nice at all."

"She assumed. That's what you get when you make an ass out of yourself." I checked the dance floor again, looking for the girls. They were having a good time, but the men had made a coordinated effort to pair off. Meredith was all smiles as she danced next to a brunette with a man bun. After the day we'd had, her happiness made me smile.

"There ya go. Now, that's real pretty."

I don't know what came over me, but I stuck my tongue out at him.

"Don't do that unless you're planning on using it."

My thoughts were all over the place. The first one instantly went into the gutter, as I imagined getting down and dirty with him. The second made me feel guilty as I thought about Matt, my cheating husband. I was pregnant, and I didn't know who he'd been with. I'd have to get the baby checked to make sure that we were both safe. Matt hadn't cared, and I wasn't sure he would have told me about the women if I hadn't found out on my own.

"What, mama? You got that look."

No witty retort came to me, so I remained silent as I pulled my phone from my pocket. I felt like I had to tell someone, and he was perfect. I didn't believe he would judge me, and I would never see him again, so there was no harm in letting him into my newfound turmoil. Opening the video, I made sure the sound was off before I handed it to him.

I didn't think he had expected a live porno, because he nearly dropped the phone on the table when it played. It was at the same time that the waitress brought over our drinks. She set a beer in front of him and a pitcher of water in front of me.

"Anything else, darlin'?" she asked him, placing her hand on his shoulder with familiarity.

I wondered just how familiar they were and then scolded myself for caring too much.

"Nope, we're good. Thanks, Dee." He rushed her away from the table so that he could continue to watch. I would have too if it wasn't my life.

The video ended, and he hit the button to play it again. "Let me guess: your husband, the groom, and a bridesmaid?"

"You're good. The bridesmaid is my cousin."

"Does the bride know?" he asked me, looking out onto the dance floor.

"No, I got lucky. She called off the wedding before I had to tell her because she said it was a bad idea not to be happy."

His gaze shifted back towards me. "You dodged a bullet there."

"It was easier to let her think she'd come up with this choice on her own. If it hadn't played out like that, I would have told her. She had a right to know, but I wanted to spare her the pain."

"What are you going to do?" I should have answered flippantly, but I didn't dodge his question like I should have. I answered honestly that I didn't know what was going to happen to me.

I felt like I had summoned the devil with one simple thought of Matt. My phone vibrated in Sabre's hand, and a cold dose of reality settled in between my shoulder blades.

Sabre stared at the picture of Matt that had popped up on the home screen as the phone vibrated with the incoming call. I thought Sabre was going to answer, but he passed me the phone at the last minute.

"Hey Matt," I said, answering. I stared straight ahead, shoulders pulled back, and my spine straight. I couldn't say anything I'd regret later on. Matt would use any tiny piece of this conversation to blow something out of the proportion, even if it was innocent.

"Where are you?" His voice sounded cold through the line, and I imagined icicles hanging off an imaginary string.

"About four hours from home. The girls were hungry, so we stopped to eat at some bar."

I was going to keep this as vague as possible. It was late in the evening, but I didn't want Matt to suddenly show up with Brandon and cause a scene with the bikers. They would be out of their league, and it would just end badly.

"You left a mess here, Grace. It's unlike you to take off with no word. Brandon's family is very upset that they paid for a wedding that didn't happen. They've threatened to sue, and your father laughed at them and walked, taking your aunt with him. You could have smoothed this all over and made Meredith follow through, but you were nowhere to be found in that shit show." His voice was still cold but slimy.

Analyzing his statement, I had to face the truth that he was right. Under normal circumstances, I would have pushed Meredith, citing some bullshit about what was best for her when I didn't have a clue. The guilt rolled over me in the same manner that the waves crested the beach. I felt drenched in cold, clammy sweat, and I was having a hard time breathing through the pain that gripped my chest.

"No, you're right. It was a mess." I hoped agreeing with him would get him to calm down.

"Wrong move, Grace. You made me look like a fool, and I didn't appreciate it."

"I looked for you, but you were missing. There wasn't any time." It was a lie.

"Hmm," he said. His tone implied that he didn't believe my story. "When are you coming home?"

"We'll probably get a room somewhere and then head back in the morning."

"Be home by noon. Don't be late." *Click.* The line went silent.

My hand shook as I slid the phone away from my ear and placed the screen down on the table. I didn't want to touch it, but my eyes wouldn't look away from it either. Matt had just threatened me for the first time in our marriage, and I wasn't sure how to react. I wasn't scared, nor did I believe Matt would physically harm me. This felt like some sort of setup, where no matter what I did, I was going to lose. It was getting harder to breathe in the dense air that surrounded me.

"Why do you let him treat you like that?"

I had forgotten Sabre was sitting next to me. I didn't know what to say, so I went with the truth. "That was new."

I'd met Matt as a sophomore in college. The girls in my program had gone out to a dorm mixer, and Matt and his friends had been the first people we'd met. We had been inseparable from then on. He had treated me like a queen, and I had gushed about how perfect our relationship was. Like a good friend, I thought I was doing the right thing by wishing the girls as much happiness as I had.

After graduation, we were married and bought a house. Our lives had moved forward together, and having a baby was just the next step.

I hadn't been honest with myself. Things had changed, and I had chalked it up to the baby. We were going to be parents in six months, and I kept telling myself that it was natural to adjust. We'd see it through and settle into a new normal. Together, like we had always done everything else. I either hadn't seen the red flags, or I had ignored them. I had a reason now to be wary.

"We have a clubhouse a few miles up the road. The four of you can stay overnight." It seemed like an innocent offer, but the smirk that settled at the corner of his lips said otherwise.

"No, thanks. I appreciate the offer, but we'll just head back and grab a hotel somewhere." I wasn't letting the girls into the clubhouse. They were old enough to make poor decisions on their own. Looking at the pairs on the dance floor, I thought that was exactly what was about to happen. They didn't need any encouragement.

"Can't blame me for trying to lure you into my bed."

It was nice to be flirted with, but I didn't take him seriously. "It was generous of you to donate your bed for the night, but I won't put you out."

He leaned forward and his eyes narrowed as he stared at me. "I wasn't donating shit. When you're in my bed, mama, you'll be lucky if you get any sleep. I'd rather you put me in." He winked at me and pulled away.

I wouldn't make a poor decision either. It was time to go. I looked out onto the dancefloor and caught Meredith's eye. She must have had the same thought because she gathered the girls, and we were back on the road a few minutes later.

We ended up pulling into a hotel and stayed the night—far away from a group of bikers.

Chapter 4

The Ice Queen Melts

Sabre

One minute she was sitting next to me, taking a drink of water, and the next she was gone. I sat there, dumbfounded. What the fuck had just happened? Trying to process what I remembered, I played the scene back in my mind, drinking my beer.

The last thing I remembered clearly was when I'd offered her my bed for the night, and she'd turned me down. I didn't think she'd really take me up on it, but it was fun to see her flustered. I doubted she allowed many people to see beyond the perfect mask. The next thing I knew, the bride was storming to the table. They had grabbed all of their things and hightailed it out of here. It wouldn't have surprised me to find out they had been practicing that maneuver over the years. It had been too fast, and I normally had better instincts than that.

Taking another sip of my beer, I watched over the edge of the glass as Grizz headed my way with the rest of the brothers a few steps behind him.

"How could you have let them go?" he asked me as he approached.

I took another long gulp of my beer. The foam tickled my tongue, which made me curious what she'd taste like in my bed. She. Fuck, I didn't even know her name. I'd just started calling her mama, and she'd gone with it. "You didn't even know what was happening, so don't come at me. They were gone in a cloud of tulle before you even knew the bride wasn't next to you."

"How the fuck do you even know what tulle is?" Grizz raised his eyebrows at me, trying to get the last word.

We'd been best friends way too long for me to take him seriously right now. He was probably pissed that they had left without a trace, and he'd have to get Cyph to work his magic. I wasn't taking my life into my own hands and telling him that his womanizing skills were rusty. He should have been able to talk her into coming back to the clubhouse. Reality hit me like a ton of bricks that I hadn't been successful either.

"Are you two going to bicker like old ladies, or are we heading out to the parking lot? They might still be here," Pretty said, standing with his feet shoulder width apart, and his hands on his hips, scolding us.

Grizz didn't hesitate. He worked his way through the tables, pushing past anyone who dared to step in his way. Reaching the front door, he nearly pulled it off the hinges as he ran into the lot. The rest of us filed out behind him, but it was too late.

A silver SUV turned out of the parking lot and headed for the highway.

They were gone.

"Fuck. Did anyone get their plate number?" Grizz crouched, rubbing his hands against his face.

"How the fuck did you expect us to see that far? It's dark." Pretty was continuing down a dangerous path by provoking Grizz, but my brother loved to stir up other people's shit.

"He was hoping for a Hail Mary but got denied," I heard Wreck say from behind me.

Grizz was staring at the road, probably willing the girls to turn around. "Let's go after them. We can probably catch them."

"Then what? Scare the fuck out of them? We're bikers, and they're definitely high society princesses. Did you see the bride's dress? It was probably worth more than my bike, and that's saying something." Count was our treasurer, and I didn't even question how he would know something like that.

"Well, we can't just stand here with our dicks in our hands," Grizz said, his eyes falling on Cyph. Grizz pointed at the phone in his hand. "Find them."

"All non-club information comes with a price." Cyph didn't even bother to look up from his phone as he happily typed away.

"I am not paying you when you could have already been done by now. You're wasting time. At least figure out where they live, fuckface." Grizz was breathing heavy, his chest pumping twice as hard as normal as he tried to rein in his temper. I thought the bride had just been a conquest, but now I questioned how fucked up Grizz was going to become.

"Not without payment. You know I don't work that way." Cyph tucked one arm into the crook of the other and continued to play on his phone.

"You're fucking with me now? What the fuck do you want?"

"Three video games for the club's Playstation and the fight night package for the TV." Cyph stuck his fist out to bump with Count's.

"Fuck, no. Just find them. If you weren't busting my fucking balls, we could have caught them." Grizz was two seconds from strangling Cyph.

"Four video games and the package for at least a year." Cyph wasn't giving up, and I was enjoying the bickering way too much.

"For a goddamn phone number? I'll just fucking do it myself." Grizz pulled out his phone and clicked the app to bring up the maps. "Anyone know where they were from?" he asked the rest of us.

I threw Grizz a bone. "Start with a four-hour radius. The husband called, and she said they had driven four hours before they stopped here to eat."

She'd held the phone to her ear in between us, and the husband had had been so loud that I had no problem hearing him. I didn't like how he had spoken to her, but I hadn't pushed the issue. She hadn't appeared to be afraid, and I was looking for a good time, not a lifetime commitment. If there had been any sign that he was getting physical with her, I told myself that I would have stepped in.

Grizz clicked his fingers at me. "Yes!" He instantly went back to the map, but he'd easily get confused when he had to bounce between the map and a browser window. Pointing at Cyph, he said, "This would have been faster if you'd just do it, but you're being a little shit since none of them were interested in you."

"At least I am not delulu. You think she really wants a little bitch like you?" Cyph retorted. "Five video games, the fight night package, and the sports network."

"Oh, that was a good one." Count chuckled, enjoying this as much as I was.

"You can't be fucking serious right now." Grizz was now whining.

"You should have taken me up on my first offer. Check your fucking phone." Right on cue, his phone dinged with an incoming text. Cyph had already figured it out.

"You're a fucking bitch, and I am going to remember this." Grizz was scrolling through the text. "Do I call her now?"

The rest of us cracked up laughing.

"For what? 'Hey baby, come back so that I can whisk you away to my rancid room in the clubhouse, and we can celebrate your honeymoon?'" Pretty was laughing so hard that he tripped over his own feet and fell into Wreck.

My phone dinged, but it wasn't unusual to get texts at all hours of the day and night.

"You're welcome," Cyph told me with a smirk.

I opened the text. He'd done me a solid.

Cyph

Grace Montgomery.

Grizz had figured out that Cyph had sent me my woman's information for free. "How come he doesn't have to pay, and I got robbed?" he complained.

With a snort, Cyph retorted, "I know where my bread gets buttered."

***

Grace

I felt like a train had hit me as I drove past each mile marker on the way home. The energy in the car from the day before had vanished. We were exhausted, and the laughter that had bounced off the windows was now gone, but the silence was not uncomfortable.

After we'd left the bar the night before, we'd headed south, stopping at the first decent chain hotel we'd found. Settling in one room, the girls had immediately gossiped about the bikers all night, like they would have done in high school. I had only interjected a word here or there, preferring to stay on the outside of their conversation.

I dropped Charlie and Stella off at their respective homes and then made my way to Meredith's condo. The girls had ridden to the church together, so when my father had called this morning, he'd said that he had taken care of their vehicle. It was currently sitting at Charlie's apartment complex.

I was a little surprised that he hadn't mentioned the failed wedding to Meredith. She'd spoken to him as I had driven, and when the conversation was over, she'd mentioned the car and then let it drop.

Halfway to her condo, Meredith turned in her seat to face me and asked, "What happened, Grace?"

"When?" I asked warily. Too much had happened, and I didn't want to guess wrong and volunteer additional information.

"At the wedding," she said, biting her bottom lip as she bent her knee and tucked her leg underneath her. She turned in the passenger seat so that she faced my profile as I drove. "Yesterday was unlike you. It was strange because you didn't push me to get married, and I know you. You would have told me to put my big girl panties on and just do it."

Despair hit me over the head like a water balloon. Had I really lived my life like that? I didn't know why I was questioning myself when I already had the answers. Meredith was right. I hadn't wanted to admit to it.

"What happened?" Meredith kept pushing for answers, staring a hole into the side of my head.

I should have word-vomited everything that had transpired in the last twenty-four hours, but I kept my secrets locked tightly to my chest. Part of me rationalized that if I didn't emotionally understand what had transpired, how was I ever going to make her see reason?

I didn't know what to tell her, but I had to come up with something or else she'd never let this go. Meredith would think that I was hiding something from her, and she'd be too close to the truth that I was trying to protect her from.

"When I walked into the bridal suite, you looked so alone sitting at that table, and then when you sobbed, my heart broke for you. I don't have an acceptable answer, but weddings are supposed to be one of the best days of your life, and you were miserable. If I have ever pushed you into something, I am incredibly sorry. No one should live like that." I meant every word.

"Why do you?" She had a point, but I wasn't sure if I was ready to analyze my situation with my sister. I'd lived my life as if I was a 1950s trophy wife, and I was better than that.

I didn't blow her off, but I had to shut down the conversation. Otherwise, I would cry in a bout of self-pity. "Not right now," I told her. "Let's get you through the fallout of the wedding. You know Brandon's family won't let this drop."

I pulled into the driveway of her condo and turned the car off. She'd bought it a few months ago, and Brandon was supposed to move in a while ago. However, he had been dragging his feet with every excuse known to man. I wondered if the real reason had been that Meredith was the sole owner. None of his stuff was here, and he didn't have the keys to the place. Meredith had dodged another bullet, I thought, the phrase reminding me of Sabre. My stomach fluttered with butterflies.

"It'll be okay. They can afford the wedding, and Brandon can threaten to sue as much as he wants. You know it would look better for their family to just play the victim. I don't care. They can paint me in whatever light they want," Meredith said. "I feel easy, like this was all wrong, and I didn't see it until now." She smiled, lost in her thoughts.

"Which biker? I asked her.

She looked at me like a deer in headlights. Her eyes were wide open, and where she'd been smiling before, her lips now formed an O shape.

"I am not blind, Mer. Which one?"

She smiled wider. "Grizz. He was the dark-haired one with the man bun. I didn't give him my number, but I told him that if he really wanted to find me, he should look up the wedding announcement. If he's smart, he'll put it together since Brandon's family took out that ad in the gossip column."

We stared at each other over the center console as we sat in my car. She smiled at me, and as my smile formed, we cracked up laughing at the situation. It'd been too long since we'd just been sisters, sharing a secret. She was suddenly quiet. "Do you think he'll call?" she asked.

"I think he'd be stupid not to." I hugged her as tight as I could.

"Me too, Grace. He'd be stupid not to fight for you." She got out of the car and walked to her front door before I could say anything.

I wouldn't pretend I didn't know who she was talking about.

I didn't know what to expect the closer I came to my home. I was anxious, and my palms were sweaty on the steering wheel as the miles seemed to pass a little too quickly.

It was a little after one, and I shook my head in disbelief as I pulled into the driveway. Matt wasn't even home, and he'd specifically mentioned that I should be home by noon. I hadn't purposely been late, but I also hadn't reached out to tell him either.

Pulling my phone out to call him for the first time this morning, I checked the screen and saw that I had a text. It was from an unknown number, and I normally wouldn't have paid it any attention, except the preview message started with *mama*. It never dawned on me to question how he had gotten my name and number as I opened the text.

Unknown

Mama, I'll be here whenever you need me. Just call.

I would never reach out to him, but I also didn't delete the number.

Walking into the empty house, I tried to pretend everything was normal. I placed my keys on the right hook near the garage door, took off my shoes, and made sure they were next to each other in the little cubicle.

"Matt?" I called out as I walked from the garage door to the living room. His car wasn't in the garage, but I wanted to make sure he really wasn't home. I waited a few seconds, listening for any response. "Matt?" I called out again. Nothing. Pulling out my phone, I checked for any message that I might have missed.

Dragging myself upstairs, I turned on the shower and stripped off the dress. I was physically and emotionally exhausted, and I wasn't in the mood to play these mind games. Matt was probably waiting for me to call and ask where he was. In reality, I didn't care. I was more concerned about the argument that would ensue when he arrived home. I didn't know if I had the strength to fight, and I didn't want to just blindly agree to any thing Matt would say. Showering, I tried to wash the building anxiety away. I threw on a pair of pajamas and climbed into bed. Releasing a moan, I felt like I was in heaven. It wasn't long before I fell asleep.

I was groggy when I woke from the nap. I didn't know what time it was, but the room was dark, and I figured it must have been past dinner. Burying myself further under the covers, I just wanted to fall back asleep. My stomach rumbled, but I ignored it. Closing my eyes, I waited for sleep to overtake me again. My stomach rumbled loudly once more, and my bladder cried. There was no point. I was up.

Standing up, I stretched and used the bathroom before heading downstairs to fix something to eat. I was in the middle of scrambling eggs when Matt walked in through the garage door. Neither of us said hello as he entered the kitchen. My eyes bounced between the eggs in the pan and his back as he stood in front of the refrigerator. I didn't know where to start the conversation, so I plated my eggs and sat at the kitchen table to eat. It might have been delicious, but I wouldn't know. It tasted like sawdust in my mouth.

Matt closed the refrigerator and walked towards the table. I pulled my shoulders back and straightened my spine, preparing for the battle that was going to start. He approached me from behind and patted the top of my head. Dropping to a crouch, he whispered in my ear, "Don't fucking think about it."

I sat at the table as his heavy footsteps made the hardwood stairs creak. I heard the water rush through the pipes as he turned on the shower. Not long after, he came back downstairs, patted me on the head again, and walked out. His car started in the garage, and he was gone. I didn't see him for three days after that, and when he walked back into the house, he pretended nothing was amiss.

Chapter 5
The Dinner Guest

It had been a month since the canceled wedding.

It had taken Brandon and his parents about a week to settle down with the lawsuit threats. Meredith had been right, and when they hadn't gotten the sympathetic reaction they wanted with threats, they had switched to playing the victim. They had told anyone who would listen that Meredith was a harlot. She'd led Brandon around for years with no concrete plans to actually marry him.

That hadn't stopped the rumor mill from running rampant in our small social circle. After the wedding, Brandon had moved on quickly with Clara, but if you listened to the gossip, no one blamed him. It was still Meredith's fault for not being able to keep him happy. Every time I caught a whisper, I wanted to come out with my metaphorical guns blazing. I was ready to fight, and I had proof of Brandon's infidelity, but I'd remind myself that it wouldn't do any good to play the ace that no one knew I had.

Meredith took it all in stride, which in all honestly, surprised me. She could become high-strung in high-stress situations, but this time, she simply let them be. She never openly refuted the lies they told, nor did she slander them. If anyone actually asked her for her side of the story, she didn't hesitate to express that it hadn't felt right and wished Brandon well. It was an honorable response, and I was proud of her. I wasn't sure I would have reacted the same way, but in hindsight, she also wasn't aware of what I had witnessed.

Meredith had been able to make a clean break, but I wasn't as lucky. To the outside world, things appeared normal between Matt and me. Right after the wedding, we returned to our regular social gatherings. We went to client functions, and we appeared together at expensive restaurants so that Matt could network. I was his pretty, pregnant wife, and he was the family man that you could trust with your money. No one knew it was all a mirage.

Over the next two weeks, it hastily fell apart. Matt always worked late, and in the beginning, he'd text not to wait up for him. I wasn't naive enough to believe that he was actually working. It was code for cheating. At first, it'd been a day here, a day there, but eventually Matt didn't come home for days on end. If he did, it was to take a shower, pack a change of clothes, and leave again.

As long as he wasn't home, I hadn't rushed to any resolutions. I figured as long as we were living separate lives, I would prepare myself for the inevitable end of my marriage. I'd started making plans and working on projects that would bring in cash so that I'd be alright when the time came.

Meredith had called a few nights ago and asked if Matt and I could attend a family dinner. I'd agreed, not thinking too much about it as I had texted Matt about the plans.

It was now Friday, and Matt would be home soon so that we could head straight over to Aunt Elizabeth's.

I was about ready to shower when my phone dinged. Picking it up from the kitchen counter, I read the incoming text from Matt.

Matt

Business meeting running late. Go without me.

I rolled my eyes as I set the phone back on the counter. I really wanted to slam it, but it'd probably break, and really, this was no one's fault but Matt's. Letting out a scream filled with frustration and disappointment, I tried to make myself feel better as I stood in the empty kitchen, but it was getting harder to regulate my emotions when things like this were becoming a daily occurrence.

I left the kitchen and headed for the bathroom to shower and get ready, but as I waited for the water to heat, I turned towards the mirror to look at myself, wondering how much of my marriage failures were my fault. Was I not good enough?

I looked at what I was wearing. A white t-shirt and jean shorts. No makeup. My family wouldn't care what I showed up in. It was only Matt who insisted I look my best, and he wouldn't be there.

***

Opening the door to my aunt's house, I could hear voices coming from the kitchen.

"I'm here," I called out, as I took my shoes off in the doorway. I'd spent just as much time here as I had at my father's house growing up. It was second nature to walk in like I owned the place.

"In the kitchen, Grace," my aunt called back.

I headed into the kitchen, but as I turned the corner, whatever I was going to say to my aunt died on my lips. My eyes bugged out. My feet stopped in the middle of the doorway, and my mouth hung open.

My sister and Grizz were sitting on the barstools at my aunt's kitchen island. She tucked her hand into the crook of his elbow as they sat close enough to be in each other's laps.

"Oh, Grace! You look good. How are you feeling?" my aunt asked, pulling me into a hug. I quickly closed my mouth, so that she wouldn't ask if something was wrong. I wouldn't know how to tell her that I'd just experienced the shock of my life.

"I'm good," I said. Kissing her on the cheek, I returned the hug. It was comforting, but my mind was reeling. Why had Meredith told my aunt to schedule this family dinner? Did my aunt know how she and Grizz had met? Was *he* with them? Why would *he* be with them? I hoped this wouldn't go to hell in a hand basket.

"Grace," my sister said with trepidation as she approached me. I noticed her voice had shook. Quickly checking on my aunt, I saw she was busy pulling serving utensils out of the drawer and hadn't noticed.

Meredith hugged me tightly, but she was running on adrenaline and couldn't stand still. She wrapped her arm around mine and lead me to the counter to make the introductions. "This is my boyfriend, Jonathan. Jon, this is my sister, Grace."

He had a twinkle in his eye, as if he were enjoying my sister's discomfort. It made me realize what a stark contrast this was. When Meredith had introduced Brandon to our family, he'd dominated every conversation. It didn't matter what the topic was, Brandon had always been right, and if Meredith tried to smooth things over, he'd take his anger out on her. Grizz was just enjoying the awkwardness of the situation. I couldn't contain the smile that was twitching at my lips.

He stood as we approached, sticking his hand out for me to shake. "Grace, it is nice to meet you. I have heard so many good things."

"The pleasure's all mine. I was not aware that Meredith was dating. How did the two of you meet?" I couldn't help it. He was not the only one enjoying watching my sister squirm.

"You never told me, Mer," my aunt popped into the conversation. She was pulling a roast from the oven, and the smell made my stomach growl.

"Why don't you tell them, Meredith?" Grizz said. I would keep the secret until they spilled, but I wouldn't call him Jon. It didn't fit him once you knew his road name.

"Uh, well. Uh..." she stuttered, trying to come up with the right words.

"I brought the dessert you wanted," my dad called from the front door. Meredith had dodged another bullet.

Setting the roast on the top of the stove, my aunt left the kitchen to grab the dessert from my dad. Once she was gone, Grizz and I looked at each other and laughed. "Lucky," I whispered to Meredith.

***

Dinner was a casual affair, and I was enjoying myself. The food had been delicious, and the conversation flowed easily.

It was towards the end of dessert that my dad dropped a bomb on the table.

"So, are you an Iron Shield or a Guardian Knight?" he asked, taking a sip from his drink.

The table went completely silent.

"I am a criminal defense attorney," my dad said. "While you look like one of those starving artist types, no one wears a long-sleeved shirt in the middle of summer, and the bottom of your tattoo is showing. Both clubs have that shield shape." He brought his fork up to his mouth and took a bite of cake.

We stared at him for several minutes, before he shrugged his shoulders and lifted his eyebrows. "What?" he asked us. "I've been dealing with the Guardian Knights for almost twenty years. This one was too easy."

My aunt was the first one to speak. "I was going to say something, but I didn't think I was right."

My dad looked at Meredith. "Why don't you tell us how you two really met?"

She didn't have a choice and told them the story about how we had headed up the coast after the wedding and landed at the biker bar.

After she finished, she smiled, and Grizz put his arm around the back of her chair. He let her have her moment, but if she needed him, he was right there. I smiled at their closeness.

"I told him that if he wanted to find me, he should look up the wedding announcement. You never did say what happened after that." She turned towards Grizz, with a smile on her face. I couldn't remember the last time I'd seen her smile that bright.

Grizz shifted so that he was looking at her. "I found the wedding announcement in the paper and went from there." He smirked.

"No, you didn't. What really happened?" Meredith pushed.

He looked at me and winked. "Grace told Sabre that you were four hours from home. I tried to draw a perimeter around that and check the local papers, but I am not good at that stuff. Cyph, our computer guru, took pity on me and had your name and phone number in less than a minute. It just cost me an arm and a leg."

My stomach knotted at the thought of Sabre.

"I am worth it," Meredith said.

"Yeah, you are. I figured you guys would drive home Sunday, so I waited until Monday. The hours went by slowly as I planned what I wanted to say to you."

"Your first words were, 'When are we getting married?' So you didn't plan too hard, did you?"

They stared at each other, each one with a secretive smile for the other. My dad stared at my aunt with a small smile, and she beamed one back at him. I was the only one missing someone else. I felt my phone in my back pocket, but I wouldn't reach out, even though I wanted to.

The night had been a success.

***

Sabre

It was a regular Friday night at the clubhouse, which usually meant the brothers unwound from the work week and someone would end up doing dumb shit. It was home, and I wouldn't have it any other way. Along one wall, we had set up an entertainment section in the main room, with large TVs, every gaming system known to man, and comfy couches to take it all in. I had plopped my happy ass in the corner of one couch and just watched the people.

Behind me, I could hear a game of pool being played, the billiard balls smacking against each other regularly. I didn't bother to turn around and ask who was winning, nor did I care to see which brothers were throwing darts nearby. Instead, I found amusement in watching the prospects assigned to the bar, running around like chickens with their heads cut off. They weren't doing a terrible job, but every now and then, a patched brother would yell for their attention. It built character, and I didn't worry about the liquor tab. We ordered enough from the distributor to get the cheapest rate, and we made a shit ton of money monthly so it didn't matter. The brothers could enjoy the booze.

We had six club girls roaming around the main room, making sure that the brothers were alright. They knew their roles and how to serve the club. In return, I took care of them financially, putting a roof over their heads, spending money, and even providing college tuitions. However, they were in direct competition with the girls who just hung around. Fresh meat was always more appealing, but those girls were looking for Old Lady status, and none of the brothers would ever give that up lightly.

"I am bored," my brother, Pretty, said as he flopped down on the couch on top of me. The whole left side of his body was touching mine, and there was no personal space.

"It's Friday night. Grab a whore and fuck it out of your system," I told him, trying to get him to scoot over.

"You should take your own advice. Oh wait, she ain't here."

"Fuck off. She's not a whore." Someone who'd been at the bar that night had a big mouth, and the story had spread like wildfire. Ever since then, the brothers had ridden my ass about Grace, but they left Grizz alone.

Pretty was actually my brother by blood, and while I wouldn't trade him, he was normally the first one in line to push my buttons. He laughed and scanned the room, and if I knew him, he was looking for a blonde to torment me.

My phone dinged with an incoming text. Pulling it out of my back pocket, I elbowed Pretty in the side just because I could. Clicking the phone to light up, I saw Grizz's name. Motherfucker was supposed to be at family dinner.

I opened the message, and there she was.

It looked like she was putting dishes away and didn't know he'd taken her picture.

Her shirt rode up in the back as she appeared to be reaching for something in a cabinet. My eyes instantly went to her visible bump. It was one thing to know that she was pregnant, but it was another to actually see the baby. A surge of protectiveness came over me, and I couldn't shake it. I would have given them anything they asked for, even though I hadn't seen or heard from her in a month.

"She's so damn hot. Did you know she was pregnant?" My brother was leaning against my arm to look at the phone.

"Fucking knock it off, or I am going to beat your ass," I told him and put my phone back in my pocket.

"I might like it," he said.

Another *ding* came through. I looked at my brother. He looked at me with a wide smile. "You going to get that?" he asked.

I pulled my phone back out and opened the message. Grizz had sent a video.

Pretty reached over and hit play. He was seriously cruising for a beat down. Shooting him a look, I turned towards my phone. She was all smiles, twirling around the kitchen, putting away dishes. It took everything in me not to make the four-hour trip.

"So, should we call you Daddy now?" Pretty smirked.

On instinct, I curled my fingers in and hit my brother hard enough in the stomach that he doubled over.

Wreck wasn't happy, but he'd get the same treatment if he intervened, and he knew it.

"Okay, no Daddy."

I hit him again.

"Why you got to be so violent?" Pretty sulked off to nurse his wounds. Wreck's eyes followed him to the bar. I didn't ask what was going on between those two. If it became a problem, then I would deal with it.

I sat back against the couch and closed my eyes, letting the sounds of the party surround me. It didn't help, as my thoughts only went to her. I rubbed my eyes, as if I could clear away the image of her pregnant body, dressed down for a family dinner. I would do anything to have her to just like that, and afterward I'd take her in my bed, knowing she was carrying my child.

I groaned as my dick hardened. Fuck!

Looking around the room, I saw a blonde chick standing nearby. I didn't know her name, but she was here often enough that I knew she'd be down to relieve me. Pointing to her, I crooked my finger, and once she stood in between my legs, I pointed to the ground at my feet.

She kneeled and placed her hands on my knees. "You sure you don't want to go to your room, Sabre?" she asked. I had learned that lesson early on as a prospect. You take a girl to your room, and she thinks she's your old lady.

"No. Take care of it here." I didn't care that I was being a dick.

She undid my belt and unzipped my jeans. Taking me out, she gave me a few strokes.

Running my hands through her short hair, I gave her a tug, bringing her lips closer to my dick so that she'd get the hint. "Suck it, or I'll find someone else who will."

She opened her mouth and took me all the way in.

She licked.

She sucked, giving it her best effort, but I was losing my hard-on.

Fucking shit.

I was in the middle of the clubhouse with a blonde chick sucking my dick. If I didn't come, I'd never hear the end of this. There were too many brothers in this room, and even though they weren't watching, they would know.

I laid my head back on the couch and closed my eyes, replaying the scene over in my head with Grace in place of the girl. I would never have treated Grace that way, but this was a fantasy. A damn hot one.

In my mind, Grace was in her t-shirt and shorts, kneeling between my legs. Her eyes locked on mine and a smile crossed her face, like she knew what she would do to me, her pregnant belly safely positioned between my legs, protecting our child.

She opened her mouth and took me completely in. It was so good. I put my hand in her hair. "That's it, mama. Take me in," I encouraged her.

She took me to the back of her throat, sucking in her cheeks to create a large amount of suction around me. It was the best blow job I'd ever received, and there was plenty to judge against.

"Make me come, mama, and we'll head upstairs." Spurring her on, I couldn't wait to be buried between her legs. To take her repeatedly in my bed until she begged me to rest. I buried my hand in her hair, lightly pulling at the roots.

I felt her hand stroke my balls, and that was it. They pulled up into my body, and I released into her mouth, spurt after spurt until I was sure she'd milked me dry. That was when I realized I'd buried my hand in short hair. Grace didn't have short hair.

My eyes shot open, and I saw the girl I had called over.

"Do you want to go upstairs now, Daddy?" Oh fuck, no.

Standing from the couch, I tucked myself in and zipped up my jeans. Stopping at the bar, I grabbed a bottle of Jack and went to my room to barricade myself in. Getting black out drunk sounded like a damn good idea.

Grace was married, and I didn't owe her any undying loyalty, but I felt guilty for what had happened.

What the fuck had I just done?

Chapter 6

Gunpowder and Lead

Grace

"I am assuming we're going to do everything red, white, and blue. Do you think that's too much for decorations?"

I had met the three other members of the community events committee at an upscale restaurant, but the night was wrapping up. I was trying to contain my excitement that the meeting was almost over. All I wanted to do was go home and pull the covers over my head. Hiding from the world seemed like the best idea right now.

"Grace?" one lady called out to me.

I had zoned out. I pretended to shuffle my papers so that I would have a few seconds to collect myself. "No, that will be fine. It's the Fourth of July, so nothing else will work. We'll grab some silver and gold to offset it, if we need to."

"We have the auction items, right?" another one asked.

"Yes," I replied. "Most of the regular donors have already confirmed. I'll reach out to the ones who haven't, and we have a new list of businesses to solicit."

"You're so good at this, Grace. Just like your mother was."

It was the last thing I wanted to hear. It had always rubbed me the wrong way when people compared me to my mother. *You look like her. You act like her.* Like they knew her personally. She was my mother, and I didn't have a clue who she was underneath the perfection.

My mother, and even my Aunt Elizabeth, were admirable women. Confident, poised, and sophisticated. It was what had drawn my father's attention to my mother. It was also what held him back from my aunt. As I grew older, I could feel the spark between them, but neither one had ever made a move.

What had been the appeal for Matt? I was a hot mess dressed in a fancy package.

I'd barely seen Matt before Meredith's failed wedding attempt, but now we lived two separate lives. He would always claim that he had a work thing that he had to stay late for. A client needed something last minute, and he wouldn't be home for dinner. Matt did whatever he pleased with no consequences. It wasn't uncommon to go days on end without even speaking. It all screamed of bullshit, and I was suspicious that there were even more secrets that would come to light eventually.

As our group walked towards the front door, a loud, high-pitched laugh caught our attention. Turning toward the sound, I immediately stopped in my tracks.

There was a large party seated near the bar.

This was a nightmare.

My cousin Clara was sitting next to my husband, laughing at something that was said. I recognized a few more couples sitting at the table as Matt's co-workers and their spouses. They'd all been to my home for one dinner party or another over the years. A few more men rounded out the table. Were they closing another business deal?

I was angry, but I managed not to show it. I kept a cool demeanor, although I wanted to rage at all of them. How many times had I been told to prepare a dinner party on short notice because they needed to show the client they were family-orientated? How many times had I attended one of those meetings so that I could laugh at the right time and make the buyer feel important? Matt and I were so good at closing deals, it had become a running joke.

"Isn't that Matt and Clara?" I heard one woman mutter behind me.

I ignored her and made my way over to the table. I felt my hands clench and a frown forming, but I reminded myself not to show my anger. If they had cared how much this was going to affect me, they wouldn't have done it. No one at the table seemed to care because they all knew Matt wasn't married to Clara.

It was no easy feat at six months pregnant and in heels, but I made my way over to them. My features smoothed out into a calm facade and my hands dangled at my side.

Matt's boss looked up from his glass as I approached, his face falling when he saw me.

"Grace," he said, looking nervous. "What are you doing here?"

I smiled and placed my hand over my stomach. "Same thing you are, Glenn. I had a business meeting to attend to." The look on his face confirmed my suspicions. They were celebrating some deal that they'd closed.

I moved towards the closest man that I didn't know. Sticking my hand out for him to shake, I said, "I am sorry. We didn't get introduced. I am Grace, Matt's wife."

He shook my hand as he stuttered, "It's nice to meet you." He looked a little green. This was probably the last place he wanted to be.

"Oh, the pleasure's all mine," I responded, still smiling. It was anything but. Matt hadn't said a word, but his eyes followed me. I turned from the man and took a few steps over so that I was directly behind Matt and Clara.

"Cousin, I didn't know you had an interest in banking. The last time I saw you, you were in a church classroom being spit-roasted." I placed my hand over my belly, my meaning coming across clearly. A few more faces were a pale shade. "Would you like the video for your adult website?"

"Cousin," she addressed me through gritted teeth, "Matt said you have been under the weather lately, so I filled in for you. You need your rest."

"Oh, I am fine, but Matt wouldn't know. What does Brandon have to say about all of this? Since you're newly dating." Brandon was in acquisitions, while Matt was in sales. Same bank but distinct divisions that worked closely together.

Clara muttered something indistinguishable.

"Or is this some new thruple that I wasn't aware of?" I questioned openly.

I turned back to the man I had briefly spoken to. "I am sure your business deal is in excellent hands. Matt works so hard to provide that he's never home." I turned my attention to the rest of the table and smiled widely. "Well, I must go rest now. Have a good night!"

I held my head high and walked out of the restaurant to my car, not saying another word to anyone.

I never turned around.

Matt never came after me.

Our marriage was officially over.

***

I was on autopilot, not even bothering to process what had happened. I remembered driving home, stopping at every streetlight and obeying every traffic sign, but beyond that, it was all a blur.

I should have opened the garage and gone into the house, but I sat in my car, contemplating what to do for over twenty minutes. The first person I wanted to reach out to was Sabre. Pulling my phone from my purse, I opened my text messages and typed a few lines, but I didn't have the heart to send it. I'd only met him that one time, and even though he had said to call, I didn't want to be a burden. I wasn't his responsibility. It was Friday night, and he was probably banging some hot chick that had a thing for leather, anyway.

I closed out my text messages and opened my contacts, debating who to call. My aunt was my first choice, but it was late, and if I called her now, she'd want to know all the sordid details. I'd end up telling her, and then we both wouldn't get any sleep tonight. I couldn't do that to her.

My father was next on the list, but I wasn't overly enthusiastic about dialing his number. I had a feeling that he wouldn't believe me that Matt was cheating, and even if he did, it would all somehow be my fault. I wasn't in the mood to defend myself. This wasn't a trial, and I wasn't guilty until proven innocent.

Meredith was my last choice, and I hit dial before I could chicken out. She answered on the third ring. "Hello?"

"Hey, Mer. What's up?" I was trying to act normal.

"I can barely hear you. Grizz and some brothers are here for the weekend. We're just hanging out, but it's really loud."

No sooner had she said that than someone laughed loudly in the background. I could hear music blasting, and I assumed they were at some bar.

"Did you need something, Grace?" She pulled the phone away from her mouth and whispered to someone, but it wasn't distinguishable over the line.

"No, everything's fine. It sounds like a good time. I'll just talk to you later."

"Alright, see ya." She quickly hung up.

I was done. I wasn't staying here on the off chance that tonight was the night Matt was going to come home. Getting out of the car, I went in and quickly packed a suitcase with essentials for a few days. Making sure I had enough cash, I decided I'd go to a hotel and start making plans for my future. Alone.

I kept telling myself that this was for the best. I wasn't relying on anyone anymore. However, I held onto my anger, so I wouldn't break into a million pieces.

***

Sabre

It had been a quiet night in the clubhouse with Grizz and the boys gone. There weren't any runs scheduled for the weekend, so when Grizz had approached me about his plans, I didn't have a problem with it.

"A few of the brothers want to come with," Grizz said. He was sitting in one of the chairs in front of my desk with his feet propped up on the corner. "You know, you could come."

"No." I looked up from the paperwork I'd been working on.

"Why? It'd be the perfect chance to see her yourself," he pushed.

"When you first started making these trips, I asked you to check on Grace. How many times did Meredith almost catch you? I distinctly remember you trying to invite Grace to lunch at a fast-food joint, and Meredith had a shit fit. What do you think is going to happen if I come with you? I don't give a flying fuck what Meredith thinks, but she excludes the one woman I am going to want to see." I bridged my fingers together and placed my elbows on the desk.

"Yeah, good point. If you still want to come see her, don't worry about it. I'll make it work." Grizz shrugged.

"No. Meredith will have too many questions for you, and when Grace's finally mine, I'll have plenty of time with her." We'd smirked at each other.

Morning had rolled around, and I was in the kitchen, drinking my coffee, and shooting the shit with the older brothers who'd gathered around the table in the kitchen.

I couldn't help but reflect on the old days when my parents had been alive. I could remember being a kid, running through the kitchen and hiding behind my father's legs as he stood in front of the kitchen sink. He'd pat the top of my head with one hand and drink his coffee with the other. I was standing in the same spot as an adult, imagining my son doing the same thing I had.

I hadn't realized I was smiling until Slate said something.

"Did someone get laid last night?" he ribbed me over the rim of his coffee mug.

"Who you kidding? The last time he tried to get some, he dumped that blonde chickie on the floor and took off running," Thunder boomed, taking a sip of his coffee.

The table exploded with laughter, and I smiled at their antics. They weren't wrong. I'd taken off running and become a monk. There was only one woman I wanted, and until I had her, no one else would compare. It didn't matter that I hadn't seen her in two months.

I was smiling as I took another sip of my coffee and crossed my legs at the ankle. The brothers moved away from my love life, but that didn't stop the camaraderie.

My phone rang.

Grizz.

"Why the fuck are you calling me?" I asked him. He was supposed to be playing house with Meredith, so the fact he'd called me meant shit was going down.

"Fucker. I need to talk to you," he said. There was a slight twinge of fear in his tone, and my body immediately snapped to attention. I braced my hand against the counter as I waited for the news. "Grace is missing."

My heart stopped.

"What do you mean, she's missing?" My voice sounded like cold steel, even to my ears. The conversation in the kitchen had completely stopped.

"We went out last night, and it was loud, so when Grace called Meredith, they didn't talk long. I didn't know she'd called until this morning when Meredith mentioned it, so I had her call back immediately. Grace's phone is off."

"So, Meredith blew off her pregnant sister." My tone sliced through the fucking bullshit.

"You know it's not like that," Grizz tried to rationalize, but it was too late. I was too livid to see straight.

"Put me on speaker," I said. The phone clicked over.

"Cyph," I said.

"Yeah, Prez. I am on it." I could hear the clicks of his keyboard. "Her cell phone last pinged at her house about 9 PM. She must have turned off her phone before she left because there's no trail of her past her driveway. Too many true crime shows. I'll find her, Prez, but I am not sure how long it's going to take."

"You have four hours. You better have a lock on her before I get there." My nostrils were flaring through my anger, my chest pounding with each rapid breath I took. "If something has happened to her. If something has happened to my baby, I am pulling patches, and I don't give a fuck who it is."

None of them said a word, and I could hear Meredith sputter in the background. She'd heard me claim Grace and the baby, and right now, I didn't give a fuck what she thought. I was no longer interested in playing around. I was done.

"Meredith, listen closely," I said to her. "You need to get it through your thick fucking skull. The Iron Shield is a family. I would put my life on the line for any of my brothers or their families. You couldn't even take five minutes to talk to Grace." I heard her gasp. "Old Ladies have to be unanimously voted in. It won't matter what you do. Beg. Sex..."

Grizz growled down the line.

"I'll never vote you in for this. That's not a threat. That's a motherfucking promise."

"I got her," Cyph said. "She emailed David McNally about 10 PM last night. All it says is, 'Check your calendar.'"

"Oh my god," Meredith whispered, but I still heard her. "Grace is getting a divorce."

Chapter 7
A Petty Betty

Grace

I stared at the ceiling of the hotel room, contemplating the meaning of my life. This was godly uncomfortable in my condition, but I didn't care. I'd spent most of last night making plans and researching options. By the time I couldn't handle anything else, it was early morning. I'd tried desperately to fall asleep, but my mind was still running. If it wasn't the scenes from the restaurant; it was thoughts and questions about the future. I was emotionally and physically exhausted, but the adrenaline had kicked in.

I mentally tried to pick at the small paint chip in the ceiling as I contemplated where I'd gone wrong. I started with our college days, looking for any signs. There were none. We had talked daily, attended classes, and hung out when we had free time for four years. His family had lived close to my father, and so we had seen each other in the summers. It hadn't been perfect. We had been too young to know what an actual relationship should look and feel like, but I didn't think it was bad either. There were no obvious signs that I could think of that would have led to this.

Moving forward in our dating timeline, I passed our engagement and went straight to our wedding. I still couldn't see anything that should have caused me alarm. It wasn't until I'd gone job hunting that the flags flew in the wind. I'd worked through high school and freelanced through college for extra spending money, so once we had moved into the home Matt purchased, I had wanted to work. That had been the source of our first fight. He didn't want me away from the house, and I didn't want to sit at home, relying on him. He'd used my safety as his reasoning, but thinking about it, it was more about control. If I had been out of the house, I might have realized sooner how much I was changing to please him. He wasn't changing at all.

A tear fell down my cheek as I thought about all the times I'd tried to celebrate my success. The first time I'd landed a client, I'd been sitting at the dining room table with my laptop. The house only had one room that was suitable for an office, and Matt had commandeered it. I'd made breakfast, eggs and sausage, and he'd been sitting at the head of the table, eating.

"Hey, guess what?" I'd looked over at him as I bit off a piece of sausage.

"Do you have to chew like an animal? If you'd put the computer down, you could focus a little more on your manners." He'd snapped off a piece of sausage from his fork, and I had refrained from telling him to look in the mirror.

"You know I had that company put together a website for me. Well, this party planner contacted me through it, and we discussed all of her needs. She just wrote me to submit a proposal for all the work we discussed and as long as it's the same, she'll book me."

"Why would you want to do that? You won't have enough time to complete the job." He went back to eating his breakfast. As far as he was concerned, the topic was over.

"It's a big contract, so I am going to go for it. She said as long as I get it to her by noon, she'll decide today. If she picks me, do you want to go out to celebrate?" I was trying not to bounce in my chair.

"No, I am not giving up my free time after work. Make sure dinner is ready on the table." He'd stood from his chair and walked out the front door, leaving his breakfast dishes on the table.

I remembered being upset, but I hadn't seen the issues like I did now. It was no wonder that after a few times of trying to tell him about my clients, I'd stopped. It was always the same thing, and I'd end up feeling worse than the last time.

However, a few nights after, he'd come home to dinner on the table. Matt had taken one look at it and announced that we were heading out. He wasn't eating leftovers, so he graciously gave me enough time to throw it all out. The rules were never fair. I had just become numb to it.

There was one small thought that floated around in my brain. Sabre wouldn't have treated me like that. I hadn't spent enough time with him to know, but somehow, I was steadfast.

Looking at the clock on the nightstand, I saw I had a few more minutes to lie there before I had to get up and shower for my appointment. Picking up my phone, I turned it on. There was a missed call from Meredith, but I didn't return it. I'd talk to her later if I was up to it.

Pulling up the text messages, I once again typed out a quick note to Sabre. I debated on whether to send it. He had told me to call if I needed him, and there was a broken piece of me that did. I needed to hear him call me mama and make me laugh at some dumb joke. However, I also knew that I was about to be a single mother, and no one wanted to be saddled with a kid that wasn't theirs.

When I was ready to leave, I reached for my purse on the chair. Catching my reflection in the mirror, I stopped short and analyzed the woman looking back at me. I was the perfect trophy wife. My hair was done, my makeup was flawless, and I even had a dress and heels on. I watched in the mirror as I raised my hand to pat a stray hair down. The woman looking back at me was real. The only thing that was missing was my smile. It'd been gone for a while. The outside was spotless, and the inside was a chaotic mess.

I drove to the restaurant, which wasn't far from the hotel I had booked. Once I parked, I couldn't find the strength to walk to the front door. The car was my haven, and the meeting that I needed to occur was anything but.

I took a deep breath and made my way to the front door. Walking in, I scanned the dining room for Mr. McNally.

"Ma'am, are you here for the two gentlemen in the corner? They said they were waiting for a third," the hostess asked me.

"No, I am only dining with one man."

"I am pretty sure they're waiting for you." She led me over to the table in the corner. On one side sat David McNally, his posture stiff and formal, a briefcase by his side—a typical image of a lawyer. On the other side, Sabre leaned back in his chair, his presence a stark contrast with his leather jacket and rugged demeanor. I didn't know what he was doing here, but I was grateful.

A surge of emotion made my heart race. I wanted to run to him, throw my arms around his neck, and bury my face in his shoulder. My feet picked up the pace, and my arms rose on their own. The clinking of dishes and murmur of conversations brought me back to reality as I approached. We were in a busy restaurant, and I was still a married woman. My arms fell to my sides, and I forced a polite smile, suppressing the urge to show how much I needed him.

They both stood as I approached the table. Thanking the hostess, I turned towards them.

Sabre was the first to move. He reached for my elbow and gently guided me a few steps towards him. Bending down, he kissed my cheek and placed his lips to my ear. "You're in some serious shit, mama. You don't disappear on me like that." He kissed my ear and pulled away.

I took a second to regain my composure before I turned toward Mr. McNally. "Thank you for coming. I know this was short notice, but I appreciate it." I held my hand out for him to shake. "Have you met Sabre?"

"We've met, but Grace, I'll need your permission to continue with this in front of him."

"No, that's fine," I said. I tried to take my seat like a lady, but my center of gravity had changed. I felt Sabre's hand on my back as he helped guide me into my chair. When I was comfortable, both men took their seats to continue.

"I am sorry, Grace, but I am at a loss on how I can assist you," Mr. McNally said. "Your invite didn't mention the circumstances."

"I am sorry. You were the first person I thought of to help me divorce Matt, and it slipped my mind," I replied. I took a quick look at Sabre out of the corner of my eye, but he didn't seem surprised.

"On what grounds?" Mr. McNally sputtered.

"It doesn't matter, but if it's important then irreconcilable differences and infidelity."

Mr. McNally puffed out his cheeks as his face became red. "Matt wouldn't cheat." He paused, trying to gather his thoughts as his tongue hung out of his mouth. "That's quite an accusation."

"Oh, it's the truth." I smiled at him.

The waitress came over and asked if we would like drinks before ordering. Sabre shifted in his chair and pulled out his wallet. Giving her a hundred-dollar bill, he told her, "I don't think we'll be getting food, so consider this your tip for the table."

"Of course, sir," she replied, like a happy little clamshell, and scampered off to another table.

Once she was gone, I looked at Mr. McNally. "I'd like you to represent me in terminating my marriage," I said, pulling out a stack of papers that I had worked on overnight. "I'd like half of all marital assets, including his 401K and investment accounts. You'll find the account numbers and current balances here."

Mr. McNally scanned each page. I didn't know if he was trying to protect Matt's privacy, but I'd made copies in case this went south. His eyes were wide as he started with the first page, but each page made them bug out even more. When he reached the last page, he sighed before setting the stack face down on the table and turning towards me. "Grace, you can't possibly take half of what Matt has worked hard for."

"This is California. I don't think that I need to explain to you I am entitled to half and more for support. This baby needs a future." I placed my hand on my bump, trying to make a bigger impact.

"Will the biker provide when the money runs out?" Sabre wasn't happy with that statement. I watched as his jaw clenched. His lips pulled back in a snarl, exposing his teeth. When I had first met him, I thought his road name was because of his ability to spring into action. Looking at him now, I realized I'd been mistaken. I now thought of a saber-toothed tiger, strong and sturdy but beautifully powerful. He remained silent, and let me continue on.

"I'd like a stipulation in the proceedings that Matt will relinquish his parental rights to this child. He had no problem abandoning me, and I won't let him do that to an innocent baby."

"Grace, you're being unreasonable. Let's say that you receive half of everything. Once the money runs out, you won't have anything. You have no provable income. Being a socialite doesn't pay the bills," Mr. McNally said. "I also can't, in good conscience, ask Matt to give up his baby."

There was a low growl. "You better walk that tone back," Sabre said. "She's not asking you for your professional opinion. She's telling you what she wants done, and you'll do it without complaint."

I didn't need Sabre to lash out at the lawyer. He had his arms crossed on the table, and I reached over and placed my hand on his forearm. I hoped that would placate him for now.

"No, I think Mr. McNally is right. It will be uncomfortable for him," I said. "I am very sorry that I dragged you out here on a Saturday. I can see what a delicate position this puts you in."

"If I were you, Grace, I'd kiss the ground Matt walks on and forget this whole thing." He rose from the table and stormed out of the restaurant.

"Well, that went as well as I expected," I told Sabre with a smile. I'd planned this meeting to create a conflict of interest. It'd worked out better than I had counted on. He was squinting his eyes at me, as if he had missed something.

"Let's get out of here," I said, as I tried to rise from the chair. It was a no-go. The chair was too low, and I didn't have enough momentum to stand on my own. I laughed at my predicament, and Sabre chuckled along with me as he helped me. Placing his hand on my back, we made our way outside to my car.

"Alright, mama. You have some explaining to do," he said as he trapped me against the passenger door of my car.

"I know. Follow me to the beach? It's not far."

He took a step back from me and pulled out his phone, hitting a button, and placing it to his ear. "Come get my bike," he said to whomever was on the other side. I assumed it was one of the men from the club. I tried not to pay attention and give him his space, but he never looked away from me. My eyes stayed connected to his as I listened to his side of the conversation.

"You're not busy, so get your ass over here…You ride bitch with Wreck all the time, so what's the problem?" He smiled. "Yeah, you do that, and I'll break your balls." He hung up the phone, still smiling.

I didn't want to question, but I was curious what had just happened. He swiped at his lips with his fingertips before he offered an explanation. "My little brother, Pretty. He has a fascination with busting my ass over you. He can't help himself. One too many times dropped on his head."

I smiled, thinking about the genuine affection clearly buried beneath the sibling rivalry. I'd never had that with Meredith, and it was probably too late to build that type of relationship. There was too much trauma separating us.

"I can't put you on my bike, and I am not letting you drive on your own," he told me.

"I am more than capable," I teased. "I drove here."

"You are, but you don't have to be." He left it at that. Had Matt ever said something like that?

I opened my passenger door and sat sideways in the seat while we waited. Heels were a necessary evil today, because when McNally ran to Matt, the first question would be about my appearance. I stifled a yawn while we waited.

"You alright?"

"Yes. I didn't sleep well last night."

Before he could say anything more, we heard the sounds of a motorcycle but couldn't see it until they pulled into the parking lot and headed for my car. There were two men sitting on the bike, but it appeared they were in sync.

The driver was bald with a menacing scowl on his face, but the passenger was stunning. He was almost too pretty for words. I scanned his face to see if I could see any familial similarities to Sabre. They had the same basic features, but where Sabre was rugged, Pretty was just pretty.

"If you're not careful, I am going to steal your girl," he called to Sabre.

"You really are choosing violence today, huh?" Sabre called back before turning toward me to make the introductions. "Wreck is the bald asshole, and Pretty's the one who doesn't know when to shut up."

"Eh, occasionally, I am quiet," Pretty said as he patted Wreck's shoulder. Sliding his leg over the bike, he stood and made his way towards us. Wreck nodded at me but didn't come closer.

"Grace," Pretty said as he bent to kiss my hand, like some sort of knight in shining leather.

Sabre shoved Pretty in the shoulder, making him lose his balance. He had to stand or risk falling over onto the pavement. "Knock it off," Sabre said.

"What?" Pretty put on an innocent face. "I was just introducing myself."

"You're cruising for a beat down, and Wreck won't be able to save your dumb ass."

Pretty looked at me again. "He's always so mean to me. Can you fix that for your favorite brother-in-law?" He pouted. The man was deadly to the right person.

I laughed. "Oh, you mean, Grizz?"

Pretty's expression instantly transformed into a wounded face, and he made a scoffing noise. "I'll remember that, missy."

Sabre handed him the bike keys. "Take it back to Meredith's and wait for my call. Chop, chop."

"I'm going to put a few dents in it."

Chapter 8
Let The Tides Wash Away Our Sins

Sabre

Grace plugged the beach into her car navigation, and I followed the instructions until we were pulling into the parking lot. Putting the car in park, I opened my car door, but before I could get to her, she was already standing in front, waiting for me.

"You're not excited, are you?" I asked her as I rounded the hood. She didn't retort, but her legs were bouncing. "Next time, stay in the car until I come get you," I said, sliding my arm around her waist and pulling her to my chest. She turned her head up to look at me, and I stole a kiss from her lips.

"I can get out of my car. I am not that big yet." Her head tilted down, and I had a feeling she'd faced more comments about being large rather than pregnant.

I raised her chin, forcing her to look at me. "I know you can. There's a difference, mama. You don't need me to help you. I want to." I pulled her tighter to me and kissed her forehead. Grace buried herself as close as she could and wrapped her arms around my waist. We stood there for a few minutes in the parking lot, lost in each other.

She was the first one to pull away. "Come on. We are going to do this the right way," she said, holding out her hand towards me.

I didn't hesitate to let her lead me to a bench that was a little way away. It was on the edge of the parking lot, but a little sand had blown underneath it from windy days. She sat down, pulling me to sit next to her. I didn't let on, but I was putty in her hands, and it wouldn't have taken much to get me to follow her lead.

Grace pulled off her heels and hissed as she rubbed her bare feet against the sandy particles.

"Warm?" I wanted to beat my own ass for acting like a high schooler on his first date.

"No, I knew better than to wear the heels, but they were a necessary evil that I am going to pay for. My feet are going to swell tonight."

"You want me to rub them?" I smirked.

Her face turned a light shade of pink, and her lips turned up into a small smile. "I can't bend that way, so you'd have to fall at my feet. You know? Princess treatment."

"You'd like that, wouldn't you?" I'd miss her quick wit. She kept me on my toes, but we bantered easily back and forth.

"Do it one day, and I'll tell you if I like it."

I clasped her cheek in my hand, stroking the soft skin under my fingers. I hadn't realized how much I'd thought of her over the last two months. Now that she was here, I wanted to take my time with her. To savor the hours until I had to go back to the club. I leaned over and kissed her again.

"It's funny you're here. I wanted to tell you what happened last night, but then I thought you might have been busy. When you showed up today, I knew I owed you an explanation," Grace said wistfully, her gaze fixed on the water. "My mother loved the beach and used any excuse to come here, so I thought this should be the spot where I tell you everything." With a small smile on her lips, she stood, holding her shoes in her hands. Pointing at my feet, she waited patiently until I unlaced my boots and took off my socks. "Come on. Let's go."

***

"You weren't planning on hiring the lawyer, were you?" I asked her as we walked down the shore, toes in the sand, carrying our shoes.

She smiled up at me. "No, but I made it so that Matt couldn't use him either. It would have been a conflict of interest anyway, but now, they can't bend the system to their liking. McNally spends his Sundays on the golf course with Matt's dad. Sometimes, they pick up tee time with Judge Dean. If I were to take this to court, I'd have to face Dean, and he doesn't like my father. No matter what the law said, I would have to spend tons of money fighting Matt, only to be shut down. It shouldn't be like that, but it's the good ole boys club."

"Who did you hire?" I was taking a guess, but I was sure there was a plan already in place here.

"I have an old friend from college that doesn't speak to Matt. They had a falling out before we graduated, so I called him. He was more than motivated to take the case." A melancholy look came over her face.

"What is it, mama?" I didn't like the dark shadow that crossed her face. She should always smile, and when she was mine, I'd do everything possible to make sure it happened.

"Do you think I am a terrible person for wanting Matt to hurt?" she asked me, watching the water as it lapped at our ankles.

"No, I think you're trying to grieve the loss, and you can't."

"I want him to feel pain. He'll care more about the money than the baby."

I let her get lost in her thoughts again as we continued to walk.

"I couldn't see it, but the marriage has been over for a long time. I am not holding onto hope that he'll come back and say all the right things. Even if he did, I wouldn't want him to. It wouldn't matter, and he'd just be telling more lies to save face. I think in all of this, I just didn't want to see that I was right."

I could understand that, and I nodded my head to acknowledge that I was paying attention.

"Why are you here?" she asked me. She tripped over her words. "It's not like I am not glad to see you, but..."

"Mama." I gently took her elbow and turned her towards me, stopping our walk. She didn't fear me, but I could sense her nervousness. I claimed her lips in a searing kiss. "I am here because you went missing without a trace. Cyph said you turned your phone off in your driveway, and it took him longer to find you. That's not acceptable to me, and I would have pulled patches if they hadn't located you. Meredith filled in the details when Cyph found the email you sent to the lawyer." I made sure she was paying attention to me. "I don't play with you or our baby. They got a lesson on how serious I am about that, and eventually, you won't question it either." I bent down and pecked her lips.

"I am not free," she whispered, frowning up at me. "You can't just claim another man's baby."

"I see it like this. You have roughly three months left of cooking." She smacked my arm, but my smile widened at her. "I am not leaving until Monday. We'll get you settled somewhere temporarily, and I'll be here every weekend until you pop. You need something, you tell me. You have an appointment, you tell me. Understand?"

"You can't skirt your responsibilities."

"I am not. I am rearranging them. It's only for three months, and Grizz can handle the rest. He's going to owe me, anyway."

"I can do this on my own." She looked like she was going to stamp her foot on the sand.

"You can, but you're mine. I take care of what's mine. Once the baby comes, you both will come live with me, and we'll make a real go of this." I was serious. They weren't living anywhere else but with me. I ran my hands along her jaw until they cupped her cheeks. I gently kissed her to show I wasn't blowing smoke up her ass.

"I can't raise my baby in an MC clubhouse." She raised her nose in the air, and I lightly tapped it.

"My mom loved my dad, but she wasn't crazy about MC life. It can be tough, but we love harder to get through it. My dad built her a home right before Pretty was born. It's on the property but sits further back. No one's used it since they passed. I have been working on it ever since that first night. You'll be safe there, and it's close enough to my...work. I get called out a lot for dumb things."

She didn't respond.

"If you don't like it, I'll get you something else," I said to her.

"Matt bought the house before we were married by himself. I didn't know until he handed me the paperwork. He never asked me if it was alright or what I wanted."

"You'll always have a choice, mama. Unless it involves your safety; that's my call." I took another look at her. The stress of the day was showing, and she looked tired. "Why don't we sit? I'll even help you up and down." I wiggled my eyebrows at her.

"Is that some sort of kinky innuendo?" she asked with a laugh.

"Nope," I popped the P. "I promise that when you're six weeks healed, I am hiring a babysitter, and we're not leaving our bed."

She looked at the sand to hide her blush. "That's five months away."

I stepped towards her and wrapped my arm around her waist. "You're not ready, Grace, and I'll wait. You're mine. I am not going anywhere. Plus, there are other fun things to do. It's just going to take a little time to clean up the mess. Besides, a baby should never see his father's dick."

"You know it doesn't work like that, right?" She laughed so hard at me she couldn't control her snorts.

Her bump pressed firmly into my stomach.

The baby kicked me.

He agreed, and that was good enough for me. For now.

Chapter 9
Matt Strikes

Grace

It had been a while since I had shared a bed with a man. As I awoke, I could feel his hard body at my back. His arm wrapped around my waist, with his hand across my belly. He took every opportunity to touch me, as if yesterday had given him permission.

I wasn't a fool. I was aware there would be good days, where everything seemed right. There'd also be not so good days, where I'd question every little thing. I couldn't move one man out of my life to bring another one in. It wasn't fair to anyone, but if I was honest with myself, I wanted this to work.

My sleepiness was waning, but I wasn't ready to move. This was too comfortable. I reached for his hand and slid our fingers together. My eyes were open, but I didn't focus on anything. I felt him brush my hair away from the back of my neck. His lips quickly descended in hot, open-mouthed kisses, his tongue licking the skin that he'd kissed before moving on to another area.

I started to squirm and slide backwards to rub against any part of him I could. I'd move back, wiggle my butt, and not hit payday. It was maddening, and I made a whining noise to show my displeasure. He chuckled against my shoulder, sliding my tank top strap with his teeth.

"Good morning, mama." He pulled me against his body and pressed his hardness against the curve of my ass. "Is that what you want?"

I slid our hands to my hip, hoping he'd take the bait and move them to where I really wanted him to be.

He chuckled again against my shoulder, sliding his left arm underneath my neck, so that I was laying on his bicep. He then took our hands and slid them back to my waist, pulling me even further into his body.

"You want something, you ask for it," Sabre whispered in my ear. He slid his right hand out from under mine and placed it back on my hip, waiting for me to say something. "You're denying both of us with this silence."

I tried the wiggle trick again. It didn't work, and I should have just said that I wanted his hands on me. To let his touch imprint on my skin. In the next instant, I felt guilty. I was a married woman, and even though my husband had cheated, I was better than that. I had taken vows.

The one thing I noticed in all my confusion was that Sabre wasn't rushing me. He was still nipping at my neck and shoulder, but his hand never left my hip.

I finally gave in. "Touch me," I whispered into the room.

As his hand slid to where I wanted him, his phone rang.

Groaning, he kissed my shoulder one last time and reached over to grab it.

"This better be fucking good," he said to whomever was on the other end.

Last night, I had called my aunt and asked if I could live in her pool house until I delivered. I hadn't given her many details, and to her credit, she hadn't questioned me. It wasn't the best situation, but I'd have my space and people around if I needed help. My father still lived around the corner from my aunt in the house that I had grown up in. It was the only reason that Sabre had agreed.

The brothers were supposed to pick up a moving truck and meet us in the hotel lobby. I assumed the phone call was them. We were late, or they were early. It was hard to tell, but I figured the faster I was ready, the quicker we could get this day over with.

Sabre was still on the call when I made my way to the bathroom and closed the door. I took a minute to stand in front of the mirror and really look at myself. It had only been a day, but I could see things were changing for the better. Today, I recognized my old self appearing. My eyes were bright, my cheeks were pink from this morning's events, and there was a small smile tugging at my lips.

I was standing in front of the mirror, pulling my hair into a ponytail, when the door opened. I only had my underwear on, but I wasn't uncomfortable.

"You are one hot mama." Sabre leaned against the doorjamb, watching me.

I didn't know how to handle the attention, so I tried to play it cool. "You didn't knock. What if I was using the bathroom?"

He barked a laugh. "You weren't. I listened at the door before I opened it, and even if you were, I am sure it'd be hot."

"No." I scrunched my nose. "That's not hot. It's just a fact of life."

"I'll make you a deal. The only time you can close the bathroom door is when you're actually using the shitter. Anything else, it stays open. Deal?" He laughed as he leaned against the doorjamb.

"Deal." I watched him out of my peripheral view. I started at his bare feet as he crossed his legs at the ankles. He'd put his jeans on from last night, and they fit him like a worn glove. They molded to his thighs, stretching the fabric. I tried to pretend like I was still using the mirror, but I was really tracing his muscular lines from his shoulders, down each forearm, to his six-pack abs.

I reached for the dress that I'd brought into the bathroom with me, but I heard him laugh.

"Drop the dress. You're not wearing that. Turn towards me." This time, I didn't hesitate, like I had in the bed earlier.

He walked towards me and fingered the lace of my bra. "This is nice," he said, "but I am going to prefer you naked." He wrapped one arm around my waist and the other across my back. Pulling me towards him, he claimed my lips in a hard kiss. I'd had plenty of kisses, but none like this. His lips molded to mine, his tongue seeking entrance. I was putty in his hands.

He instantly pulled back, and I was confused. Lightly pecking my lips, he kissed his way down my neck, through the valley of my breasts, to my protruding belly. He kissed the top and laid his cheek against the front, holding my hips in his hands.

"I know. You don't like it."

It took me a minute to realize that he was talking to the baby.

***

Sabre let me take charge of moving day, and I pointed at the items I wanted to keep. The brothers would do the heavy lifting. Any of my personal items would come with me to the pool house, and the furniture would head north with the brothers. I'd be there anyway in a few months, so it didn't seem like that big of deal to only make one move.

I didn't know if it was a new perspective or if I was finally pulling off my rose-colored glasses. The house wasn't the only thing I hadn't had a choice about. Matt had hired an interior decorator right after we'd moved in to make sure it was a showroom for his business parties. It was a dream for a magazine spread, but it hadn't been comfortable to live in. I hadn't realized that I hated most of it until now.

I was on restrictions from Sabre and the brothers, but I didn't fight them. They were looking out for my well-being, and I understood. I wasn't able to carry much, and no one was sure that I'd make it up and down the little ramp that led to the back of the truck.

I put a small box of shoes on the ledge of the truck and was making my way back to the house when Matt pulled into the driveway like his car was on fire.

I never imagined Mr. McNally would tell him of my plans so quickly. Matt was livid. He whipped his car door open and stood abruptly. I should have walked back to the house, but I froze. My feet wouldn't move as his eyes locked on me. I knew it wasn't possible, but steam seemed to rise from his skin, turning it a reddish shade. His nostrils flared, and when he smiled, his jaw clenched.

"You fucking bitch!" he screamed at me. "Are you trying to fucking ruin me? I lost that account, thanks to you. They didn't want to do business with 'someone of low moral character.'"

"It was probably for the best," I tried to placate him, but I didn't feel responsible for his actions. A man with great moral character wouldn't bring his wife's cousin to a business closing. "You did it to yourself. If you didn't want people to know you were sleeping with Clara, then maybe you shouldn't have been so public about it."

He was just warming up. "What the fuck are you thinking? You're demanding half of everything I've worked for and insisting I relinquish my rights?"

I tried to find Sabre or another brother, but I didn't see anyone. If they were in the pool house, they'd never hear us. I told myself to remain calm and not respond. I wasn't playing his mind games, nor would I give the neighbors more gossip to take to the local country club. This wasn't the man I'd married, and now, I couldn't even stomach to look at him. I just wanted to scream and rail back at him until all of my conflicting emotions were word-vomited.

"Frigid bitch! You fucking told McNally I was cheating on you. Well, there's Clara, that chick you used to go to Pilates with until you got fat, and at least a few more. The best one was when you were getting an ultrasound and I was fucking Dr. Vargas in the supply closet."

I wanted to tell him I didn't care. He was free to do whatever he pleased. Matt's choices no longer impacted me, but deep down, I was in agony. Each revelation had pierced my heart, leaving deep emotional wounds in their wake. It would take time to heal, and I hoped the scars wouldn't be too ugly.

"Does this make you feel like a man?" I asked.

"I am a man every day that I am not with you."

I didn't have to listen to any more of this. Planning to walk towards the house, I turned my back to him and took a few steps. Matt wrenched my elbow backwards and forced me to turn and face him again. I squeaked at the suddenness of the movement. It had hurt, and I wasn't sure if he had sprained my elbow.

"You were never supposed to get pregnant. I pretended you were Clara, and that's how I could even get it up. I had to be drunk to be with you."

More deep cuts to my soul.

That was when something clicked in my mind. "You slept with Michael Sullivan's girlfriend in college, didn't you? That's why he stopped speaking to us. Well, you'll be happy to know he's excited to have you served—I hired him as my divorce attorney."

He didn't confirm nor deny, but the smirk said it all. This went all the way back to the beginning of our relationship. Had Matt ever even loved me?

"That was a fucking cunt move to call McNally and not tell him what it was about." Matt still held onto my elbow and squeezed so that I would have to cower to him. I was done with all of this.

"Let go of me." I tried to pull my elbow away from his grasp.

"You think you can satisfy the biker? Yeah, I know. McNally has a big mouth. Face it, Grace. No one wants to raise another man's baby." He was still smirking.

I wanted to hit him repeatedly. It wasn't enough to ball up my fists and just pound on him until he begged me to stop. I wanted to make him hurt as much as I did, and the thought of running him over with my car crossed my mind. The only thing that stopped me was jail. I'd already been one person's bitch, and I would not do it again.

I pulled my elbow out of his grasp and tried to turn around, but I wasn't quick enough. Matt shoved me in the chest so hard that I fell backwards. Grasping for anything that I could reach, I braced for impact with the driveway, but it never came.

A muscled arm wrapped around my waist and pulled me back against something so that I could regain my balance. Once I was stable, Wreck stepped in front of me.

"Flo," he said to me. "Don't turn around. Walk backwards towards Pretty. If this motherfucker swings, I am his huckleberry."

I did as requested, no questions asked. When I reached Pretty on the porch, he helped me navigate the stairs.

"You okay, sis?" he asked me softly, his eyes never leaving Wreck's back.

"Yes," I whispered back.

Cyph came out of the house with his phone in his hand to stand on my other side. He must have caught me looking, because he said, "In case, the motherfucker gets handsy. He seems like the type."

Chapter 10

The Family Is Dysfunctional

abre

"At least she's not taking half of this shit. It's ugly," Grizz said to me as we stood in a bedroom, looking at a small desk that was coming with us. It would go in the truck with the rest of the furniture until Grace made the ultimate move.

"Where would it go? Most of this screams money, and the clubhouse is shabby chic on a good day," I retorted. It took a minute for the thought to sink in, but we both laughed at the comparison. It was true, and I hoped Grace wouldn't have culture shock.

"This should be one of the last pieces up here. Let's take it out and see what else needs to go," I said when the laughter died down.

"You think she's going to make you buy new shit?" Grizz lifted the bottom of his shirt and wiped the sweat from his face and forehead.

"No, but you better be prepared. If Meredith ever ends up moving, that sounds like something she'd do out of spite."

"As long as she's happy and not making my life hell, I'll buy her whatever her little heart wants." Grizz smiled, placing his hands on either side of the desk.

"When you're broke, and she's riding off into the sunset, I am going to remind you of this." I placed my hands on my side of the desk, preparing to lift.

"Face it, Grace. No one wants to raise another man's baby," Matt screamed. He was so loud that we heard him clearly in the bedroom. Not knowing he was here, Grizz and I both walked to the window to look out. From this vantage point, we could only see Matt's car. I had had a feeling Matt would show up today.

"Fuck. Grace is outside," I said to Grizz as I turned and headed for the bedroom door. He was right on my heels as I took the stairs two at a time, slowing down before I rounded the corner. The front door was open, and I took a quick peek. I didn't want to rush out, putting Grace further in danger.

She was walking backwards towards the porch, out of harm's way. Breathing a quick sigh of relief, I nodded at Grizz to follow me. We went out the back door and around the side of the house to the front yard. Matt never saw us coming. He was too busy screaming at Wreck, who just stood there with his arms crossed and his feet planted.

I wrapped my arm around Matt's neck, making sure that I put enough pressure that he knew I wasn't fucking around.

"She's alright, but he put his hands on her, Prez. Shoved her hard in the chest," Wreck told me.

"That true?" I asked him a friendly tone. He didn't need to know that I was picturing his torture.

"She's my wife." Matt was trying to elbow me in the solar plexus, but I had him pinned tight enough that he couldn't move.

"I knew you were a dumb motherfucker," Wreck said to him.

"Come on, Wreck. If he was smart, he wouldn't have shown up here until we were gone," Grizz said from behind me. He had stayed a few feet back in case Matt took off running.

"You fucks are trespassing on my property. She's my wife, and she's carrying my baby, so I don't know who the fuck you think you are."

"See, that's where we disagree," I chimed in, tightening my hold on him. He was coughing from the pressure against his throat. "When you're served the papers tomorrow, do everyone a favor and just sign. They're mine."

Matt laughed in between coughs. "You won't have any use for her. If you think she's going to keep you warm at night, good luck. She's so cold that no one wants her."

I shifted so that I could stare at my brother over Wreck's shoulder. I didn't want Grace to see the level of violence I was going to extend to our unwelcomed guest. Pretty figured out what I wanted and led Grace into the house. Cyph stopped recording from his spot, but he didn't move away from the porch.

Matt had pushed Grace in her chest, so I thought it was only fair that I drive my fist into his. He started to cough and sputter even harder than before.

"Not so tough now, when you're not running your mouth." As he was catching his breath, I hit him again. "You pushed my woman and my baby, and unlike you, I protect what's mine."

He looked like he wanted to say something, but he was too busy trying to breathe. Wreck and Grizz just stood there with their arms folded while I walked to the driver's side of the car and opened the door.

Matt was laying over the top of the hood, so I took a few steps and grabbed him by his neck. Shoving him towards the driver's side, I made sure he ran right into the door.

I turned him around so that he was leaning against the driver's side frame. "This brings me no pleasure, you sick motherfucker." Grabbing him by the balls, I squeezed as hard as I could. Matt's mouth dropped open, but there was no sound escaping. Twisting, I made sure that he'd be pissing funny for a few weeks.

"I don't know what you said to her, but I have my suspicions. Don't worry. I'll fix the damage you've caused when I love on her."

Twisting his balls again, I made sure he understood me. "If I ever see you near her again, I'll cut your dick off and pin it on the wall so that the brothers can throw darts at it. Trust me, Scrub will make sure you stay alive long enough so that you can walk around as the dickless wonder."

I pushed him so that he fell backwards into the driver's seat, hunched over.

"Get the fuck out of here." I slammed the door closed on his knees.

Wreck, Grizz, and I stood in the driveway as we watched Matt leave. Cyph came down from the porch to stand next to Grizz.

"Cyph."

"Yes, Prez?"

"I want a full background check on Matt. Leave Grace out of it unless it's a marital asset. He's high on something, and it ain't life."

"I caught that, too," Wreck said.

"I want to know how much of his bullshit is going to fall on Grace." With a huge smile, I leaned forward and told him, "You'll also have to clean up these cameras."

"Bitch."

***

Grace

There wasn't much left to do, and we finished soon after Matt left. I wanted nothing more from this house, and I could tell the brothers were ready to close this chapter. We were all in silent agreement.

I'd called my aunt right before we'd finished packing my things to give her a heads up we were coming. She'd told me she'd gone to the grocery store earlier that morning in preparation.

"I was just going to order takeout or maybe pizza," I'd said to her.

"You can't serve them pizza after they spent the whole day lifting and packing. They're grown men, and they need a home-cooked meal. I'll put a roast on. It's no big deal."

By the time the brothers had unloaded my personal things into the pool house, they were back to their normal selves. Pretty, especially, was having a good time ribbing the rest of them. He even asked my aunt if she'd go swimming with him in his boxers. Wreck rolled his eyes.

"I need a pool boy, if you would like the job permanently," my Aunt Elizabeth had joked back. Wreck had stopped in his tracks when he heard that.

"I am too pretty for manual labor," Pretty had retorted.

"No one said you actually had to do anything." I had never heard my aunt tease like that. She'd always been so prim and proper that it shocked me to hear her.

I'd thanked her profusely, and now I was glad that she hadn't listened to me. The entire house smelled like a roast, making my mouth water. My father and Meredith had shown up about an hour ago, and now we were sitting around the dining room table, finishing eating and chatting about nothing.

When there was a lull in the conversation, my father came out swinging with the heavy hitters. "Are you going to tell the rest of us what's happened, Grace?" He cupped his hands together and placed them on the table as he stared at me.

"I left Matt," I answered him. I had hoped that my simple answer would prevent him from interrogating me like one of his legal clients. He didn't have to like my decisions, but I was still his daughter.

"Any reason?" My father wasn't backing down. His face was a calm mask, but his eyes zoomed in on me.

"Yes." I really didn't want to have this conversation now, and I only prayed that the secrets I had kept from Meredith wouldn't come flying to the surface.

"Care to enlighten me?"

"Gerry," my aunt stepped in. "Now isn't the time."

"When's the time, Liz? My youngest daughter calls off her wedding two hours before the ceremony and shows up a month later, dating again. My oldest daughter is now leaving her husband of eight years, pregnant. That baby needs a family."

I should have known this was the mountain my father would die on. When my mother had passed, my father had put his grief first and his parenting second. He thought I was making the same mistake, putting my needs in front of my child's.

"You're acting like you didn't raise them to be independent." My aunt didn't back down. No one else dared to say a word, but our heads pinged back and forth, watching the match across the table.

My aunt wasn't done. "I am ecstatic that Grace has left, and you should be, too. How many times has she shown up in the last few years alone? He's busy. He's working. That's all a bunch of horseshit, and you know it."

I'd never heard my aunt swear, and I hadn't been sure she even knew those types of words until now. Too bad I wasn't wearing a pair of pearls to clutch. Now seemed like the best time.

"How many times since they were married, have you seen Grace dressed to the nines? Dress, full makeup, and heels? Too many times. She would come here for a family dinner like that. She's pregnant, and I know she's been standing in four-inch heels. He didn't care as long as the presentation was perfect on the outside, Gerry. He didn't give a shit, and we stood by and didn't say a goddamn word. Honey, do you even like all those charity committees and fundraisers?" she asked me.

I shook my head no.

"See?" She went back at my father. "She should run her own for-profit organization. You sent her to school so that she'd never rely on anyone. Yet we allowed him to stifle her. Never again. Never again."

"Since you seem to have opinions, what's wrong with Brandon?" My father wasn't giving up. He was sitting at the dining room table with five bikers, and he was asking about past men. They were uncomfortable, shifting in their chairs and trying to communicate silently with their eyes. I think they were honestly looking for a way to make sure that my sister and I were alright. We just kept looking at each other with our eyes wide open. We'd never seen my father and my aunt argue like this.

"You're kidding, right?" My aunt crinkled her forehead in disbelief.

"No. What was wrong with Brandon?" my father asked.

"He was a mini-Matt, and if you think he wouldn't have done the same thing to Meredith, you're delusional."

"You're delusional if you think they were the same."

I had to stop this, no matter the cost. I couldn't let my father and my aunt rip each other apart over men who were not worth either of their time.

"Mer," I said to her from across the table. Sabre must have known what was coming because I felt his hand on my leg, trying to steer the conversation.

He turned to face my father. "Does it really matter what you think of Matt? Your daughter wants a divorce, and the first thing you should have done was ask her how you could have helped. I didn't see you at the house today."

My father's face turned red, and his fist clenched on the table. I placed my hand on Sabre's leg, patting it. I appreciated the alpha male in him trying to defend me, but I didn't want any trouble. My father could say whatever he wanted, and as long as I didn't have to tell Meredith about Brandon, I'd be okay with it.

"I don't know who the fuck you think you are," my father started. "Matt's a good family man."

Any hope I had that this would end peacefully dissipated into thin air. My father was determined to not let this go until he had torn our family apart.

"Mer," I said to her. "I am so sorry."

She looked at me. Her eyes were even wider, and it reminded me of when she'd been a little kid and hadn't understood the world around her. She'd get the same look on her face, and I'd let her climb into my bed so that I could explain whatever it was she didn't know. Meredith didn't have a clue what was coming, but it wasn't hard to realize it was bad.

"Do you remember when you asked me on the way home why I didn't push you into marriage?" I asked her, but it was a rhetorical question.

"Yes." Her voice came out in a whisper, her hands shaking on the table.

"Please forgive me." My voice was breaking. Sabre let go of my leg and slid his arm around my chair. "I didn't tell you I saw Matt and Brandon spit-roasting Clara. They were having sex in one of the Sunday School classrooms, before the ceremony. Aunt Elizabeth said you were upset when I got to the bridal suite right after, and I didn't think it was important to tell you when you were already calling it off. I am so sorry. I was trying to spare you the pain."

Meredith stared straight ahead. I didn't know if she was in shock or if there was just nothing to say, and then suddenly, tears ran down her cheeks as she sobbed. Grizz tried to hold her, to comfort her, but she sat in her chair, staring straight ahead like a statue.

I wanted to reach out to her and try to make it better, but I was the person who had destroyed it all. Meredith had thought that she'd ended the relationship with Brandon on her terms, and I'd let her believe in the lies by omission. She wasn't free of the emotional turmoil, and now she'd have to grieve it all over again. It would bleed into whatever future she had with Grizz, and I doubted they were strong enough to survive after tonight.

"You've ruined everything. I hate you," she whispered at me. Getting up from the table, she went through the living room to the front door and left. Grizz followed her, but I didn't think he'd be able to get through to her. He had a fight on his hands if he was going to get her to see reason.

"Grace," my dad said.

I would not continue this conversation. I'd already hurt Meredith, and my father would not make me feel guilty for leaving my husband.

"No. I left Matt because he's been cheating on me since the beginning. As I was leaving, he told me he helped conceived this baby on a drunken bender, because that's the only way he could get it up. Is that enough of a reason, Dad?"

I stood up from my seat and collected the dishes from the table. My aunt did the same. No one stopped us.

In the kitchen, my aunt tried to apologize, but I wouldn't accept it. I loved her even more for trying to defend us. It wasn't her fault that this had all fallen to hell quickly.

We dropped the dishes in the sink, and I turned towards my aunt, wrapping my arms around her as best I could. She hugged me back just as tightly.

"I miss my mom," I told her.

"I miss her too, honey. She'd be so proud of you."

"I've made a mess of things," I said.

"No, she would be. You realized that something was wrong, and you're making necessary changes for a better tomorrow." We didn't let go of each other.

My aunt pulled back a bit, so that we were looking at each other.

With a sly smile, she asked me, "Have you told Sabre you're having a boy?"

"He hasn't asked." I shrugged.

"That should tell you everything you need to know about that man."

My smile formed at the corner of my lips. "Are you going to tell my dad that it's finally time?"

Her smile dimmed. "Honey, he's not emotionally available to me."

A heavy silence filled the room as we loaded the dishwasher.

"Do you think Meredith is going to be alright?" I asked her, putting a dish into the rack.

"I don't know, honey. That was quite an unexpected blow. I hope Grizz will get through to her."

"Do you think I should call her?" I didn't know what to do. Calling her didn't seem right, but I didn't want her to suffer in silence.

"No. Let it go for tonight. I'll reach out to her tomorrow once the men are gone. Maybe she'll talk to me." She let out a heavy sigh. "It's times like these. I really miss your mother. She could make anyone talk to her. It was a gift."

Chapter 11
That Baby Isn't Yours

S abre

"Let it out before you have a heart attack." I stared at Grace's dad, and he stared right back at me. We were in a one-sided standoff because I didn't give a fuck what he thought. There wasn't anyone left at the table he could fight with, so I was the next best target.

He leaned forward in his chair, placing his elbows on the table. I was sure he thought he could squash me like a bug, but I had news for him. I'd fought my way to the top of the MC and defeated better men than him.

"What are your intentions with my daughter?" he whistled through gritted teeth.

"I thought it was pretty clear." I gave a dry chuckle, quickly surveying each brother around the table. Cyph was playing on his phone, which wasn't unusual. Wreck was cutting himself another piece of roast, and Pretty folded his hands across his stomach and sat back in his chair, waiting for the fireworks that were sure to come.

"I am asking you." Gerry squinted his eyes and lowered his head so that he was watching me down the bridge of his nose.

"I am going to be here every weekend to see her. Guess what? I will be here for every appointment, and when she delivers my child, I am still going to be here for her."

"Your life isn't here." Gerry was a lawyer, and this was a shakedown. He was looking for any excuse for why our relationship wouldn't work, and I didn't blame him. However, I was going to shut down every argument he had.

"It's four hours." I shrugged, nonchalant.

"That's a long time to make a weekend trip."

"It's only temporary." I wasn't fooling the lawyer, but he hadn't come out swinging with the heavy hitting questions yet.

"How temporary?" Gerry was already leaning forward in his chair, but he raised his elbows off the table and crossed his arms over his chest.

"When Grace delivers, they're going to come live with me."

"I will not allow my grandchild to be raised in an MC clubhouse."

"Yeah, you know, with the orgies every night," Pretty chimed in. He was going to die. I was going to kill him. However, that comment caught Wreck's attention. He doubled over, choking.

"You're right. It won't," I answered her father. "I have a home on the property that my family will live in. It's close enough to the MC for their protection and separate enough to raise a family." I was glad I'd already made these plans early on.

"Raise a family? That baby isn't yours," Gerry huffed.

"I am getting real tired of people saying that. No wonder Grace doesn't believe me when I tell her it doesn't matter."

It was still early days, and I didn't have a problem that Grace was putting her and the baby's well-being first. She was entering a new stage in life and needed to make sure that it was right for them. However, there were clear signs where her skepticism came from. The only person who believed I'd stick around was her aunt. It was a telltale sign when all the nay-sayers used the same phrase.

"Say this works. What happens when she actually has your kid? It's different when it's your own."

I wasn't afraid to confront her father. I didn't give two shits what he thought about me or my plans. He had no say. However, it was easy to see that the man was in pain. I wasn't about to kick him when he was down. He deserved it, but I would not heap more shit on him.

"Grace is carrying my kid. It may not have my blood, but I have claimed both of them. They're mine, and that's just how it's going to be. In a few years, when she's pregnant again, that'll be my kid again. Except this time, we'll have two instead of one. If she gives me a football team, the only problem we'll have is the house only has four bedrooms."

There wasn't anything her father could say.

Eventually, Gerry left for the night. No one had heard from Grizz, and the other brothers had been bunking on Meredith's condo floor. No one wanted to be involved in that drama, so Grace's aunt offered for them to take her guest rooms for the night.

I walked Grace back to the pool house. She'd been quiet the rest of the night, and while I didn't like it, I understood. Too much had gone on for one day.

We were walking up the path when she tripped on a paver in the landscaping. I reached out and grabbed her under the arm to steady her. "Hey," I said to her, "you alright?"

"I don't know. I was fine, and then suddenly, I was really lightheaded. It was weird, but I think I am okay."

"Let's get you inside, and you can rest for tonight." I placed my hand on her back and opened the door.

When we entered the pool house, she went towards the boxes in the kitchen. I watched her for a minute to see if she was really going to unpack. I'd be gone tomorrow, and she'd have plenty of time for that. She'd just been unwell outside, and I wanted her sitting on the couch or I'd take her to bed.

She opened the lid of a box, picked something up from the top, and then set it down and put the lid back on. This went on for three more boxes, and that was when I clued in. She was trying to stay busy so that her mind wouldn't process today's events. Grace scrunched her nose at the last box, and I could see her heart wasn't in it. I wouldn't leave her alone with her emotions.

I walked into the kitchen and stood at the island in the middle. Pulling out my wallet, I grabbed a thousand dollars and laid it on the countertop.

She frowned at me. "I have money," she said, walking towards the other side of the island, away from the boxes.

I just looked at her, taking in the finer details. Her eyes were bright, but she had purple patches underneath. She was exhausted, but she gave me a small smile.

"I have money," she told me again, gathering the bills into a pile and holding them out towards me. "I am a marketing expert. Well, I was in a former life. I take a few clients a year because that's all I can manage. The money is in a business account that Matt doesn't have access to."

"Mama, come here."

She walked around the counter and stood in front of me, holding the money to my chest in one hand. I didn't reach for it, but I wrapped my arms around her and pulled her closer to me.

"I am giving you the money because it gives me peace of mind that in case I am not here, I've given you enough to provide for you. It has nothing to do with you or your capabilities. It's purely selfish on my part. If you don't use it, start our kid's college fund."

I don't know what it was, but something I said broke her.

She finally let out the emotions that she'd been holding in and laid her head on my chest.

I took the money from her and laid it back on the counter before I picked her up and walked to the bedroom. Setting her on the bed, I propped up the pillows and then rearranged us so that I could hold her. I'd had plans to rekindle the fire from this morning, but it seemed selfish to start in this moment. She needed reinforcement that I wasn't going anywhere, and something sexy didn't seem like the right move.

I let her sob against me as I held her. I didn't tell her things would get better or any of that other useless bullshit people said. When she was done, she laid quietly across my chest with my arms wrapped around her.

She shifted so that she could look at me. "Do you want to know what we're having?"

"You know?" I asked her. Grace hadn't mentioned it, and I hadn't given the baby's sex any thought.

She nodded her head yes and gave me a small smile.

"The only thing I want is a healthy mama and baby. However, I am going to warn you. If it's a girl, I am buying bigger guns, and you won't be able to stop me. Just sayin'."

"Why? So you can threaten boys when they come calling?" She rolled her eyes.

"Of course. No one's good enough for my princess, and if she looks like you, I'm fucked." I was serious. Grace was a knockout.

"Well, it's a good thing it's a boy then, isn't it?"

Chapter 12
The Iron Shield

Sabre

The morning after the family argument, I kissed Grace goodbye and thanked her aunt for the hospitality. It was early morning, and we were preparing to ride back in time for Monday morning church. As we walked out to the bikes, I reached for my back pocket, intending to call Grizz. No one had heard from him after he'd chased Meredith out the front door. Just as I pulled out my phone, I saw Grizz sitting on his bike in the driveway, waiting for us.

Riding back as a pack, we stopped for breakfast at a roadside diner.

"So, you going to spill the deets?" Pretty asked Grizz, buttering a piece of toast.

"It's over. There's nothing to tell," Grizz said, not bothering to look up as he took a sip of his coffee.

"Come on. Don't leave us hanging." Pretty never knew when to quit, and Grizz was the wrong bear to poke.

"What? You want me to tell you about how she screamed for two hours straight?" Grizz shot him a look over the rim of the coffee mug.

"Well, yeah." Pretty smiled at Grizz with chunks of toast in his teeth.

"How old are you?" Grizz said.

"Old enough for you to suck my dick, bitch."

Grizz pointed a finger at Wreck. "You better get your boy under control, or the only thing you'll be topping is your pillow."

"Who says I am the bottom?" Pretty smiled again with more toast in his teeth.

Grizz was about to stand up from his chair and reach over the table when Wreck slapped his hand over Pretty's mouth.

"Settle down," he said. Pulling his hand back quickly, he looked at his palm. "You licked me?" He wiped away the toast with his napkin.

"I licked it so it's mine." Pretty continued eating as if he hadn't just tried to claim Wreck.

I steered the conversation back towards Meredith. I wanted to know what she'd screamed about and how this was going to affect Grace.

"It boils down to Grace is the perfect one and Meredith is the fuck up."

"What the fuck do you mean?" I asked.

"I didn't stutter." Grizz took a bite of his burrito. "I don't know if it's some sick older sister idolization bullshit or what. Meredith lives her life, and when it comes too close to Grace's, she runs in the opposite direction. Grace married Matt, and until recently, it was the perfect marriage. Meredith goes to marry Brandon, realizes he's just like Matt, and runs because it will never be good enough. Not because he's a fucking cheater and didn't deserve her."

"So, where do you fall in?" I asked.

"Meredith didn't know you were interested in Grace until this weekend. When she found out, she wanted to run, but I told her it didn't matter, and that she needed to calm down because we're two totally different people. It didn't go over well. Told me I didn't know what I was talking about and threw me out. I slept on the bench in the dog park in the complex. Tried again to get her to talk to me, and she wouldn't. It's fucking over. I will not let some bitch lead me around by my dick."

I watched Grizz shut down over breakfast. No matter what any of us said, the conversation was on hold until Grizz was ready to talk again.

***

It had been a few weeks since Grace had moved to the pool house. True to my word, I drove down every Friday afternoon. I wasn't crazy about making the trip each week, but I kept telling myself it was temporary. The miles fucking sucked, but watching her walk towards me made up for it. I'd sit on my bike, and when she'd reach me, she'd tilt her head for a kiss.

I didn't miss the Thursday night warm-ups and the Friday night parties. I'd rather be with Grace, even if it meant we ate take out in front of the TV. Fuck, I was becoming domesticated.

Monday would roll around, and I wouldn't want to leave her. I wanted to pack her up in her car, leave my bike in the driveway, and just head north. I had to remind myself it wouldn't be long before they lived with me permanently.

Grizz wasn't happy. If I was with Grace, he had to be at the clubhouse as vice president.

Monday morning rolled around again, and I was pulling into the driveway that led to the clubhouse. Stopping at the guard shack, I waited for a prospect to approach me.

I waited.

I waited.

No one came.

Motherfucker better not be sleeping.

I took my helmet off and threw my leg over my bike. Putting the kickstand down, I made my way to the shack. We had a double gate system, where the first gate let you into a holding pen and the second opened into the yard. The shack was large enough to straddle both openings, with windows on either side of the gates.

I walked up to the closest window. Holding my hand up to the glass, I looked in. Sure as shit, my prospect was sound asleep, reclining in the chair, his feet crossed at the ankles, propped up on the desk. His mouth was wide open. Motherfucker was snoring.

I pounded on the window and watched him fall backwards out of the chair.

When he realized it was me, he understood perfectly that he was fucked. It was one thing if another brother had caught him, but I was the president. He'd serve punishment for this.

The prospect opened the window. "Mornin' Prez," he said.

"Open the gate."

He smiled really widely. "Sure, thing," he said, trying to play this situation off.

I pulled into the yard and parked my bike at the front of the line. Inspecting the clubhouse, I couldn't help but wonder. What would Grace think when she saw this place for the first time? When the club had first started, they'd bought an old farm and told the farmer to leave everything as is. Using the barns and the old ranch house, they'd melded it together to form the clubhouse, but it constantly needed rehabbing. The outside wasn't pretty, but a lot of us called the inside home.

I decided right there that she'd have to deal with it. The club was non-negotiable, and the clubhouse was just a part of that. I was born an Iron Shield. It pulsed through my blood, like it had my father's. It'd pulse in my boy's blood and anyone else Grace gave me. They wouldn't know anything different.

When I walked through the front doors, it was back to business. Monday meant church at nine in the morning. You better have been dead or dying not to attend.

Grabbing a cup of coffee, I dropped my phone and keys into my cubicle outside the door and made my way to my chair at the head of the table. I wasn't stupid. We lived in a digital world now, so when I had taken over, I had made sure the room deadened any digital signal once you crossed the threshold. I didn't even allow Cyph to have his computer. I only wanted to see the reports from each business, and Pretty usually brought his notepad as secretary.

The brothers trickled in, and at nine sharp, the prospect closed the door.

I banged the gavel and said, "Who wants to start with their reports?"

No one said a word.

"We're not fucking doing this today. Those of you that manage club businesses know that you have to submit your reports to the rest of the class."

"I'll go first," Grease said. He never said much, but the man knew his way around anything with a motor. Last year, he had asked me if he could have a few more men to build custom cars and bikes. I saw nothing wrong with that, as long as they could keep up with the projects.

"We're early on the bike for that whale, and he's bringing a new restoration when he picks it up. The soccer moms have started showing since we got our first Google review." He handed his papers to Count, our treasurer, to review.

It broke the ice.

Everything was running smoothly until we got to Jigsaw. Jig was a layover brother from my father's era. Too old to really be useful but not old enough to retire. The girls at the strip club thought of him as a fatherly figure, which was why he had kept his job over the years. He handed his papers over. "We're up twenty-five percent," he rushed.

Scanning the reports, Count frowned. It deepened as he read further in to the report. A math whiz, Count's favorite pastime was screwing the IRS. As our treasurer, we used the same loopholes as those other rich bastards.

"You're full of shit," Count said. "You're actually down twenty-five percent, and it looks like you have too much inventory for the volume of sales. This wouldn't have been a problem, but customers are down. How could customers be down? It's a fucking titty show."

I held out my hand for the report. Taking a quick look, I found Count was right. There was too much liquor in inventory to account for the lack of customers. We were down.

"Jig, you're being removed from manager permanently. For now, Count will have to run it and rebalance your books. How did this happen in a week?" I asked, staring at him over the papers in my hand.

He tripped over his words, and sweat was pouring from his hairline. "I don't know, Prez. Everything was fine last week, but I went to print the reports, and that's what I saw. I don't know."

"You can bounce for now. I'll have the new schedule out later today, and there will be a mandatory staff meeting." I wasn't happy, but until I knew the complete story, I wouldn't dish out the punishment. It would come later for Jig.

"Anything else?" I scanned the rest of the room, pausing on each brother's face for a few seconds. My father had done the same thing when he'd been president. He'd told me it was the little things that mattered. Reminding the brothers that you were open to them was a part of creating a close-knit family.

One of the wise men raised his hand, like this was a classroom. They no longer took part in runs, but they still worked hard for the club, and we relied on them for basic things. They'd served their time, and now they could rest.

"Yeah, Thunder," I addressed him.

"Permission to speak freely, Prez?" His loud, booming voice cracked like a storm, ensuring everyone knew exactly where he was in the clubhouse.

"What the fuck?" Did he think I was going to beat his ass over whatever he had to say? I wasn't. Thunder was normally the only one who never consistently annoyed me.

"Well, it's about Flo, and I am too old to have my ass beat."

"Flo?" I was confused.

"You know, Prez. Flo." Thunder looked at me as if I'd lost my mind. When I didn't respond, he explained it to me as if I was five. "You're the president of the club. She's your first lady, so some brothers started calling her Flo. It sounded better that way, and it's still respectful."

"You mean Grace?" I asked the room, sitting back in my chair, watching each brother nod their head. They'd never called her Flo in front of me, but it was obvious that tongues had been wagging. "Tread carefully." I rested my elbow against the table and rubbed my temple, feeling a headache coming on. It was too early for hard liquor, but I didn't know what to think about this. When my mom had been First Lady of the Club, everyone had loved her, but no one had given her a road name based on her position.

"Alright well, some brothers and I were talking. We were in the kitchen the day she disappeared. You were out the door in under ten minutes. Now, if that had been my Old Lady, I would have done the same thing."

I was getting angry. "Get to the point."

"We don't know her, and she's your Old Lady." I tried to read his face, but he was telling me the truth from their perspectives.

"What are you trying to say? You want to meet her?" I looked around the room. Almost every brother was nodding their head yes.

"Scrub, can she travel at seven months?" I asked our resident doctor. Scrub had been born in the club and was the only one of us smart enough for med school. He hadn't had a choice.

"Yes, but she'd have to stop at least once an hour to stretch and walk around, provided she's not having any complications." She had had an appointment this past Friday, and the OB had told us everything looked good.

I didn't like the thought of her on the road.

Thunder popped up again. "The Old Ladies would like to welcome her into the club with a baby shower, but they weren't sure how to bring it up to you."

I had to give them something, or they would ride my ass over this more so than they already had.

"Most of you know how I met Grace. Most of you know that she's pregnant. It's not my kid, but I am claiming them. That's not up for debate."

Grizz was angry. His hands clenched on the table, and I could tell he was gritting his teeth. He was probably cursing Meredith's name.

"When Grace delivers in two months, I'll bring them here permanently."

"Is that why you're fixing Mom and Dad's house?" Pretty piped up. It was unusual for him to be so quiet.

"Yeah. If she doesn't like it, I'll get something else, but for now, it'll do."

I steepled my fingers and rested my chin on them. Thunder was right. I couldn't ask them to give their lives for her when they hadn't met her. I'd just have to make sure she understood what she was walking into.

"We haven't had a Family Sunday in a while." I was thinking out loud. "Chef, do we have enough supplies for one?" I asked. Chef ran our diner and cooked nightly for whomever was here.

"It shouldn't be a problem, Prez."

"Let's do that. We'll have a Family Sunday in two weeks, and I'll figure out how to get her here. I don't want her on the road by herself." It placated them for now. "One more thing. We had a sleeping prospect this morning." There were moans and groans throughout the room. "How many women are in the clubhouse right now?" I asked the room.

Grizz popped up. "Just the club girls, and there's six of them."

"We're losing a prospect, but I won't have someone here that can't protect the club." There was agreement, but no one spoke. "He'll get six hits and then we'll promptly dump him on the side of the road."

Chapter 13
Friday Date Nights

It was Friday, and Sabre would leave the clubhouse soon to head my way. When he'd told me we'd make a real go of this at the beach, I'd wanted desperately to believe him. I was also a realist, and if he didn't show or made an excuse, I would just move on. I was having a baby by myself, and I didn't need to worry about a man in my life.

The first week after I had moved into the pool house, Sabre called and texted the entire week. It was the little things. He'd send me a text in the morning. By lunch, it was usually a video call while he sat in his office, and at night, he'd call me again. I'd keep a running commentary about whatever TV show or movie I was watching. I didn't know if I was distracting him from his work or keeping him company. There were always power tool sounds in the background, and I didn't want to ask for fear he'd stop calling.

That Friday rolled around, and I pretended like it was another day. I ran errands. I worked on a small proposal for a project that would need to be completed by the end of the year, and I tried not to watch the clock. Sabre had called that afternoon to tell me he was on his way. He'd never missed a Friday, even though I knew the miles took a toll on him.

This Friday was no different. I was sitting at the island counter in the pool house, answering emails and pretending count the hours. I was writing an email, but my eyes were so focused on the microwave clock, that I forgot to hit send. Laughing at myself, I grabbed my phone off the counter and headed to my bedroom.

I was puttering around the room when my phone rang. Smiling, I reached over and grabbed it. Taking a deep breath, I shook out my arms and legs. I had to play this cool. I refused to show him exactly how much I missed him when I wasn't sure what to make of our situation.

"Hello?" I said.

"Mama."

I smiled widely and held my giggle in. "Hey," I said, trying to sound casual.

"Don't give me that shit. I don't believe you're not as excited about today as I am."

"A little." I smiled as I climbed into my bed, getting comfortable.

"What are you doing?" Sabre asked.

"Shouldn't you be asking me what I am wearing?" I was trying to play coy.

"No," he scoffed. "If you start that shit, there's no way to finish it. I am not riding four hours with my dick so hard it's suffocating in my jeans."

"That sounds like a tragedy." I finally gave in to the laughter that bubbled in the back of my throat.

"It is. He'll shrivel up and die."

"Why do you talk about him in the third person, like he has actual feelings?" I didn't know why I was keeping up with this silly conversation, but it was fun and light.

"He does, and he really wants to get acquainted with you."

"That's not my fault. You did that to yourself." I openly laughed at him.

He made a disgruntled noise. "Don't know what I was thinking, but it fucking sucks."

I could hear him walking around, but there weren't enough background sounds to place exactly where he was in the clubhouse. I'd asked one time why he didn't call me from the road. He'd told me I was too much of a distraction, and he'd rather call me from the clubhouse before he actually left. Safety first. It also gave the brothers a chance to razz him if they knew he was talking to me.

"What are you doing, mama?" he asked me.

"Lying in bed. I might take a nap before you get here." I'd been increasingly tired the last couple of weeks, but it wasn't so bad that a nap wouldn't cure it. Dr. Vargas hadn't implied that anything was wrong, and I chalked it up to the baby growing.

"You're killing me," he huffed. "Grabbing a cup of coffee, and then I am on my way. You alright?"

"Don't worry about us. We're fine." I didn't want him stressed trying to get here when a nap sounded fantastic.

"You don't quite understand that you're mine. Even if you were here, I'd still worry about the two of you. It's just what you do for the people you care about. Sleep tight, and I'll be there soon."

I awakened an hour before his arrival, so I'd showered and dressed in shorts and a nicer shirt. The first Friday he'd arrived, I'd worn a dress and heels. After he had told me how beautiful I looked, he had slapped my ass and told me to go change. We hadn't been going anywhere that required that level of dress code. I'd actually been more comfortable and had a better time. Now, I didn't bother with the fancy clothes.

I waited until I heard the engine of his bike driving down the street to grab my things and lock the front door of the pool house. Walking around the main house, I made it to the driveway as he pulled in. I stopped. This was my favorite part.

He stopped the bike and made sure the kickstand was in place before balancing the bike on it. It was always the same pattern. Next, he turned off the bike but didn't stand. Sabre slid his helmet off and ran a hand through his hair. Placing the helmet behind him, he sat on the bike and watched me watching him. We both smirked at the same time.

I waddled towards him, and as I approached, he wrapped his arm around my waist, and I wrapped mine around his neck. "Hi," I said before I leaned down and kissed him. When I started to pull away, he wouldn't let me go, resting his forehead against mine.

"Hi," he said. "Each week you're more beautiful than the week before, and that's saying something, because you knock my socks off."

"Words like that will get you laid."

"Nah, I fucked myself over telling you'd I wait. I'll keep my promise to you, so that the next time I make one, you won't ever doubt that the words are true."

I didn't know what to say, and when he scanned my face, I think he knew I was having a hard time. It'd been a while since anyone had kept a promise to me. I wasn't sure I even believed in them anymore.

"Hungry?" he asked me. "I am starving, and I thought we'd head to that seafood place on the beach."

I nodded, still needing a minute. He unhooked his arm from my waist and held out his hand for my keys.

He drove us to the restaurant, and we took our meals and sat down in the sand to eat and watch the tide. When we finished eating, he reached for me, and I climbed into his lap. My back to his front.

Sabre told me about the club's shenanigans. "Cyph's been running the fight channel all hours of the day and night. He's been telling Grizz he's getting his money's worth. Of course, it's not going well, and there's almost been several fights break out. Who needs the channel, when they could just do a knockout tournament in the backyard?"

I laughed as I leaned back into him and just listened.

"Count's our treasurer, so he's been running one of our clubs until we can get a new manager. It's not a big deal. Count knows what he's doing, but it means that he spends a lot of time with the girls."

"Strippers," I corrected.

"How do you know they're strippers?" he asked me.

"You were pausing over keywords, like there was more to it than just a club with waitresses. It wasn't hard to figure out." I tipped my head back and smiled at him. He nipped at my lips before he went back to telling me the story.

"Well, Count couldn't care less, but supposedly, Cyph enjoys hanging out with the girls." He reached down to my side and lightly tickled me. "So now, I have Count teasing Cyph, who's picking on Grizz. When Grizz explodes, he'll take out at least three more brothers. I swear, it's like running a fucking frat house."

"I am sure you can handle it," I teased.

"Well, you'll get to experience it when I come get you in two weeks." He buried his face in the crook of my neck, his stubble tickling my skin.

"What are you talking about?" I crinkled my nose.

"The brothers have officially asked to meet you, so the club is hosting a family picnic, two weeks from this Sunday."

"Are you asking me to come or telling me?" I brought my hand up to rub his forearm.

"You'll be begging me to come, and I'll enjoy every minute of making you squirm." He kissed the side of my forehead as he tightened his arms around me. "Mama, I am asking if you'll come to the family picnic." I must not have answered quick enough because he quickly followed up with. "They know how we met, and they just want to see the woman who's captivated their president."

"With pretty words like that, how could I say no?"

He called it a family picnic, but it would be a family interrogation.

***

It'd be a miracle if I didn't throw up. I wanted to, but I didn't think it would make me feel better. This wasn't morning sickness. This wasn't even food related. I was nauseous over a family picnic.

I'd been to plenty over the years, and I'd even planned a few, but I couldn't shake the nerves. My mind kept shouting that I was walking into an interrogation, no matter how many times I repeated the words "family picnic."

I didn't blame the club. They wanted to make sure that I was good enough for their president. However, there was a little voice that berated me for having too much baggage to saddle him with. It would just be selfish not to let him go.

It was constant, but I put my big girl panties on and got to business. I enlisted Aunt Elizabeth to help me. I told her I was nervous and that I wanted to make a good impression.

She laughed at me and said, "Grace, you know a way to a man's heart is through his stomach." We made four coolers worth of salads, lasagna, anything that would go over well.

It was four in the morning, and I hadn't been able to sleep. To top it off, as soon as I got comfortable, the heartburn kicked in like a bitch. This kid was trying to kill me.

Sabre had told me he didn't want me on the road by myself, but I figured it was so early, I could get a head start. It only made sense to meet them somewhere on the road instead of roaming around the pool house, counting the minutes until their arrival. I texted, telling him I was going to pack the car and then make my way to the highway.

I was an hour into the journey when my cell phone rang. It had automatically connected to the Bluetooth in my car, and I hit the button on my steering wheel to answer. I wasn't expecting the growl that came down the line.

"I am not happy with you, mama." Sabre growled again into the phone.

"I told you I couldn't sleep, so I figured I'd make the trip quicker." It sounded reasonable to me, so I wasn't sure why he was so upset.

"I don't care. Your ass should have been home until we got there."

"Too late now," I replied, disappointed at how this trip was turning out already. He meant well, but so had I. What a way to start our three days together.

"Where are you?" he asked.

"About an hour in, right outside of Bentley."

"It's too late now, but don't stop. There's a roadside diner at Exit 154. Should be about an hour and a half from you. I know the owners, and your ass better be there when I get there."

I was angry with myself for not following his instructions. I was angry at him for thinking that I couldn't do this. This wasn't how it was supposed to go. I was just angry and didn't feel like responding to him.

"Mama, you know your safety is my priority. I wouldn't forgive myself if something happened to you. It was the whole reason we made these plans, and I expected you to follow those instructions."

"I don't like you right now." I frowned at the radio, showing his connected call.

"Mama."

"No," I cut him off. "I am feeling good. I have no complications, and I spent all day yesterday making food because I am not good enough for you. You don't get to be angry when I am the one who has to make a good first impression. I'll just turn around and go home."

"Your ass better be at that diner," he repeated, and I hung up on him.

I fumed all the way to the diner. I fumed as I sat in the parking lot, waiting for my detail squad. When I heard the loud symphony of bikes, that was when I realized why I was angry. Sabre honestly cared about whether or not I was alright. It had nothing to do with what I looked like or that I had cooked for today. He had cared only about me. Matt wouldn't have given two shits as long as everything was perfect. I didn't know there was a difference...until I had calmed down.

I watched in the rear-view mirror as they pulled into the parking lot in formation. I recognized Sabre at the head of the pack instantly. Pretty and Wreck were behind him, and two brothers I didn't know were behind them.

The four of them backed into a spot behind me, and Sabre pulled in behind my SUV. I thought I was calm until I saw him pull off his helmet and rub a hand through his hair. My anger flared all over again. He didn't have the right to look that good.

He sat his helmet on his seat and made his way to my window. I looked straight ahead, avoiding eye contact.

"Mama, open the door," he said loud enough so that I was the only one to hear him.

I didn't want to cause a scene in front of the brothers that I didn't know. I unlocked the door but still sat facing forward.

He opened the door and squatted down, reaching for my hands in my lap. I didn't move.

"Mama, it took me the drive here to realize what's going on. I am not Matt. I'll never be that fuck face." He rubbed my hands between his.

I didn't know how to apologize for my behavior. On the one hand, I shouldn't have to. I was an adult, and I had left my home early to be helpful. On the other, the comparison would never be fair.

He rubbed his thumb against my cheek. "I don't care what you wear. You could have had your pajamas on. I'd still think you're the most beautiful woman I've ever seen."

I finally shifted to look at him. I didn't know how to make this better, and tears leaked from my eyes.

"Hey, it's alright," he spoke tenderly. "It's just a speed bump. We're going to have those every now and again."

I swung my legs out of the car and sat sideways in the driver's seat. "Stand up," I said and waited for him to move.

When he did, I threw myself into his arms. Burying my face into the flannel underneath his leather club cut, I tried to think of what to say. I'm sorry didn't seem good enough. I held him tight to me, and when I lifted my head to speak, he looked down at me.

"I know," he said.

"You don't know shit." I was still feeling feisty.

"Potty mouth," he said as he kissed me. "I like it."

"Thank you," I whispered against his lips.

"It's alright, mama. I am not going anywhere, and neither are you."

"Can you guys just fuck already? I can't handle all this sexual tension."

I buried my head again into Sabre's chest, and he held me just as tightly. We were trying to ignore Pretty. He must have opened my passenger door because suddenly, there was a high-pitched squeal.

"You made potato salad!"

Chapter 14

Sunday Family Picnic

Grace

This was déjà vu.

I was waking up in a strange bed, and kisses were being placed on my shoulder.

By the time we had made it back to the clubhouse and unloaded my car, it was still early morning. Sabre had told me most of the brothers wouldn't be awake until noon, and the picnic didn't start until one for everyone else. He had ordered the brothers to go back to bed and then led me to his room.

Unzipping my dress and helping me with my shoes, he had made sure I was laying comfortably before he had stripped and climbed in behind me. Wrapping his arm around my waist, he had whispered in my ear, "This is going to be the best nap I've ever had." I hadn't told him I felt the same as I placed my hand over his forearm.

Now my eyes were fluttering open. My hair was to one side, and I felt him lick from the bottom of my hair line down my spine. I tried to pretend I was still sleeping, but I felt him chuckle against my skin.

"I know you're up," he whispered in my ear.

I sighed. "I bet you say that to all the women in your bed."

"I distinctly remember trying to lure you." He wrapped his arm tighter around me. "Looks like you came willingly."

"I haven't come yet," I whispered.

He laughed and placed his forehead against my shoulder blades. "Are you going to stop me this time, mama? I am not starting something you're not finishing."

"What if you're not a sure thing, and then I've started something for nothing?" I tucked my hand under the pillow, hiding the smile that was tugging at my lips. "There are plenty of other men here that could fill in for you."

He growled against my back and gently rolled me all the way over so that I was facing him. His eyes danced with excitement. This was our version of foreplay.

I pretended to go back to sleep as I snuggled closer to him. My smile gave me away, and he saw through my act. Kissing his pec, I drew random designs against it with my tongue. My eyes were still closed, but I could smell and feel him surrounding me. It was better than an aphrodisiac.

"What is this? Some sort of fucked up snuggle fuck?"

"You said fuck twice," I commented dryly. Opening my eyes, I tilted my head back so that I could look at him. "Stop talking and do it."

He sat up and arranged the pillows on the bed. When they were to his liking, he reached for me and helped me to lean against the mountain he had created. "The only thing I want to snuggle with is your warm, wet pussy."

He wasn't even touching me, and I let out a groan.

He chuckled again. "Let's see how loud you can scream."

Placing his hands on the wall above my head, he leaned in and claimed my mouth. The kiss was passionate and wet, a preview of what was to come. Leaving me breathless, he licked down my chin, past my neck, to the valley between my breasts. Making swirls with his tongue, he traced the curve of my left breast. Pulling the cup of the bra down with his teeth, he sucked my nipple into his mouth. I didn't recognize the moan that escaped me.

"That's it, mama. I want to hear you," he praised me.

When he had had his fill, he did the same thing with my right nipple. I was close to coming, and he hadn't even touched me where I needed him.

He pulled away from me. "What do you think? Should we see if you can come from this alone? I am up for the challenge." He smirked. It would have been arrogant on any other man. On him, it was mischievous.

I shot him a look through my hooded eyes. Grabbing the back of his hair, I tugged until his mouth was back at my breast.

Going back to my left nipple, he sucked it into his mouth until it became sore. It was like he instinctually knew when to switch so that I would beg for more. He'd nip at my nipple, lick his way to the other nipple, and start over. My moans were low but frequent. I couldn't hold them back. My body felt like it was riding a tidal wave. The slow, gentle climb, floating above the crest in the middle, and then the final push over. Sabre would give me a few seconds to find the shore, only to start all over.

As I came back to reality from the last orgasm, I felt Sabre's hands on my thighs, gently massaging them. I let my legs fall open to give him room. He lay in between them but stopped. Placing his fists on either side of me, he balanced on his arms, so that he was right above my belly.

"I know you don't like sharing, but just this once, give your daddy a break. I promise I won't traumatize you with my dick." Before I could make a wisecrack, he kissed my belly and continued.

If the first round of orgasms had been gentle, this was anything but. He slid my panties down my legs, and that was all the warning I had. I tried to reach him, just to touch him for some sort of grounding, but I couldn't. Grabbing the sheets was my only anchor to reality. I'd die a fortunate woman. No complaints.

I bucked my hips as much I could, but I couldn't gain any leverage. I tried to use my heels to push up, but the sheets were silky. There wasn't enough grip, and I ended up hitting him underneath his chin. Sabre laughed it off and held me down by my hips to stop any further exploring. I let my head fall back on my shoulders, not bothering to silence the sounds that were rapidly forming on my lips.

"That's it, mama. Let them hear you come for me."

Releasing one last scream, I felt like I was airborne, flying above the clouds. As I came down from my high, I watched as Sabre moved towards me. He slid his arms around my limp body and held me tight. This must have been aftercare. I didn't know. I'd never experienced it. Kissing my temple, he said, "That wasn't even my dick."

As I formed a response, there was a loud bang on his door.

"Warn the single brothers when you're going to do shit like that. Now, I have got to take care of it myself."

***

Eventually, we had to leave his bed and help with the preparations for the picnic. Sabre was outside with the other brothers, making sure there were enough tables and chairs. I wanted to be helpful and waddled my way to the kitchen. Slowly opening the door, I stood just inside, unsure of how to introduce myself to the three women working.

"Hello, I am Grace." That was dumb. "What would you like me to do?" I directed my question towards the two women standing at the sink. They turned as one when they'd heard me, smiles on both of their faces.

"You really are pregnant, girlie." I spun towards the sound, and that was when I realized that the waitress from the bar was standing at the stove. Her hair was teased out more than I remembered. She wore a similar outfit as she had in the bar. Tube top, short skirt, fishnets, and stilettos.

"Should you be standing so close to an open flame with all that Aqua Net?" I was trying to break the ice, and I hoped she would catch the awkward joke. I didn't have to worry about the other two. They howled with laughter, grabbing the counter and each other to hold themselves up. They eventually collected themselves and the older woman walked towards me.

"Hello, Flo," one of the women said. "I am Bear, and I don't think I have ever seen Dee speechless." She winked at me, pointing towards the woman at the stove.

Bear had to have been in her late fifties or early sixties, but she looked like the epitome of a biker chick. Tight tank top. Short shorts and heels. She had laugh lines around her lips, and her eyes were kind as they twinkled from her amusement. I immediately liked her.

Bear led me to a barstool at the island counter. "Sit," she said, as she helped guide me.

"I can stand. Just show me what you need done." I wanted to be helpful. Good first impression and all.

"I haven't seen that boy smile in a really long time. That's help enough," she said as she walked toward the sink.

"I am Raven," the third woman said to me, twirling a piece of her salt and pepper hair. I didn't say a word, but she chuckled. "My old man named me that many moons ago. You obviously know Dee," she continued as she nodded towards the waitress.

"We've met," I said politely.

"She thought you were turning your nose up at the club's liquor, like you were too good for it. We heard about it for days afterward until Sabre stepped in."

"I didn't mean to," I said, making wide circles around my bump.

"You weren't showing then," Dee said in a huff.

"No, not really, and the dress was puffy."

The conversation lulled as they continued to prep for the picnic, and I jumped the gun a bit. "If you give me the napkins, I can wrap the silverware."

They howled again.

"Someone would have a fork in the eye for sure," Bear piped up, still chuckling.

Raven came around the counter and wrapped her arm around my shoulders in a side hug. "Honey, you're precious. If we gave those assholes real silverware, we'd never get it back."

As they worked, I listened in, adding a comment here and there. They even let me fill the vegetable trays, making me feel included.

***

The backyard was full of people. Brothers, wives, girlfriends, parents, anyone, and everyone, and I loved every minute. The food was delicious, and I had a smile on my face all day as I mingled.

"Give it back, fucker."

I was sitting at a picnic table in the backyard, chatting with some of the other wives that lived in town. When I turned towards the sound, I had to shake my head at the sheer childishness of it all. The last time I had checked the food table, the bowl of potato salad had been sitting in the ice. It was now tucked in the crook of Pretty's arm. He was cradling it like a football.

"It wasn't yours. I am saving it," Pretty said, twisting his body so that the bowl underneath his arm was further to the back. He looked like he was ready for a fight.

"For what? Potato salad wrestling? That's not enough," Count retorted. I had met him earlier in the day, and I recognized him from his blue spikes. He tried to reach for the bowl, but Pretty moved further away from him.

"It's so good. I am going to rub it all over my dick."

"You won't need much. Now pass over the rest." Count tried to swipe the bowl again from Pretty but missed and knocked into one of the other brothers.

"That's what the girls say when they're with you." Pretty wasn't giving up. He turned his back on Count and tried to walk into the clubhouse.

"Wreck say the same thing?"

Even I knew it was the wrong thing to say. I'd heard the rumors, but I hadn't asked questions. It wasn't my business, and I didn't think gossiping would help me make a good first impression.

Pretty turned around, placed the bowl on the ground, and launched himself at Count. No one broke it up, and I didn't dare try. When the first sign of blood appeared, Sabre pulled them a part with Grizz's help.

"Family picnic. I am sure if you ask Grace nicely, she'll make more," Sabre said, holding Pretty with an arm wrapped around his chest.

When Pretty looked over at me with an innocent face, I nodded. It wasn't a big deal, and I was sure the ingredients were in the kitchen. I'd poked around in the cabinets earlier, and it looked pretty well-stocked. The women had told me that Chef was the brother responsible for the kitchen. He loved to cook, and no one minded eating.

The picnic went on after that without a hitch. I made acquaintances. I refilled drinks and played hostess. When I found a tray in the kitchen to load a round of refills, that was when I realized what I was doing. These were not Matt's business associates that couldn't do for themselves. These were Sabre's brothers. Shaking my head and smiling, I left the tray in the kitchen and walked back outside. After this round, they would have to get their own drinks.

It was getting dark, and some families were packing up to take their kids home. As they said their goodbyes, the numbers dwindled. That was when I realized women were arriving. Women dressed to bag a brother. If I thought Bear's clothes were tight, she had nothing on them. Skirts that barely covered their asses. Tube tops. Thigh highs. I couldn't help but watch them. I'd never be comfortable wearing something like that, but more power to them.

I was sitting with Bear, Raven, and Dee when they noticed what I was watching.

"Girlie, if you're a vestal virgin, go to bed now," Dee said to me.

"How bad?" I asked. I knew exactly what she meant. There were club girls that satisfied the needs of the single brothers. These women were going to get anything they could from anyone they could.

"You might learn a few things," she continued.

"You could go reciprocate," Bear said, wiggling her eyebrows. "The brothers have big mouths, and you were the talk of the morning."

I shook my head, letting my hair cover my face and trail down over my shoulders.

"Don't worry about it. I heard it was hot as hell," Raven chimed in.

"I am going to go die now," I said as I got up from the table. Their laughter following me.

I entered the clubhouse and made a beeline for the bathroom. My bladder was the size of a pea these days. As I opened the door, I saw there was a young blonde girl at the sink. She looked at me and shook.

"Hello, I'm Grace," I introduced myself. I was trying to put her at ease, but she shook even harder.

She walked towards me, as if she wanted to escape, but I leaned against the door. "What's going on?" I asked her. I had seen her when she came in with a group of women who had hung around. However, I hadn't met her, and I didn't think I'd done anything that warranted the shakes.

"Flo, I am so sorry." Her voice broke. "I didn't know, and he called me over."

"What are you talking about?" I was confused, and this conversation wasn't heading in any direction.

"The girls told me he was free, and when he called me over, I took my chance. I didn't know he was with you. If I had, I would have never done it."

"Start at the beginning and tell me everything," I told her. "You're not in trouble," I quickly added.

"I gave Sabre a blowjob." Her lips quivered, but the shakes hadn't stopped.

"That's it?" I asked. I wasn't sure what to do with that information.

"I don't think he was into it because it took forever, and my jaw got tired. I was about ready to give up when he became feral. I thought he'd take me upstairs."

She looked at the floor and dug one of her high heels into the tile.

"He called me mama. I thought I was special, and that I'd finally found a man of my own." She laughed, but there was no hint of humor. "I put it together when I heard him call you mama today. We're both blonde. He probably imagined you during the blowjob."

"I am sorry," I said to her with a shrug. I didn't miss the irony of the situation. Laughing hysterically, I just looked at her. She must have thought I'd officially lost it.

As my laughter died down, I waved my hands over my baby bump. "My soon-to-be ex-husband told me he had to picture my cousin. You're telling me that the other man in my life used me as a fantasy. I know it sucks for you, but that's a tremendous ego boost for me."

She smiled as if we were sharing an inside joke. Her shaking had stopped.

As I washed my hands, a cold sweat came over me. Were we together when this blowjob had occurred?

Chapter 15

Sunday Family Picnic, Part Deux

Sabre

The sun set over the family picnic. It had been a good day. The club had come out in full force to welcome my woman. They were my family, and I didn't realize how much their support meant to me. She'd already won over most of the brothers that lived in the clubhouse, but the rest would fall. Thunder had been right. I owed him a favor for reminding me that the club was family, and family was everything.

It was getting dark, and I wanted to be by Grace's side when the nocturnal festivities started. I'd noticed that the first round of regulars had already arrived. I wasn't interested, but I also didn't want Grace to experience culture shock. Although, she *had* watched a threesome in a church. Chuckling to myself, I scanned the yard, looking for her. The last time I had seen her, she was sitting with the other old ladies.

Walking over to where they sat, I leaned in between Raven and Bear. Mama Bear had been my mother's best friend, and I had spent as much time at her house growing up as I had my own.

"Ladies," I greeted them.

"You better not fuck this up," Bear said as she turned towards me in her chair.

"Thanks," I replied dryly.

"No, I am serious, Sabre. Don't fuck this up. She's cute as a button." Bear used her finger to drive her point home into my chest. She was the only one I would have ever allowed to disrespect me like that.

"You approve?" I asked. It wouldn't matter either way, but I was curious.

"Yeah, and your mom would have, too."

It stung in all the right ways. I'd been thinking about my parents lately, reliving the good times and wishing they were here. I couldn't bring them back, but I knew they were looking down on the club, smiling.

"You going to show her your parent's house?" Raven asked me. "I've heard you've been fixing it."

"As soon as I find her."

"Girlie took off for the bathroom," Dee said with a wicked glint in her eye. "Didn't take too kindly to this morning."

"I doubt that." I laughed. "She wasn't complaining," I said, standing up and heading towards the bathroom inside the clubhouse. Their laughter followed me all the way to the back door. I was sure they were having a good time at my expense, but I didn't care. They thrived on gossip, coffee, and nail polish.

Shaking my head, I headed for the clubhouse's bar inside. It faced the bathroom, and I'd be able to snag Grace when she finished. I didn't see her, so I sat next to Grizz to wait. He was busy trying to forget the one that got away at the bottom of a bottle.

I wasn't Meredith's biggest fan. Unless something changed, I'd never excuse her behavior. I was still pissed that she hadn't taken a five-minute phone call the night Grace had left. Not only had she brushed her off, but that stunt at the dining room table had irritated me. Grace had never said a word about either. It was like she brushed it off as typical Meredith behavior. It was a speed bump that we avoided discussing.

Looking at Grizz, I could tell he was almost to the point in the bottle where regret sets in.

"Don't do something stupid. Grace is here, and one day, they will speak again."

"Take your own advice," he said as he nodded towards the bathroom.

"Fuck!"

The blonde girl that I had called over to blow me was walking out the bathroom door.

Grizz snorted as his head hit the bar.

"Go to bed." I elbowed him in the side. "You're drunk."

"We're not together. I can fuck whomever I want. Maybe I'll go with that chick."

"That's a lie," I said. "There's only one frigid pussy you want, and she ain't here."

I stood up from the bar stool and dug my heels in, bracing myself in case he took a swing at me for that comment.

"God, she fucked me up." He took his bottle, and I watched him walk upstairs towards his room alone. At least that was one crisis adverted. I didn't need Grace seeing him fuck some other chick and then telling Meredith.

Fuck my life. Grace walked out of the bathroom. Her face was blank, and there was no doubt in my mind that they had talked. We hadn't been together then, but would Grace see it that way? I wasn't about to lose her. I turned towards her, watching her approach me. "Hey," I said, kissing her forehead.

"Hi," she replied. Her face was still blank.

"Walk with me." I held my hand out for hers. At least she didn't shrink from my touch.

I led her around the back and walked down the dirt path behind the clubhouse. My father had made sure that when he had built the house for my mother, it sat far enough from the clubhouse for privacy but close enough that it was secure. It wasn't ready, but I hoped by the time the baby arrived, it would be our home.

I tried to find the right words to say, but I'd never cared about a woman's feelings before. I didn't want Grace to be hurt over something insignificant to me. I knew I needed to grovel for her forgiveness, but I didn't know where I should start.

I glanced at her, my mind racing. "Grace," I began, my voice uncertain. "Did she say anything to you?" That probably wasn't the best thing to say.

"Should she have?" I realized Grace was well aware of who I meant. That probably wasn't a good thing, either.

As we approached the house, I had an idea. Making sure I had a good grip on her hand, I led her up the steps of the porch to the swing I had fixed. My mom had loved to sit outside, surrounded by the clubhouse sounds but far enough not to be involved. I had thought Grace might like the same thing.

Sitting on the swing, I gently pulled Grace to sit next to me. Wrapping my arm around her shoulders, I made sure there wasn't any space between us.

"Fucking Grizz," I muttered. Grabbing my phone, I pulled up the picture that Grizz had sent me the night he'd shown up to dinner at her aunt's house. "This started it." I handed Grace my phone to show her the picture.

Scrunching her nose, she turned towards me. "When was this taken?"

"The night Grizz met your family."

"Why would he take a picture of me?" She was still staring at my phone.

"To torment me," I groaned.

"Why would a picture of me putting away the dishes torment you? I am not even showing skin."

"I wanted you from the moment I sat next to you in the bar." Was she serious right now?

"I don't understand. There was plenty of time in between now and then to forget me when you have a harem knocking at the gate."

How had she gotten that impression by what I had said? I held her chin, making her look at me. "You know that's bullshit." I went for broke. "Mama, I've always wanted you. I should have tried harder that first night. You should have come here and never fucking left, but I was a fucking idiot. I pretended like you were just some out-of-towner that I'd never see again." I pulled her closer to me, and she laid her head on my shoulder.

"When Grizz started seeing Meredith, I made sure he'd check in with you. I wanted a full report the minute he stepped into the yard. Were you alright? Had he seen you? I should have known you were important, but I was busy fighting it." I scanned her face for any sign we were okay. She made no movement, and I was getting scared.

"Grizz sent that picture, and I tried to play it off. We weren't together, even though you consumed my every waking thought. She was just a blonde that night. I called her over, and she blew me. I had a hard-on when she started, but it didn't last long. She was trying, but I was going soft. If I had been anywhere else but the main room, I would have walked away, but we'd have never heard the end of it if I hadn't come. I let my mind wander to you, and I was so absorbed into the fantasy, I accidentally called her mama without even realizing it." I grabbed her chin and turned her so that she faced me. "You're not going anywhere. I am not going anywhere. This was just a speed bump, and not even a big one."

She smiled, and the twinkle was back in her eyes.

"You played me." I held her tighter to me, so that she couldn't escape.

"No, I didn't. I just didn't let you off the hook easy. You sweated." She leaned in to kiss me, breaking the hold I had on her chin. "Do you even know her name?"

I didn't answer. As long as Cyph had cleared her to hang around, I didn't need to know her name.

"It's Kelly, and she wants to be a nurse." Grace kissed me again.

"Please tell me you didn't make a new friend that's going to haunt me."

"No, but she's hoping that one of you will take notice of her."

"It won't be me. I only notice one woman these days, and she takes all of my focus." I kissed her this time, deepening it.

"Cute," she said.

"I prefer dead sexy." I couldn't help it. It was easy to tease her.

She laid her head on my shoulder as I gently rocked the swing. "I wasn't sure I wanted to know, but it wasn't as bad as it could have been. She told me what happened and how she'd put it together when you called me mama today."

"It was before we were together. You know I will not cheat on you, right?" She made a non-committal noise. That wasn't acceptable to me. I turned her chin again, forcing her to look at me. Grace was stunning in the moonlight. "Mama, I will not cheat on you."

Staring out into the yard, she rambled, "I am not afraid of that. We spend time apart, and it hasn't crossed my mind until today. I let someone else change me to fit their mold, and as I find myself again, I like who I am. I don't want to lose that. If you leave, or we don't work out, I don't know what will become of me emotionally. That's the part that scares me."

I made a noise in the back of my throat and held her tighter. I understood where she was coming from, but I didn't want to think about spending another day without her. Our current situation was temporary, thank fuck.

She was still staring out into the yard. "Tell me about your parents."

She couldn't see it, but I smiled at my memories of them. "My mom was a college senior when she lived in town with some friends over summer break. She met my dad at the grocery store, of all places, and he invited my mom to the clubhouse for a party. He told her she could bring her friends with her, but no one showed.

"The way my dad always told it was that he would ride up and down the streets looking for my mom, and when he found her, he'd 'randomly' bump into her. My mom would always laugh and remind him he chased her ass through town.

"They had a fling. My mom went back to school, and my dad continued to live the biker life. She found out she was pregnant with me the first week of school. She didn't tell anyone, but that December, she graduated early and came back here. When my dad saw her, he told her she should have listened when he said he'd keep her. It was a running joke between them. He'd tell us he'd keep my mom, but that we were expendable."

I looked down to make sure Grace was alright. She had a small smile on her face, as if she was picturing my parents and their antics.

"They sound like good people," she whispered.

"They were the best." I held her as I rocked the swing with my foot. "I was born in the club, and my parents lived in the clubhouse until my dad built her this house. By then, he had become president, and my mom supported his endeavors. However, there was always a piece of her that wanted solitude. You've seen it. There are people everywhere and constant noise. It's an amazing family, but it's not a place to actually raise one."

Maybe this was all too much for her.

"Mama? If you don't like it, we'll either build something else, or we'll buy something in town. Your choice."

She turned towards me and wrapped her arms around my waist. "Thank you."

I bent down and kissed her with fervor. I needed to know she was alright. If something was wrong, I'd die trying to make it right, but she was too quiet.

"Show me?" she asked as she pulled away from me.

"The tour awaits." I was trying to bring her smile back. I held out my hand to help her up from the swing, but she beat me to it. Leading her towards the front door, I unlocked it and flipped the light switch on. I let her walk in first, because I wanted to see her reaction. Her face wasn't as blank as it had been, but there were hamster wheels turning behind her beautiful brown eyes.

The front door led into the living room, and I stood in the entryway as she roamed around downstairs.

"It's warm in here," she said as she stood in the doorway that led to the kitchen.

I didn't think it was warm, but I wouldn't question her. I was still on thin ice, and if that meant I was going to freeze my balls off, then so be it.

"A family lived in this house. It carries warm memories," she repeated. "My mom was full of life, and when she passed away, she took all that warmth with her. It's so cold, which is why we meet at my aunt's."

I understood what was going on in her mind.

"I want to show you something," I said, gesturing for her to lead the way up the stairs. When we reached the middle stair, there was a creak. She paused, and I made sure that I was ready if she slipped. Rubbing her foot across the stair repeatedly, she made it creak.

"You didn't sneak anyone in here, did you?" she laughed.

"No. Wouldn't have mattered, anyway. The brothers would have snitched to my dad. If we wanted to…"

"Cause mischief?" she helped with a wide smile.

"Yeah, something like that. We did it away from the club."

Leading her down the hallway, I stopped at the first door on the right. I squatted, so that I was level with her belly. "This is for you," I told the baby, placing a kiss on her stomach.

I opened the door and moved out of the way. I had painted the walls a light blue, and there was furniture in the room. A crib, a changing table, and a dresser. Grace walked in and went straight to the crib. Running her hand along the edge, she turned towards me, tears in her eyes.

"My dad made these when I came along, and when Pretty was born, he used them. They've been sitting a while, even though Pretty hasn't grown up yet. I cleaned them up and gave them a fresh coat of varnish."

She waddled towards me and threw herself into my arms. Catching her, I made sure I had her attention. "What do you say, mama? Let's make some new memories here."

Chapter 16
That Sounds Like A You Problem

Sabre

My eyes were still closed, but there was a bright light trying to force its way in. Too bright, and it made me question what time it was. Last night, Grace and I had walked back to the clubhouse after I'd shown her the house on the property. It wasn't ready, and I thought she'd be more comfortable in my room. I could have sworn I set an alarm before I had fallen asleep with her in my arms. It was Monday, and I couldn't be late for church.

I wanted to roll over and forget everything, but I was afraid that I was two seconds from being wide awake. That was when I heard it. A wet, sucking noise. I'd had enough blow jobs in my life to recognize where this was heading.

A light laugh bounced around me.

"Am I dead?" My voice was rough with sleep.

"I don't think so," she laughed, stroking underneath my dick. He twitched at her touch. "He doesn't seem to think so, either."

I looked at her through my hooded eyes. "What are you doing, mama?" I rasped.

"Replacing a memory." Grace was sitting on her knees in between my legs.

I sat up and fluffed the surrounding pillows.

"What are you doing?" she asked.

"Going to enjoy the show."

"Might as well get the full effect." She arched her back and pulled my shirt over her head, not wearing anything underneath. I stretched and locked my hands behind my head. If I got close to her, I would break that promise to wait. The baby would get over it. Eventually.

Her eyes traced over my upper chest. "How come you don't have tattoos?"

"If you do a good job, I might tell you."

"Is that a challenge?" She smirked.

I shrugged. This was one thing I loved most about being with her. I could tease her, and she'd never back down. "It ain't going to suck itself."

"Oh." She made an innocent face, and her lips shaped into an O.

She bent down and licked the top of my dick from my stomach to the head, making a ring around the crown, and licked the underside back towards my body. "Was that alright?"

She was killing me. This was better than any club hookup, and we hadn't even begun.

I pretended to fall back asleep, but my eyes weren't completely shut. I could still see the outline of her body and hear how frustrated she was in the sighs coming from her lips. Me too, mama.

I settled back against the pillows, ready to enjoy the slow friction building. I never expected for her to deep throat me. My body jack-knifed forward, and I caught her off guard. She nearly tumbled backwards off the bed. Instinct made me grab her arms and swing her forward so that she was against my chest.

"You just wanted a feel."

I palmed her breast, swiping quickly at her nipple with my thumb. "Nah, I just didn't want to have to explain the thud to the floor."

She laughed and leaned even closer so that her lips were on mine. "This is not the way I planned it."

"How was that?"

"You weren't supposed to wake until the end." She kissed me, her tongue exploring my mouth.

"Nah, that's a shitty plan." I rubbed two fingers against her throat. "This. This is a good plan."

Laughing, she pecked my lips quickly and pushed on my chest. Laying back on the pillows, I watched her lean over and take me to the back of her throat. I didn't want to think about who had taught her that, but I'd be the last one to reap the rewards. I didn't know what was better, watching her work me or feeling her mouth surround me.

Hot, wet. When she needed a minute, she'd slid me out of her throat and use her tongue to make circles around my dick. Her heat engulfed me, and I became lost in it.

There was a bang on the wall. "Too loud. Knock it off." I hadn't realized it was me that was snarling and growling.

Someone yelled, "You're just pissed you didn't keep that girl."

The first brother responded, "If she's in your bed, I am coming."

"You wish you were coming." Laughter echoed through the walls.

"We should remodel, starting with the walls," I moaned into the room. I didn't really care that the brothers could hear us, but they'd see nothing. Grace was mine, and I was a greedy bastard. Her body was for my viewing pleasure only.

Grace shifted on the bed and brought her right hand up to wrap around me. She sucked in her cheeks and pulled back off of me, letting her grip slide with her. It was constant friction. I wasn't a praying man, but I thanked whatever god had brought her into my life.

When she pulled away on the upstroke, I pushed forward with my hips, looking for more. She sucked harder, and her grip tightened. I was putty in her hands, and it wasn't long before I was shooting into her mouth.

As I was coming down from my high, she pulled away from me, sitting back on her knees. When she stuck out her tongue, I could see my come. Damn, if I didn't want another round instantly. She made she sure had my attention and swallowed.

Growling, I grabbed her by her hips and pulled her against me as I sat up. Gently gripping the sides of her face, I kissed her with everything I had. It was the alpha male in me that wanted to know what we tasted like, so that I could claim her.

There was a high-pitch scream coming from down the hall.

"What's a man gotta do to get pussy? My hand's tired," someone yelled.

"That's what she said." Another round of laughter followed it.

We both chuckled at the brother's antics. I gently rolled her to her back and returned the favor. When she was screaming my name, I leaned over and whispered in her ear, "I don't like needles."

***

It was a quarter to nine when I grabbed a cup of coffee and walked into the office we held church in. It had been a good morning, and there was a smirk on my face. The brothers trickled in and took their assigned seats. They looked at me. I looked at them, but no one said anything about this morning's fun. We normally didn't kiss and tell.

When the prospect closed the door at nine, the lazy atmosphere of the morning vanished. Cyph walked into the room, placing a folder in front of him as he sat down. It was clear shit was about to go down.

"We all want to know what's in the folder, but we need to get through the club business reports first. Grease?" I started the meeting, hoping the mounting tension would ease.

"Everything's good. We're getting a lot of referral business in the garage and with the restorations," Grease said quickly, handing his report to Count for review. He sat back in his chair, but his fingers tapped on the wood table.

"If you grow anymore, we may need to look for a bigger garage, but there's enough here that I can make it work," Count commented as he flipped through the pages of the report.

No one was paying attention. Every eye was staring at the folder that sat in front of Cyph.

"Chef? What about the diner?" I tried to keep church moving, but it was like pulling teeth.

Someone coughed. There were a few brothers that kept shifting in their chairs. No one asked to speak.

"All my costs are in line. May need another waitress if it doesn't slow down, but I don't want to hire someone and then the summer business goes home." He handed his report to Count, but his eyes were still on the folder.

"Enough. If you have a normal report that you didn't get to present, turn it into Count. If there's an issue, bring it to my attention after church." Looking at Cyph, I couldn't get a read on him. "What's going on, Cyph?"

He looked back down at his folder. Taking a drink from a Red Bull, he cleared his throat. "I don't know how the pieces go together, but the strippers from the tit show were here yesterday."

"They're still here," a brother piped up. There was an awkward chuckle.

"I prefer strippers, so I was sitting with them. They thought nothing of it when they talked about our new clients that were coming in. You could tell that they were a little nervous, and I wondered if this might be why our sales were down. So, when I went to bed, I ran through the security feeds from the last couple of weeks." He took another drink.

Opening the folder, he pulled out a few pictures and laid them in the middle of the table. The first couple were of the security footage from the club. There had been a few tables of well-dressed men watching the show with drinks in hand. The second set of pictures were their licenses. This was why I loved Cyph. I didn't have to tell him to take the next step. He just did it.

"Why the fuck do we have cartel members in our club?" Grizz exclaimed.

The brothers all talked over each other. Banging my hand against the table, I instantly shut them up. I felt it in my gut. There was more. There was always more.

"What else is there?" I asked Cyph.

"We always check new employees before they work at any of our businesses. However, there's a few at the tit show I didn't recognize." He laid out a picture of a license on top of the rest of the papers. "This is one of our new employees."

The brothers instantly talked over one another again.

"That looks like Flo."

"Nah, Flo's too classy."

"Prez would know."

Grizz beat me to it again. "That's Clara. Their cousin."

"The one that was getting spit-roasted in the church by the ex-husband and the groom." I finally found my voice to contribute. "What the hell is she doing there?"

Everyone looked at Jigsaw, and I could tell we'd stumbled upon something we weren't supposed to find out. Jig's face had gone pale, and it looked like he was about ready to shit his pants.

"I....I....I...."

One minute, I was sitting in my chair. The next, I had Jig's face pinned to the table. "What the fuck did you do?" I seethed, pulling Jig up by the hair and slamming his face back into the table. No one got up to help him. They knew the club wouldn't tolerate disloyalty and that Jig would face the consequences alone.

I slammed Jig's face again into the table.

"She came in a few weeks ago, asking for a job. I gave her our normal application, but she said she was running from an abusive boyfriend and was afraid he'd find her. I let her work off the books, but I told her I'd have to have a background check. Every time I tried to ask for basic info, she distracted me."

"Help me understand, Jig. While you were getting your dick sucked, you put everyone in this room in jeopardy. Every brother, every one of our family members, and my unborn child." I slammed his head for a third time against the table. "Is she even working?" I asked him.

"Barely."

"So, you're stealing from this club, too."

Looking at my enforcers, Twig and Pint, I said, "Get him out of my fucking sight. He can stay in the cell downstairs until we decide what to do with him, but make sure none of the women see you."

When the door closed behind them, I walked back to my chair. Looking at Cyph again, I wanted to know what else there was. Matt, Clara, and now the cartel. These pieces connected, but I didn't have a clue how.

"The day we moved Flo out of her house, I started running searches on Fuckface. Anyone who was there knew he was on something, but he came up clean, until now." He stopped, but I nodded my head for him to keep going. He didn't want to talk about Grace, but we needed to know about Matt.

Cyph took another swig, and I wanted to beat him for pausing. "Fuckface actually makes shit tons of money off of his contract signings and bonuses. They paid off their cars, have minimal credit card debt, and their house has positive equity. I was thinking, if they're actually not bad off, why is he trying to take out loans? Payday loans. Loans from the bank. Anywhere that lends money."

"Has anyone given him a loan?" I asked.

"No, because the bank canned his ass over his morality clause."

My eyes twitched, and I rubbed my temple as the vein in my forehead throbbed.

"Matt lost a client on Friday night after Grace outed him for adultery. The bank then received an anonymous email with a video that following Monday. It was the perfect storm to let him go. Too easy." Cyph took another sip of the Red Bull, and I wanted to rip it out of his hand and throw it against the wall.

"Where did they get the video, though? The only one I know of is on Grace's phone. She recorded the threesome in the church. Thought she would need proof, but as far as I know, it's gone nowhere." The room was silent. No one wanted to say what we were all thinking. "Is it possible that Grace's phone is being tracked?" I asked Cyph.

"I thought of that, but when I searched it remotely last night, it was clean. I'll have to do a deep dive with it physically."

"This isn't a coincidence. I can head over to the club today and see if I can find Clara. Since I am acting manager, she won't think anything of it," Count said.

"No, it should be an older man. She'll think she has the edge because she could pull one over on Jig," Thunder said. "I can go over there and see if she'll do the same thing with me."

"Both of you go. Give her options, but if the cartel shows up, you call for backup." I looked at both of them.

They nodded in acceptance. No one was going to play the hero.

"Cyph, see if you can figure out any connection between the cartel and Matt. I don't see it, but I am not ruling it out. I also want to know why Matt is playing hardball over the divorce. Grace filed for half of their marital assets and sole custody of the baby. If he were to just sign over his parental rights, she'd release the money. He has to know that."

"Meredith still talks to Clara. I'll ride down there and see if she has any information," Grizz said, rubbing a hand over his face.

I inspected my best friend. He looked like last night's bender had done him in. "Call her," I said. "You're not fit to ride."

"She won't answer. I'll have to make her talk to me." He didn't look thrilled at that prospect.

"Take a few brothers with you," I told him. "That goes for the rest of you, too. No one rides alone until we know what we're dealing with." Every brother nodded their head in agreement. "I am not losing anyone over this shit show."

***

The smell of breakfast hit our noses when the first brother opened the door to leave church.

I caught Chef's eye. No one used his kitchen without asking permission unless they were getting a drink. He looked back at me and shrugged as if to say, *I have been with you this whole time.*

As we walked into the main room, I saw there were tables grouped together with a smorgasbord of food.

Eggs.

Bacon.

Pancakes.

Biscuits with gravy.

The brothers helped themselves to plates, but I headed towards the kitchen. As I approached the door, I could hear loud music playing. It was some pop princess that I only knew because we played it to keep the club girls quiet for a few minutes.

Cracking open the door, I paused. The club girls were putting platters of food together. The girls that had stayed over were cooking, and in the middle of it all was my woman, directing traffic. They were all singing as they worked. I took a step further into the room.

It was a domino effect. One girl saw me, and they instantly bolted into the main room. When I caught Grace's attention, she leaned against the counter, crossed her arms over her chest, and looked me up and down. Walking over to her, I kissed her until her arms uncrossed, her hands unfolding, reaching for me.

Pulling back, I asked her, "How did you get them to work together? They don't fight, but they don't listen either."

"That sounds like a you problem," she told me with a wide smile. Kissing me again, she whispered, "I told them they couldn't eat unless they helped. It took little convincing to get them all on the same page."

Pretty burst into the kitchen and shoved me to the side.

Grabbing Grace in a bear hug, he swung her once but thought better of it.

"You made me potato salad with my name on it."

Chapter 17
The Interrogation

S **abre**

No sooner had my brother burst into the kitchen than he was gone in a flash.

Grace was laughing as she turned back towards me. Stealing a kiss, I held her hand and led her out to the food line. I couldn't believe the girls could work together. There was always friction between the club girls and the hang-arounds looking to catch a brother. It made me wonder how much they'd actually listened to Grace, or if she'd really strong-armed them.

They'd arranged tables in a row, creating a buffet line from both sides, even setting up the rest of the tables so that everyone could sit together. Putting Grace in front of me, I silently awaited our turn.

I noticed Grace had only grabbed a small scoop of eggs and two strips of bacon. I didn't think that was enough, considering she was eating for two, and I put two more strips of bacon on her plate.

I watched as she threw them back in the pan. I grabbed them again and put them back on her plate. "You need to eat, and that doesn't look like it's enough."

"I can't have extra bacon. It'll give me heartburn," she said as she threw them back in the pan again. She suddenly grabbed the hand that wasn't holding my plate and held it to her belly. I could feel just the slightest bit of pressure. The baby was kicking.

"See!" she said happily. "He agrees." She was still holding my hand to her when she looked down at her protruding belly. "Tell Daddy we like bacon. but it doesn't like us. He worries too much." There, in front of the bacon, she made my heart stop. She looked up, quickly kissed me, and moved down the line like nothing had happened.

She didn't realize what she had said, but I treasured it. It was the first time she had accepted my claim on them. No matter what happened, that was the moment they were officially mine.

I caught my brother's eye. Pretty was already sitting at the table with two full plates in front of him. He made sure Grace wasn't watching when he wound his fingers into a heart shape. Pretending to pump his heart over his t-shirt, my brother gave her his seal of approval and teased me in the same motion.

My eyes circled around the room, and every brother that I landed on gave me a sign that they approved. Damn. I was going to have to hold it together or risk being called a pussy. She had wrecked me with one word. Daddy.

Breakfast continued on as if we did this every day. The brothers were joking with each other, and the girls interjected here and there. It was light-hearted after such a heavy church. I sat back in my chair, drinking my coffee, and took it all in. Grace even joined the conversation every now and again.

Eventually, the girls who had stayed overnight cleaned up the food and took off. Our club girls knew it was time to go and made excuses to head towards their rooms. Grace was the only woman left, and as she stood from the table, I placed my hand on top of hers.

"Mama, we need to talk."

"Oh, so is this the part where they interrogate me?" She'd turned to face me, but her expression was earnest. She really believed the brothers would question her, when in reality, I needed her help.

"What are you talking about? I asked her.

"Well, you said they wanted to meet me. I have been waiting for the inquisition." She shrugged.

I must have looked at her funny because she continued to ramble. "You know? Where they rapid-fire questions at me. Yes. No. To get to the other side."

The brothers chuckled at her antics. If the rambling hadn't given it away, I just had to look into her eyes to know she was serious. She thought she wasn't good enough for me, and I'd kill Matt for that, given the chance.

She turned towards the brothers at the table. "It's okay. I am ready." She squared her shoulders like she was going into battle. This wasn't what I had meant, but I'd let it play out for now.

Once the brothers clued in, they started aiming questions in her direction. Birthday? Natural hair color? Shoe size? Bra size? Did the curtains match the drapes? Most of them were just stupid, but it was breaking the ice, so I didn't put a stop to it. She had a smile throughout the ordeal, so as long as she was good, I was good.

It wasn't until my brother piped up that the questions took a different turn.

"What's going on with your divorce?" Pretty asked, his arms crossed over his chest and his elbows planted firmly on the table.

"I hired a lawyer that has a personal vendetta against Matt, so he's motivated to make sure that this goes through. As far as I know, the county sheriff served Matt right after I moved out, but he won't sign. His lawyer keeps sending back unreasonable demands. Even if I agree with one of them, he just updates it to something even more asinine."

"What happens if you never get a divorce?" Pretty slid his elbows forward so that he was leaning over the table.

"I don't know," she said. "I have never thought that it wouldn't go through, eventually." They stared at each other, both losing the previous humor. "My marriage is over, Pretty."

They continued to stare at each other.

"Ask me what you really want to know," she said.

"What happens when that baby comes, and you decide club life is beneath you? Or Matt comes to his senses and tries to win you back? I won't let my brother suffer." There was movement underneath the table, and Pretty winced.

"Matt's not coming, and even if he did, I wouldn't go back. However, this is his child, and even though I am fighting for sole custody, I don't know what will happen," she answered. They were still staring at each other.

She surveyed the brothers around the table. Crossing her arms and laying her elbows on the table, she mirrored Pretty's position as she went down the table. "I have no clue what club life entails. If I do something wrong, all I ask is that you tell me. I don't mean any harm. I just don't know. Like I know that you've been calling me Flo, and I do not know why." There was a chuckle around the table, and I felt myself smiling. "Is someone going to clue me in?" Grace prodded gently.

The chuckles escalated to a low roar as the brothers laughed and ribbed each other. There were even a few comments directed at me to "clue her in."

"Mama," I said, getting her attention. I pointed to the President patch on my club cut. "President."

She stared at me as if I had two heads and was speaking a foreign language. "Okay, you're president, but what does that have to do with me?" She was skeptical, and her brow puckered.

I ran my fingers through my hair to avoid reaching out and grabbing her. She was adorable in her confusion, and I really wanted to take her upstairs and break my promise to the baby. "The president's woman is usually called the First Lady. You're mine." I watched as she worked through the implication.

"I understand now why this is so important." She looked at Pretty. "I can't promise I won't hurt him. I can't promise he won't hurt me. However, there will be speed bumps along the way, some bigger than others. I am politely asking you to butt out, and that goes for all of you. Stay out of it." She took a drink of water, and as I looked at my brothers around the table, I knew she had earned their respect like the First Lady she was.

My brother didn't know when to stop. When he had first started his line of questioning, I'd allowed it. I'd thought that they were questions that the club would need to hear to further accept Grace into the fold. I would have never forced her to answer, but as long as they weren't too awful, I'd let it continue. I didn't want any lingering resentment.

"What happens if Matt wants all the money and gives up the baby? You going to sponge off my brother?"

Pretty was my brother, and even though he was a pain in the ass on a good day, this went beyond my brother trying to protect me from a gold digger, which Grace wasn't. I wondered if something was going on with him I didn't know about.

"You can't be serious," she said.

"Like a heart attack."

I was about ready to step in, but Grace placed her hand over mine. She never looked at me, but her message was clear. Let her handle this. I scraped my thumb under her palm, and we disconnected.

"I actually had a business prior to being a trophy wife. I am not a dumb blonde, and I have money set aside that Matt doesn't have access to. If he were to take everything, I can rebuild without your brother's help. Did you know he gives me money each week? Not because I ask for it, but because it makes him feel better. It's all currently sitting in a freezer bag in a duffel I have packed for emergencies. Now, I have a question for all of you," she said. She wasn't backing down either. I was proud of her, but this was my family. I didn't want them at odds with each other.

She stared at Pretty and then let her gaze move to each brother. "There's no denying that this is my child. Let's assume, in a few years, Sabre knocks me up. Will you treat my child any less than you'll treat his? That's a deal breaker for me."

I waited with bated breath for their responses. I had assumed that when I claimed Grace's baby as my own, the club would automatically recognize him as my son. The Iron Shield was a family, and I hadn't considered that the club might treat my biological children differently in the future. My brother's questions had opened up a canyon-sized hole I hadn't thought about or prepared for.

Pretty had become the spokesperson for the brothers. He leaned forward again so that more of his upper body was on the table. Staring at Grace, he smiled. "I have conditions." There was another movement underneath the table. Wreck was trying to save my brother. "You make me the favorite brother-in-law. Grizz ain't shit."

Grizz's nostrils flared at that.

"You make sure that my brother is a much happier person." He wiggled his eyebrows and stuck his tongue in his cheek. If Grizz didn't get to him first, he was a goner if I caught him.

"You make me potato salad at least once a week with my name on it."

***

Grace

I hoped I had addressed their concerns, but I refused to back down anymore. I didn't think I had been disrespectful, but I also had been very clear about my stance. If I'd let them push me around, they would have always thought they could get away with anything. Those days were long gone.

I understood Pretty's concerns. If the roles had been reversed, I would have liked to think that the new me would have asked Meredith's partner the same thing. I wasn't upset, but I could tell that he had put some thought into this, and I didn't want trouble. He wasn't the only one. They were protecting their president. I could respect that, but I wasn't a gold digger. Maybe I should have moved here sooner so that they could get used to our situation. It was too late now.

Sabre took over the conversation, and I was grateful when he steered it away from the twenty questions. "That was interesting, but it wasn't what I wanted to talk to you about," he said to me. He slid forward in his chair and reached for his back pocket. Pulling out a few papers, he laid them in front of me. "Do you recognize any of these men?" he asked me.

I picked up the papers, scanning each page before flipping to the next one. They were printouts of state licenses. I sat them back down on the table and asked, "Do you know what Matt does exactly at the bank?"

I looked at Sabre, and he was watching me. He hunched in his seat, ready to spring into action like a lion. "Walk us through it," Sabre said. "Please."

"Matt is the head sales agent for the entire bank. He originally started with minor projects such business renovations, new equipment, things like that. He eventually went into large-scale projects, including land buying and new construction. It wasn't uncommon for him to close at least one multi-million dollar deal a week. He's that good. The bank didn't care how he came by the contracts, so he would take prospective clients out to dinner, drinks at a bar, or even invite them to the house for a dinner party. Anything he needed to close the deal."

I picked up the pictures of three of the men. "He invited these men for a home-cooked meal. Matt told me they lived in Mexico but they had been working on this project with him and hadn't been home in months. They missed 'real' food. I made their acquaintance, and they brought their wives. The deal was supposed to close the next day, so Brandon and Meredith were there as well." I placed my hands on my belly, trying to hold us together.

"What is it, mama?" Sabre always picked up when I was in distress.

"That dinner was the same night." I took a quick peek at him, but he hadn't put it together. "It was the same night," I emphasized.

"Aw, fuck." Now he understood. Matt had taken the couples out to a local bar for after-dinner drinks, but I had stayed home. When he had come back, he was so excited that things had gone well. He had led me upstairs to our bedroom to celebrate. I hadn't known Matt was drunk. I also hadn't known I had been the wrong woman.

"It gets worse," I told them. Picking up another picture, I said, "This is the man that I introduced myself to at the restaurant the night I caught Clara and Matt. This deal fell through, and that's the one Matt was screaming about on the driveway. I don't know what happened."

There was uneasiness surrounding the table, when Cyph piped up from halfway down. "I do. The deal fell through on Friday night, and the bank received an anonymous email with a video. They canned him on Monday morning."

"What video?" I asked. Dread settled in my stomach.

"The one that's on your phone," Sabre answered.

I turned towards him. "How did they get it from my phone? You're the only person who knew it existed."

"Another mystery. You'll have to give your phone to Cyph, so he can check it for a tracker."

"Is this Matt?" I asked. This didn't feel like something Matt would do, but I hadn't really known my husband in the last few years.

Sabre reached for my hand and interlocked our fingers. "I wouldn't normally tell you this, but you're involved. There are more pieces, but we don't know how they connect." His thumb tried to soothe my panic. My chest felt tight, and I was taking fast, shallow breaths. "Your cousin Clara is working at our strip club."

"Clara?"

He nodded in agreement, shocking me. "She told my former manager that she was running from an abusive boyfriend. She was afraid that he would find her, and she needed money."

"That's a joke. Clara has never worked a day in her life. My aunt and uncle pay for all of her bills, and she gets an allowance." I tried to take deep breaths, but nothing was working.

"The other problem is these men." He pointed to the pictures on the table. "We know them as cartel members. They've been visiting our strip club."

"Cartel? Like drug lords and big guns?" I was freaking out. These connections all had one person in common: Matt. What had he gotten us into?

"We need info," Sabre told me. "Cyph's going to check your phone, and we'll have to work our connections to see if there's anything unusual. This isn't a coincidence, as much as I would like to think it is."

"Do you have a phone I can use?" I asked.

"What do you need?"

"I need to speak to Meredith, and it can't wait until tomorrow. She has the phone numbers for the wives that were at that dinner. I don't know if she still speaks to them, but I can't have her in danger."

"Is there anyone else that bitch is talking to she shouldn't?" Grizz was hot, and he was two seconds from jumping out of his chair.

"She's hurt," I said. It was a weak excuse. My sister had made questionable decisions ever since our family argument. However, she was still my sister, and I would not let Grizz speak badly of her.

"She's a brat. She only thinks of herself, and she's going to do something stupid that puts someone else in jeopardy. More than likely, you. That shit never falls on the dumbass it's supposed to."

He was right, and I didn't have an answer for it.

"I'll try to get a hold of her," I repeated.

"She's got less than an hour to contact someone, or I am going to go get her. If she can't keep her mouth closed, then she can be a prisoner here."

Chapter 18

I Am Keeping You

Grace

Sabre had dismissed most of the brothers at the table. It was their day off, and he told them he'd call an emergency church if there was any news. Once they were gone, it was just us and the rest of the officers at the table.

Cyph had run to his bedroom for a burner phone so that I could make some calls. I wanted to help put the pieces together, but I'd had no clue the lies that had circulated around me while I'd been with Matt. There was no other explanation. Somehow, all of this was connected.

"Here," Cyph said to me, as he handed me a phone. "It's just a burner, but I programmed it so that it'll show your phone number to whomever you're calling. I'll work on your actual phone this afternoon to see if I can pull anything from it."

I thanked him. I was dreading this. This wasn't the first time that I'd taken the blunt end of Meredith's anger. It probably wouldn't be the last either. Life had changed the minute my mother had passed away. Over time, Meredith had figured out that if she cried wolf, she'd get her way. It didn't matter if I was the one who took the brunt of the punishment. She had been too little to know any better, and I hadn't been old enough to know not to placate that behavior. We had all been dealing with our grief differently, and my father had spent most of the time in his office, working late.

It was always the same cycle. Meredith would throw a tantrum, usually because I'd overstepped. My father never asked questions. He just doled out punishment based on our ages as he saw fit. I'd end up at my aunt's pool house to wait out the storm. It wouldn't take long for a reprieve, and then it was just a waiting game until the next time.

Trauma shaped everyone differently, and where I could excuse Meredith's behavior toward me, I'd never allowed myself the chance to reciprocate. I didn't resent her as my little sister, but I also didn't stoop to her level. Maybe I should have. It would have evened the playing field.

Instead, I had been the third parent she didn't want. I made sure she had clean clothes, lunch for school, and her homework was done. I didn't know where I had developed my sense of familial responsibility, but I had grown up too fast. She hadn't grown up fast enough, and we had clashed. I was trying to help my father, and Meredith saw it as parental authority.

My heart had broken when she'd said she hated me. She had never expressed hatred before, and it felt like a red flashing signal that our relationship had severe damage. I had played it off like typical Meredith behavior, for the same reason that I'd answered Pretty's questions. Sabre would destroy me if he openly disrespected my sister, and I hadn't given Pretty a reason to come in between us either. I still felt responsible for her, and I hoped that this was just another bump in the road.

I understood why Meredith felt hurt at not being told right away. Meredith always had to know what was going on around her. She'd been napping when my mother had left the house. My mother had been there one minute, and when Meredith had woken up, she was gone. In my mind, she was already calling off the wedding, and there had been no reason to heap more on the situation. I had wanted to make it easier for her, like when we'd been kids.

I dialed her work phone number and waited. I could feel everyone watching me, but this had to be done. It rang. Once. Twice. Three times before she picked up.

"Hey, Mer, it's me. I need to speak to you," I said into the burner.

"I am sorry, but that project is currently on hold." I heard her reply, but I didn't know if she was speaking to me or to someone in the background.

"Do you have a few minutes?" I asked.

"No."

"Okay, then just listen for a second. Do you remember that dinner party that you came to a few months before your wedding? The one where you helped me make a taco bar because we were doing a home-cooked meal for Matt's clients? I know you traded phone numbers with the wives, but I need you to stay far away from any of those people."

"That's going to be hard, considering I am having dinner with Brandon. I have to go. Bye."

I held the phone to my ear until I heard the dial tone. I'd messed up by not making her speak to me right after that family dinner. There was no one-size-fits-all bandage to stick over the gaping wound, so I'd been silent. It'd been a mistake. I should have stood at her front door and not taken no for an answer until we fixed this. The guilt pierced through my heart.

I immediately called my Aunt Elizabeth.

"Hey, honey," she answered. "Are you having a good time?"

"Hi, Auntie. Yes, I passed the inquisition with flying colors." I could hear the men shifting in their chairs. I didn't think they had expected the questions to take a turn like they had. Continuing on, I asked her, "Auntie, have you spoken to Meredith?"

"Not lately. Why?"

"I just called her, and she told me she was going to dinner with Brandon."

Grizz was sitting at the other table, but when I said Brandon, he stood up so forcefully that the table flipped over. There was a loud bang, and it echoed through the main room.

He might have said he was over Meredith, but his actions had just proven his words were a lie. When he went to throw the chairs around, Twig and Pint pinned him against the nearest wall, and I could see Sabre trying to reason with him, but they were too far for me to hear what was being said. Would their relationship have survived if I had just told her? Grizz had been guilty by association.

"Why is she seeing Brandon? I thought that was long over," my aunt asked me.

"I don't know. That's just what she said, and when I tried to question her, she shut me down," I replied.

We continued to talk about nothing for a few minutes more before I said my goodbyes. Hanging up the phone, I set it on the table in front of me. I didn't really want to raise my head to see what was happening.

How could my sister be so stupid? I wasn't really the person to be the voice of reason with her when I had lived a farce for way too long. I just prayed that she wouldn't be in danger.

I finally had the courage to look around the room.

Grizz was pacing from left to right on the other side of the table from where I sat. Sabre was sitting on the table, slinging one leg back and forth with his arms crossed. The other two men had moved back to their seats, but they were on alert in case something else happened.

Grizz turned towards me. "What the fuck is her problem?" He threaded his fingers through his hair, causing the bun to fall apart.

I shook my head. I had an answer, but I didn't think Grizz would appreciate it.

"Cyph, is Brandon still employed at the bank?" Sabre asked him.

"Yes. Someone edited the video, so it only showed Matt's ass." He chuckled.

Sabre then turned to look at me. "What does Brandon do exactly for them?" he asked me.

"Government regulations. Making sure that the transactions are legal before they clear the bank," I responded, sitting back in my chair. I'd try to help, but I was reeling.

"The cartel has money. Why do they need the bank?"

I could tell Sabre was thinking out loud, but Count piped up. "Legitimacy. If I am up to no good, my money is only going to buy me so much leeway. If the bank backs me, there are no questions asked as long as the check clears. It wouldn't matter if I turned around and paid them off the day after signing. They're still on the project."

I sat and watched them try to piece together the puzzle. There was no doubt in my mind that they would figure this out.

"Okay, so did they buy Matt off?" Sabre questioned Count.

"If it was me, I would have done a deal with him. If it goes well, do another, but make it a little bigger. They probably didn't have any pushback, or he could smooth things over for them." Count's spikes bounced in his excitement.

"Yeah, but he was high. There's no way that habit was brand new," Wreck said.

"Matt doesn't do drugs," I piped up, confused.

Sabre turned to look at me. "The day we moved you out, he was high on something. You had to look closely at him to notice that his eyes were red-rimmed. I would bet that whatever he's on, he needs more to maintain normalcy."

"Could they be supplying him in exchange for deals?" Pretty asked. "They'd own his ass."

"I have a feeling they already own his ass without the drugs," Sabre replied, and there were a few head nods.

"Why are they here, though? You said they've been to the club, and Clara works there. The only connection both of them have is Matt." I wasn't sure if I was supposed to join in, but this was as much my mess as theirs.

"All roads lead to Matt," someone said.

"Cyph, do we know who pulled the plug on his last transaction? The one from the restaurant?" Sabre asked.

"Hang on," Cyph said as he typed on a laptop. "It looks like it was a mutual agreement. The bank let the 'customer' know that Matt wouldn't be handling the deal, and they backed out on their own."

Sabre dangled his leg. "Anyone else think the bank is a front-end deal only? They came in, and Matt got it done. On the back end, there was more money exchanging hands."

"Where's the money, though? Before I left, I made a copy of every bank account I could find. Some of them I didn't even know about. There's a record of everything in the divorce, which is now public record." I watched as he shrugged his shoulders. We still felt lost.

"How is Brandon a part of this?" Grizz seethed.

"What do you mean?" Sabre asked him.

"It's a little too convenient that he's waltzing his way back in after the wedding was called off. He may not be as dirty as the other players, but he's trying to play a game that he has no clue how to win."

I rubbed my eyes. Grizz was right, and Meredith would get hurt because she was mad at the world.

"You going to give me permission?" Grizz asked Sabre.

"You would do it anyway, even if I said no. I'll stay here but take four and a riding buddy with you. Count, you're at the club with Thunder."

"I am leaving in twenty minutes if anyone wants to go." Grizz stormed off towards the bedrooms. The rest of the men dispersed.

"Come here, mama."

I was exhausted, but I didn't hesitate. I stood up from my chair, walked over to his side, and stopped in between his legs. He placed his hands on my hips and pulled me further into his body. My arms instantly wrapped around his neck.

"Guess what?" he whispered in my ear.

I nuzzled my face into his neck.

"I am keeping you."

I had come to the same conclusion. There was no going back to the pool house.

***

Grizz

I let my anger build as each mile rolled underneath my tires. There were too many issues to figure out what I was exactly livid about, but they all led back to Meredith.

I'd let her yell and scream for two hours as I sat on her living room couch the night of the family disfunction. I hadn't said a word, and she wouldn't have heard me, anyway. Her hands had flailed as she paced in front of the back patio doors, ranting and raving, and I'd lost track if she had even had a point by the end. I couldn't understand why she thought her life was a mess, when she needed to open her goddam eyes and see the world around her.

I'd tried to move on, but even the club girls didn't entertain me. Meredith was blonde, so I thought if I fucked anyone who wasn't a blonde, it'd work. I had tried. I had grabbed a pink-haired club girl, taken her to her room, and by the time she was undressed, I wasn't interested. She had done me a solid when she didn't tell anyone as I just walked out of the room.

As we exited the highway, I took deep breaths, trying to calm down before I saw her. We were almost there, and I wanted answers. Why would my woman go to dinner with her cheating ex?

I knew where he would take her. The little Italian place with the grandmother that sung while she was cooking in the kitchen. Meredith loved that place, and I had taken her more times than I could count. The food was good, though.

Pulling into the parking lot, I instantly honed in on her car. I shook my head at her stupidity. She'd parked at the back of the lot, furthest from the door. Pulling into a nearby spot, I made sure that we would all fit, side-by-side. It was easier to observe from here, and no one would easily see us.

I called Cyph to get the license plate for Brandon's car. He confirmed it was the one right next to hers. Instinct told me to go check his car, and I signaled to the brothers that I was going to look.

Creeping behind the other cars, I made my way over. It was still light enough to see, but I cupped my gloved hand around my eyes and pressed on the windows. The front seat was clean. I did the same thing with the back windows, and that was when I saw it. Brandon had a gun in the car. It was sticking out between the driver's seat and the console.

I made my way back to my brothers and told them what I had found. "Why would a banker have a gun?" Wreck asked.

"I am going to get her. This isn't right." I strode towards the front door. Pretty and Wreck were both following me, and the other three were standing guard over the bikes. "What are you doing?" I asked them.

"Watching the fireworks." Pretty whistled.

Walking through the front door, I instantly saw her. She would always be a beacon for me, calling me to her like a siren.

The hostess tried to ask how many, but I ignored her. Meredith was sitting with her back to the door, so she never saw me coming as I walked straight to her. Brandon didn't even lift his head as I approached. Fucking pussy. There was no way he could protect her when shit went down, and it fucking would. I briefly wondered if he even knew how to fire that gun in his car.

Sitting next to Meredith in the booth, I helped myself to a piece of bread on the table.

"What are you doing here?" she asked me. Her tone was ice cold.

"Saving your ass." I dipped the bread in the olive oil and brought it to my lips. Taking a bite, I let out a little moan. I wouldn't normally do that for food, but I enjoyed watching her face change. She wasn't as unaffected by that sound as she thought she was.

"You need to leave," she told me as she tried to slide further into the booth. I'd purposely sat so that we were touching, and she had nowhere to go.

"Why, so you can tell me to go fuck myself? Nah, I'll pass. I'd rather be fucking you." I took another bite.

"Go to hell, Grizz." She tried to push me out of the booth, but I was too big for her to move on her own.

"You notice Brandon has said nothing?" I asked her. If another man had done what I just had, there would have been no words as I drove my fists repeatedly into him. Brandon was sitting there with his mouth wide open. His eyes pinged back and forth as he watched us.

"What in the fuck did you see in him, anyway?" There was nothing about Brandon that impressed me.

"More than I saw in you."

Direct fire. I'd had enough of her bullshit and giving her space had only let Brandon weasel his way back in.

"Now, baby, you're just making shit up to irritate me. Trust me, I was already livid when I heard about this little party. You should have invited me personally."

She looked at Brandon, and although she hid it pretty well, the disgust was clear on her face. "Get up, so that I can go home," she said to me as she tried to push on my arm.

"Tell Brandon this will be the last time he ever sees or hears from you." I was locking her ass in my room at the club until she came to her senses.

"Fuck off, Grizz." She tried to push my arm again, and when I didn't move, she blew out a breath that whistled through her hair.

"The next time I fuck off, it's going to be with you. I am already hard thinking about that tongue thing you do," I said. I was actually keeping my cool. Taking a peek at Brandon, I saw he still sat there like a chump. If someone had said that to my woman, I would have launched myself over the table. "Tell him, baby. Tell him you're mine."

"I am going home. You both can go to hell. Now move," she huffed.

I only had a few minutes before she'd start making a scene.

"Why is there a gun in your car?" I asked Brandon, crossing my arms and leaning my elbows on the table.

"What in the ever-loving fuck? You have a gun?" Meredith was two seconds from screeching at everyone, and I had to wrap this up.

"Protection," Brandon said.

"From whom?"

He didn't answer. Brandon stood up, threw some money on the table, and left.

"Nice date. At least he bought you dinner before he left."

I pulled my phone out and texted Twig. He and Berry needed to follow Brandon and report. Shit was going down, and that ass wipe had a shit stain a mile long. He didn't come here to win Meredith back. Someone had sent him.

"God, I swear. What are you doing here?" Meredith covered her face with her hands.

"The only God you swear to is me when I am fucking your pussy raw. Let's go." I stood from the table and held my hand out to her.

She was angry. Her cheeks had red tints to them, and her eyes squinted at me. "I am not leaving with you. I am going home, and you better not follow me."

I didn't know what it was, but I'd had enough of her. I picked her up by her arms, stood her in front of the table, and threw her over my shoulder in a fireman's carry.

It was time to go.

Chapter 19
Listen Up, Buttercup

Grizz

I was in a restaurant, for fuck's sake. The moment her ass was over my shoulder, the room went eerily quiet, but no one stepped in. They didn't ask if she needed help, nor did they whip out their cell phones to record.

"Put me down, Grizz," she yelled at me, hitting my back with her fists and kicking her legs.

I waved to the grandmother in the kitchen as I walked towards the front door. She smiled at me and waved back. No one would have stepped in if Meredith had been in serious trouble. Fucking shame.

Meredith continued her tantrum as we walked across the parking lot towards the bikes. I heard her call out to Pretty and Wreck as they walked behind me. She thought they would rescue her. I could have told her that was a lie. Pretty was enjoying the excitement, and Wreck was only here to protect Pretty. They wouldn't step in. She wasn't their problem.

Suddenly, Wreck whistled low. "Shut her up. We have company."

I smacked her ass, and she instantly went silent. When we had been dating, it had been fun to tame the attitude. She was a spoiled brat on a good day, but I didn't mind. A few good spankings, and she'd melt in my hands. However, Meredith the Bitch was wearing on everyone's last nerve, including mine. It was hard to sympathize with someone when all they did was spew hate.

We double-timed it to the tree line where the bikes sat.

I sat Meredith on her feet, turned her around, and placed my hand over her mouth. I didn't trust that she wouldn't try to run. Crouching with her in front of me, I whispered in her ear that she was alright. I'd make sure of it.

A black SUV with tinted black windows pulled into the parking lot. It drove down the aisle where Meredith had parked her car and pulled into the spot that Brandon had vacated. They knew exactly who they were looking for.

Two men exited the SUV and walked over to the driver's side door. They popped the door open with a Slim Jim and swiftly silenced the alarm. These were professionals. As one man hot-wired the car, the other went back to the SUV. Once he closed the door, they sped off, Meredith's car in tow.

Brandon had been up to no good. Meredith had dodged another bullet.

I should have started calling her Tef because nothing dangerous ever stuck to her. Yeah, she'd hate it, but it made me smile on the inside as I tried to process what my next step was going to be.

She pulled my hand away from her mouth. "What the fuck just happened? That's my car. Why didn't you stop them, Grizz?" she whined.

I ignored her. I had planned on staying at Meredith's condo, but that wasn't an option anymore. Looking over at my brothers, I could tell we were all on the same page.

"I recorded it so that we can send it to Cyph, but we have to get out of here," Pretty said. "Not just a pretty face." He framed his face with his hands and smiled wide. It was cheesy but typical.

"Where do we go? We can't go to the Knights without an introduction," I said. "I can't call Sabre until we're somewhere secure."

"I don't want to be you when you call him. He's going to be livid," Pretty sing-songed with a smile.

"My aunt's," Meredith whispered.

"I am not putting her in danger." I liked Aunt Elizabeth, and I wouldn't include her in this fucked up mess.

"You won't. There's a back way in. If you walk your bikes, you won't make noise, and you can hide them in her garage."

I didn't have a choice. It would have to do. I grabbed the extra helmet I had brought and plopped it on her head, making sure the chin strap was tight. She looked at me with tampered fury. This wasn't over yet, just postponed.

As she was swinging her leg over my bike, Pretty called out to her. "Hey, Mer?" She turned her head to acknowledge him. "If you're thinking about jumping off the bike, don't. Flo makes me potato salad. I have no problem running your ass over." He smirked.

***

Meredith

What the fuck have I gotten myself into?

This was a high-speed roller coaster that was going to go off the rails, and I wanted off. I wasn't a thrill seeker, and I'd unknowingly planted myself in the middle of a TV drama. I wasn't handling anything well, and it felt like I was drowning in a sea of despair.

I should have burned my wedding dress to ward off bad omens. Instead, it was hanging in a closet upstairs in my aunt's home. Nothing had seemed off the morning of my failed wedding. My hair was done, and I was dressed, sitting in the bridal suite, waiting for my time to shine.

I didn't know why I did it. I wish I hadn't, but I had stood from my chair and walked towards the mirror. The girls chattered with each other, not even realizing that I was having an internal crisis.

The woman in the mirror had been stunning as she looked back at me. She wore a lace wedding dress that was fitted to every curve until it flared out into a satin skirt at her waist, stiletto heels on her feet, because when she had suggested white ballet shoes, her fiancé had told her no. She'd argued that no one would see them, but he'd said it was appalling. I didn't think she was real. She was perfect, and I had raised my hand to wave at her. Her hand came up at the same speed and angle as mine to wave back at me. She was real, but all I could see was my sister.

I was selfish. I'd never asked Grace if she was happy, even though I'd never seen her fully smile. Staring at my reflection, I had tried to smile. My lips had turned up at the corners. I tried again, but instead of a smile, I frowned. I wasn't happy, and I hadn't been for a while. All I could see, laid out in front of me, was the monotony.

I'd promised myself not to stifle my desire to flee. Yet, here I was again, stifled and unhappy, walking into my aunt's. I called out as we walked into the main living space from the garage.

"Meredith, honey? Is that you?" I'd sent her a text to warn her we were coming so that she wouldn't think the house was being robbed.

"Yes, and I have unwanted guests with me."

"Nah, your aunt loves me," Pretty posed. "I should have been a pool boy," he sang. "Should have learned to clean and skim." He added some dance moves. Wreck just shook his head.

Aunt Elizabeth came around the corner in her robe and grabbed me in an enormous hug. I couldn't hold it in anymore. I shook. "Oh, honey. What's going on?"

"Brandon tried to kidnap me," I answered into the collar of her robe.

"You let him live?" she asked Grizz. My aunt was serious.

"For now," he replied. When I pulled away from my aunt, she hugged each brother. When had our lives become infiltrated by a motorcycle club?

"Is anyone hungry? I have enough for sandwiches." She didn't even stop to get their responses before she set out a spread on the dining room table.

"Hey Aunt E? Do you have potato salad?" Pretty asked her.

She laughed as she said, "That good, huh? I told Grace if she didn't win you over, the food would."

Of course, Grace was the star, and the MC hated me. It was fine. I didn't care.

I wasn't hungry, but I sat at the table, patiently waiting. I just wanted to go home and pretend that nothing had happened.

Grizz sat at the head of the table and pulled his phone out as the rest of the brothers made sandwiches.

"It was nice knowing you," Pretty said to him.

Grizz rolled his eyes as he hit a button on his phone. He could only be calling one person—Sabre. Grizz didn't shit without Sabre knowing. Now that he was with Grace, I wanted nothing to do with it. It wasn't jealousy. I didn't care what she did. It was more like I was so afraid of becoming her I had run in the opposite direction as fast as I could. It had landed me in the same boat.

The phone rang.

"Hey, I need to put you on speaker," Grizz said. He clicked a button, laid his phone on the table, and then detailed the night's events.

"Where are you?" Sabre asked.

"Aunt E's."

"Did anyone follow you?"

"No."

"Have Twig and Berry checked in yet?" Sabre asked.

I hadn't known they were along on this trip. Twig and Berry were both enforcers that I had met before.

"No."

"Fuck. Shit's going to go down."

"Yup."

Wonderful conversation they were having. It didn't explain how I was going to get home.

"I need a ride home," I said.

"You're not going anywhere," Grizz retorted.

"I am going home." He'd called me a brat in jest, but Grizz was really going to get the full effect.

He leaned on the table with his arms crossed. "What the fuck is your problem?"

"I am going home." I was digging my heels in.

"Brandon was supposed to kidnap you tonight. He would have succeeded. Do you get that, Meredith? If you had gone willingly with him, he would have dropped you off on the cartel's doorstep and washed his hands of the whole thing. They were making you disappear. That's why they took your car — so that you wouldn't leave a trace. I would have never found you, and it wouldn't have been for lack of trying."

"Point for Grizz," Pretty popped up, making a tally in the air with his finger.

"Why do you care what happens to me?" I didn't care what happened to me as long as I could go home.

"Eh, point for Meredith. Although it's under duress." Pretty made a tally mark a little further away.

"Guess I shouldn't." Grizz leaned back in his chair.

"Nope." I popped the P sound. I would never tell him he'd been the only man in my condo. If I used my imagination, I could pretend that it still smelled like him. I could picture him throughout the place. It was my haven.

"Meredith," Sabre said through the phone.

I didn't say a word. He wasn't my biggest fan, and it stemmed from the night Grace had gone missing. Sabre thought I should have paid more attention. How could I have? I wasn't a mind reader, and she'd sounded fine when she'd called.

"Listen up, buttercup. You better thank your fucking lucky stars that Grizz still gives a shit. He's the only reason that you're sitting there, all high and mighty. Most of us have already written you off."

"Why should I care what you think? Go play house with perfect Grace." I stood up from my chair and walked out of the room.

"Don't leave this house," Grizz called after me.

I turned into the den and paced the length of the room.

My aunt walked in a few minutes after I did, sitting on the couch. She said nothing as she watched me walk back and forth.

"Are they still on the phone?" I asked her.

"Yes, they're trying to come up with a plan. They're not really sure what they're up against."

I sat next to her on the couch and she wrapped her arms around me. I curled into her body and laid my head on her chest, like I had as a little kid.

"It's alright. Let it out," she soothed me.

The tears rushed down my cheeks. It was much easier to be flippant than to tell Grizz the truth. I was pregnant.

Chapter 20
Things Are Starting To Come Together

When Grizz had called, I had excused myself to my office. I didn't need to have this conversation in the main room. I'd make it up to Grace, but I didn't think she'd be uncomfortable. When I had left, she was looking at Chef's recipe books. He was in his element, showing her all of his creations.

I was sitting in my office chair with my phone on speaker, but no one was really saying anything. Grizz had heard from Twig, and they were on their way to Aunt E's. I suspected it wouldn't be good news.

Count and Thunder had checked in from the tit show a few hours ago. There was no sign of Clara, although Count had confirmed she'd been there. He had asked some girls about Jigsaw's hires. They had been eager to talk. Those girls were taking tips away from them, and not even working regular hours. They showed up, made money, blew Jig, and left. I'd have to be more diligent with the club's legit businesses. No more relying on just the accounting reports.

Cyph hadn't emerged from his room, so there were no fresh developments there. Although, I had sent up a case of Red Bulls. I hated doing it, but the alternative—him crashing—would have probably been worse.

There was a knock on my office door.

"Come in," I called.

Grace stuck her head in. "I don't mean to interrupt, but I wanted to see if you need anything before I head to bed."

"Come here, mama." I smiled as I watched her shut the door and waddle towards me. She was beautiful, and I didn't deserve her. Maybe one day I would tell her when we were more secure in our relationship. For now, I would show her exactly what she meant to me and hope that it would break down some of the walls she carried around.

"Is this the start of a dirty movie?" I didn't know if he worked on it or if it came naturally to him, but Pretty always interjected at the worst time.

"You need to get laid," I told my brother through the phone, like that would even help.

"Maybe," he agreed. "When this shit is all over, I'll go on a bender, and you fuckers better watch out." I could hear a distant growl.

Grace reached my side of the desk, and I slid my chair back, giving her room to sit in my lap. She curled her upper body against me, and I wrapped my arm around her back, kissing her forehead.

"Are you going to christen your office?" My brother didn't know when to stop.

I shook my head, but before I could respond, Grace answered him. "Of course, just not right now."

"Why not? That'd be hot listening through the phone. It's not like it would be the first time." Pretty made noises that sounded as if they belonged in the soundtrack of a porno.

She looked at me with a huge smile. "I am pregnant," she answered him.

"Yeah, so? It's not like he can knock you up again." Aw, fuck. I knew where this was going. I was about to be the punchline of their teasing.

"A baby shouldn't see his father's dick." She couldn't hold it in and busted out laughing. I could hear the laughter coming down the line. I was the only one not laughing.

"You didn't." Grizz coughed. "You seriously didn't say that shit."

When I said nothing, Grace stroked my chin and placed a light kiss on my lips. "You know he did," she answered Grizz.

"Fuck, Sabre. You're supposed to be banging that shit every chance you get. Maybe that's Meredith's problem." Grizz was still chuckling.

"My problem is that you won't leave me alone," we heard her say, but it was faint. She must not have been sitting with the brothers at the table.

"No, your problem is that you have a corncob stuck so far up your ass that you can't see straight. Let me fuck it out of you, and you might lose the attitude," Grizz replied.

There was a distant door slam.

"That went well," Pretty said.

"Yeah, she wants me," Grizz sighed.

Grace looked at me and shrugged her shoulder. She wouldn't speak badly of Meredith, but she was just as clueless as the rest of us.

I heard Twig and Berry in the background through the phone. They must have walked in from the garage. There was chatter, but I couldn't distinctly make anything out. I'd wait until it died down to ask what had happened.

"Prez?" Twig said. He was closer to the phone now, and I figured he must have been sitting at the table.

"Yeah, Twig. What happened?" I tightened my hold on Grace. This would not be good, and I wanted to make sure she had my support.

"Berry and I followed Brandon out of the restaurant to an industrial district. Dude seemed extremely scared or stupid as fuck. He went straight to a warehouse and paced outside his car. It looked to us as if he was waiting for someone, and a black SUV pulled up. A silver car pulled in right behind it. Brandon tried to explain something. He was waving his hands around, but they didn't want to hear it. They set his car on fire and put a bullet in his brain."

"Oh my God," Grace whispered, one hand coming up to cover her mouth, while the other went to her stomach. I wrapped my arm around her tighter so that my body supported her.

Twig was a matter-of-fact kind of man. If that was what he said happened, it was exactly what had happened.

"Grizz," I said. "You think that's the same SUV you saw?"

"Probably, and the silver car was probably Mer's."

There was another knock on my office door.

"Come in," I called. Cyph peaked in this time with his laptop. He looked at Grace and instantly said he would come back.

"Nah, she already knows, and Grizz and the boys are on the phone. They're holed up at Aunt E's. Tell us what you found." I waved him in.

As he walked into my office, I inspected him. His eyes were red-rimmed, and his hair was standing up on end. I hadn't seen him since this morning, so it was safe to assume that he'd spent the whole day at his computers. When this was over, he'd crash, and I wouldn't see him for a few days. I needed to remind Scrub to check on him.

"Oh, okay." He sat in the chair opposite my desk and placed his computer on the surface. He waited for confirmation, and I nodded my head to start.

"It took me a while, but I found the tracker on Flo's phone. It's pretty ingenious, and I copied the code so that if we ever need to duplicate it, we can." He rambled about all the nerdy things it could do. He was strung out on Red Bull, and I felt terrible.

"Cyph," I said, cutting him off. If I hadn't cut him off, he'd ramble for hours about all the cool shit the tracker could do. It would mean nothing to the rest of us, but he'd be happy.

"Oh yeah, so anyway. Flo runs a marketing agency, which is pretty badass. You do pretty well. I had to go through all of your emails and accounts. Sorry."

Grace shrugged. It wasn't worth arguing about.

"They imbedded the code into an email and asked for a status update on a project. I checked the email date, and you would have already been pregnant."

"Who sent it?" she asked.

"Alejandro Rodriguez."

"El Sombra Roja?" Wreck popped up. "You work for the Red Shadow?"

"Who's that?" Grace asked him through the phone.

"The most dangerous man south of the border," Wreck answered.

"I have had lunch with him. He's very nice." She was earnest, and the hairs on the back of my neck stood up.

"What the fuck?" I turned towards her and tightened my arm around her back.

"I started working on marketing campaigns when I was still in college, so that I would have extra spending money. I couldn't ask my dad, and Matt would pick expensive places and not cover the bill. You know Matt comes from money, and he made me sign a prenup to protect his family's assets. That's why he's fighting so hard. It didn't include any marital assets. He didn't think the agency would be worth a damn, so he let me make a provision that he receives nothing from it, and if it fails, I take all the risk. That's why I told you, Pretty, that if I had to, I could start over without help.

"A few years ago, Alex hired me to market his club in LA. It went really well, and now, he sends me work two or three times a year. Matt didn't care because I worked from home, but the more clients he gained, the more time I spent away from the agency. I had to cut down so that I could balance it all."

"Alex? You're on a first name basis with El Sombra Roja?" Wreck asked, skepticism laced his tone.

"How did you meet him?" I asked her the question that was on everyone's mind.

"He initially reached out through my website as a prospective client. He hired me, and when I finished with the club, he told me I had exceeded expectations. It just became a thing. I would finish one project, and the next was sitting in my email the following day. This went on for a few years, and one day, he emailed he was passing through town, and asked if he could take me to lunch. It's been a thing ever since."

"Fuck me," Grizz sighed. "How is it you and your sister are still alive?"

"Cyph, are the men that have been showing up at the tit show known associates of this Rodriguez?" I asked.

"Not really. Like, they're all cartel, but they're in separate factions. Those factions are not warring with each other. I checked," Cyph answered with a shrug.

"Mama, are you working on any projects that we need to know about?" I looked at Grace. I was proud of her. She could hold her own out there, and if she'd been terrible, Rodriguez would have never rehired her. However, I was livid at her. She hadn't thought about doing background checks on her clients. Grace had gone to lunch with this man without knowing how dangerous he really was.

"No, I am currently not working." She made a motion with her hands in front her bump.

"That still doesn't answer why Brandon tried to kidnap Meredith tonight." Grizz came through over the line.

"As much as I hate this, grab Meredith. We need to know how this went down." I wasn't looking forward to this conversation.

There was a shuffle and then silence from the other end of the line.

"Are you sure about this?" Grace whispered in my ear. "I don't think she'll cooperate."

"She doesn't have a choice. We need to know what Brandon said to get her to that restaurant," I whispered back. Grabbing a quick kiss from her, I waited until we could hear the argument brewing between the ex-lovebirds.

"I don't want to do to this," Meredith screamed.

"You don't have a choice. What did he say to you?" Grizz spat.

She didn't say a word, but they had moved closer to the phone, so their voices were louder, clearer.

"What did he say to you, Mer? What the fuck did he say?"

Silence.

"God dammit, Meredith," Grizz yelled back.

There was a sob.

"Come on, baby. I can't protect you unless you tell me what's going on." I noticed his voice had gentled. Grizz had earned his road name because he always wanted to rip through whatever obstacle came his way. I had never known him to be a patient man, but he was trying for her.

"Grace?" she sobbed.

"I am right here, Mer," Grace said to the phone. My hand was sitting on her knee, and she laced our fingers together.

"I am really sorry," she sobbed harder. "I am so sorry."

"It's alright. You're my sister, and I love you, but you have to tell us what Brandon said. Please." Grace leaned forward, so that she was closer to the phone.

"I haven't talked to him since the wedding, but he called the other day. I didn't recognize the phone number, so when I realized it was him, I hung up. He called me back, and before I could hang up again, he said he had something important to tell me. When I pushed for answers, he told me I would have to meet him. I figured it was a public place, so there was no harm. He sat down across from me, and I pushed again because I really didn't want to see him. He said that Matt was—" She hiccupped and tried to catch her breath.

"It's okay, Mer. What's Matt up to?" Grace tried to coax her.

"Brandon sounded scared. He said that the cartel was coming after him because Matt's missing. I didn't believe him, but his face was a little green and his hands shook."

"Did he say anything else, Mer? We can all work together to solve this," Grace asked her gently. I could hear in Meredith's voice that she was barely hanging on.

"He said that Matt had solicited the cartel as clients because they were trying to expand their legal businesses. Matt would work the deal, and Brandon would make sure that it went through without red tape. Everyone was ecstatic, but then the bank fired Matt. I didn't understand, but I guess the firing triggered an audit of Matt's transactions. The bank canceled any pending deals. They foreclosed on any of the properties that the bank still had the titles for and kept any cash payments, labeling them as fraud. They legally took whatever they could. Brandon said the cartel was furious, and now, they want Matt to repay them. You guys don't have that kind of money, and since Matt's missing, they put the screws to Brandon."

"I can't say that I am surprised anymore," Grace said. "Mer, why did Brandon call you, though? He should have my number and could have reached out directly. I could have pulled some money from the accounts that I have access to."

She was actually getting through to the bitch over the phone.

"I don't want to hurt you." Meredith hiccupped. I gently squeezed Grace's fingers to get her to talk again. We didn't need Meredith to sob her head off. We'd get nowhere.

"It's ok, Mer. I love you," Grace reiterated.

I looked at her face, and I knew she meant it. No matter how much Meredith had spewed hate her way, Grace wasn't the type to waiver.

"Tell me, so we can figure this out as a team."

"After the first couple of deals, the cartel was happy, but they asked for more. More money. More property. Just more. Matt was having to jump through hoops with the lies. Brandon said the jefe's wife can't have children, so Matt made him a deal as a sign of good faith to keep their business at the bank. I know little about it, but the deal depended on that dinner party you threw with the taco bar.

"Matt used you as the bait. You played the perfect hostess, and they went back to the jefe, singing your good graces. According to Brandon, he told them to make the deal. They would get a baby, and Matt would continue with the business deals through the bank.

"Clara was supposed to get pregnant that night. She looks enough like you that no one would have questioned it. She's busy partying, and her parents have recently cut off the gravy train. Matt offered her pay for the nine months, and then they would turn over the baby. When we went out for drinks at the bar that night, Matt got drunk, and Brandon tried to cut him off, but he wouldn't listen. Clara showed at the bar later to take him home with her, but he had already ordered a rideshare to head to you."

"You don't have to fill in the rest. I already know what happened that night." Grace rolled her eyes at me. She was just as tired of Matt as everyone else.

Meredith took a deep breath. "I was trying to leave the dinner on a good note when Grizz showed up. I didn't want Brandon to find out that I am pregnant."

Chapter 21
This Is Better Than Reality TV!

Grizz

"What do you mean, you're pregnant?" I could barely breathe. Grabbing Meredith by her forearm, I dragged her to the farthest corner of the kitchen, away from the spectators.

"You heard me, or do you need a refresher in the birds and the bees?" she said, trying to push me away.

If she kept this up, I'd bend her over the kitchen island and remind her how we had created the baby. It wasn't an immaculate conception.

"Cut the attitude. I am not in the mood to deal with the bitchiness you've been dishing out lately."

"I am not your problem. Stop acting like I am," she replied, her hands on her hips.

I couldn't help it. I laughed in her face and caged her against the wall with my hands. "That's a lie," I mumbled. "I made you my problem when I couldn't walk away. Don't get me wrong, Tef. I should have run, like you do, and never looked back." I dropped my forehead to hers. "My kid?" I asked. I already knew it was, but I wanted her to say it.

"Cut the lights. We have company," Berry said from the living room. I flipped the switch in the kitchen, and Wreck turned them off in the dining room.

"How many times does the cartel drive by before they shoot up the place?" Berry asked.

"Shoot on six," Wreck answered. If I had been thinking straight, I would have asked him how he knew that. We'd only crossed the cartel's path recently.

"They're on their second pass. Black SUV with black tinted out windows," Berry said, standing near the front window with the curtain barely pulled to the side.

"We have to get out of here." I took charge. Walking to the dining room table where my phone was, I told Sabre I'd talk to him later and hung up. Putting the phone in my pocket, I made plans. "We can walk the bikes through the kitchen, out the back and into the woods, but we'll have Aunt E and Mer. The garage faces the street, so we can't take a car for them."

"What about my dad?" Meredith asked. "He's on the next street over. Can't you walk your bikes through the trees to him and pick up his car?"

"They just made another pass. That's three," Berry called.

"Your dad isn't home, Mer," Aunt E popped up. She'd changed out of her robe into jeans and a sweatshirt. I'd never seen her dressed down, and it looked weird on her. "He's at some function for the firm."

"Mer, I hate it, but you're going to have to ride until I can get a car." There was no other option, otherwise, I would have taken it.

"I can't ride on the back of your bike pregnant." Her voice was rising.

"You didn't have a problem with it on the way here, so stop being difficult. It's not like you're showing," I pointed out.

"Pass four," Berry called out.

"We have to go. You will have to ride on the back of my bike," I said. I wrapped my arms around her tightly. Pulling her into my chest, I whispered into her ear, "It'll be alright, Tef. I won't let anything happen." I let her go and helped the other brothers as we moved the bikes through the kitchen.

We walked them down the stairs of the back porch, past the pool house, and into the line of trees at the back of the property. We had reached the road when the cartel opened fire, shooting directly into the house. Using the sound of the shots as our cover, we started our bikes and took off in the middle of the night, never looking back.

***

Sabre

I wasn't prepared to fight a two-front war. We weren't model citizens, but we weren't one-percenters anymore. I had contacts but not enough that most of the club wouldn't end up in jail or dead.

I looked at Cyph as he sat on the other side of my desk, plucking away at his laptop. Cyph was a skinny nerd with glasses, but he could throw down with any brother. My conscience said he was too smart to spend the rest of his life in jail.

I panned the room until my eyes settled on Grace. She had stayed up as long as she could, but her eyes had gotten heavy, and I heard a soft snore. She'd fallen asleep sitting on my lap with her head on my shoulder. I had kissed her forehead and tried to send her to bed, but she wouldn't go. She wanted to be close in case we needed her. We'd compromised, and she was sleeping on the couch in my office. I smiled as I watched her.

My eyes searched for her bump underneath the cover. She was laying on her side, and I didn't know if that was comfortable for her. Watching her chest rise and fall, I reminded myself that they were safe. I'd burn the world down to keep them that way. They were mine, and no one was going to take them from me. It was only a matter of time before Matt resurfaced.

There was a knock on my office door. It quickly opened, and Count's mohawk appeared in the crack.

"Come in," I called to him quietly.

He walked in, stopping right in the doorway to look at Grace. He smiled as I had. Continuing to my desk, he plopped his ass into the other chair on the opposite side of me.

"You didn't buy a new couch?" Count asked me.

"No, it's comfy," I answered nonchalantly.

"I am pretty sure my cum is on that couch."

"Fuck! We're buying a new one as soon as possible." A few years back, the club girls had taken a stand for new main room furniture. They had complained that their knees were knocking on the wood beams, and it was easier to just buy new than to let the brothers go without pussy. Some of them could be real assholes when they weren't getting any.

I hadn't told Grace, but I'd bought a brand new bed for my room. It might have been my manly pride, but I couldn't bear the thought of my woman laying where others had been.

"How're Grizz and the boys?" Count asked.

"Holding up in a sleazy motel. He said it's cozy and there's no room to move, but they're okay for now. We'll ride out at daylight to meet them on the road," I answered.

"They actually got all six bikes in one motel room? It's not like we ride crotch rockets." Count's face showing his disbelief.

"No, they had to get connecting rooms. Grizz said they spread the bikes out between the two and leave the door open. How was the tit show?" I asked.

"It's actually not as bad as we thought. It's down in sales, and there's a shit ton of inventory, but with a couple of good nights, we could get it back on track. The girls are still happy. They're making decent money, so this only started recently."

"What did they have to say about Jig?"

"There are at least two other girls and Clara that are on the Jig special. Ironically enough, they never show when the 'new clients' are in." Count shook his head and rubbed at his eyes.

I picked up my phone and texted Pint to prepare Jig. We had a few hours to kill and questions to be answered.

"If you want to go, I'll stay with Flo," Cyph joined the conversation. "I am cross-referencing some details, but I think I am onto something." He continued to type quickly without looking up from his screen.

"When this is done, we're going to talk about the Red Bulls," I said. I didn't know which would have been worse, the energy drinks or drugs.

"Yes, Daddy."

"Fuck off," I said to him. It then hit me like a ton of bricks. "Fuck, I am going to be a dad." I looked over at Grace again. "I am going to be someone's dad."

***

Pint texted everything was ready.

"You in?" I asked Count.

"Sure, I am not doing anything."

"Yeah, because a certain blonde isn't here right now," Cyph said.

Count hit him in the shoulder as he stood. "I am ready for a good old-fashioned beat down."

I followed him out of the room, stopping to kiss Grace on the forehead. She lay still, and I hesitated, not wanting to wake her. The blanket was still covering her, and I figured it would be enough for now.

Count opened the door to the basement and let me go first. I walked past the cells that the original club had built and strolled through the last door at the end of the hallway.

The Playroom.

It was anything but a good time.

Pint was leaning against the back wall, waiting for me. As I surveyed his handiwork, I felt a sneer forming. Jigsaw was hanging from chains in the middle of the room. He stood on his tiptoes, only wearing his boxers.

I shook my head at him. "You sat at my mother's kitchen table drinking your morning coffee daily. You were my father's secretary, Jig. When it was time to pass the records over, you taught Pretty how to keep the club's secrets. Why turn your back now?"

"Fuck off."

I took off my club cut and hung it on a hook by the door. Rolling my sleeves up to my elbows, I turned around and surveyed Jig again.

"What happened? Tell me, and I'll let Pint take you back to your cell. No harm, no foul."

Silence.

"Have it your way." I hit him with an uppercut to his stomach. He couldn't bend over to relieve the pain, so he wheezed.

"Hey, Count," I said over my shoulder. "Call Scrub. Jig's getting old."

"On it." I heard him reply from over my shoulder. I stood a few feet away from Jig and watched him struggle. If I wailed on him now, he'd never survive it, and I'd have to answer to the club for killing him without a vote. Jig had been a member too long to be disrespected, even though it appeared he was betraying the club.

While we waited for Scrub, I started off with the question I was most interested in. "Why does the cartel want my baby?" I asked him.

I wouldn't have cared that the cartel was visiting our tit show. It was our business, and as long as they were spending money without an issue, the club wouldn't have any problems with that. We didn't have a beef with them, so there would have been no reason to defend our territory. They could share the wealth for all we cared, starting with the bar and the girls on the stage, but now we had an enormous problem. They were only soliciting our business to get closer to my son.

Silence.

I hit him again in the stomach.

As I waited for him to catch his breath, the playroom door opened, and Scrub walked in, holding his medical duffle. It was his magic bag of tricks, and he never left home without it.

"You know I love the first hit. You should have called me sooner," he whined as he went to stand on the other side of Count. Their fists bumped before they turned back to watch the show.

"Why is my baby so important, Jig?"

Silence.

Pint had set up a table full of toys. Grabbing the blowtorch, I clicked on the flame and walked back towards Jig. "You have two club tattoos. I can't remove those until the brothers vote you out. I believe in the traditions of this club, but they won't stop me from removing the rest."

"Oh, shit. Hang on." Scrub went into action. "Give me a few, and then he's all yours."

I'd known Scrub since we were in diapers, running around the clubhouse. He may have looked like a mild-mannered doctor, but he was just as ruthless as any of us. His loyalty ran deep, and I knew he was getting a kick out of this. In Scrub's mind, you were with the club, or you were against it. It was absolute, but he had a hard time reconciling that there were gray areas.

When he was done with an IV, he turned to look at me. "Low setting, Sabre. It'll still hurt like a bitch, but he shouldn't go into shock, and I can nurse the wounds." Scrub smiled at me and held his knuckles out for a bump.

"I am not playing, Jig. Why does the cartel want my baby? Last chance." Silence.

I stood behind him and started with the large tattoo of the interlocking puzzle pieces on his shoulder. I outlined it with the blowtorch, and then filled it in, like a picture in a coloring book. Once the skin had completely burned, I set down the torch and grabbed my knife. It was the same one that my father had given me when I prospected. I'd give it to my son when the time came.

I started at the top of the tattoo and peeled the skin in strips. Jig had been trying to hold in his cries and screams with the torch, but with the first slice, he lost the battle.

"You fucking bitch," he cried. There was a string of profanities.

We should have officially retired him a long time ago, but he'd slid under the radar. He was weak, or he had become weak over the years. I wasn't sure right now, and I didn't really give a fuck.

"Tell me what I want to know. Why, Jig?" I went back to pulling at the tattoo with my knife. Once the puzzle pieces were gone, Scrub bandaged him up, and I moved on to the pinup girl on his side. Starting the process again, I burned her legs off. I wasn't even to her waist when he talked.

"I didn't know they were cartel when they first showed up. They walked in one day, ordered private dances from the girls, and paid for the top shelf liquor. That's how I ordered all the extra bottles. They were good-paying customers, and they were coming in four to five nights a week. I didn't want to run out." Jig was panting, as if the pain was too much, but he continued to talk. "They set me up."

I was silent as I outlined the top of the pinup girl with the torch.

He tried again to get my attention. "They set me up. I swear, Sabre."

Finishing the tattoo, I pulled my knife out. Starting at the bottom, I fileted the skin, waiting for Jig to hang himself some more. He was doing a good job of that, and I hadn't even had to prompt him.

"Clara isn't the first girl I've allowed to work off the books," he cried, and the tears were running from his eyes.

I poked at the redness underneath the skin until it bled. His screams bounced off the walls of the playroom. I wasn't the only man relishing the punishment.

Jig talked through the pain, but he had to stop and take a breath every other word. "One night, a girl came in to the tit show while I was managing. She had a sob story, and I gave her a job, like the other ones. She thanked me on her knees, but it all fell apart the next night. The cartel came in with pictures of us. I don't know how they got them, but they said she was sixteen. It wasn't like I could come to the club for help, and the last place I wanted to be was in jail. I swear she was eighteen, but I didn't ID her."

I went for the kill. Lowering my voice to soothe him, I asked again, "Why, Jig? Why an innocent baby?"

The tears finally streamed from his cheeks. "The men that come to the show are mid-ranked cartel. They were drunk one night and let it slip. There's an arranged marriage between their jefe and the daughter of El Sombra Roja. The only obstacle is that they can't merge the cartels until they seal the covenant with a child. The jefe plays too rough with his bride, and she can't conceive." Jig hung his head. His eyes focused on the ground in front of my feet.

"Why my baby?" I pushed.

"They said that Clara agreed, but Flo got pregnant instead. They don't care who does it as long as they get the baby."

"Patch him up, Scrub, and when he's ready, he can go back to his cell."

I looked at Count, and he looked back at me. I still didn't want a two-front war. We were going to have to eliminate Matt first and hope that Clara went with him.

I would not go down without a fight.

Chapter 22
Safety In Numbers

Grizz

I was standing at the window, peeking through the blinds. We'd driven about an hour north before we'd found a rundown motel that rented by the hour. We hadn't asked questions, and neither had anyone else. The cartel wouldn't come looking here, and even if they did, the pimps would drive them away. We'd only rented two connecting rooms, and by the sounds, their business hadn't been affected.

It was snug in the room. We'd rolled the bikes in, and there wasn't much space to maneuver. Twig was laying in the tub. He'd complained that there was too much noise, and he was a light sleeper. On one bed, Wreck was spooning Pretty. They needed to decide what they were doing, since they weren't actively hiding anything anymore. Sabre wouldn't give a damn, and anyone who dared to object would face his violent wrath. On the other bed, Meredith and Aunt E were sleeping. Berry and Snake claimed the beds in the other room. They said it was better than sleeping on the floor. I'd grabbed Snake on the way out as my riding buddy.

What a fucking night. It was far from over, and I had a feeling this was just the beginning. Looking back out the window through the slats in the blinds, I noticed the sun coming up. I'd give them a few more minutes, and then it was time to go.

I had already talked to Sabre. The plan was to text him when we left, and he'd ride out with a calvary to meet us. Safety in numbers. I planned on sorting this out when we got back.

A little guilt crept into my stomach. I'd made the decision to come get Meredith, but I shouldn't have included the other brothers. This was my mess, and my need to clean it up had only trapped the other men into this situation. At the same time, I didn't give two fucks. She wouldn't escape me. I would not let her outrun her shit. She was going to stand and fight it. I wanted to know what was going on, and at the end, she'd realize she belonged to me.

As my mind wandered to my kid, a small pair of hands wrapped around my middle, holding me tight. She laid her head in the middle of my back. I didn't want to move, but there was a still a part of me that was severely pissed off.

"I am sorry," she whispered.

"Later." I wanted to get back to the clubhouse, work all of this out, and then fuck her silly. I didn't share Sabre's dumbass philosophy. I had no problem fucking Meredith while she was pregnant. Hell, I'd probably fuck her more, and that was saying something. My kid was going to have to learn to share, and now was as good a time as any. I wrapped her hands in mine and brought them closer to my lips. Leaning over, I kissed her knuckles, and then broke our hold.

"Time to roll out."

***

Grace

I was laying on the couch when Sabre walked back into his office. I'd been awake for a little while, but I hadn't moved. Cyph was still clicking away at his computer, not really paying attention to anything but his screen. It was easy to see that he needed an intervention.

"Hey," Sabre said, as he patted him on the shoulder. "Head to bed."

"Nah, I got a few more things I want to look at." Cyph didn't even look up, nor did he stretch.

"Give it a rest," Sabre told him. "Head to bed. We'll work on this when I get back." There was no give in his voice, and Cyph packed up his laptop and walked out of the room, his decision overruled.

"You should have told me you were an experienced parent." I smiled as I shifted onto my side to look at him. He walked over to me, kissing my forehead.

"Mama," he sighed. "I feel kind of bad for my kid. He won't be able to pull any shit."

"It'll make him work harder." I laughed as I fluffed the pillow and lay back down. Sabre chuckled with me and sat on the floor near my belly.

"You hear that?" he said to my stomach. "Don't even think about it." He placed a kiss on my belly, laying his hand gently across the spot. "I know," he said, still talking to the baby. "You'll wrap your uncles around your little pinkie. Heaven help them when your mama gives them a niece." He raised his eyes to meet mine. "Grizz called, and they're okay. They spent a few hours in a seedy motel."

I said nothing as I reached down to interlock our fingers. He gave mine a squeeze but didn't let go.

"Are you ready for the ride?" I asked.

"Mostly. I've already spoken to the brothers who will ride out with me. They'll be ready in about an hour. Once Grizz calls again, they'll leave the motel, and we'll leave the clubhouse. Meet somewhere in the middle." He squeezed my fingers again. "There's no work today. I've closed the club businesses, so every brother has their assignment. The ones not riding with me will stay here to protect the club." He looked down at our hands and sighed. I could see that he was worried. These were his men, his brothers, and he took responsibility for them as their president. It made my heart want to reach out to comfort him. "I hate leaving you, mama. I absolutely despise it." He was still staring at our entwined fingers.

"I know, but I am safe here. They need you more right now." I was worried, but I wouldn't show weakness. This was the first time that Sabre needed my strength, and I wouldn't let him down.

"Mama, I've talked to Thunder and Chef. They're both former military, and I've asked that they be your personal bodyguards until I get back." Sabre sighed. His brow furrowed.

"Alright. If you think that's best." I wouldn't argue with him.

He laid his cheek against our hands. "I honestly don't know, and I think that's what's bothering me. I have these little pieces, and I have no clue how they go together. If I can't figure it out, how do I protect you? How do I protect our family?"

"I watched the officers work together earlier, spitting ideas back and forth. When you get back, you'll lead them again. It may not be in the next few days, but you'll figure it out. From there, I have every confidence that'll you know how to move forward. We have to. There's no other option."

He raised his head to look into my eyes. "You're right. We'll figure this out together." He leaned back over and kissed my belly again. Letting go of my fingers, he stood up from the floor and leaned down to kiss me. "Thank you," he whispered against my lips.

***

As I stood on the porch, my stomach was upset. It rumbled in time with the hum of the bikes. I couldn't shake this feeling of intense dread that today wouldn't be as simple as Sabre had made it seem. My heart pounded as negative thoughts took over my mind, the what ifs playing havoc on my emotions. I could't let him leave without giving him a piece of me to take with.

I stood between Thunder and Chef, but my feet moved on their own. I walked down the porch stairs and made my way in between the bikes that were lined up in two neat rows.

"Wait!" I called as I tried to move as fast as I could. It wasn't more than a waddle, but I tried to pick up the pace. "Wait!" I called again.

I could see Sabre up ahead, putting his helmet on. The rumble of the bikes blocked out any other sound. He wouldn't hear me. I tried again as I kept walking. "Wait!" I screamed.

The brothers must have heard me the last time because the bikes shut off in pairs, like a symphony. It was eerie as the yard went deadly silent. I didn't know if this was an omen of what was to come, but I tried to run to Sabre.

As the last couple of bikes turned off, Sabre realized that something was off. He quickly scanned over his men, looking for any reason they wouldn't be ready to ride. I called out to him, and this time, he turned toward me. A smile played at the corner of his lips. Laying his helmet on his seat, he made his way towards me.

We met in the middle, and I threw my arms around him. I tried to wiggle my way closer, but this was a bad angle. He shifted me to the left, and like puzzle pieces, we clicked together.

"I couldn't let you leave without telling you," I said, catching my breath. My chest was rising and falling in rapid succession. It might have been exertion or emotion. I didn't know which. "I need to tell you."

"Tell me what?" he asked. He held me tightly around my waist.

I looked up at him. The words wouldn't be enough. I needed him to know how much he meant to me. "I love you." It came out clear and crisp in the yard's silence. "I need you to know. I love you."

He swooped down and kissed me like tomorrow would never come. Right now, it didn't feel like it would. I could hear the brothers whooping and hollering, but I grabbed Sabre by the neck and returned the kiss.

His phone dinged with an incoming text. It had to be Grizz. They were ready to head out.

Sabre didn't check his phone, but he pulled back from my lips. Resting his forehead against mine, he drank me in as if he was thirsty, and I was the only glass of water he wanted.

"I love you," I whispered to him. "Bring them home." I kissed him lightly. "Come home safely." I pecked him again. "We'll be waiting for you, Daddy."

***

Meredith

How could I have been so stupid? I was well aware of the fact that I had fucked up, but so had Grizz. I was still angry, and until I could figure out how to let it go, we'd be in this constant battle.

My aunt and I were sitting at the picnic table that was in front of the roadside diner we'd stopped at. There was a low roar rapidly approaching us. We watched as Sabre led the club into the lot, parking near the rear. He quickly dismounted and made his way over to us.

Sabre hugged Grizz, and I watched as they exchanged a few words. Turning together, they made their way over to the rest of the brothers. Sabre hugged Pretty, and I couldn't help the jealousy that deepened within my chest. Had Grace and I ever been that close? There were a few more words said, but we were too far to hear.

Sabre walked towards us, and my aunt stood to greet him. I didn't bother. I would not treat him like the white knight that rescued us. Fuck that!

"How are you, Aunt E?" he asked as he hugged her.

"I am fine, Sabre, but it has been quite the night. I am not sure I've ever had that much excitement," she said with a smile as she hugged him back. "How's my girl?"

"She's worried but good," he answered. Turning towards me, he nodded. "Meredith."

"Sabre," I said, just as coldly. Fuck you, asshole.

"We've brought a car so that the two of you will be more comfortable." He turned and whistled through his fingers at the rest of the club. "Pulse! Come here." I'd expected a kid to turn around, but I couldn't place Pulse's age. He had a baby face, like life hadn't kicked him around yet. However, his eyes told a different story.

When he reached us, Sabre clapped him on his shoulder. "Ladies, this is Pulse. He'll drive you back to the clubhouse." He turned towards the prospect. "You fuck this up, you won't patch in." Pulse turned a shade of green, and I almost made a wisecrack. My aunt stepped up to diffuse the situation.

"It's lovely to meet you, Pulse. We appreciate the ride," she said as she smiled at him.

"My pleasure, ma'am." The prospect had manners. What was he doing riding with a motorcycle club?

I was ready to be done with this shit, so I walked towards the car. I didn't know where they had gotten it from, but it smelled like old hamburgers when I opened the back door. Grace hadn't even bothered to lend us hers.

As I climbed in and went to shut the door, an enormous shadow passed over me. Grizz was blocking the door, and he crouched down so that he was at my eye level. "You're not going to say goodbye?" he asked me.

"We're going to the same place," I retorted with a snort.

"You're cute. I am going to have fun breaking that sass out of you." He was bouncing on his heels, his hands touching my thigh on the seat.

"Not interested."

"I am not walking away. Fuck, Mer! I am not letting you push me away, either. Once this is over, you're going to submit to me because that's what we both want."

I tried to close off my emotions. I wanted it with him, but I also wanted more. He was waiting for me to agree, but I didn't say a word. Shutting the door, I could hear him mutter every single curse word known to man.

It didn't take us long to move. My aunt was sitting in the passenger seat, Pulse was driving, and I was sitting with my back to the window behind him. The radio was playing some rock song, but I wasn't paying attention.

I was in my little world when the car turned to the left, suddenly. Pulse had turned around in the middle of the road, using one of the emergency turn-arounds.

I tried to gauge the situation. My aunt was talking to Pulse. The brothers that had been behind us were following us, and at the back of the pack, I saw Grizz.

When I turned around again, that was when I realized what my aunt had been saying. She was trying to talk Pulse off a ledge as he balanced a gun on his knee, pointed at her.

Chapter 23

The Past Is Trying To Kill US

Meredith

"I am sure this is all a misunderstanding. Why don't you explain it to us, Pulse?"

My aunt was using the same tone she'd used on me as a child. I clearly recognized the sweet soft tones that lured you in, only for you to tell your secrets. She'd then hit you with the disappointed tone. By then, it was too late. You were in trouble.

"Shut the fuck up. They'll probably just kill you or send you to the brothel. Have you even been on your back, you old hag?"

Pulse wasn't very good at this. He was trying to watch the road, but when he glanced to check the gun in his lap, the car would swerve.

I wasn't sure what to do, but I wasn't going down without a fight. No one spoke to my aunt that way, including me.

"Pulse," I said. If my tone had a name, it would have been Resting Bitch Face Meets Pissed Off Pregnant Woman. "Real talk. What the fuck is going on?" I wasn't sure he would take the bait, but if I could get his attention, maybe he'd forget the gun.

"They want you," he said, as he met my gaze in the rear-view mirror.

I flippantly said, "Yeah, get in line. I am a hot commodity right now." Tossing my hair over my shoulder gave the right impression. His eyes widened as he watched me through the mirror. I didn't know how to steer this conversation, but we needed information.

"You sure know how to pick 'em. Shitty taste in men, sweet cheeks." Pulse clicked his tongue against his bottom lip as he refocused on the road. I could do this. I could keep him talking.

"Tell me about it, stud." Come on asshole, give me what I want so we can stop this car.

"You were going to marry Brandon. That's pretty self-explanatory. How he ever got it up, who knows? They put Rosetta in front of him, naked, and he didn't even have a chub." Pulse kept looking behind us, but I could have told him the MC would maintain their distance until they came up with a plan. They had Bluetooth helmets and were probably chatting.

"He did alright. Nothing spectacular, but it got the job done." I went in for the kill shot and said a silent apology to my aunt. "I bet you could do better."

"Boss won't let me fuck you. I tried to explain it wasn't a problem, but the jefe had his reasons." He side-eyed my aunt. "No one cares about you."

"I'd break you in half." My aunt was playing the bad cop to my good cop. I didn't know she had it in her.

I leaned forward and shifted in my chair so that my feet were on the floor mat. I pretended like I was interested in this conversation, but I really wanted to know how far I could reach. Aunt E and I side-eyed each other. We were on the same mental page. There was no plan, but we were buying ourselves time.

I was out of ideas, but I needed him to talk, so I started with the obvious issue. Grizz would be so proud. "So, Pulse, you know the brothers will never patch you in now."

"I never cared about their patch. It doesn't mean shit since they're not one-percenters." He glanced in the mirror, out the back windshield. The brothers must have been too close because he stepped on the gas. I didn't want to know how fast we were going.

"So, how did you prospect? You obviously passed the background check." I threw in a laugh that I hoped sounded sexy. Less scared, more sex bomb.

"It wasn't hard. They didn't dig deep enough." The gun was pointing down, like he'd forgotten he was holding it. I leaned forward a little more to create intimacy, and my belt rubbed against my skin.

Something in my mind clicked, and I focused on one keyword. "Who are you related to?" I asked him.

"El Sombra Roja."

"The Red Shadow," my aunt whispered. I did a double-take. What secrets was Aunt E hiding? I telepathically sent her a message that we would have a chat later. "I have a past," she said to placate me.

"Okay, who wants to fill in the rest of the class?" I truly did not know what was going on, but it seemed like these were pieces of the mystery. Sabre would want to know, and it might get me a few brownie points. I quickly scolded myself. I didn't give a shit what Sabre thought.

"Story time, sweet cheeks. Pay attention." We'd already passed four exits, heading in the opposite direction. How much longer would this continue? I'd felt safer on the back of Grizz's bike than in this car.

"El Sombra Roja used to be the most powerful man in Mexico, but he decided a few years ago to expand his legit businesses. That's all fine and dandy-like, but you still have to reign supreme over the not-so-savory ones. It's what gives you power. Control." He looked over at my aunt. "Right, Mom? You dated him."

My head pinged back and forth between them as I tried to grasp what was happening. My finger pointed in each of their directions in tune with my head, while my mouth hung open. I didn't look down, but I could feel my toes tapping their own beat. Aunt Elizabeth was Pulse's mom? If she was, then that would make him my cousin, right? I'd heard of people finding relatives they didn't know existed with DNA kits. This was too much, and I loved other people's drama. "What in the fuck are you talking about? That has to be a lie. Aunt Elizabeth, what's he smoking?"

Pulse was well aware that he had the upper hand in this conversation. He sneered at my aunt, who'd gone pale. She looked like she was a few seconds from passing out.

My aunt turned in her chair to face Pulse. "I met your father when he was in college," she said to him, ignoring me in the back. "Back then, he was just Alex. I knew nothing about the cartel or his family history. He kept it from me." She still was pale, but now it appeared as if she wanted to cry. Her eyes never left the side of Pulse's face, looking for any family resemblance.

"Peter," she breathed, "I only spent a few hours in your life. People always say that if a loved one returned, they would recognize them instantly, but you were only a baby. I should have looked closer when you were first introduced. It's easy to define where each of your features come from."

She brought her hands around her neck, massaging the muscles in the back. "I loved your father, but he lied to me. When you were born, he couldn't maintain those lies. He walked right out the front doors of the hospital with you in his arms and vanished back to Mexico. I wouldn't understand until much later why the hospital let him. They didn't have a choice." Now there were actual tears in her eyes, but she quickly wiped them away.

"I tried to contact him. I called, I wrote, and I even planned to cross the border with my father's help. Right before the trip, an invitation came in the mail. It was your father's wedding to Lucia." She chuckled dryly. "The note stated that if I fought for you, they would send you back to me. In pieces." She choked on a sob. "I didn't have a choice. I let you go and hoped for the best."

"That's a great sob story there, Mom. Don't worry. I've made my way, and when this is over, I'll be the most powerful man in Mexico. I can probably bury the fact that I am half-gringo."

"What's going on, Peter? The truth." My aunt reached out to place her hand on his forearm, but he pulled away from her. She dropped her hand back in her lap, her bottom lip quivering.

I tried to lean to the side to look at Pulse, but my best viewpoint was through the rear-view mirror. As I listened to them, I could see the family resemblance. He was dark-haired and had a darker complexion, but if you looked closely, you could see my family's bone structure in his cheeks and forehead. He also had my aunt's turned-up nose.

"Lucia's dead, and dear old dad has decided that he wants to put the family back together after twenty-seven years. Speaking of which, Uncle Gerry really needs to stop taking cartel cases. He's missing the minor details. He needs to be put out to pasture before the cartel gets a hold of him." Pulse's eyes shifted to the back of the car. "Your boyfriend is at the back of the pack, sweet cheeks. Doesn't he want to protect his baby?"

"How do you know about the baby? I didn't tell anyone until last night."

"Dr. Vargas is very resourceful. She's banging one of the sicarios, so when you booked your first appointment, you stepped into the hornet's nest. They really wanted Grace, but you'll do for now," he sneered at me through the mirror.

"I am always second fiddle to Grace." I was in the middle of an identity crisis, so there was some truth in my voice.

When the first pregnancy test had come up positive, I had grabbed my phone to call Grizz. I had wanted him to know immediately, but something had stopped me. It was this intuition that maybe the test was false. I ran out to the store and bought ten more. I was still in disbelief when they all turned positive. That was when I'd made the appointment with Dr. Vargas. Since I was Grace's sister, she'd put two and two together.

It was all Grizz's fault. I'd wanted to tell him the weekend that everything had fallen apart. When he was about to leave the clubhouse, he'd called me and let me know some brothers were coming with him. It'd ruined my plans, but I couldn't tell him to ditch them. There would have been too many questions, possibly an argument, and I would have had to tell him over the phone. I was going to make the best of it, and when I had a moment alone with him, that was when I was going to spill. That moment never came, and we never discussed the future.

My life had imploded when I'd watched Sabre put his arm around Grace. I'd heard him claim her and the baby, but I hadn't thought about the ramifications of what they really were. They hadn't seen each other in two months, and I hadn't thought there was any way something was going on. I hadn't thought she'd even called or texted him back.

It was all predetermined from that moment forward. It didn't matter that Grizz was my perfect match. Sabre wanted Grace, and watching my sister, she was going to let it happen. All my hopes and dreams with Grizz had crumbled into dust, to be swept away into the trash. My life had become too entangled with Grace's, and I needed to distance myself. Brandon had called the next day, and I took it as a sign to run in the opposite direction. That was when I knew my relationship with Grizz was over. I didn't think twice that I hadn't told him about the baby.

I probably should have unpacked years of trauma and seen a therapist, but it was easier just to play the selfish bitch. I was good at it, and no one questioned it. It was what I knew best, but I'd picked Brandon when I'd seen his name pop up on my phone. He was the one I had run to, even if he was the worst likely choice.

"Why are you doing this if your father is trying to expand again? I haven't talked to him since the day you were born." My aunt was pleading with Pulse. I thought she really wanted him to pull over and just hug her.

"See, that's the thing, Mom. Men in power forget how they got it. I don't plan to make that same mistake."

"What have you done, Peter?"

"It's not what I have done. It's what Dad has forced me to do. The Lopezes rode into town and slowly took business away. Dad should have gone to war then, but he didn't. He figured hitting a few random targets of theirs would work. Newsflash: it didn't, and the Lopezes just grew in money and in power.

"Arranging a marriage between two cartels didn't work either. The only thing that will work is for me to help legitimize the Lopezes. They'll start the war. El Sombra Roja will be dead. I'll be so distraught that they killed my father, I'll wipe them out completely. Win-fucking-win."

I leaned forward again in my chair. My belt buckle rubbed against my skin as I shifted. It was uncomfortable, but it gave me an idea.

"What do you need a baby for if you have this amazing plan, cousin?" The word burned on my tongue. Though we shared the same blood, I would never claim him. He'd be lucky if he didn't see the inside of a body bag after all of this.

"Manuel Lopez plays too rough with Lucia's daughter. She's already had a hysterectomy." He smiled as if this was funny, but my heart went out to the girl. "Manny needs the baby, so the arranged marriage will seal the covenant between both factions. Dad will never see the war that's already brewing on his front lawn."

I tried to catch my aunt's eye as I slowly slid the strap of my belt through the buckle. I didn't want to make a sound, and as long as Pulse didn't completely turn around, he'd never see what was coming.

I paused. Checking on my aunt again, I saw she wasn't paying attention to me either. In any other circumstance, I would understand. However, her demon spawn was trying to kidnap us.

I went back to my belt and loosened it so that both flaps were open. Checking on them again, I found Pulse still staring at the road, and my aunt was still staring at him. I pulled the belt through the loops in my pants, giving a silent cheer when it came free.

I looked for the gun. In all the excitement, Pulse had set it down on the console. He was too busy telling my aunt what a horrible mother she'd been. My aunt, like the poised woman she was, sat there and took it.

I waited.

I shifted forward and curled my body over my knees. I didn't want him to see the belt until it was too late.

I waited some more, gripping each end of the strap in my hands.

When Pulse turned to look at the road again after his last diatribe, I struck. Wrapping the belt around his neck, I pulled as tight as I could. He was trying to keep the car steady while reaching for the gun. My aunt fought the gun out of

Pulse's hand. I held on to the straps as tightly as I could, digging my knees into the back of the chair for leverage. He was quickly losing the battle to breathe.

A shot rang out.

Pulse slid back against the seat, losing control of the car.

He was dead, but his foot was still on the accelerator.

"Mer, open the door and jump," my aunt screamed. "Now!"

I said a silent prayer. *Please protect my baby and make sure Grizz knows I love him.*

I tried to land on my back, but when I hit the pavement, everything went black.

Chapter 24
How Are We Getting Out of This?

Grace

Grizz had texted. It was time, but I didn't want to let go. I wasn't superstitious, but there were too many signs that I couldn't ignore. The men had mounted their bikes, preparing to ride, but there was a silence that hid among the hum of the machines. They shifted on the seats of their bikes, but nothing else moved. Not even a small dust devil dared to dance across the yard.

I found the strength to kiss Sabre one last time and held my head high as I turned away from him to walk back to the porch. He'd warned me that when there was an upheaval in our lives, we would simply love harder to get through it. I had taken him seriously, but I hadn't understood the magnitude of those words. I stood at the porch rail, in between my two guards, smiling as I waved goodbye to the men as they drove through the gates in pairs. In reality, I just wanted to curl into the fetal position and beg for Sabre's return. My stomach tightened. My baby agreed with me.

No one moved from the porch, even though the last pair of bikes had crested the hill and were out of sight. I didn't think any of us wanted to be the person who openly speculated. The unknowns lingered in the air, and these men only dealt with facts.

Count was the only executive team member left in the clubhouse. He eventually ushered everyone back into the main room, but before he entered, he glanced at the horizon. I didn't know what he was looking for, nor did I ask. However, when he caught me watching him, he offered a small smile. His eyes held shadows that had seen too much.

Count tried to get the remaining brothers to relax, but no one wanted to pretend that everything was normal. On a regular day, there were always a couple of people playing pool or watching TV. The club girls would wander around the bottom floor, flirting and teasing. Today, we all waited with bated breath.

I sat on one couch, with Chef on one side and Thunder on the other. Count came up behind me and squatted so that his elbows rested on the back of the couch.

"Are you alright, Flo? This might be a little much for you, in your condition." His gaze flickered to my bump, a silent reassurance that he was looking out for his brother's child.

"I am fine. Please let me know if there's anything I can do to make this better." I meant every word. If I could relieve the tension in the room, I'd do it, but we all knew that wouldn't happen until the men returned.

"Nah, we're fine. Just take care of yourself. I'm not taking a chance that Sabre beats my ass if I tell him you didn't sit down." He smiled at me and stood from his crouch. "You two, guard duty. Keep her safe," he addressed the men next to me and went to sit at the bar facing the room.

The silence from the yard settled into the clubhouse's main room. We were statues, waiting for any sign.

As the two-hour mark approached, my phone dinged with an incoming text. Before I could pull it out of my back pocket, Count's phone went off, signaling another. It could have only been from one person. I turned towards Count, and he winked at me as he looked at his phone.

Checking mine, I breathed a silent sigh of relief.

Sabre

> *Just wanted you to know we're here, and everyone's fine. Don't worry, mama.*

"They're getting ready to head back," Count addressed the room. The only sound was the ticking of the neon clock that sat above the bar.

Count's phone rang. As I turned back to face him, I noticed everyone else in the room had done the same thing. We were waiting for some piece of news that would make all of this simply disappear.

"What the fuck are you on?" Count said into the phone as he cradled it against his ear. The light in the room bounced off the silver rings on his hand. His eyes focused straight in front of him, not seeing any of us. "Are you fucking serious?" He nodded his head yes to whatever was being said. "Alright, lock the gate from the shack and haul ass in here." He hung up the phone and set it on the bar to rub at his eyes. His body was tight as he slid off the barstool and dictated orders.

"OP stand at the door, and when the prospect gets in here, seal it behind him." Count's eyes bounced to Cyph. He'd been sleeping on one couch with his head in the lap of a club girl. The excitement in the room had woken him. "I need you, man. Can you brace and lock the main gate from here?"

"Yeah, I'll do it from my room." Cyph stood quickly and ran up the stairs to the second floor. Count didn't stop assigning positions, even though he hadn't said a word on what was going on.

"How and Zook, I need you guys to run to the artillery and bring out the big guns. We have company. Zone and Lightning, grab rifles and hit the roof. I need to know what we're really dealing with." Each man moved immediately to comply.

Count finally addressed the rest of the brothers who were waiting for an update. "The prospect said that there are two blacked-out SUVs running up and down the road in opposite directions. I am not taking any chances. Man your battle stations, and we'll show them a warm, bullet-filled welcome."

There was a flurry of activity in the room, but before I could shift to stand, Count was at the back of the couch again. "Flo, they're here for you, and I am not letting them get close."

"You think it's the cartel?" My heart dropped into my stomach. The look on his face confirmed my thoughts.

"Unless they break through the gate, they can't do a drive-by. The clubhouse sits too far back from the road." Count looked at Thunder first and then Chef. "What are they really here for?"

"Intimidation?" Chef said.

"You can just say it. They're here for the baby." I was done with the guessing games.

"What's the easiest way for—" Count said.

"Count!" Cyph screamed from the balcony on the second floor that overlooked the main room. "They have automatic machine guns! They won't break the gate, but they'll be able to light this place up."

"Fuck! We can't defend against that." Count looked up at Cyph. "How comfortable are you putting everyone in the vault? Our bikes are out front, and we can't leave. They'll chase us."

"It'll be hot, and there's no light in there, but it could work." Cyph shrugged.

"We can't rebuild if we're dead." Count stuck two fingers into his mouth and whistled. All the frenzied activity in the room stopped immediately. "If you didn't hear Cyph, the cartel is here with machine guns. We won't be able to defend against them without the entire club here, and I am not losing anyone today. We're headed to the vault." When no one moved, he screamed, "Now!"

People were everywhere, and as I tried to stand from the couch, the room spun. I felt as if I was underwater, with no lifesaver to bring me to the surface. Quickly closing my eyes, I reopened them, hoping this feeling would go away, but it didn't. It only made it worse, and I felt as if I was falling into the abyss. Trying to reach out, I found nothing to ground myself. I was going to fall without a safety net.

"Whoa, missy. Not so fast. I got ya." Two hands reached out and grabbed my elbows to steady me.

"We need to get her downstairs before they shoot," someone said.

"She needs to go to a hospital," another voice chimed in.

"She'll die there, and then we'll die when Sabre kills us. Didn't you watch that show about how people go to the hospital and never leave?" I could hear panic in that voice through the fog.

"Flo, can you hear me?" It was Thunder with his boisterous voice.

I nodded, even though it was fuzzy between my ears.

"You guys are fucking stupid. Her blood pressure is probably sky high," one of the club girls chimed in. "Flo?" she asked me. She put her hands on my cheeks and made me look at her. It was Pebbles. I recognized her by the hair buns she always wore. "I need you to breathe with me. Ready?"

I hadn't realized that I was breathing heavily until I tried to follow her lead. It was a challenge, but I followed her pattern. As my heart rate slowed, my breathing became normal again, and the haze subsided. I sent a silent prayer to anyone who was listening. Now was not the time for this.

"Thanks, Pebbles," I said, when I could see her clearly. Thunder was still holding my elbow to steady me, but I backed away from them and tried to follow the rest of the club. Thunder guided me down the stairs, and Chef was directly behind me, but when I reached the bottom step, I had to pause.

The MC had a prison in the basement, complete with bars.

These were legitimate cells, or what I imagined the inside of a prison to look like. I'd never had the privilege of visiting one. The lights had a yellow hue to them and made the white walls seem dirty.

"Let's get you to the vault," Thunder said to me. "If Sabre doesn't answer your questions about all of this later, I will."

When we reached the last cell on the right, I saw a man sitting in the bed, leaning against the wall. He was in terrible shape as he wheezed with every breath he took. It whistled through the hairs of his mustache.

"There she is," he said, directing his statement at me. "The bitch that started this whole fucking mess."

I turned to fully look at him, and that was when I noticed the bandages wrapped around his arms and legs.

"Your boyfriend did this, bitch," he said to me, when he caught me staring.

"Knock it off, Jig. You did this to yourself by betraying the club." Chef placed his hand on my back and tried to help guide me forward.

"I didn't do fucking shit. You know how much money they want for that baby? We could all live like kings, and she could fucking have another one. No one wants her, just the kid."

Pain snaked its way through my body. It started at my head and lodged a migraine behind the bridge of my nose. All I could see was the white light, as I tried not to collapse from the intensity.

"She's nothing special. Sell the kid, and Sabre can play with her until he tires. Look at her. It probably wouldn't take much to break her."

I swayed back and forth, trying to grab onto Thunder's arm before I toppled over. His words brought up all the pain that Matt had inflicted. I wasn't good enough. No one would ever accept me for who I was. My chest hurt, and I couldn't breathe. This was it. This was going to be the end of me. I wrapped my arms around my bump, not giving up in defeat. I would protect my baby from this monster, even though the haze had crept in around the edges of my vision.

"Can't even hack it, and this is supposed to be your first lady," Jig taunted from his seat on the bed.

Whatever I meant to say to him died on my lips as a shot rang out.

Thunder grabbed me in a modified bear hug. At seven and a half months pregnant, there was no way he could reach around me completely. The bump was the size of a basketball, making it no easy feat to be gentle while still ensuring I was protected. His body covered mine, but as we hit the floor, I turned to look at the man they'd called Jig. He had a bullet hole in the middle of his forehead.

Lifting my head to see over Thunder's shoulder, I saw Luna had a gun in her hand. Before I could call out, Pebbles overtook her from behind. They wrestled to the ground, evenly matched. Luna threw a punch, but Pebbles dodged it and grabbed Luna's arm with the gun. It went off. Chef had been too slow to duck, and the bullet lodged itself into his shoulder. He fell to his knees as we heard a loud popping sound.

Pebbles had dislocated Luna's arm from the shoulder and easily overtaken her. Grabbing the gun, she said, "My daddy was a cop, you stupid bitch. This is going to leave a nasty scar." Pebbles pistol-whipped Luna out cold.

Thunder picked up his head and screamed into the void for the rest of the brothers. The haze hadn't rescinded, but I could see a familiar set of blue spikes running my way.

"We got a problem. Her water just broke," I heard Thunder say as his chest bounced against mine with the words.

"How do you know?"

"My pants are wet."

No sooner did the word wet leave his mouth than there was a loud popping sound coming from upstairs. The cartel had opened fire.

Chapter 25
My Worst Nightmare

Sabre

I hated hospitals with a passion. White wall. Closed door. Sit. Wait. I was a man of action. I'd never been good at sitting on my hands and waiting for someone to grace our presence. Grizz was sitting next to me, and he was having a hard time sitting and waiting, too. He would stretch his left leg, and then he would bring it back in, only to bounce it a minute later. Once his left leg stopped, his right leg would do the same thing.

We'd ridden out of the diner's parking lot in formation, so no one in front of the car would know anything was amiss. It wasn't until the brothers in the back had yelled at the rest of us that there was a problem.

***

The car made a U-turn onto the emergency service road, but we were clueless about anything else. Following at a distance had been my order, but I heard Grizz in the earpiece of my helmet screaming that we should just overtake them. I couldn't remember what was exactly said, but I didn't want the women to be hurt on my watch. It wasn't until both of their car doors opened I realized it was going to happen anyway.

It was like watching a movie, where you knew exactly what was going to happen, but you were yelling at the screen, hoping for another outcome. The passenger door opened first, and we watched as Aunt E flew and rolled once she hit the pavement. Meredith came soon after, but she took most of the impact on her left side. The car continued speeding until it hit the guardrail in the middle.

Grizz laid his bike down in the middle of the road, not caring about the damage he'd just caused. He ran towards Meredith, but she was unconscious when he'd reached her. It was a nightmare. Grizz screamed at Scrub to do something, anything. He then turned back to her lifeless body and started screaming again about how she made him crazy. He went on a tirade about how she needed to wake up, so that he could make her see they were perfect together. I had known it was serious for him, but I hadn't paid attention to how serious it was until then. It was Old Lady serious.

Scrub parked his bike and immediately jumped in at the scene to take over. Assessing the situation, the first thing he did was plan for an emergency flight lift for the women. The club would eventually end up paying dearly for that one day, but at that moment, it might have been the difference between life and death for them. Watching Grizz lose his shit, I chose life in a heartbeat and worried about the bill later. If we lost Meredith, Grizz would never be the same, and I was just now understanding that.

Scrub had run to Meredith first, but when his preliminary check yielded nothing, he ran to the other side of the road to check on Aunt E. I saw the anguish on his face. It was bad, and he didn't have the right equipment, but he did the best he could.

The club stood to the side of the road and let Scrub and the paramedics work. We didn't move for fear that we would be in the way. As we stood there and watched, no one mentioned Pulse. He could have been alive at the time of the crash, and we wouldn't have known. No one cared enough about him to check. He wasn't getting a patch now, so he was dead to us. When the helicopter left, I walked towards the car with Wreck right behind me.

There was just enough space for us to walk in between the car and the guardrail. Approaching the driver's side door, I motioned for Wreck to wait. The window was still intact, so I tapped on the glass with my knuckle. There was no movement inside. I tapped a little harder. There was still no movement. Grabbing the door handle, I opened the driver's side door. Pulse was sitting straight up with a belt wrapped around his neck. The blood vessels in his eyes had burst, and there was slight bruising beneath the belt. He was dead.

"That's Tef's belt around his neck," Grizz said over my shoulder. I hadn't been aware that he had been following us to the car. He appeared to be hanging in there, for now. I'd eventually have to ask how he was holding up.

"How do you know?" I said over my shoulder.

"I bought it for her. It's a running joke. She has no ass," he said, lost in his own world.

"She was in the back when we left the diner, right?"

"Yeah, she was sitting right behind Pulse. She was being pissy and stormed over to the car to avoid everyone. I demanded to know why she didn't say goodbye, so I crouched so that she couldn't close the door." Grizz wiped his hand over his face.

"Grizz," I said, "she did this to protect them. Why they needed the protection is the more important question."

"There's a gun in his hand, Prez," Wreck said. "He was holding them at gun-point."

"Tef," Grizz whined and doubled over, trying to grasp a breath. His body gave out as he bent over the guardrail and violently threw up.

"Wreck, help me pull his cut off of him, and we'll have to take the belt and anything else they left behind."

***

The news played on the hospital waiting room's TV. No one was watching, but we were all paying attention to the broadcast. Someone coughed. Another brother slid forward in their seat, with their hands in between their knees. A knee bounced somewhere in the room. Once the reporters went from the local news to sports, we were in the clear.

When the helicopter had left, the club had taken our time to make sure that we cleaned the scene. Pulling the plates off the car, I had made sure that we grabbed any personal items before burning the car. There were no cameras on that stretch of highway, and the car wouldn't yield any evidence once the highway patrol found it. The case, if it was ever even opened to begin with, would be closed. Either way, it wasn't important enough for the news.

The wait was killing me, and I traced what had happened, starting from the time we'd pulled into the diner. Halfway through, I realized I was just as lost as before and went back to staring at the opposite white wall.

"What if she doesn't make it?" Grizz said softly.

"She's too much of a bitch not to," I whispered back. If I blatantly displayed my hostility towards Meredith in front of the brothers, they would never give her a chance to prove herself.

"Yeah, but she's my bitch. Just don't let her hear you call her that."

"Are you going to beat my ass for calling her one?" I asked, trying to liven up the mood, at least for a second.

"No. She's bitchy, and she hasn't earned the club's support, but she's mine." He took a deep breath and wiped the back of his hand against his lips. "She's mine, Sabre. Pregnant or not."

I didn't want to address his claim on her in the middle of the hospital's waiting room, but I had to keep him talking. It was better than the lifeless body that had sat next to me for the last hour. "You think she lost the baby?"

"Yeah. There's no way she could protect it. You saw her jump." He took another breath and wiped a few tears from his eyes. "She had her arm wrapped around her stomach. Protecting it. Just tells me that no matter what she said, she wanted it."

I sent a silent prayer of thanks that I knew where Grace was and that she was safe with my baby. I didn't know if I would have been able to handle it as well as Grizz, even though I knew he was numb. Settling back in my chair, we both went silent, deep in our own thoughts.

Two hours had passed, and I was still staring at the white wall when a flurry of activity took over at the emergency room's check-in desk.

I wasn't sure if they were doctors, nurses, or just personnel, but people came rushing out of the double doors. Standing in a line, they faced the ambulance bay. They were waiting for someone to come through the sliding double doors. I didn't know why I stared at them as hard as I did. I didn't care about anyone else, but I couldn't look away.

The overhead intercom crackled. "Dr. Andrews, please dial code 0014. Dr. Andrews, please dial code 0014."

"How many Dr. Andrews do you know that work in this hospital?" I asked Grizz, still watching the staff at the entrance.

"Just one, and she delivers babies," Grizz said, sliding to the front of his chair.

Fuck. That was what I was afraid of. I immediately stood up and walked over to the waiting room reception desk. As I approached, an older woman with a pink volunteer jacket stood up. "May I help you, sir?" she asked me.

"I just heard you page a Dr. Andrews. You wouldn't be paging Dr. Alison Andrews, would you?" I tried to smile, but I'd been staring at the white walls for too long and didn't have any fucks left to give.

"I am sorry, sir, but I am not at liberty to release any information," she answered, placing her hands on her hips.

"Look, I am an old family friend of Stands," I said.

"Who?" The lady looked at me over the top of her glasses and down the bridge of her nose. Fuck, she was going to bust my balls.

"Dr. Andrews. We're old family friends." I again tried to smile. This was more Pretty's department than mine. I wasn't having any luck trying to charm the pants off the old woman.

"I am sorry, but I am not at liberty to release any information. Perhaps give this Dr. Andrews a call, since you should have her number *as a family friend*."

Well played, lady.

I didn't immediately sit back down in the waiting room. I was done with that shit, and if someone didn't give us an update soon, I'd demand one. Standing in front of the waiting room's reception desk, I turned to watch the people still waiting for the ambulance.

It wasn't long before the ambulance backed into the bay. The staff were leaning forward, ready to sprint at a moment's notice. Finally, the paramedic in the back of the bus opened the doors. The first person I saw was Thunder.

My brain went into overdrive. I blinked rapidly to make sure I was really seeing Thunder. Why was he here? What had happened that he needed an ambulance? If Thunder was here, who was with Grace? I'd put the fear of death into both of her bodyguards before leaving this morning. Maybe Chef was with Grace, and she was safe at the clubhouse. Thunder didn't look injured, but he was wide enough that I couldn't see behind him.

"Sir! Sir!" I heard, but the noise dulled into the background. "You can't be there. You need to sit back down."

"Prez," Thunder said to me as he took a step to the side. There was a hospital gurney in the back of the ambulance. All I could see was the swell of a pregnant woman's belly. The paramedic in the back of the bus jumped down, and started to pull the gurney forward. Blonde hair spilled down the sides, and there was a bracelet on the woman's right hand. It was Grace's. She'd told me that it was her aunt's, and that she'd stolen it, with permission, permanently. Thunder was here with Grace. This was my worst nightmare coming to life.

A scream echoed from the back of the ambulance. Grace was in pain, and they weren't moving fast enough. "Move!" I tried to command them, but they looked at me like I was crazy. "What the fuck are you doing just standing there? Fucking move! She's in pain."

I didn't know what I was planning on doing, but I took a step towards them, and Thunder blocked my path. Holding me against the wall, he tried to call me down. "Let them save her, Prez. We did the best we could."

"What the fuck happened?"

He didn't answer, just shook his head no.

As the paramedics rolled Grace out of the back of the ambulance, the staff took over.

"Thirty, female. Thirty-four weeks pregnant. Blood pressure 161 over 80. Shows signs of hypertension. Reported dizziness and blurry vision," I heard the paramedic rattle off.

The doors to the emergency room popped open, and Dr. Andrews ran out. Stands, Bear's daughter, that wanted nothing to do with the club.

"Grace!" I raised my voice, hoping she would hear me over the chaos.

I saw her head turn in my direction, but she was lying on her back and couldn't see over her bump. "Sabre?" she asked.

"I am right here, mama." I tried to get closer to her, but between Thunder blocking me and all the staff, there was no room.

Stands' head popped up when she heard me. "Is your name Grace?" she asked.

"Yes." I heard her voice laced with pain. My heart broke to hear her like that.

"Well, Grace. You're in expert hands. I have the best delivery rate in this hospital, and that's not me bragging. That's just a fact. Plus, I am club. Feel like delivering today?"

They were rolling Grace through the double doors when I heard a dry chuckle. "Not like this," the words fell from Grace's lips in painful strikes to my heart.

The doors slammed shut. I'd have to sit in the waiting room, staring at the white fucking walls.

My legs buckled, and I slid down the wall until my ass hit the tile.

"I love you," I whispered, pretending she could hear it behind the door.

"Come on, Prez. Let's get you back to the waiting room." Thunder reached down and helped me back to my feet.

"Thunder? What the fuck happened? She was supposed to be safe."

"The cartel happened, Prez."

Chapter 26
White Walls Caving In

Sabre

I was the one now numb, sitting in the waiting room chair, staring again at the fucking white wall. They'd wheeled Grace back to the abyss, and naturally, there were no updates. I had tried to get the older woman behind the waiting room desk to tell me something, anything, but she shot me down every chance.

Pretty had taken pity on me and tried his best. He had walked up to her and handed her a coffee. I didn't know what he had said, but it had worked. There was nothing in the system except that Grace was there. The woman had assured Pretty that she would inform him as soon as there was an update. It'd been over an hour.

The sound of motorcycle engines reverberated off the walls of the waiting room, and our heads instantly turned to look out the large window at the back of the room. The rest of the club was here, and I could finally get answers.

I stood and tapped Grizz on the shoulder. His eyes focused on the bikes that were parked and stood. I'd taken it easy on him as we waited, but this was club business, and he was still my vice president. He needed to be present for whatever was about to go down.

Thunder stood. He wasn't a club officer, but he'd been around long enough to know that he was going to be put in the hot seat, and he better have had the answers that I wanted to hear. He'd preferred to wait until the rest of the club was here. It probably was a smart move on his part.

Heading towards the parking lot, I saw my brother stop and speak with the volunteer again. He must have told her we were heading outside because I saw his finger point towards the doors. She nodded feverishly and gripped his forearm before letting him go. She'd never been that nice to me.

As we walked towards the bikes, the regular brothers dismounted, nodded at me, and slinked off to the waiting room. Count and Cyph were the only two who stayed seated with their bikes still running. Whatever had gone down was bad. This conversation would need to be masked underneath the sounds of the engines.

Count shifted in his seat directly facing me. "Did Thunder tell you what went down?"

"I am asking *you* what the fuck happened." My tone showed that I didn't want to hear any fucking bullshit. I planted my feet shoulder width apart and crossed my arms over my chest.

He detailed everything, from the time I had texted until they'd loaded up to drive here. There had been no flaws in their execution. If I'd been at the clubhouse, I would have done the same, and I couldn't fault him.

"We took Chef to Bear's, since she's a retired nurse. The wound isn't bad, but she'll have to dig the bullet out and bandage him up. He'll live. Couldn't tell the paramedics that we had a gunshot wound, so Chef hid until they were gone. That's why I sent Thunder with the ambulance."

"No, you did well, Count." I lowered my eyes and rubbed the back of my neck. I took a minute to calm down. My heart raced, chest tightening with anxiety. I needed an update before I lost my shit.

"Pretty?" I asked my brother. "Is the volunteer going to call us if something changes?"

He nodded. "Delores and I are good friends. I remind her of her late husband. She said she'd send someone out here if there was a change, even though she's not at liberty to give me any information." He rolled his eyes.

"Fuck. How long is that going to take?" I was getting frustrated with this whole situation.

Pretty shrugged. "I don't know, but my work is already done. You're welcome."

"I doubt it's a coincidence that all of us are here at the hospital. What happened to you guys on the road?" Count stepped in, trying to diffuse the mounting tension.

"We didn't know Pulse had made the U-turn until the brothers behind the car started yelling. From what we can figure out, he was trying to kidnap the women. They actually saved themselves and jumped out of the moving car."

"What? Pulse didn't jump?" Cyph asked.

"No, Tef strangled him with her belt." Grizz was proud as he puffed out his chest and raised his eyebrows. "That's my girl," he said with a slight tilt of his head.

"Scrub made the arrangements to have them airlifted here from the scene. He's been with them ever since." Scrub was the only brother who had direct permission to work outside of the club. He'd applied at the county hospital right after med school so that we would have an in for situations like this. There had been a few ER visits over the years, but this was the first time we were seriously going to cash-in. It was hard not to text him every two seconds to check in.

Cyph yawned for the third time since we'd been standing out here.

"Have you slept?" I asked him.

"It doesn't matter." He yawned again. His eyes were red-rimmed, and he constantly rubbed them in between the yawns.

"Do you remember anything about Pulse's background check?" I didn't want to put pressure on him, but this was serious. We needed to know what we were dealing with.

"No. It was standard stuff. Broken home, like most of us. Did some not-so-nice things but nothing that we couldn't handle. He might have had some college, but I am not sure. It wasn't enough to flag him." Cyph yawned again.

"How did Pulse get behind the wheel of the car? Did you tell him he was driving, or did he ask?" Count asked me.

"I threw the keys to the car at him and told him to drive. He was in the clubhouse when I was passing out assignments, and I didn't think twice about it.

Pulse was our best prospect, and if he'd survived a few more months, we would have patched him in."

"How did the cartel know that the club was going to be split?" Wreck broke into the conversation. Wreck was imposing on a good day. He wasn't the largest brother in the club, but he gave off the most menacing vibe. My brother didn't know when to shut up, but Wreck hardly spoke. If he did, we paid attention.

"Go on," I told him.

"Count said they drove two blacked-out SUVs down the street with a machine gun. They planned that, but how did they know who would be in the clubhouse?"

Pretty tucked his hand in the crook of Wreck's arm. "They might not have. It could have been a lucky guess," he popped in.

"Nah, they had a general idea of the numbers, even if they didn't know who exactly. Think about it," Grizz said, staring off into space. "They hit Aunt E's last night, and I bet they ransacked the place, looking for us when it was all over. When they didn't find anyone, they hit the club. Someone's running the show and quickly regrouped."

"What if Pulse tipped them off?" Thunder tried to lower his voice, but it still bounced around us.

"Yeah, where do you get a machine gun that quickly?" Count asked. He counted on his fingers. "It would take me at least three phone calls and a favor to get one."

"Seriously? I can probably name that tune in under two," Cyph said, yawning again.

"Well, the next time we need one, I'll let you handle it." Count laughed.

"The machine gun doesn't matter. They had plenty of time to get one, or they had it and just waited. I want to fucking know what happened in that car." Grizz let out a low growl. He was coming back to life.

"Until one of them is awake, I wouldn't bet on that happening soon. They're going to need time to heal, and Aunt E isn't going home. She probably doesn't have one left," I said.

"Tef's not going back to her condo either." Grizz stamped his foot and crossed his arms over his chest. All of us just looked at him, trying to see what he saw. No one wanted to tell him that Meredith would fight him tooth and nail.

"Something's not right with this," Wreck popped up again. "If Pulse tipped them off, why did they not search the clubhouse? They could have come in and fought their way to Flo. They're after the baby." Wreck caressed Pretty's knuckles.

"If Pulse was working with the cartel, why did he need Meredith? It was Meredith they were after. We took Aunt E with us for safety," Pretty followed up.

"I can answer the one about why no search. They wouldn't have been able to penetrate the gate without a battering ram, and even then, it wouldn't have broken open. When Sabre took over as President,"—Cyph looked over at me—"it was one of the very first upgrades that we made, and I keep up with the software so that it's not outdated."

"Ah, so that's why the upstairs looks like a fucking pincushion. They only shot at the middle because the gun could only hit the first floor," Count said.

"I can answer the one about Meredith. They need a baby, and as long as she was pregnant, they would take either or both." Grizz sighed and pulled the tie from his man bun to redo it. It was a telltale sign he was jittery.

"How did they know she was pregnant?" Wreck said. "You didn't even know."

"I don't think any of us will truly know what their plans are or how it all connects until we personally have to deal with them. Don't forget, we have a club girl now involved in all of this. Luna didn't wake up this morning and decide to shoot Jig. That shit was planned," I said.

"Maybe he let her in on his plans, and she took it upon herself to seize the moment. You guys were trailing the rest of the club into the vault," Count said to Thunder. "If she had been quick enough, she could have eliminated all of you and taken Flo. What do we do now?"

"Nothing. It's not like we can call the cartel and ask what's up," I said. "For now, we wait to see how the women pull out of this." I shuffled my feet and looked at Count. "What did you do with Luna?"

"Pebbles hit her pretty good, so she was out when we threw her in the same cell as Jig. Zook is standing guard to make sure that she doesn't get any bright ideas." Count smirked. "I left a few of the men with the club girls. They wanted to come, but we couldn't have protected them on the backs of our bikes if the cartel had hit us on the road."

I was shaking my head when I noticed Pretty nod to someone behind me.

Standing in the doorway was the volunteer in her pink coat, flagging us down. There must have been an update.

Chapter 27

Always The Bridesmaid

Sabre

Grizz and I walked side-by-side behind Pretty as we crossed the parking lot. Fear spread over us as each step brought us closer to the older woman who'd stepped outside to flag Pretty down. Sweat dripped off my forehead, and my hands felt clammy to the touch. Grizz kept curling his hands into fists and then releasing them. Each step felt like a thousand pounds dropping on our shoulders.

"Dr. Matthews requested that someone show you back to the waiting room. He said nothing else." She squinted her eyes at me, officially warding off any questions I'd try to get her to answer. "He said he'd be with you shortly." She turned and walked back through the double doors to her desk.

"Dr. Matthews," Pretty snorted. "She wouldn't be so uppity if she knew he liked threesomes."

"You will not tell her," I said. "Scrub has to work with these people."

Taking our seats, we waited, staring some more at the white fucking walls. This day would never end.

It was a half an hour before Scrub walked out of the double doors that led to the emergency room. I couldn't help but notice the irony that he now wore a pair of blue scrubs, a surgeon's cap covering his auburn hair.

He took the chair next to me and swung it around before sitting so that he could see all the brothers behind us.

"Aunt E is out of surgery, but she's going to have a long recovery. Broken bones. Jarred ribs. Cuts and bruises. You name it, she has at least one. However, luck was on her side. She had a few internal bleeds, but we stopped them. The rest of her injuries will heal." He hung his hands in between his legs and lowered his head, taking a minute.

"What is it?" I knew him well enough to know that he wasn't done. He was only gearing up for more.

"This is the worst part about it. I made sure she was alive when we arrived. Now, they're assessing her in the back, and she's still unconscious. There's no way to know if she has a concussion or the severity of it. Neurology is flying blind, because they can't safely evaluate and treat her. They're making accurate guesses based on the data, but no one will know what damage has already been done. She may need severe help."

"I am not worried about it. We'll cross that bridge when we get there, even if it means hiring a nurse or some shit like that." I was serious, and I wouldn't let Aunt E hurt. I'd make sure she had what she needed to move on. "For her safety, how long will she be here?" I asked him, turning to face his direction.

"At least a week or two, maybe more. Since she was going to be in severe pain anyway, ortho made a plan to reset her broken bones in order of severity. She'll have at least one or two more surgeries, depending on how well she's healing. When I left, they were working on temporary casts for the first round. Since they don't expect her to regain consciousness soon, they're confident that she wouldn't cause any further damage. When they're done, she'll head to the ICU."

"I want to do right by Aunt E. Can we keep a guard detail on her in the ICU?" I asked him.

"Eh," he said, thinking out loud. "The ICU has standard visiting hours. I think it closes at either nine or ten. A brother can sit with her."

"I'll do it," Thunder volunteered.

"Later," I told him, shaking my head. Brother was probably feeling guilty, and I wouldn't let him overdo it.

"The ICU is round, so the nurse's station is in the middle, with each room around the outside. The front is all glass, but the problem will be when visiting hours are over. Someone could sit in the waiting room, but they will only see the entrance." Scrub took off his surgeon's cap and twiddled it in between his fingers.

"What are her odds of pulling through, Scrub?" I asked.

"She'll have a better chance at a full recovery, depending on the damage from the concussion. However, that's a long, drawn-out road of doctor's appointments, physical therapy, and the like. The hospital did a quick search. Her next of kin is sitting in the triage room right next to her." He rubbed his eyes. "Speaking of which, did anyone call their father?"

"No. I'll have to do that." The longer I could wait, the better off I'd be with that phone call. Grace's father, Gerry, would blame me when it was Matt who'd set this whole thing into motion.

"What about Meredith?" Grizz asked Scrub, leaning back in his chair.

Scrub looked at Grizz and shook his head. "I will tell you what I know, but it's not much. When Meredith jumped, she turned and landed on her left side. It's not surprising that most of the damage is on that side, since it took the most impact. No broken bones. No internal bleeding. Dislocated shoulder and a sprained knee. She's actually not doing too badly, but she has severe road rash. They're not sure if it's going to heal on its own or if they are going to have to skin graft certain parts of it."

"The baby?" Grizz pushed.

Scrub rubbed at his eyes again, as if he didn't want to answer or didn't know how much to tell Grizz.

"Tell me. That was my kid, too." Grizz tipped his chair back. It was a good thing I was in between them, in case Grizz tried to beat it out of Scrub.

"Again, this is what I know. They wheeled both Meredith and Aunt E into surgery when we first got here. It's easier and quicker to fix things when you're assessing. That didn't surprise me. However, they called Stands down to check the baby. I swear I know little after that."

"That's it? Did she lose it or not?" Grizz was flexing his left hand, preparing to reach over me and knock Scrub out.

"I wasn't involved in Meredith's care." Scrub sat straight up in his chair. He'd recognized the same thing I had. Grizz was a ticking time bomb.

"They wheeled Grace in, and the residents have been running back and forth to ask Stands questions. She can't leave Grace, but they don't have anyone to replace her to look after Meredith. It's the best they can do for right now, and it's working."

"Why aren't you in there?" Grizz was two seconds from an all-out war in the waiting room.

"I am not specialized enough to be in there. Pregnancy is not my thing, and I didn't check for any new updates before coming out here."

"Hey, Grizz. You should name your kids Tick, Tick Two, and Boom. You know, because you're about ready to explode," Pretty said out of the blue, trying to diffuse the situation. Grizz did not find it amusing.

"If you and Wreck ever adopt, I am naming them Run, For, and Cover." Grizz raised his middle finger at Pretty.

"What about Grace?" I quickly asked to change the subject.

"Last I heard, they were going to do an emergency c-section. Grace's blood pressure is spiking, which is putting the baby in distress. Stands hasn't left her." Scrub patted me on the shoulder.

"Grace fucking wins again. It's getting easier to see why Meredith runs in the opposite direction. There's no use competing with someone who's perfect." Grizz stood from his chair.

"Sit your fucking ass down." I wasn't in the mood to hash this bullshit out. He was hurting, but I would not let him take it out on Grace. Meredith had done enough of that.

He crossed his arms and tried to kill me with his stare. Maybe they were perfect for each other.

"When will they transfer Aunt E to the ICU?" I turned back to Scrub. I was done with Grizz for now, and I knew he'd never take a cheap shot with my back turned.

"In an hour or two. They're prepping her room, so she's sleeping in recovery."

"Chef's out of commission, so Thunder, you'll switch off with How. One of you will be here every 12 hours until we can get her settled." No one said a word as I gave orders. Taking out my phone, I let How know his assignment. He'd taken the second shift since he was at the clubhouse.

"When I head back, I'll put them on her visitation list. No one will say anything to them. You know, Aunt E might like some flowers to brighten up her room." Scrub looked at Cyph.

"Yeah, I think her favorite flowers are daisies. I'll get her some," Cyph commented.

How did Cyph know what Aunt E's favorite flowers were? It took me a minute to realize that Scrub had just encouraged Cyph to wire up a camera in the flowers for Aunt E's room. Cyph had just picked something, letting us know that he'd caught Scrub's message. I clapped Scrub back on the shoulder, not wanting to voice how smart that was.

Scrub stood from his chair and walked over to Grizz. "The next time you want to play favorites, pick another fucking brother. I don't do that shit, and you know it. It's how I lost my woman." He pivoted and walked back through the emergency room doors.

I watched Grizz drop his head in between his legs. It was getting harder to breathe, not knowing what was going on.

Scrub never came back out to the waiting room, and I finally made the call that I had been dreading.

Chapter 28
Matt Strikes Again

Sabre

I dialed Gerry and put my phone to my ear, waiting for it to connect. I wasn't dreading this phone call, but it would not be on my top five favorite things to do. The three most important women in Gerry's life were all in the same emergency room. As much as I didn't want to speak to him, he had a right to know. If it had been the other way around, I would have hoped he'd do me a solid by calling.

The phone rang.

It rang some more in my ear as I stared at the fucking white wall in front of me. Somewhere in the background, the front doors slid open. I was still waiting for Gerry to pick up. Fucking idiot.

Grizz elbowed me in the side and abruptly stood up. I looked behind me at the rest of my men. They were all standing, feet planted, arms crossed. They all had their battle faces on. Holding the phone to my ear, I surveyed the area to see what would cause this type of reaction.

I didn't need to call Gerry anymore. He was walking through the front door with Matt by his side. Son of a bitch.

I quickly stood, not really sure how to address this. Grace and the baby were mine, but she was still technically married to that fucking bitch. No matter what I told myself, he'd fathered that baby and had a better claim on them than I did.

No one said anything as they approached us. They must have discussed their entrance because Gerry stopped right in front of Grizz and me, while Matt continued to the older lady that was still sitting at the waiting room desk.

"It didn't have to be this way, but you two need to leave and take the riff raff with you." Gerry mirrored our stance, planting his feet and crossing his arms as he stood in front of us. There was a murmur among my men. They didn't appreciate that comment and neither did I.

"We're not going anywhere," I said, leaving no room for argument.

Matt walked back over to us. "There's no update, Gerry, but I made them aware that we're the next of kin and to only address us. Delores said she'd make a note in their files."

"Delores and I are good friends. Why don't you go back to the expensive trailer you crawled out of?" My brother was honestly jealous that the old woman had helped Matt. Pretty considered her under his control, and it was playing mind games with his charisma.

"Like fuck you are. There's no chance in hell you're her next of kin," I said to Matt. "She was divorcing you, and instead of just letting her go, you played games. How are your buddies in the cartel? I hear they're threatening you for money you don't have." I let the smirk that was trying to form settle on my lips.

"We're still married, and there's not a damn thing you can to do about it. I'll even make them do a paternity test just to prove the baby's mine. What are you going to do then, when we both know I am the daddy and you're just a pussy in a leather vest?"

I wanted to beat Matt into a bloody pulp, but there were too many eyes and ears in the room, especially considering their cartel alliances. I should have seen it the night the family imploded. Gerry's allegiance was to the cartel, not his daughters. I didn't know how I had missed those warning signs.

Grizz let a smirk form that he'd been trying to hold back. "Meredith and I got married last night, so technically, I am her next of kin."

Fuck! Cyph was going to have to forge those papers quickly in case we needed them.

"You weren't even speaking to each other, so I highly doubt that happened," Gerry said.

"You know your daughter. She's kind of bitchy when she doesn't get her way. Meredith's going to be pissed that she didn't get to tell you herself. When she saw me at the restaurant last night, she couldn't help herself. We patched it up and got hitched. I am her next of kin. Sorry, Pops." He was now smiling, pleased as punch with himself.

I had to admit, if we could get all the pieces aligned, it was a pretty genius plan on the fly.

"You lying sack of shit." Gerry spat his words, his voice filled with venom. "She would have never agreed to that. Meredith and Brandon were back together, and you couldn't take it." He pointed his finger at Grizz.

If he wasn't careful, Grizz would show him exactly why they'd called him Grizzly since he was a prospect. His face was hardening, and his smile turned into a sneer as he swatted Gerry's finger away.

"Don't spit that shit in my face. You won't like the result. When the hospital asks for the paperwork, I'll make sure they get a copy. Until then, take a huge fucking step back, old man."

We were at a standstill. Grizz and I would not move, and there was no way in hell these two fucks were ever going to share the same space in the waiting room with the club.

The double doors to the emergency room opened, and Stands walked out. I watched her as she surveyed the room, not impressed with our show of aggression.

"Are we done here, or are you going to whip it out and see who is bigger?" she asked.

"How's my wife?" Matt demanded.

"I am not at liberty to say," she answered him.

"She's my wife, so you better talk, or I'll own this hospital."

Stands laughed. "I've already looped in legal, and they're expecting you. You can discuss your situation with them. My only concern is my patient and her wishes."

Gerry turned to her, suddenly realizing that Stands had alluded to Grace being awake. "She's my kid. Is she alright?" His face looked as if he'd aged twenty years in a matter of seconds.

Stands turned to look at me, completely ignoring Gerry. "I need to speak with you." She looked back at the other two. "Privately."

I shared a quick look with Grizz, and he nodded back at me. He'd take care of anything that came through while I was away. The rest of the executive team had shifted to flank each side of him, with the rest of the brothers providing backup, if it came down to that.

I followed Stands through the double doors, past a nurses' station, into what looked like a small conference room.

"You so owe me," she said, as she turned to face me.

I waited for her to continue as I let the door close behind me.

"I stuck my head out and saw the mess in the waiting room. No one saw me, so I came back in here and pulled some strings to help you out," she told me, taking a deep breath. "My mom likes her. Says she reminds her of your mom. That's the only reason I did this. It has nothing to do with the club, and I don't want any of your favors." Stands emphasized the word "favors."

"Sure, and you're going to tell me you're not club either in a second." I smirked. Stands was trying to outrun what she'd been born into, and it would eventually suck her back in. If Meredith survived, they could be good friends. They were both runners.

"I am not, but even I get to hear the best gossip." She smiled. "She does kind of remind me of your mom."

We shared a brief smile, both lost in memories.

She shook her head, clearing it. "I pieced together what's going on from what I know and what I've heard. That's the soon-to-be ex-husband, right?"

I nodded my head yes, not willing to give a voice to that question.

"I figured," she said. "Flo is awake. I wasn't lying about that, so I went to her and asked some hospital-related questions. Does she have a power of attorney? Is there anyone she doesn't want her information released to? She caught on quickly, but I didn't tell her the whole situation. She gave me the answers I needed to get some paperwork in place. It won't help you, but it will help the hospital keep him at a distance.

"I also took another liberty, but I don't think you'll mind. I asked her point-blank if you were the father of her baby. She caught the meaning and said yes. It's the only way I can put you on the birth certificate. It's another roadblock for that jackass to get through. I don't want to know if you are or not, but she said you were. Plausible deniability."

"I thought you weren't club." Stands was doing me a solid when I had done nothing to help her.

"I am not," she answered with a defiant glare. She'd walked out of the clubhouse and sworn never to return.

I didn't want to argue with her, but I'd check in with her more regularly when this was over. "How is she, really?"

"I almost lost her on the table," Stands said, wiping a tear from her eye. "Her blood pressure was skyrocketing when she got here. You don't wake up one day and suddenly have issues like that. This has been going on for a while, and either her obstetrician missed it or didn't care enough to monitor it. Either way, it's pure negligence."

"Wait. She goes to a Dr. Vargas. Never misses an appointment. Each time, we were told everything was good." I struggled to understand.

"Vargas? Camiya Vargas?" Stands frowned. "She's under investigation for baby harvesting. It's not the first time, but the board never finds enough evidence to pull her license. Clients have reported missing babies or were told they didn't survive, only for them to be found later on. How did Flo get recommended to her?"

"I don't know," I said. "She was going there before I met her, so either she found Vargas, or Matt introduced her. I have my suspicions."

"Yeah, so do I. Once we could get the situation under control, everything fell into place. I am monitoring her blood pressure, and we did an emergency c-section. The baby was in distress, putting her at greater risk. It's actually a lot of stress on the body, so that's why she's resting in recovery. I've been checking on her every half hour."

"The baby?" I gasped, clutching my chest.

"He's healthy. Four pounds, six ounces. He's a tiny guy, but he's a fighter, like his mom. For being early, it's not as bad as it could have been. He'll have to stay in the NICU for monitoring until he reaches his due date. It's more to prevent complications. You won't be able to take him home until it's safe. I can't keep him with Flo, but I added a few select people to his visitor list. You have enough names for round-the-clock visitation." She wiped another tear from her eye. "Come on, and I'll take you to her. You should be able to stay with her for a little while." Stands walked towards the door and opened it, gesturing me to follow her.

"Stands," I said to her.

She glanced at me over her shoulder.

"Thanks for them. I owe you." I meant it. We were her family, but we'd been too stupid to defend her. I'd bring her back into the fold.

"For my mom. Not for you." She crossed the threshold, and I followed her down the hallway. She made a series of turns before she came to a curtained room. "Let me check first." She walked in, and I could hear her talking to Grace.

"Hey, Flo. How are you feeling?" she asked.

"Like I was cut open." There was a slight chuckle.

"I bet. I have someone who wants to see you. You up for a little company?" I heard Stands ask her.

"Only if it's Sabre." I had to take a minute to calm down. Grace wanted me as much as I needed to be with her. Any doubt I had that this wouldn't work melted away.

Chapter 29
Hi Daddy! We're Waving At You.

When I heard her call out for me, I didn't hesitate. I walked through the doorway, slid the curtain aside, and then my feet stuck to the floor. Emotions swirled around me, making it hard to grasp anything. My eyes instantly sought hers as she lay in the middle of the bed. Locking onto her brown irises, relief drained from my body.

Her lips curled in a pain-filled smile when she saw me. I'd almost lost her, and any remaining relief transformed into grief. I couldn't bear the thought of being without her. If I'd lost her, I would have lost myself. I took a minute to scan her from the top of her blonde head to the two bumps underneath her blanket that I figured were her feet.

My hands rose instinctively, trying to reach out for her.

"Sabre," she whispered to me.

I wasn't a praying man, but I stopped to say a quick thank you to whoever might be listening. I vowed never to take her for granted. We'd joked about princess treatment, but I'd treat her like the queen she was. Silently, of course, because she'd never accept it. I'd fooled myself into thinking she was just some chick in the bar. She was so much more. Somewhere along the line, I'd ripped out my heart and handed it to her.

"Hey." I rushed to stand by her side, reaching for her hand.

"Yeah, you two don't even know I'm here." Stands chuckled, fiddling with the machine. "I'll be back around to check on you, Flo. If you need something, just hit the emergency call button on the bed."

I heard Stands move the curtain and slide out of the partition, my eyes never leaving Grace's.

"Hey." Grace slid her hand closer to mine and tried to scoot back on the bed, making room for me to sit.

"Don't hurt yourself. I am right here, and I am not going anywhere." I locked our fingers together and rubbed my thumb along the back of her hand.

"I don't want you far away," she said. Her hand gripped my fingers as tightly as she could. Fear was settling in. Her eyes were wide, and there were shadows buried deep within them. Her bottom lip quivered.

I kissed her forehead, letting my lips linger to remind myself that she was here. She'd been through hell, but she was alive. I leaned down and pecked her lips lightly, careful not to touch her. I didn't want to cause her more pain inadvertently. Grabbing the chair that was in the room, I dragged it to her bedside.

"Are you alright? I was worried," she whispered.

"You've been through hell, and your first thought is to ask me if I am okay?" She stumped me. I should have been the one asking her.

"I love you. Of course, I need to know that you're alright." She frowned, but it twisted into a grimace.

"Easy." I stood to peck her lips lightly again. "Right now, you're my primary concern."

"I'm good. Nothing to see here. It's not like they cut me open or anything like that."

I chuckled lightly, and her lips tipped up into a smile. "I bet the scar is going to be pretty damn sexy."

Her smile instantly faded.

"I am going to pounce on you every chance I get over that thing. Consider yourself warned." I didn't mention that the scar would always remind me of today and how close I'd come to losing her.

"Seriously? You're insane." She was blinking constantly, and I could only imagine the pain she was in. The shadows I'd seen earlier remained in her eyes.

"No, I was a fool. I should have told you first thing this morning that I love you. I know what it's like to be without you now, and I can't go through that again. You own my heart, Grace. You're mine, mama."

"Your timing sucks," she said as she yawned.

"Yeah, I'll tell you again and again. Don't worry about it." I lightly squeezed her fingers in mine.

"The baby?" she asked, fighting another yawn. "No one told me anything, except that he's doing better than expected." I was going to have to make this quick before she succumbed to sleep.

"He's doing well, but he has to stay in the NICU. His uncles can visit him, though, and when you're awake, I'll make sure they bring him to you."

"Don't let Matt get close," she whispered, her eyelids fluttering. "Promise me he won't get close to our baby. I don't care about me, but you have to protect him."

As her eyes closed, I made a silent promise to take care of everything. "I love you," I whispered.

With her hand still in mine, I retrieved my phone from my back pocket. Sitting back in the chair, I began working, taking advantage of the quiet moment.

The first text was to Grizz for an update.

Grizz

Cyph picked up what I threw down.

He's hiding somewhere working on my paperwork.

Dipshit one and two are still here.

They keep asking for info but there isn't any.

I shook my head at the sheer stupidity of all of this. Matt should be dead, and Gerry should wait like everyone else.

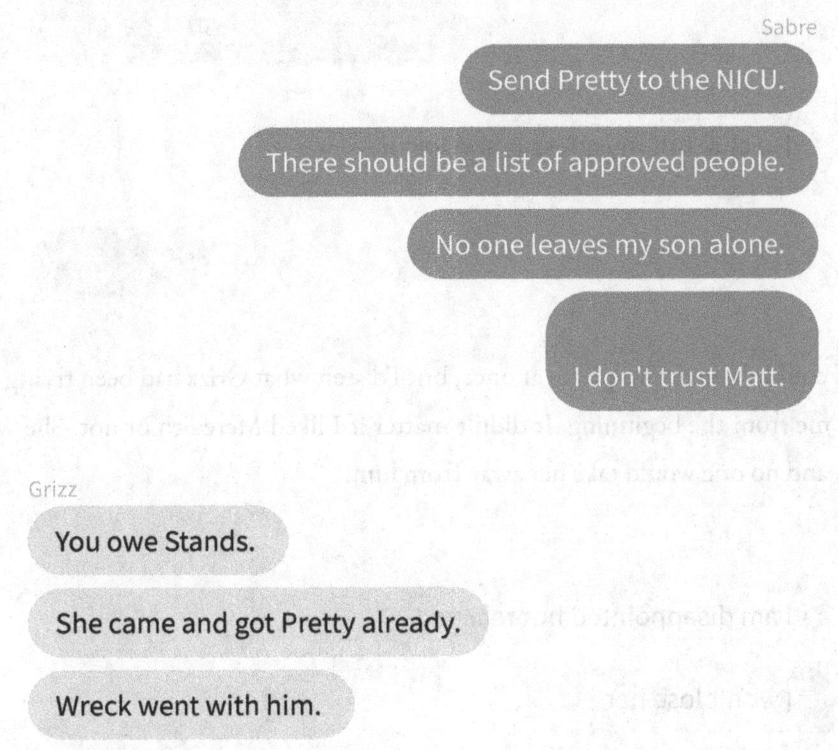

I breathed a sigh of relief. Wreck wouldn't let my brother out of his sight, and Pretty would make sure nothing happened to my son.

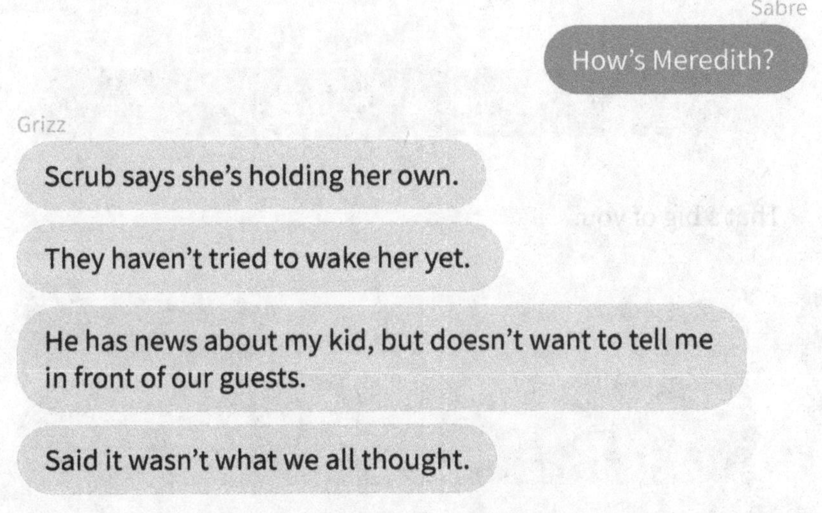

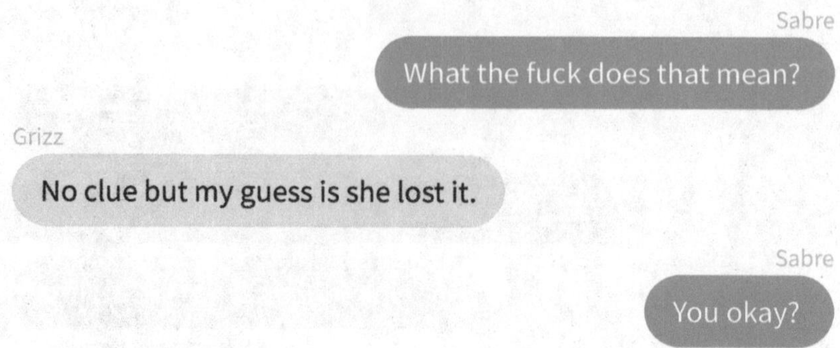

I couldn't be in two places at once, but I'd seen what Grizz had been trying to tell me from the beginning. It didn't matter if I liked Meredith or not. She was his, and no one would take her away from him.

Looking at Grace, I couldn't help but sympathize with him. If I'd lost her, life would have been over for me. Meredith wasn't my choice, but if he was happy, I'd try not to kill her.

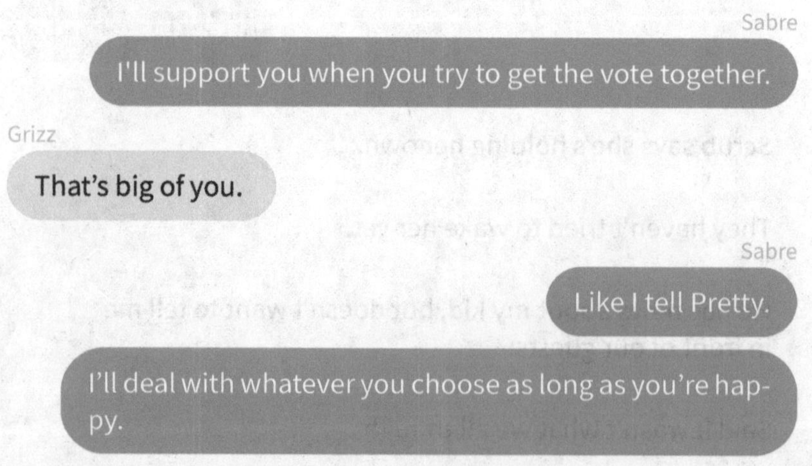

Grizz quickly moved on. He probably thought I'd back-peddle on my offer if he brought it up some more. I was serious. When he got the vote together for Meredith, I'd support it, but she had a long way to go at winning the club over.

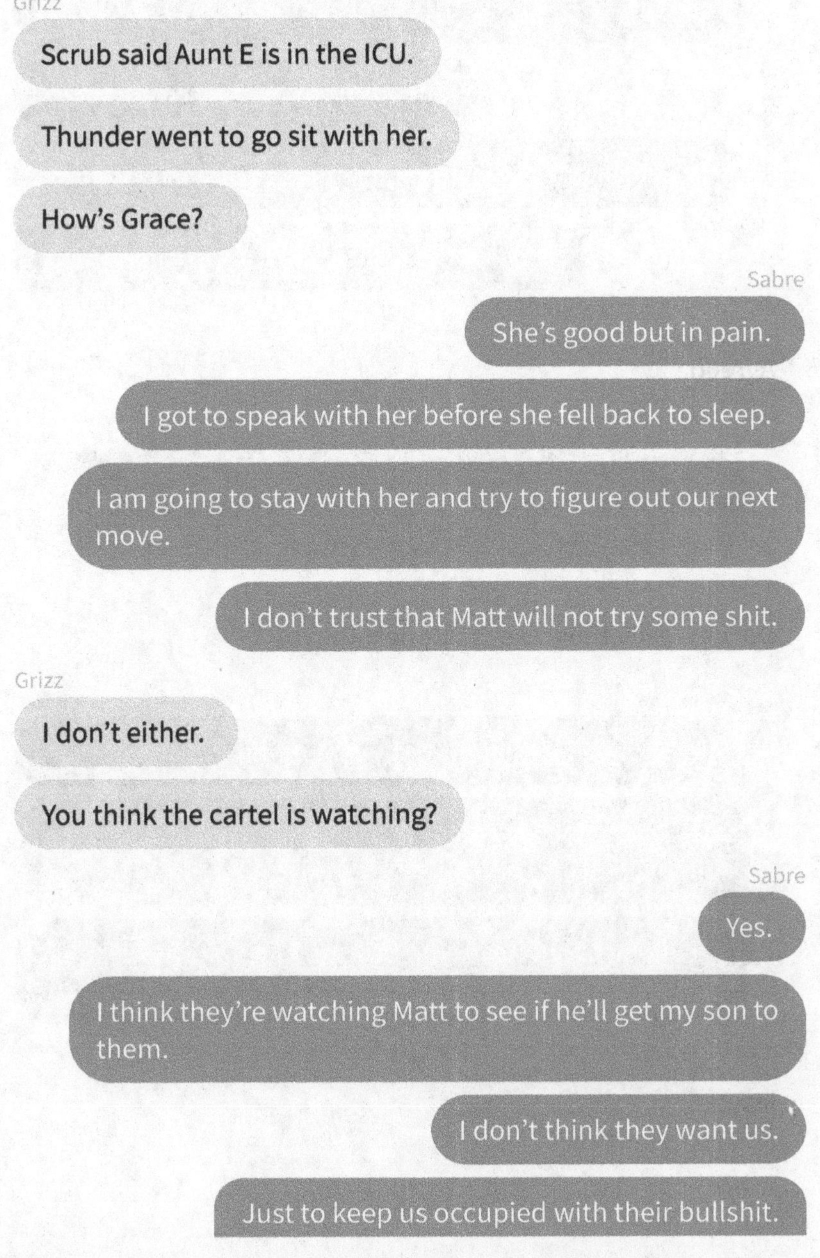

Grizz

What do you want done?

Sabre

Have Count silently send the brothers back to the club-house.

There's nothing they can do here.

The cartel isn't going to hit us unless Matt can't deliver.

They would rather him fuck up than them.

Grizz

Agreed.

Sabre

I am thinking about having Cyph put out feelers to meet with El Sombra Roja.

Grizz

Do you really think that's our next move?

Sabre

I think bare minimum we can use him as a resource.

He wasn't putting Grace in danger when he tracked her phone.

I think he might have caught wind of what was going on and kept tabs on her.

Grizz

Maybe.

I'll let him know.

Marriage license first.

Sabre

Good luck with that.

I smiled as I reread the last message from Grizz. Looking over at Grace, I could understand his enthusiasm. Knowing she was mine was enough for now. I wouldn't have to trap her. She'd come willingly, and our relationship would be real. Grace had already accepted my claim on them, and in my mind, a ring was just a formality. Although I wasn't against marriage, I wouldn't hurry into it either. Now wasn't the right time. I didn't think Grace would disagree with me on that.

My thoughts shifted to Grizz and Meredith. I didn't know what her problem was, and I didn't care enough to figure it out. My biggest fear was Grizz succumbing to the madness that was only caused by a woman. He would never survive if she couldn't get her shit together. He'd constantly chase her, trying to save her from herself. Meredith would hate that she'd been tricked into marriage, but I didn't think it would last long. They were good for each other. They just needed to get on the same page.

I sat back in my chair and watched Grace sleep, my hand still holding hers. She wasn't resting peacefully, but as long as she wasn't crying in pain, I could let it go. Her brow would furrow every so often, and it made me wonder if she was worrying.

"It's okay, mama. I am right here, and Pretty's with our boy." I tried to soothe her, not making any promise that I didn't plan on keeping. "It's rough right now, but remember what I told you. We love harder to get through it, and I love you something fierce."

Her brow smoothed, and I took it as a good sign that she was at peace for at least a few minutes.

My phone vibrated in my back pocket. Pulling it out, I had to chuckle quietly. You summon the devil, and he appears. Pretty had sent me a message. I didn't want to analyze Grace and Meredith's relationship, but as much as I gave Pretty flack, I'd never trade him in.

Spare Parts

Sabre?

Drew?

Hey asshole! You there?

You better not be ignoring me.

It must have been serious for Pretty to call me by my real name. I couldn't remember the last time someone had done that, and I wasn't sure if Grace even knew what it was.

Sabre

What's up?

Spare Parts

Thank god.

I wasn't sure if I could call you in here.

Nurse Smush Face is looking at me funny.

Wreck's outside, and Smush Face thinks this our kid.

That'd be something, wouldn't it?

I quickly texted him the same thing I'd told Grizz.

My heart thumped. My brother had officially accepted Grace into our family of two.

I must have waited too long because there were a series of vibrations, one right after another.

The next vibration brought a video. I clicked the play button and made sure to turn the sound on low. As it played, all I could see was my son's tiny hand. As I watched, my brother's blue-gloved hand rubbed his thumb along the back of the baby's hand.

"Hi, Daddy. We're waving at you."

I wanted desperately to be there, but I wouldn't meet my son until Grace was ready. I could wait a little longer.

"Last chance, Drew. If you don't want to see him, stop this video now."

I waited. Pretty liked dramatics.

He eventually panned the camera over so that the baby's face filled the screen. He was the most beautiful thing I'd ever seen, after his mother. I'd been so overcome with emotion that I squeezed her hand. She made a squeak, and I quickly released the pressure.

"Sorry, mama. You did amazing. He's beautiful, and I can't wait for you to meet him." I leaned forward and kissed the back of her hand. I didn't want to jar her.

Clicking play again, I waited for more.

"Drew?" my brother commented through the video. "We're so fucked. He's adorable. How are you going to say no to that face? Don't worry, Little Man. Uncle Luke is going to give you everything your parents say no to. Shit! I need to go shopping."

I shook my head at his antics, not really surprised. The last thing I heard from the video as I tilted my head back and closed my eyes was my brother saying that the baby looked just like Grace.

Chapter 30
IV Poles Are Dangerous Weapons

Grace

I didn't know how many hours had passed since this nightmare had first started. I'd been anxious in the ambulance, not sure what would happen and knowing that Sabre was nowhere near. Thunder had made the best of the situation, but it hadn't been the same. My heart only beat for one man, and we were missing him.

My initial anxiety had faded into relief as soon as I heard his voice. Nothing mattered anymore. It would all work out because Sabre was here. I should have stopped and asked why he was at the hospital, but I'd been too overwhelmed to think straight.

Now relief had morphed into anger. They had transferred me from the ER to one of the private rooms on the NICU floor. The only problem was they had done it in the middle of shift change. The original nurse had stopped by for a few minutes. She had said that once the new nurse finished preparing for her shift, she would come get me for a walk. It had been hours, and no one had shown up. I was so close to him and yet so far. As each hour passed, my anger grew until I was about ready to lose my shit.

"What is taking them so long? I was supposed to get out of this bed four hours ago." I tried not to take my anger out on Sabre, but I wanted to see my son for the first time.

"Is that just a gown, or did they put a robe on you downstairs?" Sabre asked me, pointing to where the hospital fabric peaked out from underneath the sheets.

He had stayed with me the entire time, holding my hand and reassuring me he would take care of everything.

"You can wait a little longer to get me naked." How could he be thinking about sex?

He laughed. "You should see your face. That wasn't the plan, but I figured I'd help you stand. You need to walk anyway, and we can head down to the NICU window."

"Oh," I said, embarrassed. I felt out of control, and everything sounded wrong to my ears.

"Yeah, *oh*. If you don't have your back covered, I'll have to go get you something. I don't want anyone else to see what's mine."

I took a few deep breaths to settle my emotions. I didn't know if the breathing exercises helped, but I figured it was a good sign that my fighting instincts had calmed down for the moment.

"No, I have a hospital robe on. No free peeks today."

"Mama, I am sure the reality is much better than my imagination." He stood from the chair and leaned over me. He kissed my forehead and wiggled his eyebrows in my direction.

"Ugh, what am I going to do with you?"

"Fulfill all of my fantasies." He laughed and dropped his forehead so that it was the only part of him touching me. "Just promise me we'll grow old together on our porch swing. You're mine, mama, and if you're ready, let's go see our son."

The tears fell down my cheeks. It was all too much for me, and I wondered how I had been so lucky to find him.

He stepped around the bed to the other side. "This might be easier if I help you sit on the edge. When you're ready, we can get you on your feet. You okay with that?"

I shook my head, the tears still falling.

He collected my tears with his thumbs and sucked the moisture between his lips. "If you hurt, you need to tell me immediately."

I shook my head again. He didn't need to know that I wouldn't say anything.

Sabre pushed the covers away from my legs. "How can I help you?"

"Hold my hands." I reached out for him, and he flipped my hands over and grabbed me at my wrists. Following his lead, I grabbed his wrists for more stability. When I was comfortable, I slid my right foot off the bed until my knee bent. Doing the same thing with my left, I slowly sat up on the edge of the bed. The pain ripped across my stomach, but I was determined to make it down the hall. I took a few minutes to adjust.

"You alright?" Sabre asked me, watching my face for any potential twinge of pain.

I held onto him as I scooted my butt towards the edge of the bed. When my feet hit the ground, I grabbed onto him to pull me up. It hurt like a bitch, and I had to bite my lip not to scream out in pain. Staring into his eyes, I knew I wasn't fooling anyone, but he let me hold on to him until I was sure I wouldn't topple over.

"How come you're not fighting me on this?" Even though the nurse had told me to walk, I wasn't sure we should do this unsupervised.

"I wanted to give the nurse plenty of time to take care of you, since it doesn't appear to be busy on this floor. We haven't seen her, so I texted Scrub to ask. He's still in the ER, but he texted the basics. You'll be okay to walk as long as we take it slowly." He unplugged the IV machine from the wall and held out his arm for me to hold. "Let's go, mama."

I took one step at a time. Shuffle right foot. Slide left foot. Rest. Start again. We'd made it to the door and had turned the corner into the hallway when I heard someone running towards us.

"She can't be out of bed. What are you doing up? You need to get back to bed!" a female voice yelled from down the hallway behind me.

I ignored her, and with Sabre's help, we kept going. I didn't care if it was her job, or if I was breaking some sort of protocol. Wreck was standing halfway down the hallway. When he'd heard the commotion, he'd stood straight up, and that was when I saw the glass window. The NICU unit. My baby was there.

"Ma'am, you can't be out of bed," the voiced continued to yell, as feet sounded on the floor.

I kept going. Nothing was going to stop me.

"Ma'am," the nurse said as she ran past us and stood in front of me, "you can't be out of bed."

"I'm supposed to be walking," I said to her. "No one has helped me in over four hours, so I am walking on my own." I took a step forward, but she didn't move. "I am sorry, but you can't stop me. Try it, and I'll run you over with my IV pole." I tried to soften the threat with a smile, but I wasn't sure it worked.

If she had a problem with it, she could just look the other way. I was done with letting people push me around.

"No one let you see your baby?" she asked, and I shook my head no. "You should have said that first. IV poles don't scare me." She looked at my arm wrapped around Sabre's and asked me if I was comfortable. I simply told her I was okay. I wasn't sure if she'd try to stop me again. "Liar, but I get it. Can you hold her here, and I'll grab a wheelchair? When she gets to the window, she's going to need to sit." The nurse was already running back down the hallway, not bothering to wait for an answer.

"Let's make a run for it before she comes back," he said to me. I rubbed my cheek against his arm, using his strength to keep me going.

We continued down the hall until we were in Wreck's vicinity. "That was impressive," he said to me.

"I don't know what you're talking about."

Wreck smirked as he tapped the glass lightly to get Pretty's attention, and when Pretty looked up, he smiled and waved. Standing from his chair, he stretched and made his way to the nurse that was in the room. She had her back to the window. We watched as he spoke with her, gesturing at us.

The nurse turned and looked in our direction, smiling widely. She held up a finger to show that we should wait a minute. We watched as she took the folding chair he'd been sitting on and replaced it with a nicer chair that had a thick padding. She then said something to Pretty, and they both walked toward the exit door. She unlocked it and let him walk into the hallway first.

"You're looking good, Mommy. Let's introduce you to your baby boy," she said, tucking her arm under mine to support me as I shuffled through the door. "I'm sorry, Daddy. You'll have to wait here. The hospital has a one person per visit policy, and they don't let me make the rules," she added to Sabre, locking the outside door behind us. "Alright Mommy, we'll get you settled, and then you can stay as long as you're feeling up to it." She patted me on the hand.

"Thank you," I said to her.

"Did you walk all the way down here?" The nurse searched my face, but I didn't tell her the truth. I wasn't going back to bed without meeting my baby. "Oh, honey. I bet you drove the charge nurse nuts when she caught you. You have that guilty look on your face. It doesn't help that the charge nurse has radar when someone's up when they're not supposed to be." She happily chattered along as we made our way to the incubator. "If it was them, they'd want to meet their babies, too."

"Thank you," I said again. "I thought I was being unreasonable."

"Oh honey, don't worry about it." She guided me to sit in the chair in front of the incubator. "It's been a slow birth week. Right now, he's the only one in here, but he's so cute that I don't mind." She pulled out a pair of blue gloves from the box underneath the incubator. "Put these on, and you can touch him."

I didn't hesitate to put the gloves on, but I panicked at the thought of touching the baby. Placing my hands in my lap, I just stared at him. I didn't believe I deserved this happiness, and I didn't want to transfer my fears and doubts to my baby. He would only know love.

"He's doing really well, considering he's early. He's small, but with a little help, he'll grow."

I stared at him, not really seeing anything in front of me.

"You alright, honey?" The nurse stood above me. I didn't raise my head to look at her. I didn't want her to know that I was afraid. The baby cooed. "He won't break if you touch him. In fact, he probably doesn't understand why you're hesitating. He just wants his mommy." She chuckled. "Although, his uncle swore to buy him a premie-sized dirt bike."

I scrunched my nose and finally looked up at her, not quite believing what she had said. "He didn't, did he?" I asked. "No, don't answer that. He did."

She laughed and patted my shoulder. "Every parent in here is afraid of the unknown. You're not alone, and your baby is right there when you're ready. Just don't keep him waiting long." She walked to the nurse's station at the back of the room. I was sure she could hear everything I was going to say, but she had given me enough space to pretend this was a private room.

"Hi," I whispered to him as I stuck my gloved hand through the opening in the incubator's side. Fear choked me, and I didn't know what to do or what to say. Walking my fingers towards him, I gently touched his. "I can't believe you're actually here. I've been waiting for you. Do you know who I am? Oh my god, that just sounds weird." I stroked his fingers, and he seemed to smile at me. "I am your mom. Grace. You and I have had such an adventure, and when you're older, I'll tell you all about it."

He cooed again, mesmerizing me, while I stroked his fingers. I racked my brain for something else to say. "Your daddy is right outside. One day, he'll probably tell you how we met, but just know this: he loves you just as much as I do." I tucked my finger underneath his little hand. He didn't have enough strength to grip it.

"Your daddy doesn't know that I've already named you. Would you like to know what your name is?" The baby made a noise, and I took that as an affirmative. "James Robert Hudson. James and Robert for the two men that protected your mommy in a time of...we'll call it uncertainty. I figured we'd shorten it to JR." The baby made another noise. "That's good, because it wasn't up for discussion." I chuckled, moving my hand to his stomach, lightly tickling it. "Hudson for your daddy. It's his last name. When you meet him, don't tell him. He doesn't know."

I sat there a few minutes more, just touching him, watching him move and coo with no baby cares in the world. "I think this is the part where I promise you the world and everything in it. It doesn't seem like enough. I promise that I'll always love you unconditionally. I'll support you in everything you decide to do in life. The sky's the limit, and I can't wait to see what you make of it. Just don't grow up too fast. I don't think I'll be able to take it. Promise me one thing, JR. No matter what, you'll always be your authentic self. That's important. I love you."

***

Sabre

I watched as the nurse guided Grace to sit in the padded chair. I couldn't put my finger on it, but I didn't like what I was seeing. Her face was blank, reminding me of the family picnic, when she'd purposely made me sweat over that blowjob. This time, though, she looked lost in her own world. Only one person could visit at a time, and I couldn't help her through the struggle. I told myself that if she reached out and touched the baby, everything would eventually be alright. Watching through the glass, I silently begged her to touch him.

"She okay?" Pretty asked me, frowning as he watched Grace through the glass.

"I am not sure," I responded. I didn't know what was going on in her head, and I didn't want to make a bullshit, generic claim that it was just hormones. Matt had dismissed Grace enough during their marriage. I wouldn't do that to her, but I was worried. It wasn't until she stuck her hand in the incubator that I breathed my first sigh of relief. If this continued, I'd make her talk to me and go from there.

Once she touched the baby, Pretty took it as the sign that everything was fine. He rambled about how cute the baby was, how small and how perfect.

"Wreck, when this is all over, we have to go shopping. Little man needs a bike," Pretty said, bouncing on his toes.

"They don't make bikes his size," Wreck replied.

"Bummer. I'll talk to Grease and see if he can make one." Pretty would not give up on this foolish idea.

"You do that," Wreck said.

I wasn't paying too much attention to them as I watched Grace. It wasn't until Pretty abruptly cut off mid-sentence about the paint scheme that I realized something was off. He nudged me with his elbow and pointed down the hallway. Matt and Gerry were heading our way.

Chapter 31
Matt Won't Go Away

Sabre

"What the fuck?" I muttered underneath my breath as I planted my feet and crossed my arms over my chest. I wasn't in the mood to deal with either Matt or Gerry. The only reason Matt wasn't six feet under yet was because I didn't have a plan yet to make it look like an accident or pin it on his cartel buddies. If he suddenly disappeared, there would be too many questions that I wouldn't have suitable answers for. I would not go to jail for his fucking stupidity.

No one said anything as they approached.

"You almost pulled a fast one," Matt said, smirking. "I have to admit, you had me for a second. Grace pissed off the charge nurse, and it all fell apart." He tapped on the glass. "Don't worry, that shit stops now. The charge nurse and I are well-acquainted."

The NICU nurse came to the door and cracked it just enough for her to stick her head out. "Can I help you with something?" she asked.

"Yeah, I want to see my son," Matt demanded.

"You are?" Her eyes bounced between the five of us, as if she wasn't sure whom to trust. I didn't blame her. I didn't trust Matt either, and he'd just confessed to cheating on his wife in front of her father. Grace had tried to tell Gerry at the family dinner, so if he couldn't see what a piece of shit Matt was now, then there was no hope of ever changing his mind.

"The baby's father." Matt tried to push past the nurse, but she stood her ground and closed the door just enough to block his entrance. Wreck shifted so that his body would block Matt if he tried to charge again. Wreck wasn't the biggest brother, but he was enough sometimes to deter trouble.

The nurse's eyes flicked to Wreck, widening slightly at the sight of him. She straightened, but her shoulders sagged a bit, a deep breath escaping her lips. The determined spark in her eyes dimmed, replaced by a wary resignation. We'd won ourselves an unexpected ally.

"Your name is?" she asked Matt, not letting him push her around. There was a bit of a bite underneath her tone. The nurse had better things to do than to ask questions that Matt should have voluntarily offered from the beginning.

"Matthew Montgomery." He tried to walk through the door again, but Wreck didn't move and the nurse would not back down.

She held her ground. "I am sorry, sir, but you're not on my visitation list. If you would like to visit, you will need to speak to a member of the hospital staff so that they can process that for you."

"I am the baby's father, and that's my wife in there. How much is this going to take?" Matt made a show of reaching for his wallet.

The nurse closed the door, but before she could get it to latch, Matt screamed into the opening, "You fat fucking bitch!"

I'd had enough. Grabbing him by his suit coat collar, I shoved him against the opposite wall, away from the door.

"The last time we met, I promised I'd make you a one-ball wonder before I send you back to your little cartel buddies. That's a promise I firmly plan on keeping," I whispered through gritted teeth. I didn't need any of the hospital cameras picking up this conversation. "What do you think they are going to do to when you can't pay, and there's no baby? Your missing dick is the last thing you'll be thinking about."

Matt shoved off the wall, closing the distance between us. "I am the master at this game, and you have no clue what the rules even are."

"I know why you need the baby. Why didn't you just knock up Clara once you realized you had the wrong woman?"

"Clara's too loose. If they wanted loose pussy, they had plenty of blondes that could have gotten the job done. Grace was exquisite the night she hosted the dinner party. The perfect trophy." He laughed in my face. "You think Grace is the prize, and maybe, to your redneck ass, she is. Grace will never be completely yours, because she'll always be comparing the two of us, and you'll always come in second." He smirked, assuming that I would smash his face in. I would. It just wouldn't be here. "Do you realize I can take the baby from you and walk out of this place?"

My voice lowered another octave. "You're on borrowed time, but if you touch a single hair on my son's head, you'll be screaming for your mama." Backing up a step from him, I made a show of smacking his shoulder with my fist as if we were just having a friendly conversation. "Good chat."

Matt flipped Grace off through the window, turned on his heel, and made his way to the elevator. I wasn't sure what his next move was, but I needed to get ahead of this. Quickly.

Gerry was still standing in the hallway, staring through the glass at Grace. "Do you have anything to add to that?" I asked him. I was done, and if he even thought about crossing me, I'd make sure his ass was on a bus south.

"Is she alright?" He didn't direct that question to anyone in particular.

"Do you care?" I asked him.

"She's my daughter," he said, as he tried to make himself appear bigger than reality as he faced us again. "When my wife died, things became chaotic for a bit, but I've always done what's best for my girls." He frowned as his mind slid into the past.

"You continue to push her towards a man who doesn't have her best interests at heart. What are you really doing with him? I don't believe for one second that you're completely innocent in all of this."

Red crawled up Gerry's neck, to his throat and into his cheeks. His nostrils flared, and his eyes shined with anger. "If you're going to accuse me of something, you better have proof, you son of a bitch."

"I don't need proof when I can see it clearly. What happened? Did Matt come to you the day Grace moved out and ask for your help? What did he promise you? I can't see you needing money." Something in his expression shifted, and I would have never seen it if I hadn't been looking directly at him.

"What did you do? Gamble it all away?" Pretty interjected. He was watching Gerry just as closely as I was.

"That's it, isn't it? You need money," I confirmed.

His knees buckled, and Wreck reached out to steady him. "You don't get to pray for salvation. Stand there and take it up the ass like a real man," he said.

"My girls don't need me anymore. I've always been careful to keep the cartel at a distance. I'll take their cases, but I am not overly friendly with them. They kept inviting me to their illegal casinos. When I went one night, that's when they had me. Before I knew it, I was broke, and they owned me." Gerry stared at Grace through the window.

"Do they know about your connection to Matt?" I asked. They had to, otherwise, they would have left Gerry alone, but some sick part me wanted him to confirm it. He'd wanted to tear into his daughters for their sins when he wasn't perfect.

"Yes. I think that's why they actually set me up, and like a fucking idiot, I let them."

"Did they give you any instructions?" I kept pushing for any piece of information that would help.

"They told me to keep a close eye on Matt. They said that he owed them several million dollars and that it would clear my debts if I kept tabs on him. You know, make sure he wasn't in any kind of trouble."

"You can't fucking be serious, Prez. I don't believe that he didn't know about the baby." Wreck squeezed Gerry's arm hard enough to leave a bruise.

"I don't either. You put your daughter and grandson in danger. I originally thought Meredith had been involved because of Brandon. Now, I am wondering if it was really because of you. Last I heard, she's still unconscious."

"What about the baby?" Gerry turned towards the window. He honestly looked shocked, but he was sweating in fear. It was an odd combination.

"Matt is trying to sell your grandson to wipe his cartel debts away. Why do you think he's here when he normally abandons them?"

"He sold my grandson?" Gerry was trembling as he was trying to reconcile the pieces of information. "I've been watching him so that he could take the baby?"

"How did you know the baby was born today?" I asked.

"I got a message this morning that said I needed to make the trip up here. It was probably from a burner phone because when I went to reverse look up the phone number, there wasn't anything there. I made the trip and got a hotel room to wait out the next message. They only send me one at a time, and it's short snippets of what they want done." Gerry wiped the sweat off his forehead with the sleeve of his dress shirt. "A few hours after that, they messaged me again. It said that Grace was on the way to the hospital, and if I wanted to wipe some debt off, I should call Matt. He answered right away, and we came here."

"Aww, fuck. Are you supposed to meet up with them?" Pretty piped up. This was the longest I'd known him to be quiet in a long time.

"I don't know what the next message will say or when it will appear. They work on their own schedule." Gerry dropped his eyes to the floor and shuffled his feet back and forth.

"Hey, Wreck? Call Twig and tell him he has a package to pick up." I saw Wreck pull out his phone to make the arrangements. "Gerry," I said, "you're on your own with the debt. I will not help you pay it off because the minute you give the cartel money, they will continually ask for more. It will never end." I ran my fingers through my hair and stared at the broken man.

"You have to protect me. They'll kill me," Gerry cried.

"I don't have to do shit. You shouldn't mistake my kindness for weakness because I can flip that switch. When Twig gets here, you're going to be good friends. He'll take you to the club and make sure you have a room. Your phone is going to go to Cyph for processing." I made sure Gerry was looking at me before I continued. "You will help me keep your grandson safe. Consider it the parenting you should have given your daughter."

Pretty and I watched as Wreck wrapped his hand around Gerry's arm and led him to the elevator. Twig would take care of him until Gerry atoned for his sins. It was more than likely that the cartel would come for him. I hoped there was a resolution before I had to sacrifice Gerry for his daughters' safety.

"Wreck wears those jeans so damn well," Pretty said out of nowhere, smacking his lips. "They mold to his ass just right."

My eyebrows shot up, and my eyes widened. "I told you I didn't care, but you're making it weird."

"Eh, it would be weird if I told you all the things I wanted to do with that ass. I didn't." Pretty smiled widely at me. "You needed a break for a second, Drew. It worked. You're welcome."

He was still smiling at me as I shook my head at him and punched his forearm. "What are you going to do, Sabre? You can't leave, and Grizz is in no place to run a church. That's even if you could get him to leave Meredith."

"I have an idea, and Gerry just gave us a way to track the cartel. We have at least five weeks before they release the baby. It'll give us time to iron out our plans."

"Grace will not want to leave the hospital while he's still in here. Do you want me to go across the street and book you a hotel room?" Pretty asked.

"Not yet, but you'll have to book a room for the four of you that are staying. Someone will have to arrange for more clothes. I'll stay with Grace until they release her, and then we'll get a room."

"Would you have still sat next to her if you knew this was all going to head our way?"

"Was I worth it?" The door to the NICU unit was open, and the nurse was helping Grace cross the threshold.

"I should have never let you leave that night, no matter what it would have cost me," I answered her honestly. We'd wasted so much time pretending that the other hadn't existed. I should have just camped out on her front lawn until she came to the same conclusion I had. Now that she was here, I was never letting her go.

"Charmer," she said with a grimace as she tried to shuffle her way into the hallway.

I held out my arm for her to hold and gain some traction. Once she was stable, I leaned down and whispered in her ear, "You shine brighter than any diamond I could ever put on your finger. Everything's going to change because you're mine, and one day, you'll honestly believe me when I say that."

"Do you want to meet him?" she asked, looking up into my eyes.

"I do," I told her. "I don't feel right meeting him without you. He's ours, and that should be something we do as a family. Not one person at a time."

She laid her head on my shoulder as the tears flowed down her cheeks. "He already likes his name, so I'll wait until the day we're reunited as a family."

Chapter 32

Code Pink

Grace

It'd been four days since I'd delivered JR, and time seemed to crawl. In the mornings, I'd walk down to visit him with Sabre's help. He'd send Wreck to sleep at the hotel across the street, then sit in the chair outside the NICU window. When I was almost ready to head back to my room, I'd raise my thumb and let Sabre know to call Pretty for the swap. We never left JR alone. None of us trusted Matt.

I was getting stronger by the day, and it was only a matter of time before the hospital told Stands to discharge me. Once the baby had been born, my blood pressure had slowly returned to normal. I could move around and walk. It was slow, but I could do it. I was still in pain. My body was sore, and if I moved wrong, I screamed in agony, but they told me that was normal and there was nothing further that they could do. I clenched my teeth, trying to breathe through the pain, but it didn't make it suck any less.

JR was the most beautiful baby I'd ever seen. A tiny miracle I could hardly believe was half my doing. He was small, but they weren't concerned that he wouldn't grow. They just couldn't give me an accurate date of when I could take him home. If I asked, they would just say that they would reevaluate every Friday. That wouldn't work with Matt constantly lingering, but we didn't want to tip them off that something was wrong. For now, Sabre was on JR's birth certificate, and no one had questioned me.

"Hey, Mommy. Look at you, up early," the NICU nurse said as she came to the door when she saw me waiting. Wreck had been sitting on the chair outside of the glass window.

"Hello. Am I too early?" The NICU had visiting hours, but since I was the only parent who had a baby in the room, they let me come and go as I pleased. I also think it helped that Sabre would slip them money at the end of their shifts.

"Nope, you're good. Come on in! He's been cooing up a storm this morning." She slid the door open further so that I could step through with my IV pole. "I think he missed you and has figured out your schedule."

"I missed him," I said, sighing. I waved to Wreck and squeezed Sabre's forearm before I let go of him and walked into the room. At first, the nurses had told us it was one person in the room at a time. I think they were afraid the brothers would bum rush the door, but that wasn't the case. Whomever was outside the window had their own chair across the hall. They would be out of the way, but they could see both directions of the hallway and into the window.

"I'll leave you be. Take your time, but if you need something, let me know." The nurse walked to the station at the back of the room as I settled into the padded chair and put the blue gloves on.

"Good morning, sunshine. Did you sleep well?" I whispered to him. It was quiet in the room, and I didn't want to disturb the peace. I liked to carry on a conversation with him, even though I had no clue what he would have said. "Did you dream of toy cars?" He cooed as if he could understand me. "You did. My smart boy. Bikes are going to consume your world, eventually," I chuckled.

Time slipped away as I stayed with him, chatting softly or simply watching him wiggle. I cherished every moment. It wasn't until there was an overabundance of movement at the back of the room that I realized something was happening.

"I think they might send me home, but I'll still be here every day to see you until you bust out of here," I whispered, tickling the bottoms of his feet lightly.

I watched as the nurse approached. Her expression confirmed my fears. "I hate to do this to you, but I have to send you back to your room. There are discharge papers in the system for you, and the charge nurse for the floor today wants to get started. She can't officially boot you though until Dr. Andrews gives you one last exam. Just let her blow hard. I already let your man know to call his brother."

I turned towards the window. Pretty was standing next to Sabre across the hall. I didn't know what they were talking about, but neither was smiling, and their hands were flailing around. "Thank you," I said to the NICU nurse, standing up from the chair and preparing to wheel myself back to the door. She held it open as I walked through, catching Pretty and Sabre's attention.

"Did he tell you that you're looking pretty good today?" Pretty smirked.

"Hospital gowns are the new black," I replied, smirking.

"What am I, chopped liver, pretty boy?" the nurse teased him.

Pretty kissed my cheek and turned to walk into the NICU. Visiting hours had officially started. "Nah, Nurse Needle, but I've got to keep up with my favorite ladies," he said with an innocent smile. The nurse chuckled and made a beeline for the nurse's station.

"I thought he had a thing for Wreck?" I asked Sabre, puzzled.

"Yeah, I am not sure what's going on with those two, and I am trying hard not to pay attention." He stood from his chair and walked over, offering his arm.

"You only have a thing for me," I told him.

"I'm done playing games, mama. If you leave, I'll hunt you down and drag you back to my bed." He laughed as we walked back to my room.

"You make it sound like such a tragedy," I said, enjoying the light-hearted banter for a moment. "The nurse said they're going to discharge me today, and the charge nurse wants to start the process. That's why I have to go back to my room."

We walked a little further. "Pretty booked us a hotel room across the street, next to the room the brothers are sharing. We won't be far from the baby, so you can come and go as you please," Sabre said with a shrug. We both knew it wasn't a perfect solution, but it was the best we had for today.

"Are you leaving for the clubhouse tonight?" I asked, knowing he had responsibilities but hoping he'd stay. If he left, I'd do my best not to show my hurt.

"No, I'm here until we go home as a family. Count's running the club and keeping me updated. Everyone understands, so don't worry." He kissed the top of my head.

"Thank you," I whispered as we reached my door, feeling a sense of relief.

Sabre and I waited patiently for the discharge, but it seemed to never come. He tried his best to remain calm, but I could sense his agitation as he sat in the recliner next to my bed. His leg bounced repeatedly. He'd place his hand over his knee to calm it, but then he'd forget and rest his hand against the arm of the recliner, and his knee would start bouncing again.

I was no better. When we had walked into my room, Sabre had helped me lay in bed facing him, but every few seconds I would shift, pretending to find a comfortable spot. We tried to fill the silence with small talk, but as each minute passed, the tension in the room grew tighter.

The charge nurse had been in and out of the room, ignoring me each time. She would give me a hostile look, fiddle with the equipment, and then leave in a huff.

"I don't understand. They made such a big fuss about discharging me, but now we're just sitting here," I said to Sabre, frustrated. "I could have stayed with our baby, and Pretty wouldn't have had to arrive early. This is silly."

"I'm just as much in the dark as you are. I sent Stands a message, and she's on her way in. She's coming on shift anyway, so she said it wasn't a big deal to show up a little early. Stands didn't know you were being discharged today, but she said it was only a matter of time." I watched as Sabre ran his hand through his hair. "I didn't want to have to tell you, but they've given me no choice, and you'll be safer if you know. Do you remember the first time we walked down to the window?"

Apprehension poured over me as I tried to sit up in the bed.

"Hey, it's not about us. We're good." Sabre stood and approached the bed. He held my hand and rubbed his thumb over the top. "You pissed off the charge nurse when you told her you'd use your IV against her. She threw a fit, and Matt figured out which floor you were on. He took it upon himself to smooth it over with her."

"You mean he slept with her?" I asked. "He's done it before. It's just a little surprising that it doesn't hurt."

He chuckled and tucked a piece of my hair behind my ear. "What Matt does outside of the baby doesn't affect you anymore. It doesn't hurt because you're mine, and I wouldn't do that shit to you. You need to be careful around her today. Supposedly, she's the one that told the NICU nurse you needed to come back to the room, but she's nowhere to be found."

"Do you think you should head to the nurse's station to check? They told me Stands would have to evaluate me before I got the boot, but this seems ridiculous. It's been three hours, and I don't even have clothes."

The charge nurse entered the room. She took one look at us, and her nose crinkled, as if we were beneath her. Sabre watched her as she moved around the room, hemming and hawing. I watched his face as the planes shifted with each thought that ran through his mind. I didn't want any trouble. Squeezing his hand, I waited until he looked down at me. We were on the same page, and the quicker she left, the better off we'd be.

"You'll need to leave," she said to Sabre.

"I am not fucking going anywhere," he told her.

"You'll need to leave so that I can prepare Mrs. Montgomery for discharge."

I had Sabre help me sit up in the bed, trying to distract both of them from fighting over who was more dominate. The nurse would win, and I had visions of the hospital security walking Sabre out in handcuffs.

The intercom in the room buzzed and then turned off. We each stared at the speaker in the wall, waiting for it to turn back on. "Code Pink, NICU." It buzzed again. "Code Pink, NICU. All staff need to man their stations." The charge nurse took off running.

"Fuck," Sabre said, looking around at the posters on the wall. "I don't know what a Code Pink is."

"It doesn't matter. Our baby is the only baby on this floor. Go check on him." I was panicking. There were feet running down the hallway towards the window, and all I could think about was JR. It would take me too long to get out of bed and follow them. "Please, go."

He dropped a kiss on my forehead and ran out of the room. I twisted the sheet between my fingers. I was eager for any bit of news, and I kept staring at the speaker in the wall. Smoothing out the sheet, I twisted it again. I needed to know what was going on, but I didn't want to be in anyone's way.

"Did you know that a Code Pink is for a baby abduction?" Matt walked through my hospital door. "Your boyfriend is down at the window with his brother, trying to figure it out. How could you have picked someone so dumb?"

"I picked you, so that should say something." I was livid, wondering if this had been an elaborate ruse. JR was healthy for his size, but fear consumed me that he would take a turn for the worse. I thought about begging Sabre to buy an incubator so that we could take him now. He would be much safer at the clubhouse.

"Don't worry, wife. Our child is still in his incubator. It doesn't take much to excite people around here. All you have to do is hire some big, scary Mexican to stop in front of a window for a second." Matt leaned against the table at the front of the room, facing the bed.

I'd had enough with the games, and the words were leaving my lips faster than my brain could keep up. "I despise you. You can say whatever you want about me and our marriage, but he'll never be your son. God willing, he'll never even know you existed. My son doesn't even have your last name. His surname is the same as the two men down the hall who would give their lives for him. When have you ever done something that wasn't for your own gain?"

"I raised your social status and kept you in the life you've become accustomed to, and this is the thanks I get. Did you forget you were begging me for more? To fuck you with abandon? Telling me how you much you loved me? Oh, how the mighty fall." He crossed his legs and placed his hands on the table.

"You wanted a trophy, Matt, and I was dumb enough to think that's what love was." Staring at him now, I realized that no matter what I would have done, it would have never been enough. I would have worked myself into a frenzy trying to fit into his perfect mold when it wasn't my issue. It was his. "My only regret is that I've waited this long to see what's always been there. You're a snake, and you're never going to be a better person. There's too much blood on your hands, and you've sold your soul to the highest paying devil. They're going to catch up with you, and I hope they pay you back in nothing but the pain you've caused. Sooner rather than later." I gripped the sheets tightly in my fists. "When you're out of our lives, I will never think about you again. Your name will never pass my lips, and I'll legally change my last name to my son's."

Matt stood straight up and rushed to the side of the bed. He placed his hand on my neck and forced me backwards, squeezing to cut off my air. I balled my fists and tried to fight back, but it was a futile effort. I took shallow breaths, but I was too weak to cause any damage. The only thing keeping me focused was the adrenaline coursing through my veins.

"Do you really think the biker wants used goods? You come with baggage." He laughed. "You're probably still tight from the kegels, but the rest of you isn't looking too hot. Flabby skin is not sexy on anyone. It's what people are going to make fun of as you're pushing the stroller. 'Look at her. She used to be hot until she had a baby. Now, it's just sad.' You think he's going to fuck you? Nah, he's going to use you and fuck anything that moves. Like I did."

I gripped his hand, trying to loosen it from my neck. I struggled with the words but managed to release them in large, breathy clouds. "You know, I am tired of you calling him a biker. Every time my son calls him Daddy, I am going to laugh, knowing you're watching from the depths of hell. I hope it burns."

He squeezed my neck harder, causing me to gasp for air. "If you have any hope of keeping him, get some pointers from the club girls. You're boring in bed." Matt used his other hand to smack me across my cheek. "If I am going to hell, I am taking your boyfriend with me. No one will want you, and your son will be with the cartel. They'll make him a sicario at four."

He let go of me and walked out the door. I hadn't told him, but I'd wanted to thank him for being so awful. It only made me appreciate Sabre more. At thirty, I could honestly say I knew what love looked and felt like, and it was because of the biker down the hall. Matt had only approached me because of his scheme. He wouldn't get another chance after today. My resolve steeled further. I would protect my son from this monster, no matter the cost.

Chapter 33

The End of What We Once Had

Grizz

I was going crazy, staring at the white walls in the waiting room. I'd begged to sit with her, even though she wasn't awake, but they had denied my request. When I pressed for an explanation, they just turned their backs on me and walked away. They rejected every plea I made, and I didn't have Pretty's charm to sway them. I even considered texting him to work his magic, but I didn't want to pull him away from the baby.

Desperate, I approached the older woman in the volunteer jacket, pleading for any information. She glanced at me, wished me well on my new marriage, and then returned to whatever the fuck she was doing. I couldn't understand why no one would tell me anything. I was her husband, for fuck's sake.

I tried to keep my temper in check. They were looking for any excuse to throw me out, and I wouldn't voluntarily give them one. The thought of being separated from Meredith made my blood boil, but I knew I had to stay calm. If they tried to force me out, I'd probably tear this damn waiting room apart and ask questions later. The only concession they made was letting me stay with her when they had transferred her to a private room, still unconscious.

Scrub wasn't her primary doctor, but he told me to just play along, and he'd help clarify things as more details became available. It was a good thing he'd said that to me because the doctor who visited every day was a tool. He was young, and I refrained from asking him if he was sure he was a doctor, since he looked twelve. His white medical coat was three sizes too big, and the drawstring of his scrub pants hung to his knees. He didn't introduce himself to me, nor did he try to talk to me about the situation. Dr. Creepo just kept running his fingers through his side-swept hair.

The first couple of days, Dr. Creepo had visited Meredith once in the morning and once at night. I might have believed him if he had been checking for activity behind her eyelids or performing another similar test. However, I quickly realized that he only wanted to get in her pants when he had rearranged the blankets to touch her legs. He wasn't looking for reflexes, and I was afraid to leave her, fearing he'd sneak in to take advantage. She was mine, and I'd kill him if I found him trying to touch her again.

Dr. Creepo told me it could take a few days for her to wake. They'd taken her off the sedatives, and now it was up to her. As night turned into day three, things weren't looking good. I didn't have to be a doctor to know that they were worried. The longer it took Meredith to wake, the more she might suffer long-term effects. I tried to force Dr. Creepo to just be honest with me. He gave me some song and dance about how things take time. I didn't know who he thought he was talking to because I understood her more than he did.

***

I'd been standing at my bike, preparing to ride, when Grace had approached me.

"Thank you for going. You'll make sure no harm comes to her, and I'll feel better when I know she's safe," Grace had said to me. She had placed her hand on my forearm so that I couldn't turn away from her.

"Why the fuck does she do this shit? She should have never told Brandon she'd meet him," I'd vented. Grace was the one person who would understand.

"I am not sure what she's thinking right now, but you know Meredith marches to her own drummer. You can't rush her if you expect her to listen to you. She does things on her own time," she'd said right before I'd left to interrupt Brandon's invitation.

"I know, but she has to learn that the world doesn't revolve around her," I had grumbled. Who the fuck was I kidding? My world revolved around her, and I didn't want anyone else in that bubble.

***

Meredith

Beep.

Snore.

Beep.

What was that incessant beeping noise? My eyes felt heavy, as if someone had glued them shut. I struggled to raise my hand, thinking I could rub them open, but it was no use. Every sound was muffled, as if I was underwater, and my body felt as if there was a thousand-pound weight pinning me down. I tried to fight my way to the surface, but I wasn't strong enough. Every time I thought I was close, the weight would suck me further into the deep.

"Baby, I am here. I haven't left, but I need you to wake up. I don't even care if you throw a fit. Wake up for me."

Grizz was here. He would make it alright. I felt my body sink back further into the dark abyss.

***

Beep.

The beeping was back, or maybe it had never left, I wasn't sure. I felt lifeless, adrift in a sea of despair. I floated to the pitch-black surface and laughed, a hollow sound echoing off the empty chambers of my heart. The sound was more of a cackle than anything else.

"Baby, you're scaring me. I need you to wake up. I don't know if you're trying, but you can't leave me. Therapy, whatever you need, we're going to make this work. I need you too badly."

Grizz's words were a lifeline, pulling me towards consciousness. His voice wavered, thick with emotion. I wanted to reach out, to tell him I was trying, but the darkness was so strong, and I felt so weak. I needed him, too. Otherwise, I wasn't sure I would survive this.

Beep.

***

Snore.

Who the fuck was snoring? Didn't they know I needed my beauty sleep, for fuck's sake? I had to go home, shower, and then try to get my job back. I didn't know what day it was, but I hadn't been there since Monday. They'd probably fired me for abandoning it. Fuck!

Snore.

I wasn't dealing with this shit. Grizz needed to shut the fuck up, or I'd stick cotton balls up his nose. I wouldn't care if they suffocated him, as long as the noise stopped. This better have been a onetime deal, or he wasn't sleeping in my bed. I didn't care how much he begged, or how good the makeup sex was going to be. Shit. What if it was fantastic? I could picture myself whispering promises into his ear that he'd make me fulfill.

"Shut...fuck..."

"Baby? Mer?"

"Too...loud. Shut...up."

"Yeah, baby. I am too loud. You tell me."

I tried to open my eyes, but they remained glued shut. This was fucking annoying. I needed to open my eyes and get on with my life. I needed to go home, check my bills, and make sure that I wasn't losing everything I'd worked hard to build. There was no room for error. I tried again to raise my hand to rub at my eyes, but I barely picked my palm up off the sheet before it fell back on its own. There was moisture on my cheek. It rolled down the curve and fell into the pillow, but I was getting aggravated that I couldn't just wipe whatever it was away.

"Mer, you're almost there. Just a little more, baby."

I felt a kiss on my forehead. He'd make it better, if only I could tell him what was wrong.

"Gri...zz"

"Yeah, baby? What do you need?"

"You."

***

Grizz

"Mer, it's time. Baby, I know you like your sleep, but enough is enough," I said to her, squeezing her hand. "What's it going to take to bribe you? A beach house?" I wouldn't let her go back to her condo, and I was afraid if I told her, she'd never wake up, just to spite me. "Breakfast in bed?" Hospital food would have to do, but I doubted she'd eat. "New furniture, like you talked about?" I'd buy her whatever she wanted. "Come on, Tef."

Her eyelids fluttered, and she cracked them, revealing her brown eyes.

"Hate..."

"Yeah, you do." I wanted to drop my head to the edge of the bed, letting my forehead touch the hand I was squeezing.

"Don't call..."

"There you are. Can you open your eyes a little wider for me? Let me see my beautiful brown-eyed girl." I tried to hold back my sobs, but I was gasping.

She was awake, but she closed her eyes and barely shook her head. An overwhelming sense of relief washed over me. She'd turned the corner, and no matter what happened, she'd heal. Meredith wouldn't leave me.

She opened her eyes completely, blinking a few times. "Too...bright," she said, closing them again.

"Give me a sec, and I'll turn the lights off." I let go of her hand and rushed over to the switch, flipping it off. "Better?" I asked her.

She nodded, her eyes fully open.

Pouring her a glass of water, I offered her the straw to sip. I didn't trust Dr. Creepo, so I'd have to text Scrub soon to come check on her. I was in conspiracy mode, and in my mind, Dr. Creepo worked for the cartel. Who the fuck knew if that was true, but I wasn't taking any chances, and he hadn't been paying close enough attention to her medical status.

"Better," she said. "My throat was dry." She scrunched her nose."Feel nasty."

I wiggled my eyebrows at her. "I'll scrub your back."

"I bet you would. Settle down, horn dog." A dry chuckle escaped her lips.

The sound was music to my ears. "How do you feel?"

"Hurt. Everywhere." She coughed. "Not in the dark abyss. It was scary there without you."

***

"Look who's awake," Dr. Creepo said as he walked through the doorway, pausing at the hand sanitizer. I understood the importance of cleanliness, but he would not get close enough to touch her, so there was no point in trying to kill us with the stench. It was only a matter of time before Scrub overruled Dr. Creepo. I'd already texted him to get his scrawny ass up here.

"Hello," Meredith whispered.

"How do you feel?" he asked her, licking his bottom lip. What the fuck did he think was going to happen? I was sitting right here, and she was mine. He wasn't shooting his shot. I'd throw him out before he even got a chance.

"I don't know," she said, looking at me.

I didn't know if he was giving her weird vibes or if I was being too sensitive, but I hated this doctor. He needed to go. As I stood from my chair to show him the way out, Scrub walked in. He took one look at Meredith, and his smile widened. Scrub was genuinely glad that she was awake.

"Hey, I can take this from here. I was told the emergency room was going to get a flood of patients from a car accident, so that's why they allowed me to visit now. Why don't you head down and prep? This will only take a minute."

I loved Scrub.

"Yeah, whatever," Dr. Creepo said, hightailing it back out of the room.

"Is there a car accident?" I asked Scrub.

He shrugged and sat in the recliner on the opposite side of Meredith, positioning himself to see both of us. "Somewhere there might be. I didn't like the way he was acting, and you looked like you were going to physically escort him out of the room."

"I would never," I said, my hand flying to my forehead in exaggeration. Scrub flipped me off, and Meredith gasped.

"Dr. Matthews over there isn't as wholesome as he appears. Scrub is one of my club brothers, so that should fill in all the blanks," I said to Meredith.

"Oh, good. I was afraid they'd kick you out for being rude," she rasped. A look of relief came over her face.

"I'm not going anywhere, wifey." I smiled at her, knowing she didn't have a clue of what I'd done.

"We're not married," she said, her face scrunched up like she was deep in thought. She turned towards Scrub. "The baby. Tell me about the baby," she begged him.

"That's why Grizz texted me to come up and see you," Scrub jumped in. "He's been waiting for you, so that you could receive the news together. Did you go to an obstetrician, Meredith?"

"Yes, I went to Dr. Vargas, the same one that Grace went to. She told me everything looked good." She looked at me. "I meant to tell you before you found out, but it was the weekend that Grace moved out. It was the last thing on everyone's mind."

I reached for her hand, mindful of the moisturizing glove she wore. She couldn't bend her fingers, but she didn't pull away from me.

"Did you have an ultrasound or anything that showed you the baby?" Scrub asked. His face was a blank canvas, but his eyes danced. This wasn't good, and he was gathering the facts before dropping us with the bomb.

"I don't think so. She said that I wasn't ready for an ultrasound but what she heard was good. The baby had a strong heart." Meredith was picking up on Scrub's cues. Her eyes watered.

"I don't know how to tell you this, so I am going to go with clinical first, and then as your friend." Scrub turned and faced Meredith head on. "You had what's called an ectopic pregnancy. It's when you have a fertilized egg, but it never implants into your uterus to grow. When they did your triage from the car, they found it in your fallopian tube. Based on the size, it'd been there awhile, and you were very lucky. It was so large that if it had grown just a few inches more, it would have burst your tube. They removed the mass surgically, and you still have full function to reproduce." Scrub shot me a look over the bed. I wasn't sure if he was looking for me to explode.

"The mass? I lost the baby?" Meredith looked in between us, the confusion written all over her face.

"No. You were pregnant, but it would have never developed into a baby. You would have eventually had the same procedure, but Vargas should have caught it sooner, not later." Scrub tried to reach for her other hand, but she pulled it back towards her, and he let it go.

"There's more, but this is from the accident," Scrub continued. "No broken bones. The only injury you incurred is a sprained knee. We have it in a brace, but as soon as you see an orthopedic, I am sure they'll remove it. If you had a concussion, there's no lasting damage. Your body just took a little longer to push you back to the surface. It's like it knew how long you needed to heal." Scrub ran his hand through his hair and shifted in his chair so that one leg crossed over his knee.

"You're probably wondering about the glove," he said to Mer. "The only major injury that you sustained from the accident was a severe case of road rash. You weren't wearing any protective gear, so your skin took the brunt end when you hit the road. There are certain areas where the surgical team could graph skin from your legs to cover what you were missing. However, they are putting salve on it to help it heal faster. You'll have to wear protective covering on that side of your body until the skin hardens and you don't have any pain. It could scar, though, and it runs the length of your left side."

"How long is that going to take?" Meredith tilted her head back, looking at the ceiling.

"It could be a year or more. They'll send you home with lotion that you will have to apply daily. You may end up wearing the coverings just because it feels better that way, forever." Scrub shifted in his chair, not sure how she'd react.

"No baby? Scars? I jumped from the car for nothing?" The tears flowed down her cheeks like two rivers.

"Meredith, you're alive, and that outweighs everything else," I told her. I couldn't handle losing her.

Chapter 34

Stop Playing With Your Food

Grace

It had been five long weeks since JR was born. True to their word, the hospital re-evaluated him every Friday, but they always found some reason to keep him. It made me question whether or not they were doing it on purpose, even though JR was making huge strides. He was putting on weight and growing inch by inch.

I had told Sabre how Matt had orchestrated the code pink, detailing the entire timeline. Sabre had sent Wreck to track down the man involved, to confirm if it was part of Matt's desperation. When Wreck confronted the worker, the man had begged to be left alone. He explained he would never have kidnapped the baby, but he couldn't pass up five hundred dollars just to walk the floor and stop in front of the window. He had kids to feed, and it seemed like easy money. Wreck had given him another five hundred and warned him never to do it again.

When I'd brought up my fears to Sabre, he'd let me vent before he talked me off the ledge.

"It fucking sucks. I know you want to take him home and worry about it later, but we can't. The hospital has done us a solid by looking the other way. They didn't have to," Sabre said, running a hand through his hair. I had noticed the bags underneath his eyes and hugged him, thanking him for listening. I loved him too much to dump any more of my frustrations into his lap.

The Code Pink flipped a switch in Sabre. He'd always been a man in control, but this went beyond anything I could have imagined. In the morning, he'd walk me across the street to visit JR and check on everyone else, but at night, he tried to exert any sort of dominance over our situation. He hardly slept, and I'd caught him mumbling as he wrote notes on the hotel's notepad.

One night, I had awakened to Sabre was sitting in his boxers at the little table in our room. "Come to bed," I had called to him.

"I can't. I have to get this right so that the two of you are safe," he'd said. He hadn't bothered to look up at me.

"You're exhausted. Please, come to bed," I had pleaded, trying to get him to see reason.

He had rubbed at his eyes and stood from the table before climbing into bed. I had wrapped my arms around him as best as I could, trying to comfort him.

"What if I fuck this up, and Matt wins?" he had whispered to me as his eyes had fallen shut.

"What if you win?" I had whispered back, kissing his forehead and never letting go.

We had a silent agreement. It wasn't hard to figure out what would happen to Matt. He'd made the deals with the cartel, and he should be the only one to pay the consequences. I had made my peace with it, but I didn't want to know any of the specifics. I thought Sabre felt the same way. We only discussed details that pertained to me or JR. He wanted nothing to tarnish me, the baby, or our relationship. It only made me love him more.

***

I must have fallen asleep before Sabre last night because I didn't remember him coming to bed. JR was coming home today, and the anxiety affected us differently. I was more anxious about starting our new lives as parents, while Sabre was more concerned with our safety. I understood, but if I dwelled on the cartel, I wouldn't be able to function. Rolling over to look at the clock on the nightstand, I noticed it was early. We didn't have to be at the hospital until nine, and it wasn't even six. I could hear the shower running.

My imagination slowly painted a picture behind the bathroom door as I lay in bed, listening to the water run. In my fantasy, he leaned forward into the spray, letting the droplets run over his head and down his shoulders. I wanted to collect them on my tongue as they clung to his pecs. I dreamed about falling to my knees and tracing the lines of his six-pack abs. Letting out a small moan, it clicked. There was nothing stopping me from living this out. I just had to seize the moment.

Opening the bathroom door, I slid into the corner to watch him. Sabre was standing in the middle of the shower. The water was running over his back. His head hung low, but he wasn't touching himself. As I watched, he let out a groan. I didn't know where his mind was.

My feet moved on their own as I raised his shirt over my head. I pretended like he wasn't aware I was in the room, but the muscles in his back had shifted. Sabre leaned his arm on the shower wall and watched me out of the crook of his elbow. I ignored him and tried to be sexy when I approached the shower door. When it slid open, it made a loud scraping noise in the bathroom's silence. The sound reminded me of nails on a chalkboard, but I slid the door shut and wrapped my arms around his waist.

"If you're not interested in carnal activity, you need to leave," he said to me, dropping his head down so that his eyes fell to the floor.

"Carnal activity. That sounds like a crossword clue," I whispered.

"Mama, if I turn around, I am going to bury myself inside you, and I am not sure I am going to take it as slow as you need right now. I don't want to hurt you," he said, letting a sigh get washed away by the water.

My hands tightened around his middle, digging my nails into his muscles. "They cleared me yesterday for carnal activity."

He laughed, but it sounded foreign to my ears. A dry hollow sound. "This is a weak moment right now. I want you too badly, and if I turn around, that's it," he sighed. "I don't have condoms, so I can't even protect you."

"I thought bikers were supposed to carry a few in their wallets," I teased him. "Some hot chick has a thing for leather, and you can just reach for one as you whip it out."

"I think you like to kill me. It's a specialty of yours." He straightened, breaking my hold, and turned around. In those few seconds, his face had transformed into the animal that was buried beneath his skin and had flooded his veins. His eyes darkened as they scanned me from the tip of my head to my toes. There were deep frown lines in his forehead that only made him more ruggedly handsome. I was the prey, and Sabre would devour me until he had his fill.

I'd never experienced this type of primal energy. There was nowhere to run, and with Sabre fixated on me, I was a little overwhelmed. Taking two steps back, I plastered myself against the back shower wall and let the remaining water trickle over me. I needed a minute to calm down.

He lunged at me, our chests colliding as he leaned against the shower wall, his arm above my head. "Are you sure about this?" Sabre cupped my hip in his hand, but he never looked away from my eyes.

I didn't answer as I wrapped my arm around the back of his neck and brought his lips down on mine. The water sprayed around us as he kissed me, growling into my mouth, "Mine."

"Yours," I said with equal intensity, nipping at his bottom lip. Using him for leverage, I wrapped my leg around his hip and tried to bring him closer to me, but the water made it slippery. He held my hip and wrapped his other arm around me, pulling me into his body for stability.

"No, if we're doing this, you're not getting hurt. 'How did you break, Grace?''Oh, she fell in the shower trying to climb my dick.'"

I couldn't help the laugh that trickled out. "It'd more likely be, 'How did you kill, Grace?''Oh, her pussy shriveled up and died, waiting for me.'"

He barked a laugh. "No. I'll never live it down, and neither will you." Pinning me against the shower wall with his body, he ran his hand down my back until he cupped my pussy from behind, plunging two fingers inside me. Lightly pumping a few times, he whispered in my ear, "You're warm, but you're not wet. Let me take care of you."

"Princess treatment," I reminded him.

"You just want to see me on my knees." His forehead dropped to mine, our eyes locked in an intimate embrace as he pumped his fingers within me.

He hadn't left me much room to move, but I pushed off the shower wall and reached for his shoulders. I pressed my fingers into the muscles, trying to push down with urgency. I had waited too long in our relationship to stop him now. Sabre had made a promise to me to wait, and while I appreciated the sentiment, I wanted him to make it up to me now.

"Good things come to good girls who wait," he said directly into my ear, suckling the lobe. I wanted him to suckle somewhere else, but the man was taking his sweet ass time. He kissed and licked at my neck and the crease where it met my shoulder. His fingers maintained the same slow pace deep inside me.

I pressed against his shoulder again as a moan escaped my lips. "I am done waiting. Stop teasing me, Sabre."

He chuckled against my neck. The vibration shot from my neck straight to my pussy, but there was no relief. Sabre kissed the middle of my throat. "You accept me for the animal that I am, but I wanted you to know the real name of the man who loves you. It's Drew Hudson."

"Drew," I said reverently. "I have a confession."

He didn't answer me but continued to kiss and lick the middle of my throat.

"I wanted our family to be united. When Stands asked me if you were the father, I instantly said yes. However, when she asked me JR's name, I could only give her his first and middle. She asked me if I planned on changing my name to Hudson. I told her, 'Eventually,' realizing that she had given me your last name." I placed my hands on his cheeks and pulled him back so that I could look into his eyes. "It doesn't matter what my last name is. I'll legally have it changed, but I want you to know that I love you with all that I am, with every fiber of my being."

He dropped to his knees and positioned my leg over his shoulder. I watched as he kissed my mound, laying his cheek against me. "I am going to hold you to that, Mama."

I felt Sabre lick the outside of my lips. First one, and then the other. Light, feathery touches that made me question if they had even happened. I needed more. Running my fingers through his hair, I grabbed at the roots, hoping it would sting. I heard him growl against me, and I did it again. He let another growl loose within the shower walls, but he continued the slow torture. Up one side, down the other, in slow laps with his tongue. It left me craving more.

"Do I look different? You're going so slow, and it's making me wonder what the problem is," I directed at the top of his head.

He parted my lips and held them open with his fingers. "Looks like breakfast to me."

"Stop playing with your food." I yanked on his hair, trying to steer him back to where I needed him the most.

A dark chuckle surrounded me. "You asked for this, Mama. I have been a starved man for far too long."

"You only have yourself to blame for that. Now, eat." I pushed the back of his head forward, hoping he'd get the point.

The gentle lapping was gone. Sabre flattened his tongue and darted as deep as he could within me, using it to make broad strokes. There was no rhyme or reason to his probing. I'd feel him in one area, and when he had his fill, he'd move onto the next. If I had only been warm before, I was now drenched. A low groan escaped from me.

Sabre never gave me enough friction to push me over the edge that I was desperately trying to seek. When he pulled away from me, I let out another low groan to show my displeasure. He chuckled at my torment. Using his tongue to savor me one more time, he made a show of licking his lips. "Still tastes like oranges, but if you don't want to topple over, you better hold on," he said. I tried to slide down the wall so that I could be closer to him, but his hands held me in place by my hips.

Sabre liked to say that I was good at killing him, but the man was going to be my demise. I used banter as my weapon of choice, but Sabre was doing a superb job with his tongue. He surprised me by curling it and repeatedly making a stabbing motion deep within me. If the pleasure hadn't consumed me, I would have laughed. Sabre was using his tongue as a dagger.

I was at his mercy, and he decided what I needed and when. There was never any consistency, as he switched back and forth from the dagger-like motion to the broad strokes and back. I couldn't think straight and there was nothing to ground me in the shower.

"Come on, Mama. I want to hear my name drop from your lips in between those screams."

He picked up the pace, and I slammed my hand against the shower wall. "Yes. Yes. Right there." I didn't know what I was even saying, but I didn't stop. My stomach tightened as my orgasm rapidly approached. My body thrashed against the wall. "Drew," I whined. I felt as if I was free falling, and he was the only person alive who could catch me.

I could feel him smile against me, and then he sucked my clit into his mouth. It launched me into the sky without a parachute to catch me.

He placed my leg on the shower floor and stood, gathering me into his arms. "Round two," he whispered into my ear. Picking up my legs, he wrapped them around his waist. His hands held me from below, but I felt trapped in the best way possible. He pushed his upper body against my chest, holding me in place. I wrapped my arms around his neck, but I was his limp doll, to be used as he saw fit.

"Last chance. I can't protect you, and if you tell me no, I'll drop your legs and finish you again with my tongue." He stroked the skin at the back of my thighs. "If you get pregnant, I'll be there. For you. For my kids."

I rubbed my nose against his, twisting left and right until my lips fell on his. I shoved my tongue in his mouth, trying to recreate the heat that he'd made me feel below. "Fuck me. Don't stop until you can't remember your name."

"I know what my name is. It's yours," he whispered.

He was holding himself at my center, but I wasn't sure why he'd stopped. I wiggled in his arms, trying to get better acquainted with his dick. I didn't want to fall, but I hungered to be connected to him. Feeling his head part my lips, I wiggled some more. In my clouded mind, I laughed. The wiggle move had finally worked.

"If you hurt, you need to tell me."

"I'll only hurt if you stop." I bopped him at the back of his head. "Don't stop."

"Yes, ma'am." He made sure that I was flush against the back shower wall and then pistoned into me.

We both let out loud groans.

"Do it again," I commanded him.

He didn't stop until we were both howling underneath the shower spray.

As my body came down from the high, I held onto him tightly. I feared that if I let go, he might vanish before my eyes. I didn't want to voice those concerns into the universe in case I accidentally gave them credibility. Instead, I placed my forehead on his, staring straight into his eyes. Silently giving him a piece of my heart to hold, I tried to convey everything that a simple "I love you" couldn't. "I didn't know what an actual relationship should look like, feel like, until I met you. Thank you."

Chapter 35
Breaking Out Of This Place

Sabre

I never wanted to see another fucking white wall in my life. If there was one in the clubhouse, that fucker was getting painted as soon as possible. I'd spent too many days staring at them, and it felt good knowing this might all be over soon.

Pretty and Wreck were the only brothers left on guard duty. Meredith had been released three weeks ago. Grizz was afraid she'd run back to her condo, so he'd made plans to keep her at the clubhouse until he could sort out their situation. When I asked how things were going, he brushed me off, insisting everything was fine. However, Count told me they were snipping at each other all the time. It probably meant I was walking into a shit storm.

Aunt E had just been released last week. Grace hadn't left the hospital in five weeks, and with a new baby, she couldn't possibly take care of everyone without running herself ragged. The baby needed to come first, but Grace would still try to be everything to everyone. Thankfully, Pebbles had offered to step in and help with Aunt E. We had found an empty bedroom on the main floor of the clubhouse to help with the transition. It wasn't ideal, but for now, it was alright. I'd probably end up moving her in with us and hiring a full-time nurse until she got back on her feet.

The four of us were waiting outside of the NICU window, eager for any scrap of news. We'd been told that the staff was processing the paperwork, but they'd gotten a later start than normal. Whether it was a lie or just incompetence, we'd already been here an hour past the expected time, and I was anxious.

When we walked onto the NICU floor, Wreck was still awake. He hadn't been to bed yet. When we were told they weren't ready, he fell asleep, sitting straight up in the guard duty chair. Grace sat next to him, bouncing her leg in time to the intercom music. I tried standing by the window and even sitting next to Grace, but I had too much energy to burn. We were too close to the end, and I could feel it deep in my bones. Pacing was the only way to clear my mind. As I made another lap, Pretty saw the opportunity to annoy me. He started pacing in the opposite direction, making a different silly face at me each time we crossed paths.

Finally, there was movement in the NICU room, and I immediately stopped pacing. Pretty had turned around, and when he saw me, he faced the window. I felt a small hand on my forearm and glanced down to see Grace standing between us, her other hand on my brother's arm. The three of us stood watching as a family, our eyes fixed on the nurse as she unplugged the cords from the incubator and removed the top cover.

"He knows he's coming home. Look how fast his feet are kicking," Grace said, squeezing my forearm.

"He wants to race. Do they start kids off in go-karts? I'll have to figure it out and go shopping." Pretty rubbed the stubble of his beard on his chin.

"No. You need to settle down and let him be a kid. If he wants to race, we'll handle it when the time comes," Wreck interjected from behind us. I turned to look over my shoulder at him, but his eyes remained closed.

"You're no fun," Pretty retorted, turning around and sticking his tongue out at Wreck.

"Careful. I was told not to do that unless I was planning on using it," Grace teased, her eyes twinkling.

Our eyes met, and I let my lips curl into a smirk. Back then, I was just looking for a hookup, but she bulldozed into my life and made me a family man.

"Is that why the shower in your room ran for over an hour this morning? I could hear the water running through the pipes, and it woke me. I couldn't get back to sleep because I was straining my ears to hear anything else. FYI, the walls in the hotel are thick, unlike the clubhouse." Pretty smirked, thinking he had her cornered.

"Blame your brother. He was in there first and woke me." She shrugged. "I had to make sure he wouldn't drown." She patted Pretty's arm sympathetically.

"Nah, he'll just beat my ass and call it brotherly love. Next time, can you at least wait until I have a bed buddy in the clubhouse before you get your freak on?" Pretty looked at Grace and winked.

Grace laughed softly. "I make no promises."

Our humor slowly died as the NICU door opened. "He's almost ready, but this is the part where you can spend time with him," the NICU nurse said, gesturing for us to follow her across the hall.

"Hey, Little Man. You're busting out of this place today," Pretty said, letting the baby try to grab his finger.

"It's about time." Grace tickled the bottom of his feet, and the baby made a happy cooing noise.

I followed them across the hall, but my feet felt glued to the doorway. This was the first time I was going to meet the baby, and I didn't feel worthy. I watched as Grace naturally picked him up and placed him on her shoulder, kissing his forehead and whispering softly. My brother stood behind her, making the baby coo and laugh. The baby was used to them, but he'd never met me.

When I'd told Grace that I would wait, it was purely because the NICU had a one-person rule. I hadn't wanted to take the visiting time away from her. I probably could have arranged a time to visit, but the longer the baby was in the NICU, the longer I could avoid the dread that had settled over me. *What if he found out later on that I wasn't his biological father and blamed me for the end of his parents' marriage? What if he hated me for it?*

"Prez, one foot in front of the other. Don't keep them waiting," Wreck said from his chair. His eyes were still closed.

I took a deep breath and walked into the room.

Grace looked up at me over the baby. "Come here and meet him," she called to me with a smile on her beautiful face.

Wreck's words echoed in my head as I approached. I would never keep them waiting for me again.

"He's been waiting for this just as long as you have," Grace said, softly.

I stood in front of them, looking down at the baby. I could pinpoint the exact features that had come from Grace and her family. His eyes were blue, which I'd read could change over time, but I imagined they would eventually be brown like Grace's. His nose had a little bubble at the end. If it eventually upturned, it would remind me of the women in Grace's family. They all had the same tilt at the end of their noses.

"If you curl your arm like you're carrying a football, you can hold him," Grace instructed.

Instinctively, I curled my arm and brought my other arm over to hold it in place. I remembered holding Pretty as a baby, but it had been so long, I didn't know if I was doing this right.

"A little closer together. He's still small but growing," Grace said, waiting for me to adjust. "He just wants his daddy, so there's no need to be nervous." She placed the baby in my arms and stepped back.

"Hi," I said, looking down at him. "Shit, that's lame."

Laughter filled the room. "Don't worry, I did the same thing. He's used to it by now." Grace kissed my cheek. "JR, this is your daddy," she said, directing the words towards the baby. "Sabre," she said, looking back up at me. "This is James Robert Hudson, your son."

I didn't respond fast enough, and Grace nervously rambled on.

"I think Thunder already knows, or at least he's suspicious," Grace began, her voice soft. "On the ambulance ride over here, I asked him what his real name was. I told him I needed a distraction, and I sold him on the idea that I was in so much pain, I'd never remember what he said. The only names off-limits were yours and Pretty's. Don't tell him I lied."

I shook my head, a smile forming. "I don't have a problem with that at all."

Grace continued, smiling at me, "I've been trying to get JR used to his name, but I think he likes it. He responds to it, and eventually he'll grow into a good man like the people he's named after. God, I don't want to think about that." She leaned forward and kissed me. JR nestled between us. "I love you, and when this is all over, we'll look back at this as one big speed bump."

She turned to walk away from me, but I called to get her attention. "Grace." I said, when she'd turned back, "You did good, mama. He's beautiful." I looked back down at him. He wasn't wiggling, but his feet were kicking. "I don't know what to say."

"It's okay. I did the same thing. We'll be in the hallway if you need us." She kissed me again and then tickled JR's foot. "Take it easy on Daddy. He's a little overwhelmed right now, but he knows how much we love him." She turned and looped her arm through Pretty's, exiting the room and making sure the door was closed.

All the times I'd heard someone say I couldn't raise another man's baby echoed through my mind as I watched him.

"I don't know how to be your father, JR. I have no fucking clue, but I will tell you this: your mother is the most important person in my life, and I love her with every fiber of my being. I promise you I will treat her like the queen she is. You'll probably hate that when you become a teenager, but it's just how life is going to be." I bounced him in my arms.

"Now, for the man-to-man chat." I chuckled, shifting JR in my arms. "We'll probably have a few of these over the years, but this is what I want you to remember: you were my son from the moment I got my head out of my ass and claimed your mother. I will not hide the fact that we don't share blood from you. I hope that you'll know how much you mean to me, how much I love you, and that it will never be an issue. You'll always be my son. If you ask, I promise, I won't hold back, but at the end of the conversation, nothing will change between us."

I shifted my arms again to bring JR closer so that I could kiss his forehead. As I approached, I felt his little hand hit my cheek. I took it as a sign that he agreed. We were good.

Chapter 36
Buh Bye

Sabre

"Thunder and Chef are here," Grace said as she walked into the waiting room, where I'd been holding JR. "The nurse went over the instructions with me, so we're free to go whenever you're ready." She approached me with a mischievous smile on her face.

"What?" I asked her.

"There's just something about a handsome man holding his son that does something to a woman."

"Does this mean you're going to jump my bones later?" I teased. It was fun to play along, even though I wouldn't hold her to any of it. When this was all over, it wouldn't surprise me if we crashed hard.

"You can't say things like that in front of a child," she laughed.

"He's going to see and hear worse things as he grows up," I reminded her.

"I know, but he'll grow up around good men, and that trumps everything else." She kissed me. "The quicker we get this over with, the quicker we can get to bed."

I kissed JR's forehead and placed him in his car seat. Watching as he wiggled, I said, "Take care of your mama."

Grace's hand wrapped around my bicep, and I raised her fingers to kiss the backs of her knuckles. "Stay with Thunder and Chef, and I'll see you later."

"We'll be safe, and I know to call when we get to the clubhouse." She pecked my lips. "We'll see you later."

Thunder reached for JR's car seat, and Chef offered his arm to Grace. The brothers had brought over one of the club's spare cars and parked it on the opposite side of the hospital. Matt would only look for Grace's SUV, and I hoped they could slip away undetected. I'd designed this plan to keep my family safe, but I didn't enjoy watching them walk away from me.

"It's time, Prez," Wreck said.

***

Tilting my head back against the headrest of Grace's SUV, I soaked in the quiet. If I was right, the next few hours would be anything but peaceful. If I was wrong, I'd be spending the next several weeks or months chasing Matt when I needed to be home. This had to end today. A deep melancholy feeling settled into my bones. The thought that if Matt hadn't fucked up, Grace would have never been mine didn't escape me.

Turning on the car, I waited for my cell phone to connect to the Bluetooth network that ran through the brother's helmets. It didn't take long, but as the ready light turned green, Pretty came through loud and clear.

"Hello, Big Daddy," he laughed.

"You're poking the tiger on the wrong day." I heard the disappointment in Wreck's voice.

"Nah, this could work out in my favor. If he beats me today, I'll milk it for all it's worth. When I go on my bender, there will be plenty of people ready to take care of me. Unless, Wreck, you want to play naughty nurse first?"

"What the fuck is wrong with you?" I chimed in.

"Hey, don't knock it until you try it." I could hear the smirk in Pretty's voice through the Bluetooth.

"Alright, focus on something else besides your dick. I am going to pull out of this parking space and see if Matt follows me from his hiding spot. He's here. I feel like he's watching, waiting."

"I do too, Prez," Wreck said. "If he actually buys that you're alone, this is his prime opportunity."

I had made a show of walking out of the hospital, carrying a baby doll in a car seat. If anyone was watching, I looked like a new dad trying to get his family home. I hadn't wanted to ask one of the club girls to pretend to be Grace. I wasn't sure of the level of danger, and I wouldn't put them in the line of fire. Instead, I'd asked Pretty to come up with a plan.

"I dressed the blow-up doll like Flo. It'll be fine." Pretty had sounded impressed with himself.

The doll was sitting in the passenger seat of the car. I didn't know where he'd gotten it from on short notice, but it looked lifelike, and that creeped me out even more.

I tuned them out and headed towards the main road. If Matt was watching, I wanted him to think that we were by ourselves, heading to the clubhouse. If he wanted to run me off the road, the path I'd charted was his best option. Wreck and Pretty would follow at a safe distance behind me, and then How and Zook would pull in front of me before we reached the exit for the highway.

I made a right and then a left, checking the surroundings, but nothing stood out at me. Matt drove a red convertible, but I couldn't see him wanting to stand out. I made another left. This was it. Matt had five miles before I reached the highway. "Is he there?" I asked through the Bluetooth.

"No, Prez. What the fuck is he waiting for?" Wreck said.

"I don't know," I said, looking out the rear-view mirror.

Three miles past and nothing. I made a right.

"How and Zook, checking into the party," I heard How say through the radio.

"You're not missing much. Fucknut hasn't shown," Pretty answered.

"He can't be that stupid. If Prez gets to the clubhouse, it's over for him. Does he really think he's going to walk up to our gates and demand we hand the baby over? Fat fucking chance," Zook said.

"We're down to a mile. Anyone see anything?" I said. My gut was screaming at me. I was right. He was here, but why couldn't we find him? Could he actually have grown a pair?

"Jackpot, motherfucker." How sounded as if he'd pissed his pants with excitement. "Zook and I are in front of him, and he's three car lengths in front of the SUV in the red car. I caught it because he swerves every time he looks out the rear-view mirror at you, Prez."

"If Wreck and Pretty move up, we can drop back and box him in. He won't see it coming if we time it right. Clueless motherfucker," Zook strategized.

"Whatever you do, don't shoot. I am not collecting shell casings off the side of the road. When Pretty and I get close to his back bumper, we'll just pop one of his tires," Wreck said.

"Aye, aye, Captain," Pretty said. "Scratch that. I want to play pirates with sword crossing."

"I don't even want to know what the fuck you're talking about," Zook scoffed.

"No, no, you don't." Pretty laughed through his helmet. "When are we doing this?"

"Go now. You only have about a mile left before we reach the highway," I commanded, speeding up the SUV so that I could pull in behind Matt once he stopped.

"Aye, aye." Pretty laughed again, and I heard the engine of his bike revving up.

My brother cut me off as he sped past me. Fucker was living on borrowed time, and I wasn't sure who was going to get him first. Wreck at least was ahead of me before he switched lanes. I watched as they easily pulled in behind Matt. Pretty knocked on the back of the trunk with his knuckle.

"Stop playing and just do it. He's sweating, and I think he's going to swerve," Wreck scolded Pretty.

"This was supposed to be way more fun," Pretty commented dryly, as he reached for his back pocket, pulling out the knife my father had given him when he'd prospected. "Gotta do what a man's gotta do," he said as he flipped his knife open and stabbed the back tire of Matt's car. The tire went down quickly, and if Matt didn't stop soon, he would tear the rim apart.

This was it, except the fucker sped up, and when Matt put all that pressure on the blown tire, he ended up sliding and flipping the car over onto its roof.

"That was one way to get him to stop." How laughed as he and Zook approached the front of the car.

"I am probably up, considering this is my specialty." Zook took off his cut and handed it to How. Walking over to the driver's side door, he laid in the dirt and shined the flashlight of his phone into the window. "He's alive. Trying to kick out the front window. Give me a minute, and I'll have him out of here."

There were no cameras on this stretch of road, and we pulled the license plates off. City patrol would eventually pick up the car, but with no identification, they'd junk it for parts and move on.

***

"Why the fuck am I here?" Matt tried to spit at me, but I was too far away. It landed on the floor a few feet from where he hung, nailed to the wall, naked. A white wall that I would paint red.

"That's disappointing. I know you're smarter than that. Not bad for a pussy in a leather vest." I smirked at him, and laughter filled the room from the brothers that had been allowed to attend. "You gave me too much time to protect my family." I walked over to him and curled my gloved hand into a fist, hitting Matt in the stomach.

"Hey, Cyph, why don't you explain to our guest where we are," I said, smiling.

"Seriously?" he asked. His eyebrows shot up and his eyes widened like Christmas had come early and I had given him the best gift ever. He clapped his hands and then started talking a mile a minute. "I was curious why the bank fired you so quickly," Cyph directed at Matt. "If you take the timeline, and you deduct the weekend, it was really only a couple of hours. Corporations don't work that quickly. HR has to be involved, and it's a whole thing. The other problem was the bank used the 'moral turpitude' clause in your contract on every termination document. They stuck to it like peanut butter to jelly. Huge red flag. So I went through your last couple of transactions. You didn't cover your tracks very well." He bounced on his toes. The anticipation was coursing through his veins, and Cyph couldn't stand still.

"They fired me because Grace is a fucking cunt who made a scene in the middle of the bar in front of important clients." Matt was shooting daggers at Cyph.

"Nope. Wrong thing to say." I walked back over to Matt and hit him in the stomach again, following it with an uppercut to his face. The rest of the brothers hadn't liked it either, and there was a low mumble spreading about the room. Grace had earned their respect, and they would protect her with their lives.

"That's not actually true. Would you like me to explain?" Cyph paused for dramatic effect, rocking on the backs of his heels.

"The floor's yours until they call," I said.

"Flo unknowingly set your downfall into motion. She's a badass." Cyph shifted to the tips of his toes.

Matt lunged at Cyph, but he wasn't able to release the nails in his hands. When we had brought him to this office building, Grizz had handled the rest. I thought it was a nice touch, considering Matt wanted to play God.

"The client that she made a scene in front of was none other than Diego Lopez, third-in-command to his brother, Manuel. There's no way you didn't know that. He's here in the states to build the Lopez Cartel's businesses and make contacts, legit and otherwise." Cyph ran a hand through his hair. "For the rest of the class, the men that have been visiting our tit show fall under Diego's authority."

Matt's face wasn't pale. He bypassed that shade and went straight to white. I wanted to make a wisecrack about him blending into the wall. Cyph was getting closer to unraveling Matt's mysteries, and I couldn't tell if we were about to uncover something damaging or if Matt was simply an incompetent criminal.

"I wish I had a Red Bull," Cyph said. "Anyway, I thought it would be poetic justice to bring you here, and I talked Prez into it. This is the first building that Diego purchased five years ago, but he fucked up and paid cash with cartel money.

No one wanted to touch this place, and he couldn't get the permits to renovate it into offices. It's been empty ever since."

Cyph pointed at Matt. "That's until you came along and talked him into a refinance. He'd be able to use the bank's name for legitimacy, and they would give him the equity, which he didn't need, but it was a perk. You didn't know that Brandon was putting a percentage of each transaction into Meredith's name, did you? There's a paper trail a mile long."

"What in the fuck?" Grizz launched himself at Matt, hitting him in the mouth. I grabbed him before he could take another swing.

"If you do that again, you'll break your knuckles open, leaving DNA. Meredith needs you more than this fucker does." I let Grizz go when I thought he wouldn't attack Matt again.

Cyph turned towards Grizz. "You were right. Brandon didn't care about Meredith. She was a means to an end, but he fucked up and got himself killed."

Matt spit the blood from his lip at his feet. "Brandon was a fucking dumbass. He would have inherited his family's money, but he wanted to build his name up quickly. The only way to do that is to have a bankroll." He spit another glob of blood. "That's why they canned me so quickly. Brandon was taking real estate, but I took cash for each transaction."

"You both were stealing from the cartel?" Someone asked what we were all thinking, but none of us could believe what we were hearing.

"They were," Cyph answered for him. "That's why Matt was so keen to give them the baby. It would seal the last deal, and the cartel wouldn't go looking for his missing percentage." He smiled and clapped his hands. "That's where Flo fucked you over. When she prepared for the divorce, she logged into the bank accounts from an unsecure network. Just the logins triggered internal audits, and the bank finally figured out what was going on. You shouldn't shit where you eat."

"Cyph, how deep are Grace and Meredith involved in this?" I asked. I couldn't fight a two-front war when it had just been Matt and the cartel. If the bank came for the girls, I didn't know what I would do. This was out of our league.

"Well, the bank has been foreclosing on anything and everything they can claim fraud on. I've been helping them along the way with accounts and transactions they've missed that didn't affect anyone. Fucknuts can't give Flo a divorce because he can't sign over half of the accounts. The ones under investigation are probably going to roll back to the bank, if not all of them. The bank knows Flo is not involved, and they're not pursuing her. However, the jury is out on how much of the funds they're going to take from her."

"What about Meredith?" Grizz asked. He was popping his knuckles.

"That one is a little harder. Brandon was signing Meredith's name to the paperwork, so it appears she's actually involved. When the bank walks the transactions back, they are technically foreclosing on the properties. With her name on the paperwork, Meredith's taking the hits for the percentages Brandon signed over to her. They've done it three times already, but I am watching it. We might have to claim fraud, so that she's not financially ruined. However, they may claim that she's a co-conspirator in this mess and then it becomes a legal battle. They could take everything from her as they clean house."

"You motherfucker," Grizz yelled at Matt.

As he went to take another swing, my phone rang.

Chapter 37

Buh Bye Now

Sabre

"The party's about to start, Matt," I said, pulling my phone out of my back pocket.

He yelled for help, but no one was in the building besides us.

"Tape his mouth. I don't need him yelling something obscene that Grace might hear." So far, I'd kept her from knowing about today's excitement. She was smart and knew Matt was going to disappear. She'd never pushed for the specifics, and I was okay with that. I waited until Berry had shut Matt the fuck up. I answered the call and put it on speaker.

"Prez?"

There were murmurs around the room at how loud Thunder was. He'd never be stealthy with his loud, booming voice.

"Yeah, Thunder?"

"The packages are at the clubhouse, safe and sound," he confirmed.

I breathed a deep sigh of relief. I'd planned for today, but knowing the two most important people in my life were safe lifted an immense weight off my shoulders. "Were you followed?" I asked him.

"Chef and I aren't sure what happened. We were on the ramp entering the highway when a black SUV with tinted windows started tailing us. They were already on the highway, but it didn't take a genius to know they were following us. Chef took a couple backroads to see if we could shake them, but they never changed their distance, always two car lengths behind us. I called Snake at the clubhouse, and he grabbed a few of the older brothers to ride out and meet us. As soon as the bikes surrounded our car, the SUV took off."

"I don't know what that was. We'll need to discuss it on Monday at church." The thought of them being pursued made my stomach churn, and I wanted to projectile vomit all over Matt. It could have been nothing, but the vehicle screamed cartel. I repeatedly reminded myself that Grace and JR were safe in the clubhouse.

"Thunder? Should I speak to him?" Grace's voice came through the phone, even though she wasn't speaking directly to me. I heard them exchange a few words.

I looked at Matt and smirked. "It's okay, Thunder. Hand her the phone," I said. I waited until I could hear her thank him. "You can't be ordering my men around like that, mama."

She laughed, and it was my favorite sound in the world. "I said please. Thunder and Chef did an excellent job. Focus on bringing everyone else home safely. JR and I are fine." This was the closest we'd ever come to talking about today.

I heard the phone *click*, and I hit the red button on my end. "Did you catch that, Matt? She's only thinking about us and our safety." I used my finger to circle the room, including the rest of the brothers.

His eyes were furious, and he made muffled sounds behind the tape. I was sure he wanted to call me some choice colorful names, but I didn't give a fuck. He wouldn't last much longer. I looked around the room, and there were smiles or smirks on each brother's face. She'd included them, and it just solidified everyone's belief that she belonged. Voting Grace in as First Lady of the Iron Shield was only a formality.

"I have nothing further to say to you, but I wanted you to know they're thriving. When you get to the bouts of hell, you won't have to worry about them because they sure won't be fucking worried about you." I looked around the room until my eyes fell on Scrub. "You ready?" I asked him.

Matt made more muffled sounds behind the tape. He tried to pull away from the wall again, but there was no give.

"Finally. I've been waiting for this." Scrub was smiling as he slid the zipper open of his medical travel duffle. I wasn't sure how much action that bag had seen, but Scrub never left home without it.

"Calm down, dude. It's just a dick," Cyph said to him.

"Do you know how much research I had to do for this? Optimal cutting positions and everything." Scrub didn't look up as he laid out a few tools. "This is the highlight of my week. You know, for research only, you fucking freak."

Scrub had directed that at Cyph, but Count answered. "You're the psycho excited about cutting a dick off."

When Matt heard their conversation, his eyes widened and sweat dripped off his forehead. He tried to scream, but the tape muffled any sound that might have escaped.

"Yet you bid on the length of it soft. Go fuck yourself," Scrub mocked Count.

"It was a sucker's bet, and six inches was available when I looked. I figured five was too small. I am seven, and there's no way to disappoint, even if you ram it home. Besides, I need bike parts." Count shrugged.

"I took the five-inch bet. I figured if he had small man syndrome then he was lacking." Pretty chimed in. "It's not the size, but the motion of the ocean," he said, swaying his hips in a circle.

"Does that work for the back door, too?" Count taunted Pretty.

"Nope, twerking does." Pretty bent over, stuck his ass out, and started to pump his back and hips.

"If you're not careful, you're going to hurt yourself. If that's the case, we'll just drive by the hospital and throw your ass out. None of us want to walk back in there," How said, laughing.

"Speaking of which, tomorrow starts my bender, so if you see something, no, you didn't. If you hear something, you just mind your fucking business." Pretty pointed at each brother individually until they acknowledged him.

"Did you approve that?" Grizz asked Wreck.

"You put a muzzle on your bitch yet, Jonathan?" Wreck uncrossed and re-crossed his arms over his chest, feet shoulder-length apart.

"At least I can claim her as my bitch." Grizz balled his fist up but took one look at Wreck and decided not to hit him. It was probably a wise move.

"Enough. Let's get this done and get the fuck out of here," I interrupted them. "Scrub?"

Matt screamed again behind the tape. He had shut the fuck up once he heard the brothers ribbing each other, probably thinking they would forget about him. Like Zook had said on the road, fat fucking chance.

"I didn't know if you wanted to use your knife, so I brought a couple of scalpels and a pair of scissors. I thought a machete would be too easy." Scrub looked towards me for an answer.

"No, I'll use my knife. I had Grizz sharpen it specially for today." I pulled it from my back pocket and made sure that Matt focused on me before I said, "My father gave me this knife when I first prospected for the Iron Shield. When my son does the same, I'll pass it onto him."

Matt's face had been pale throughout this ordeal, but now, there was red appearing on his cheeks and forehead. He was angry at me, and I didn't give a fuck.

"As soon as I put an IV in, you can cut either his dick or his balls off. Don't do both at the same time. It'll be too messy, and he'll lose too much blood. You told me he had to be alive." Scrub gathered the supplies for an IV and approached Matt, working quickly. Pulling the tape off of Matt's mouth, Scrub took a step backwards, admiring his handiwork.

"You're a doctor? Didn't you take a fucking oath or something? You can't let them do this to me. This is unethical, and I'll have your license," Matt screamed. He still hadn't realized that no one would help him escape. The brothers didn't give a fuck what would happen to Matt.

"Oh, like Dr. Vargas? Did you know she was purposely trying to kill Grace?" Scrub stood in front of him with his arms crossed over his chest. Matt stopped running his mouth, but his eyes hid secrets. "You fucking did. If Grace had died, you could have harvested the baby easier."

"It wasn't like she was doing me any favors. I would be a widower. You know how many women would have thrown themselves at me knowing my wife was dead and the baby was gone? Grace fucks up everything."

Scrub kicked him in the knee, snapping it backwards. Walking back to the table, he handed Pretty a water bottle and paper towels. "He's your brother. You're on cleanup duty. Squirt this until I tell you not to and then pat it dry. It's just water." He grabbed the blow torch and clicked it on and off a few times. "I am ready. Let's do this."

"You're not touching my dick with that!" Matt hollered. "Don't fucking touch me."

"Or what?" I asked him.

He shouted more choice words about me, the club, the blowtorch, and anything else he could think of. It wouldn't change anything.

"You should have taken me seriously when I told you to stay away from her. We protect our own, and you will pay for your sins against them." I pulled off my riding gloves and put on a pair of surgical ones, smacking the edge against my skin. I wasn't touching his dick bare-handed. "It didn't have to be like this, but the storm is coming, and you're just a pawn in this game," I said, walking straight towards him.

"Every time you fuck her cold pussy, she'll be thinking of me. We have a child together."

I didn't let him say anything else as I grabbed his dick and squeezed with all of my might. He wouldn't need it anyway. I shifted the knife in my hand and pulled the shaft away from his body. I was about ready to make the first cut when my brother yelled, stopping me.

"Measure it. We have a bet going," he said.

"You have got to be fucking kidding me." I shook my head at their stupidity.

"That's not a good choice of words, considering you're holding it." Pretty smirked.

"Here, I brought a ruler. I didn't think we would need much." Scrub handed me a school ruler, and I just looked at him. He was usually one of the saner ones, but I'd let his inner psycho free, and this was the thanks I got. Putting the ruler straight into Matt's groin, I said, "Five and seven-eighths inches. Not even six. That's pathetic."

I didn't know who won the bet, but I heard one brother yell, "Yippee!". Grabbing Matt's dick, I held it out and made the first cut.

Matt's shrieks echoed off the office walls.

"Hurts like a bitch, huh? Guess you shouldn't have been a cunt, then." I made another cut straight down until I reached halfway. Blood pooled around the open wound and ran down the shaft of his dick, past his balls, to the floor. Pretty squirted the water bottle and used the paper towel to dry the area. I took a heavier swipe and this time, his dick fell to the ground.

There was a collective groan around the room, and a few of the brothers grabbed their own dicks to make sure they were still intact.

"That was easier than I thought it was going to be," I said, watching as Pretty wiped the remaining blood with a paper towel. Scrub clicked the blow torch on and cauterized the hole where Matt's dick had previously hung. The smell of flesh burning filled the office, and a little steam released from Matt's skin. Matt's shrieks became low moans, and tears ran from his eyes. Checking on him, Scrub raised his thumb. We could continue.

"How come he didn't pass out from the pain?" I asked Scrub.

"I gave him just enough morphine through the IV to tolerate the pain but still be coherent enough to know what's going on." Scrub flipped Matt off. "You're welcome, you fucking cunt."

If I thought removing his dick was easy, his balls went even smoother. I sliced the knife through the scrotum, and his balls fell to the ground on top of his dick.

It was done. Matt was officially a dickless wonder. Any fight he had had was gone. He tilted his head up so that he wouldn't have to see the damage I'd caused and sobbed. The tears didn't stop as Scrub sealed the wound.

"Grizz, you're up," I said, waiting for him to bring his tools forward. Grabbing the balls first, I held them against the wall, and Grizz put two nails through them, one in each. We did the same for the dick, and then I pulled the gloves off.

Berry and Twig would stop at an old campground on the way to the clubhouse. The place had been closed for years, but they still had burn pits out in the open.

"Hey Matt," I called to him, "last chance to watch. The brothers have been practicing their darts."

He didn't even look at me as he continued to sob.

I was the first one to step up to the imaginary throw line. Grabbing a dart from the desk, I lined up my shot, and it pierced Matt's dick so that the shaft was now pinned to the wall.

"Not bad, Prez," someone said. The brothers talked over each other.

"We should have brought a real dart board to pin the dick on. We could have scored points and bet on who gets the most."

"No, it should have been a donkey poster. You know? Pin the dick on the donkey."

"You didn't have friends as a kid."

"Where would you get a donkey poster?"

"Same place you order everything else for delivery."

Grizz, as Vice President, took my spot in front of the imaginary dart board with a dart in his hand. "Too bad I can't do this to Brandon. Fucking prick." He whipped the dart, landing it Matt's left ball.

The rest of the brothers lined up to throw darts. No one missed. After they finished, we packed up and headed towards the door. "Hey, Matt," I said.

He looked at me, a broken man. I felt nothing for him. He'd done this to himself. "Gerry says thank you. Diego Lopez put a bounty out on your head, dead or alive. No one knows you're here, but when we get back to the clubhouse, Cyph will take care of it. Gerry was playing you to pay off his gambling debt. We'll make sure he turns your location in. The reward will be enough to clear the debt."

"What will they do to me?" Matt asked.

"Make an example out of you," I answered, closing the office door behind me.

Chapter 38
Unveiled Wounds

Grace

Standing in front of my closet, I went piece by piece, trying to put together a date night outfit. I picked up the hanger, held it against myself, and then flung it onto the bed. My black polka dot dress lay on top of a pair of mom jeans. The little black dress's hanger had caught the edge of a frilly blouse, keeping it from sliding off. I was making this harder than it should have been. If I didn't decide soon, I was going to be rushed for time. I hated being late, especially when the night promised an evening alone with Sabre.

Picking up my phone, I scrolled through my contacts. Bear's name was the first one that came up. I didn't doubt that she'd rush over and help me, but I was concerned that she'd talk me into tight clothes that revealed way too much skin. I wasn't ready to part with my mom jeans. My body was slowly bouncing back from pregnancy, but I still had trouble areas. The weight I'd gained was falling off, but my stomach was soft. I had no regrets about delivering JR into the world, but every glance at the scar was a reminder of the trauma. It was my issue to deal with. Sabre didn't have a problem worshipping my body.

I was still scrolling when I stopped on my sister's name. She'd be the perfect one to ask for help, but I didn't want to cause her unnecessary strain. She was still trying to figure out which side was up, often triggering an emotional outburst at whoever was trying to help. Grizz took the brunt end of her anger, and I felt awful for the role I'd played. Deciding to take a chance, I hit CALL and waited.

"Hello?" she answered.

"Hey, Mer. What are you doing?" I asked her, chewing on a hangnail as I waited for her response.

"Imagining throwing darts at Grizz's ass."

I heard some commotion in the background. I assumed it was Grizz, but he was too far away from the phone for me to hear clearly.

"You can't marry someone while they're unconscious, Jonathan." Meredith's voice echoed with frustration. She must have just pulled the phone away from her ear before speaking.

I sighed. Meredith thought that if she provoked Grizz enough, he'd eventually get angry and let her go. She'd flee back to her condo, though none of us had the heart to tell her she wasn't safe there. It'd been the first thing that she'd secured on her own as an adult, and she wanted to maintain that independence. It was her haven, and I often wondered if the real reason was that it held warm memories from the beginning of her relationship with Grizz.

Grizz was the type to move forward and ask questions later. However, he never raised his voice at Meredith. He never yelled at her, even though we all wanted to at some point. She was difficult to deal with, and the brothers thought it was disrespectful when she used his real name. Sabre had had to intervene a few times to keep everyone in line.

"At least you're looking at my ass and not trying to kill me. I'll call that a win, Tef," I heard Grizz tell her through the phone.

"Mer." I stepped in to grab her attention. The last thing they needed was another blowout in the clubhouse. Their volatile relationship had already become club gossip, and it wasn't painting a positive picture.

The brothers couldn't understand why Grizz put up with my sister's shit. They thought that when she'd had the ectopic pregnancy, he should have given her money and sent her home. It didn't help that they constantly compared us, feeding into her anxiety. *Flo does this. What does Meredith do?*

Most of the club girls talked openly to her face or behind her back. Some of them had been in similar situations and didn't understand why she was taking it so hard. They thought she'd dodged an unwanted pregnancy. The only people who understood were the Old Ladies and me, but we were the minority. No one could break through the ten-foot walls Meredith had built around her heart. Not even Grizz.

"Where are you?" she asked me.

"At home. I'll leave the front door open for you. Just come in." The call dropped. She hadn't even said goodbye.

I was standing at the bottom of my bed, looking at the piles of clothes, when I heard her call out from downstairs.

"In the bedroom," I called back to her. She must have heard me because her feet were clomping up the stairs a few seconds later. JR was laying on a play mat at the top of the bed to keep him entertained.

Meredith walked into the room. "What the hell are you doing?" she asked me as she took in the piles of clothing. Standing next to me, she thumbed through a couple of pieces. "There's more leather here than I would have expected from you."

"Trying to get dressed for a date, but we're probably going to take his bike, so that limits the choices. I want to look good, but nothing is sticking out. So, I called you. Hi." I didn't hug her, but I did turn and made sure she saw me smile at her. I didn't know how to help, so I killed her with kindness, which rarely worked.

"Oh, I didn't realize that was tonight. Put the prissy shit away." Meredith pointed towards the pile of dresses. "He'd make you change, so there's no point getting dressed twice." She flipped through the other piles, and every third piece she'd throw on the ground.

"What are you doing? That stuff's clean." I picked up the clothing, trying to figure out what was wrong. My floors were clean, but I didn't want to have to do laundry because of Meredith.

Bending over the bed to reach a pile of clothes, she turned to look at me over her shoulder. "He's going to take his bike, and you can't wear anything that won't protect you. God forbid, we both have road rash." She held up her gloved hand, a reminder of the scars that lay underneath.

"Mer," I said. I wasn't sure how to have a conversation with her without an argument. We were having a decent time, and I didn't want to ruin that.

"Let's just get this over with," Meredith dismissed me and continued to flip through the clothes on the bed. I stood behind her and watched, trying to tamper down my emotions. I couldn't help the excitement that bubbled in my stomach. Glimpses of Meredith before the accident were poking through all the despair that she used as a cloak. I almost wished I could video this and send it to Grizz. It was a bit of hope that we'd both hold on to with both hands.

Meredith would pull a few things out, but when she didn't like how something lined up, she'd throw it on the floor. I didn't care. I'd gladly wash everything three times if it meant that Meredith was getting a brief reprieve. "Here," she said, taking a step back. Laying on the bed was a pair of jeans that I wasn't sure when I'd worn last and a leather corset that the girls had bought as a gag gift.

"I am not sure that stuff's going to fit. Are you positive it will look alright?" I scrunched my nose at the outfit. It looked good, but I wasn't sure how it would look on me.

"You're shitting me, right? What do you care if it doesn't fit as long as you can breathe? You won't be wearing it very long anyway," she said, shooting me a look. "There's a bet on how fast Sabre can get you out of those clothes after dinner. Please hold out until an hour after you get back to the clubhouse. I'd like to win."

"Nah. It has to be within the first half an hour. Diapers are expensive, and JR needs formula. I figured if they were going to bet, then I was going to win." I winked at her.

"You bet on your own sex life?" Her eyebrows raised as if she couldn't believe that I'd played along.

"Of course I did, and then I ran to Sabre and told him not to bet, so that we'd have better odds." I laughed, but it died quickly when she didn't return it.

"The dumbasses invited the strippers from the club so that there are enough girls to go around when they get to listen in. Text me when you get back. I don't want to know if you're getting your freak on." She stared at JR.

Meredith never touched JR. She never picked him up, offered to hold him, or even feed him. She'd look at him for a few minutes, and then her gaze would abruptly shift. I wasn't sure if it was because he was a baby or if the news from Scrub about her pregnancy not being viable had dealt her a tremendous blow. Grizz had told her it was alright. He had been more concerned about losing her. Those words hadn't penetrated Meredith's walls.

I had tried to get her to open up to me right after we had brought JR home, but she had shut me down quickly.

"You had your baby. What would you know about one that was never meant to be?" As hurtful as her words had been, she was right. I had kept my smile in place, not letting her see how much it had affected me.

"You'll have more children if you want them," I said, trying to open the conversation again as she watched JR on the bed. I couldn't sit by and let her wallow like this. I flirted with the line between sister and third parent, and it was only a matter of time before it burned me. It always did.

"Why? So Grizz can trap me here? No, thanks." She turned to face me, her expression closed off, signaling the end of the conversation. "Go shower, and I'll do your hair. You've never worn a helmet." When I didn't move fast enough, she grabbed me by my shoulders and turned me towards the ensuite. "Go."

I showered and dressed quickly, knowing that JR was in the other room with Meredith. I would have never left him if I thought he was in danger or she wasn't emotionally stable enough to handle it. Walking out of the bathroom, I was towel-drying my hair when I realized there was a standoff happening. Meredith was sitting in the middle of the clothing piles at the bottom of the bed, having a visual stand-off with Kelly, who was rocking JR in her arms. I didn't know when Kelly had shown up, but the tension in the room was palpable.

"Hey," I greeted Kelly.

"Hi," she mumbled, still facing off with Meredith. "I am going to take him downstairs so that you can finish." She promptly turned on her heel and exited the room.

"Did you say something to her?"

"Nope." Meredith blow-dried my hair and braided the back, tucking the tail in with a few pins. "You're all set. Grab your jacket on the way out." My sister walked out of the bedroom, and a minute later, I heard the front door close.

Chapter 39

Grace's First Ride

Kelly was standing behind the couch, bouncing JR in her arms, listening to Grace ramble.

"The bottles are on the rack. The formula is in the cabinet next to the microwave. I wrote all of our phone numbers down and left them on the refrigerator. If you need something, you call me first. I don't care what it is. I'll have my phone on."

"Mama, she's babysat JR before. It'll be fine," I attempted to intervene.

Wrong move. Grace turned to me, fire building in her eyes. "I've always been nearby, and we're leaving the clubhouse. What if he needs me?" She placed her hands on her hips and tapped her foot at me. The fire hadn't smoldered, and I was sure that she would have burned me alive for even suggesting a thing. If I made one more wrong move, she'd let her inner mama bear loose, and I'd be sleeping on the couch for a week.

I walked over to Grace and placed my hands on her cheeks. "JR will be fine. He won't even know you're missing for a few hours, and the clubhouse will be full of people for Kelly to call."

"I am his mother. He needs me." Her eyes watered and her lips quivered.

"Yeah, and my di...I need you, too." I was lucky. I'd caught that before it had slipped out. It was one thing to be crude with Grace. She'd laugh it off and give it right back to me. Kelly was a different story.

Kelly haunted me. I didn't feel guilty over the blowjob. I had been a free man, and we had both been willing participants that night. Once Grace had heard about it, nobody had ever mentioned it again. Like we had said, it was a speed bump during a time when we hadn't been together. However, every time I looked at Kelly, I couldn't help but think what an asshole I'd been to her. She hadn't deserved to be treated like trash, and I knew I wasn't the only one who had. She'd had enough of the emotional abuse and had sworn off men. Kelly only came to the clubhouse to visit Grace and JR, not as a hang-around.

Kelly placed JR in his bouncer in the living room and walked towards us. She hugged Grace from behind and then ushered us towards the front door. Grace tried to turn around, but Kelly's momentum didn't give her the option to dig her feet in. "Peanut and I are fine. We're going to watch reality TV, and I'll give him his next bottle in a few hours."

Grace tried again to stop. "Promise me..."

"If I need anyone, call Wreck first, since he always answers. If he doesn't, call Count next, because he'll answer for me. Forget them and call Scrub, if I think it's something medical. Don't call Grizz or Meredith unless it's a last resort, and don't tell them that."

I opened the front door and stepped out onto the porch. Grace was right behind me, but she was trying to stop the inevitable. I had visions of her gripping the door frame and holding on for dear life. She didn't have a choice, and when she hit the threshold, Kelly smiled and hugged her again.

"Seriously! You're like the older sister I never had. I won't let anything happen to Peanut. Enjoy your night!" She closed the door in our faces, and we heard the lock turn.

"Remind me why I like her," Grace said, huffing at me.

I wrapped my arm around Grace's shoulder and tucked her into my chest. "It would be a crime to waste this." I ran my finger underneath the jacket, over her shoulder, and down to the curve of her breast. "A fucking shame."

She ignored me. Pulling away, she turned back towards the front door and tried to open it.

"Didn't you hear the lock turn?" I asked, smiling.

"Yes, but I was hoping it was just a figment of my imagination." She sighed and yelled at the door. "Fine! We're leaving."

We heard, "Good," muffled through the door.

I laughed as Grace wrapped her arm around my waist, still huffing and puffing. She was more upset about being man-handled out the front door than anything else. Steering her down the porch steps towards the dirt path that led to the clubhouse, I looped my arm around her shoulders. We reached the front of the clubhouse, and as I made the turn toward my bike, Grace stopped.

She plastered herself along the side wall, hands flung out to her sides. Grace was breathing hard, and I had to remind myself to focus on her face as she turned left and right, trying to see who else was outside. Her breasts bounced with each labored breath in the corset, and I didn't think she'd humor me. I was a man, comfortable knowing that she was mine.

"What are they doing out there?" she questioned me, her cheeks bright red.

"Are you embarrassed?" I asked her.

"No," she answered, but her cheeks were redder against her pale skin.

"They're probably waiting for us so that they can watch you mount my bike for the first time. With the bet, they're just trying to have a little fun."

"At my expense, Sabre. Look at me." She opened the jacket. "I look hot, and I'd like to maintain this level of hotness. What if I miss the pedal, and I go flying over the seat?"

I laughed so hard I couldn't catch my breath. I had to grab my knees and double over before I passed out. Looking up at her, I found she was still standing there, holding the jacket wide open. The corset pushed her breasts up, but slimmed out the curves in her waist and hips. The jeans molded to her legs, like a second skin. She was sexy without even trying. If I died right now, I'd go out a very happy man. "Mama, you're going to be lucky if you make it to dinner."

She searched my face, and when she found what she was looking for, she let the flaps of the jacket go and walked around the corner. I had to give it to the brothers on the porch. They didn't catcall her, even though they probably wanted to.

When I turned the corner, I watched as they all averted their eyes. She was smoking, but she was mine, and everyone on that porch knew it. She didn't pay them attention as she walked over to my bike at the front of the line and waited.

"Anyone else trying to not say something? Just me?" I heard.

"Nah, she's a smoke show, but I won't be any good later for the ladies if I get my ass beat."

"Like any lady is going to want you."

"They won't want me if my dick doesn't work."

I chuckled to myself and walked over to my bike. I'd taken her to buy a helmet earlier in the week, but this was the first time she would actually ride on the back of my bike.

"Wave to your adoring fans," I said, trying to lighten the mood as I buttoned her jacket closed. No one needed to see her like that but me. I didn't know how I was going to get through dinner, but I wouldn't dampen her confidence. I could defend us if some asshole acted inappropriately. Most of them saw the club cut and thought better of it.

"I heard they invited all the women they could think of for tonight. They just want to listen in to their president getting his freak on."

I bent so that my lips were near her ear. "Only with you. That's assuming we make it through dinner."

"Why have dinner, when you can eat dessert first?" she whispered.

I grabbed the helmet off the passenger seat and handed it to her. Waiting for her to get it on her head, I made sure that the straps were tight enough.

"Put your foot on the pedal and swing your leg to the other side. You can use my shoulder to steady yourself. You got this, mama." I put my helmet on and mounted my bike. Making sure the bike was steady, I held out my hand for her.

She ignored me and held onto my shoulder. I didn't see her pop her leg over, but I felt it as she sat down behind me. "You alright?" I asked her through the helmets.

"Yes," she said. "What do I do with my hands?"

I reached behind me, and she placed her hands in mine. Wrapping them around my stomach, I felt her breasts hit the square of my back. This was going to be agonizing torture. "You leave them here and don't let them stray."

"I can't wander south of the border?" she laughed.

"JR needs his parents. You do that shit when we stop."

"Yes, Daddy." She was still laughing at me. I could feel my dick hardening behind the zipper of my jeans. Trying to adjust, I knew I didn't play it cool when the brothers started cackling like old women. They saw through the act. I was hard as fuck.

Walking the bike backwards, I waited until I cleared the line before I headed for the gate. This was going to be a long ride.

***

When I had visited her before JR was born, I had taken her to fancy restaurants, but most of the time, we had grabbed something and headed towards the beach. I figured she'd enjoy the same type of date, and I'd checked the beach's website. They were supposed to have food trucks in the parking lot. I pulled in, and we walked among the rows, picking out random food to make a hodgepodge dinner. It was perfect. Grace's smile fell.

Grace thought nothing of it, but when she removed her jacket, every man in the vicinity turned in her direction. I didn't blame them, but they'd never have a chance with her. Several wives made comments, leading to marital disputes. When the men caught my eye, they quickly lowered theirs. She was my woman, and she didn't have eyes for anyone but me. It was the only thought that kept me cool.

We sat, watching the waves crash in and the seagulls dive for any scraps they could find. I was looking out into the waves when I felt before I saw Grace climbing into my lap. She wrapped her arms around my neck and pulled me close.

"I am ready for dessert," she said.

"Huh?" I was confused, my arms wound around her, holding her tightly to me.

"We need to get out of here." She kissed me. "If we stay, we're going to end up in jail for indecent exposure. Everyone's watching, so they'll find us."

"I've been hard since we left the clubhouse." I laughed. "They're already going to know, and this doesn't help," I said, pushing up against her so that she could feel what she had done to me.

"We will not make it to the clubhouse. Is there somewhere close?" She rubbed against me. I wasn't sure if it looked innocent, but I let out a slight groan.

I didn't let her finish that thought. It was time to go.

***

I drove to a hidden clearing among the trees. It was far enough off the road that no one would see the bike. Grizz and I had thoroughly tested this spot over the years. We'd get the girls to follow our bikes here.

Parking the bike, I made sure it was steady before I helped Grace stand. Removing our helmets, I laid them on the ground. "Perch up here and spread your legs," I told her, sliding back in my seat to give her a little room.

She looked at the bike, then at me, her confusion clear in the wrinkle between her eyebrows.

"It's alright. Hold tight," I told her, pulling her towards me and lifting her just enough for her to swing her leg over. I held her a little longer as she found her perch, following my instructions.

"You're the only woman I've ever put on the back of my bike. You going to let me fuck you out here and fulfill my fantasy?" My breath was coming out in pants, as I tried to control my racing heart and keep my dick in my pants in case she said no.

She took off her jacket in silence and laid it over our helmets. Leaning behind her, she placed her arms over the handlebars and arched her back. The corset barely confined her breasts.

A moan escaped my lips. I ran my finger through her cleavage until I reached the bottom of the corset. "Is this going to slide for me?" Tucking my fingers underneath, I used both hands to pull it. It gave way to the pressure, releasing her breasts. I tried to lean over her, but I wasn't able to reach where I wanted. Gripping her waist, I helped her up, and placed her in my lap, so that the seam of her jeans rode the length of my dick. Rocking her hips against me, she only made me ache for her.

Bending down, I suckled at her nipple.

"Fuck me," she sighed in frustration. "Fuck me, right here."

"Not until I've had dessert." I took my time worshipping her. "I've made you come like this before. Think I can do it again?" I asked her, licking and sucking around her left breast.

"This isn't a challenge. You've already won," she moaned. She gripped the back of my head and tried to hold me tighter to her. I refused to be controlled. This was my fantasy. When it was her turn, I'd play the dutiful Old Man, and she could have her way with me.

I bit her nipple, and she moaned as I licked across the valley to her right breast. I took my time, savoring the taste of her, until she couldn't handle any more. The last couple of passes, she'd ridden my dick through my pants, and if I wasn't careful, I'd end up coming too early.

"Lay back." I unzipped her pants and shimmied them until they reached her calves. Putting her legs around my neck, I found her soaked, and I shoved two fingers deep within her. "Don't fall off the bike," I told her, smirking.

She took one hand off the handlebar and wrapped it around her breast, squeezing it and circling the nipple. "If you don't make me come soon, I'll just do it myself."

"You want my dick too badly." Raising my hips from the seat, I unzipped my pants and pulled them down far enough for my dick to spring free. Pumping my fingers in and out of her wet pussy, I grabbed my dick and smacked it against her. Wiping my pre-cum on her mound, I watched my fingers fuck her. It didn't take long before my dick wanted to be where my fingers were.

She was wet enough that I slid home in one smooth stroke, and we both hissed at the friction. Pushing in, I wanted to make sure she would feel me everywhere. Not the men on the beach, but me. Scratching the backs of her legs lightly, I placed my hands on her hips and pistoned myself within her. I lost myself in her heat, her sounds, and when I gazed into her eyes, they burned only for me.

Using her hips for leverage, I pumped in and out of her. It was fun to know that a woman enjoyed what you were doing to her, but there was something about Grace. I wanted every noise from her lips, her body arching because she couldn't control herself. I wouldn't stop until she melted against my bike.

Rubbing her clit, I could feel her gripping me tightly from the inside. "That's it, mama. Take me with you," I told her.

"Drew," she moaned.

"Yeah, mama. That's who's fucking you."

I watched as she held on to both handlebars and arched her back again as she tried to push her hips further into me. I picked up the pace and slammed my dick into her repeatedly. She wouldn't last long, and I needed her to make me come. "Grip me. There you go," I praised her.

Her head tilted back and forth, and I watched as her grip tightened, her knuckles turning white.

"Drew," she moaned, and I felt her tighten the inner walls of her pussy.

I raised my hips from the seat on my bike and pushed harder and faster into her until I felt her break. She screamed my name into the clearance of the trees. With one last groan, I emptied into her, falling forward until my head lay on her stomach. I didn't know how long we laid there, but I picked her up and held her against me, her head resting on my shoulder.

"We have a bet to win, and I can't feel my legs. How are you going to handle round two?" she asked.

I traced the curve of her breast. "It's twenty minutes back to the clubhouse. With you pressed against me, it won't be a problem."

Her hand dropped from my chest to my dick as she cupped me. "You'll be the one screaming."

***

Scan the QR Code for a bonus chapter and preorder your copy of *Unveiled Wounds*, Book 2!

Also by J. Wine

Fall in Love with J's Universe

Mafia Romance
Silent Syndicate
Meet Odin (Prequel)
Odin

MC (Motorcycle Club) Romance
Iron Shield
Unveiled Desires
Unveiled Wounds

About the Author

J. Wine is an exciting new author in the world of dark mafia romance, specializing in her own brand of messy and complicated tales. In her world, love is never a straight line, and J. herself is no stranger to those complexities. Her own love story could easily fall into several tropes – best friends to lovers, second chance, and much more.

J loves the escape from reality that reading brings and hopes she can give that bit of peace to someone else. She has a list of favorite mafia and motorcycle club romances, if you need a recommendation.

It's not a coincidence that all of J's mafia romances are set in Chicago. A native Midwesterner, she escaped the blistering winters for the sun and desert. Goodbye Chicago! Hello Phoenix!

Acknowledgements

T: This is the only place where I try to wax poetry about how much you mean to me. We are the only people who truly understand each other. I hate you for telling me to suck it up, but I love you when you raise your eyebrow and just look at me when I ask if people are going to read my words. You never doubt me, and you make sure I am okay a million times a day. I am a lucky girl.

Vicky: I posted my editor was more excited about my book than I was. You should have seen all the people who told me that was rare. You take care of my book babies as if they were your own, and for that, I am eternally grateful. I mean, come on, who else is going to tell me they didn't expect chapter thirty-seven so early in the morning? In hindsight, I probably should have given you more warning.

Dee: I am snickering as I write this, because I know you will not be happy with my mushiness. It's not as smooth as the other ones, because I don't know how to describe our friendship. All I know is that I love our brand of snarky sunshine. It makes me laugh, and I think it's kismet that I named the waitress Dee. If anyone asks, I am going to say I named her after someone I didn't know I needed in my life.

Liberty: I hope you see this. I wasn't lying when I said you should read the entire book. You were my first author message, ever. In fact, I had to read it three times to make sure you were talking to me. Thank you! You gave me courage to continue when I thought writing was hard.

The Vella Readers: Thank you so much for taking a chance on the Iron Shield. There are no words to describe the journey that we've been on since last October.

It's been amazing and exhilarating, and I am glad I got to do it with all of you. You never gave up on me. You never doubted that I wouldn't finish the story, and I hope I did you proud.